SATELLITE

NICK LAKE

ALFRED A. KNOPF
NEW YORK

To Hannah, who inspires all my stories.

To Ann-Janine, who taught me most of
what I know about building them.

Finally to Lyra and Henry. Only one of them
is a constellation, but they are both the stars
round which I orbit.

/begin transmission

i love, like the moon loves the earth

PART 1

orbit

1

a wider space

the sun is rising for the 14th time today, firing the Saharan land-mass like a match flame in darkness.

i am sitting in the cupola, watching the earth spin below me, desert rolling past the window of the Moon 2 space station, dunes like waves, sunlight flooding westward.

i don't move. soon, we're over the coast of Africa. sketches of towns. u don't c them so well in the daytime, which means that they almost extinguish before my eyes, the tracery of light blinking off as the wall of sun advances.

then sea.

it's always the sea.

people down there call their planet the earth, but it's mostly water. i know every fifth grader knows that. it's just, when u're in orbit, it's really obvious. sometimes Grandpa vidlinks me from down there & he asks me where we are & i don't even look out a porthole, i just say over the ocean & usually i'm right.

Grandpa says it's called the earth because of how farming shaped modern people, or something. he says we learned how to grow things 9,000 years ago & raise animals, & it tied us to the land, like tight. like love. he says when the soil is warm from the sun & u hold it in ur hands, let it run thru ur fingers, u feel a sensation like it's ur mother u're touching.

i wouldn't know. i was born up here.

& my mother is not the touching type.

soon i'll be there tho. that's why i'm in the cupola instead of in class. in a couple of months it's my 16th birthday, & Libra & Orion are already 16, which is the age they always said we would be strong enough. strong enough to go home. they call it home, even tho we've never been there.

in fact: i just had a medical & they think my weight is ok now. my bone density. so it looks like we will be going back on the next shuttle.

back: another strange word, for a place we've never been before.

click: "Leo?"

it's the intercom system. i push up, float over to the nearest terminal. "yes?"

"i've got a problem with the auto cargo docking parameters for the day after tomorrow. u want to help?"

it's Virginia. i've known Virginia all my life. she is 1 of 2 baby-sitters, we call them. there's vid footage of Virginia encouraging us to crawl, as babies, on the station's treadmill. strapped down, to simulate gravity. then to walk. sometimes we watch the vids in class, to remind us that we have had to learn everything that comes naturally to those on earth. but i can remember anyway, or at least i think i do: i remember the weights, the straps, the monotony of putting 1 foot in front of the other, again & again.

she's been here 3 months this time, but she rotates in every year for a couple of months. usually people don't visit for much longer than that. even my mother only comes for 1 month a year. they worry about bones. about eyes. about the body going soft in the wrong places. hard in the wrong places.

Virginia is here for that, in part—to test the limits. a human guinea pig. they take all kinds of data from her body, send it back to Nevada. every 24 hours she has to have an ultrasound of her heart. sometimes she lets me do it. she knows i'm interested in that kind of stuff. by that kind of stuff i mean: everything.

also we test her eyes every week, & when she gets back to Nevada, she's having a spinal tap for the second time, which she says is going to suck in more ways than 1. she's a scientist & a subject at the same time: long-term effects of 0 g.

i always say: they should really look at me & Libra & Orion if they want to study that.

oh don't worry, she says. they will.

"u in the command module?" i say to Virginia over the intercom.

"affirmative."

"u mean yes?" it annoys me when they speak like astronauts. i mean they are astronauts. but still.

"yes."

"ok, i'm coming."

i leave the cupola & torpedo thru the station. *torpedo,* verb: to move across different modules, floating, arms in front, grabbing handles to pull oneself forward, crouching to touch down on a corner, pushing off again. i've seen vids of people swimming, & i suppose it's a little like that.

but faster.

but freer.

i cross a couple of experiment modules—infrared absorption arrays; alpha spectrometer; solar radiation measurement—& take a shortcut up thru the relaxation module where we watch vids & read & hang out. the station is arranged like a big plus sign, with huge solar panel wings on each of the 4 ends, & now i'm in the vertical arm. vertical is a pretty conceptual idea, of course, up here.

i fire past the entertainment consoles & grab an instrument panel that i use to propel myself thru a hatch into the conservatory, which opens up around me. they called it the conservatory after some kind of structure made of glass that people used to have hundreds of years ago, but really it's a big module full of plants, on tables, with UV lights hooked up above them & drainage in the tables.

the plants are to eat, & also for making oxygen. we have other systems too—there's 1 that gathers & condenses all the moisture we breathe out & sweat out, & splits it into hydrogen for fuel & oxygen to breathe. but Moon 2 is big on efficiency, so there are the plants too.

no one is surprised, & especially not me, to c Libra in there. she dreams of being a botanist. i mean that literally; she probably really does dream about it. that's how much she wants it. if Libra ever disappeared, which is unlikely in the confines of a space station, i know, but bear with me, & the authorities asked if there was anywhere she might go, u would say somewhere with plants.

that's mean of me. she's actually very sociable. more so than me & Orion, really.

when i scoot closer to her, i c she's planting seedlings. i think, anyway.

i'm more equations & velocity & the relative motion of objects; Libra is more growing things, & animals. often she watches these old documentaries about lions & chimps & elephants & coral reefs. a lot of those things are extinct now because of everything getting too hot, but it doesn't stop her.

"hey," i say.

"hey."

"where's Orion?" i say.

she shrugs. "his bunk, i guess."

they're twins, but u wouldn't know it to look at them.

Libra is pushing tiny plants into this kind of foam stuff

that the plants grow in. u can't use soil—it would disperse, float around, get into the vents. "weeks now," she says. "days."

"uh-huh," i say.

"i'll be touching the *earth,* Leo," she says. we're all named after constellations. i got lucky with mine. it's a pretty normal name.

"yeah."

"imagine. imagine how it will feel between ur fingers. between ur toes." she lifts her hand to her necklace—she doesn't even realize she's doing it. it's a little metal tube & inside is some soil from Florida, where her mother was born. her mother brought it up years ago. Libra wears it like it's precious. she & my grandpa should get together down there, i think. talk about mother earth.

me: i want to feel *gravity.* not earth. i want to throw a ball & c a parabola drawn in the air, not just watch the ball float away from me. i want to c & feel the equations i have learned. but i don't say any of that.

Libra puts down the foam & drifts over to me. her fingers brush my arm. "u ok?"

i nod. i don't know. "just nervous, i think."

she smiles. she's pretty. she is. freckles, oval face, brown skin. but i can't meet her eyes. "u'd have to be crazy not to be nervous," she says. "we've been here all our lives."

"yes."

"but it's exciting too," she says. "think about it. air on our faces! breeze. the sea. our toes in the sand." behind her is a porthole & she turns to it. she gestures at the star-filled universe beyond, as if to disperse the blackness of space, like smoke. "real sky. clouds."

i nod. "waves," i say. "low-pressure systems. precipitation. the sound of an echo."

she rolls her eyes. "i'm talking about sensations. not physics."

"sensations *are* physics."

"yeah, yeah. tho i think Orion would agree with u about the echo."

"about what?" says another voice. deeper.

that's Orion: floating down in a ball from the module above, unfolding, landing neatly beside us. he's holding his flute, like always. he plays it ok. he never seems to get very much better, or rather, he never learns very long pieces: just little snatches of tunes.

but anyway, he says, the purpose of art is art, not accomplishment. me, i think he says this only because there's a difference between playing & practicing. practicing takes work.

Orion leans in & looks at the plants. same oval face as Libra, but stronger, thicker, the jaw firmer. same freckles. "what would i agree with?" he continues.

"Leo was saying about echoes. how he'd like to hear 1."

"when we're down there?"

"yeah."

Orion smiles. it's like he makes his own light, inside him. he plays a few notes on the flute. they ripple thru the module—u can almost c them, silver on the air. "i can't wait," he says. "proper acoustics. music needs a wider space."

"we all need a wider space," says Libra.

Orion & i don't say anything. because now there's a hope-tinged sadness in the module, almost audible, like the little tune from the flute. Libra & Orion ended up here by accident. it was a big joint-venture flight—a load of Russian cosmonauts & Americans too. the most people ever in space, for the longest time. it was when they first found an earthlike planet within a few generations' travel distance: there was a whole plan to send a ship up there & colonize it, because it had fresh water, unlike the earth, which was slowly running out, & so step 1 was to c how long people could manage to live in 0 g.

1 of the results of the experiment was unexpected: if u put male & female astronauts in a confined space for 2 years, they will eventually have sex. & 1 of the women, in this case, will end up having twins on board.

they hadn't thought of the regular cardiovascular ultrasounds then either: with the 2 years in space, & the pregnancy, Libra & Orion's mother's heart ended up shot. she's been up here a couple of times since, but she can't do it for long. they vidlink all the time tho. especially Libra.

me, i was more deliberate. my mother was an astronaut to the core. 2 PhDs, military-flight tester, astrophysicist. she was in every accelerated program NASA ever had & then Moon 2 when NASA was privatized. she says she didn't know, when she finally got the call to go up to the station, that she was pregnant; she'd had a fling a few nights before she launched, some Russian ritual involving vodka. so maybe i'm half-Russian; i don't know.

Grandpa says, if it was a fling, it was the only fling she ever had, in her whole entire life.

anyway, she'd had all the scans already, so just before the mission began they gave her the usual physical, blood pressure & resting pulse rate & chest scan for embolisms & that was that.

until i came along.

in space.

9 months later.

& since then we've all been stuck here, for the same reason they wouldn't let our mothers fly back during pregnancy, because they say that a child's body can't handle reentry, can't handle landing, so we've always known we had to wait till we were 16, & everything i know about anatomy says they're probably right.

a hand crosses in front of my eyes. "Leo, u with us?" it's Libra, frowning, looking concerned now, which i suppose is better than looking sad.

"sorry," i say. "just thinking."

"about earth?"

"um," i say. "yes."

Libra leans forward & gives me a hug, & i tense, so she pulls away, still smiling tho. "soon," she says.

yes. soon. soon the waves, soon the wind, soon all the things we have seen on vids but never felt. even just a big room: the acoustics of it. a full day, not 1 that swings around every 90 minutes. colors that are not metal gray, or plastic white. what it feels like to be pulled down to the ground—in the station there is no up & no down & no weight, we all just tumble around. even liquids, they turn into balls, into globules, & float in front of u—u can suck them up with a straw from the air.

the intercom: "Leo, u coming?"

i give Libra & Orion an apologetic look. "c u," i say.

"Virginia need u?" says Libra.

"yeah, she wants some help with the cargo docking or something," i say.

Libra smiles, but it doesn't reach her eyes. "go on then," she says. "work ur math magic."

Orion nods at me & starts playing the flute again. his expression, like always, is hard to read. u can't really c into him, he's like a device screen in bright daylight. i c the muscles around his mouth tighten as he purses his lips; a short phrase of music falls like liquid from his flute, flows—not that i've ever seen anything falling, or flowing, except on a vid screen, but still.

when we were kids, we were close, me & Orion & Libra. u c that, on the vids of us crawling, of us walking. & we still come together sometimes, like for the aurora.

but now Libra is always studying. Orion is always . . . doing

Orion things. if Orion disappeared & the authorities asked where he was, i'd say look for anyplace where there is poetry. or movies. or music.

anyplace where there are no people but there are things that people have made, to tell stories.

which makes it ironic, then, that i'm the 1 telling this 1.

2

bodies

i kick off & haul on a handrail & float up thru the hatch & thru another couple of modules & then i'm in the upper command module, right next to the solar wing, 1 of them anyway. Virginia looks back at me from the terminal where she's working.

she's young, Virginia. maybe 40. she's not 1 of the hard ex-military astronauts like my mother. she & Lakshmi, who rotates with Virginia, are more the maternal kind, which is weird to say, since it's my mother who's the actual mother.

still, even tho my mother is dismissive about Virginia & her skills, Virginia is here because 1/ she's a qualified air force pilot, just like my mother, & 2/ she has a doctorate in math from MIT & 3/ she's getting those medical tests all the time to c what being up here for a long time does to someone who wasn't born here & 4/ someone was needed to look after me & Orion & Libra. which is more than my mother has ever done.

of course, these days, we need very little babysitting. which means that the Company is using the regular rotation astronauts for more & more testing.

specifically, right now, Virginia is here because the day after tomorrow—shortly after my mother & some engineer guy called Brown arrive—there is going to be an unmanned cargo ship bringing long-term supplies & docking with the station. the idea is that, in the future, they can send stuff up here without using a rocket or any kind of piloted craft; they just fire off an unmanned vehicle & it takes care of everything.

& Virginia: Virginia helped to develop the program that's going to handle the automated docking. she's hardcore. sometimes i wonder if it bothers her, that she's so qualified & yet she ended up spending years feeding us, making up games to get us to walk a little further on the treadmill, teaching us to read & write. but it's not the kind of thing u can ask.

"hey, V," i say.

"hey, u," she says.

"hey, x," i say.

"hey, q," she says.

it's a stupid game. a game from when i was a kid. but we still play it.

Virginia is the most beautiful person i have ever seen & that includes in movies. if she went missing & the authorities asked me to describe her, i would say she has green eyes & cheekbones that could cut you & she is so impossibly gorgeous that a person who didn't know her would think song would come out of her mouth, instead of speech.

it doesn't. actually her voice is kind of raspy. i think she smokes, down there on earth. not up here, of course. that would be a death risk in a whole other way.

Virginia's hair is spiked & pink, & she has tattoos of snake scales over her neck & some of her jaw. she points at the screen with an olden-days pencil—my mother says they don't really use them on earth anymore, but they're useful up here. there's a legend that the Russians spent millions developing a pen that would work in 0 g & then the Americans just took up pencils, but i don't think it's true. i think it was just a story to make us look clever during the space race, which is lame & also unnecessary, since we won.

won. well, that's debatable, now.

Virginia, the point is, gestures at the screen in front of her with the pencil. i c she's chewed the end of it to pulp. a small bubble of her spit floats between us, glinting in the sunlight coming thru from the earth side of the module.

"so i'm running the h-infinity model, & there's a problem," she says.

"now?" i say. "the docking is in 2 days."

"yeah, well, when we designed this we were on the ground. now there's . . . stuff we didn't anticipate."

"like?"

"like this thing"—she touches the side wall of the module—"is vibrating. u feel it? 1 of the gyroscopes is off. faulty bearing, i think."

there are gyroscopes built into the 4 arms—it's 1 of the things that keeps us in the right position, relative to earth. there are systems that are constantly measuring the angle of incidence of the sun, the height of the horizon, the position of the moon & stars, & a dozen other parameters, then instructing the gyroscopes to turn in their gimbals, absorbing undesired momentum, making sure we stay in a consistent orbit & orientation.

"&?" i say.

"& it's screwing the outputs from our control system," says Virginia. "the cargo container's gonna fail to lock to the hatch & it's going to crash into us."

"hmm," i say. "that wouldn't be good."

"ur talent for understatement continues, i c."

i come & hover by the terminal next to her. "show me."

she pulls up the g graph of the gyroscope vibration. i c where it's spiking, when it should be flat.

"it's under 0.2 g, so it's not triggering the automated command to take it out of the steering law," she says. "but it's still upsetting the z output of my model. we need to swap it out really, & we have a spare gyro ready to go, but we can't install it till Flight Officers Brown & . . . & ur mother are here to do the EVA."

EVA: extra-vehicular activity. a space walk.

"i could do the EVA," i say. "i already did 1 with Chang." this is true. the Asian astronaut took me out of the loading bay for a 10-minute walk. it was the greatest experience of my life—the unbounded sky around me, the blue ball of the earth below, the stars jeweling the dark.

"for like 4 minutes & Chang's gone now; no way u could do it alone. & i'm not doing my first EVA with a kid. no offense."

fine. ok. 4 minutes.

but it felt like 10.

it felt like 100.

it felt like forever, like i'm still there in some way, floating in nothingness.

i frown. "so take the gyro out of the steering law manually & use the boosters instead." we can adjust our attitude using rocket power, if the gyroscopes fail, or if they saturate because their combined momentum is smaller than the external torque on the station, say if u get hit by an asteroid & u've already got atmospheric drag & gravity gradient operating on the ship.

"i thought of that," she says, "but the boosters aren't finetuned enough; u can't micromanage the orientation. the z output would get worse. plus, this thing uses single gimbal gyros because some genius figured they were simpler to maintain, which is true, but with only 3 running, there's also a risk of getting a singularity & canceling out the gyros completely."

"& then the cargo container crashes."

"yes. & then the cargo container crashes."

"u told Nevada?" i say.

"not yet. but they can c the vibration, i guess."

i turn to another screen, where her program is running. "show me the outputs," i say. she's using an h-infinity model, which is basically a piece of genius that the Russians came up with decades ago, another thing that undermines the whole pen story. in essence, u envision the motors controlling the cargo ship not as a system intended to produce the right results but as a system intended to minimize the wrong results. the outputs from the system are ur undesirable results & u try to minimize them by feeding in the right data.

u make the whole program about stopping the cargo container from *not* docking; not about making it dock.

like i said, it is kind of brilliant.

i look at the outputs. the vibration of the ship is messing everything up, just like Virginia said. in the model, it's making the cargo ship run off course by .08 of a degree & fail docking.

i think for a second. i think about docking, 2 bodies coming together in space. in my head, it's Orion & Libra's birthday again. Virginia carries a disk of a cake into the cupola, which she brought up here in a can. on it are 16 LED candles, & when the twins blow, she presses a hidden button somewhere & the candles switch off.

"for my 17th," says Libra, "on earth, i'm having the whole deal. limo, restaurant, club."

"i'm in for the restaurant part," says Orion. "club: no."

"we don't need a club," says Virginia, & she floats to a panel & presses a switch.

then music, & then dancing: me & Libra twirling each other around the glass module, spinning, Virginia laughing as she somersaults in the air. & at a certain moment, me, flipping over & reaching out to stop & my hands closing on Orion's arms & for a moment we dance together, he & i, round & round, faster & faster, until we bump into the wall & are pressed together & Orion hugs me & grins—

& i feel something different, like Orion's body that i have known since i was born, more or less, has been swapped for something else, something more . . . physical, something more present.

i pull away, & feel my face go hot, & he looks at me, & does he pull back a little? i wonder if he knows, if he feels uncomfortable now; unsettled.

or if he felt it too.

"um, earth to Leo?" says Virginia.

i snap back into the command module.

"harmonics," i say.

"what?"

"take the g output from the faulty gyro & run it thru a Fourier transform & u've got the frequency of the vibration. then u just need to reverse that & feed it into the other gyros & a couple of boosters maybe & they can adjust the yaw & pitch of the ship rhythmically to cancel out the vibration. then the vibrations disappear from ur z output."

she nods slowly. "huh," she says. "complicated. but that could work."

"yeah, but what if it doesn't?"

she winks & taps my hand. "then u're going home early. & most probably on fire."

interlude
gifts

on Libra & Orion's birthday, i hand Libra her gift. it's a sunflower seed, set in a ring. Grandpa sent it up for me when Virginia rotated in.

she puts it on. "i love it," she says.

then i give Orion his. a slim, leather-bound book: the poetry of e. e. cummings.

Orion stares at it. "wow. i never had a real book before."

"it's old," i say stupidly.

"obviously. & i love cummings."

"i know," i say. "i mean, i remember u reciting 1 of the poems."

"'Space being (don't forget to remember) Curved,'" he says. he pauses for a moment, looks around. "cummings really would have understood living up here, i think."

he hugs me, & this time—thank god—i don't feel anything but a body, next to mine, no strange & extra awareness.

"this is our last birthday up here," says Libra.

"yeah," says Orion. "next year we'll have candles that are on fire."

"we'll burn up the dance floor," i say. "instead of hovering above it."

"i'll . . . um . . . bring the heat with my moves," says Libra.

Orion groans.

& then we're laughing, the 3 of us, spinning & holding each other's hands & laughing so hard.

later, Orion & Libra go to their quarters to give each other their gifts. i guess they don't want me to c. i don't know why. i guess that's how it is with twins. sometimes they're so close together, there's no crack in between for anyone else to fit in.

3

how it all works

i check my watch. it's an Omega Speedmaster from the early 2000s that Grandpa wore on the international space station, the ISS. space is in my blood, in more ways than 1. i have an hour before our vidlink call, so i say bye to Virginia & torpedo to my quarters—my record is 1 minute 14 from the command module, & i do it in 1.20, which is not bad.

i strap into my bunk & close my eyes for a moment. when u do that in space u c stars, just like when u look out the porthole on the dark side of the station—bursts of light, flickers, meteors, from radiation particles hitting ur cornea. sometimes i worry about all that radiation we've been absorbing since we were born & i know the doctors down in Nevada worry about it too because they're always asking on vid about whether we have any nausea & stuff, especially Dr. Stearns.

i get bored of lying there with my eyes closed, so i sit up & eat a freeze-dried cereal bar—everything i eat, pretty much, is freeze-dried; 1 of the things i'm looking forward to on earth is real food—& then i try to read. Walt Whitman. it's an assignment from Mr. Obiekwe, the English teacher who vids us from Connecticut somewhere. Libra will get an A on it, i'll get a B, like i generally do on anything that's not math or science, & Orion will fail. Orion always fails. even tho he has read more books than Mr. Obiekwe, probably.

i stare at the page, try to follow the words, but it's hard work—it mostly presupposes being in a body in a world with sky & ground & birds & fish & leaves on trees. & colors.

here, we're more like ghosts in an attic. & everything is white or black or silver.

plus, there are a lot of distractions. like noise. sometimes little meteoroids—really tiny ones—hit the outside of the station & they ping & bang; it drives Orion mad when he's listening to Bach or what have u. also there's no gravity, so air doesn't move or rise when it gets warm; it just sits there, & that means there are pumps whirring all the time & air-conditioning & cooling systems & the gyros turning & the net result equals a ton of creaking & hissing & grinding constantly.

also the view.

1 of the things they did when they built this place out of the ISS was to create these new modular units with more portholes so that people could c out more easily, which they figured might make those astronauts like my mother & Libra & Orion's mother less likely to go stir-crazy & kill each other. instead they had a romantic view of the blue-green earth below, & Orion & Libra were conceived.

good for me, i suppose. it would be really lonely up here without my sort-of siblings.

the view of the earth is beautiful too. islands scattered on blue seas, cloud formations above swirling like milk in water, mountains rising up, snow. entire countries & continents swinging past, sometimes black & laced with lights, sometimes lit with sunshine. sometimes u get the aurora too—mostly it's at the poles—& we only c it as a kind of halo, but every now & then it flames across the sea, the land, & then we always call each other, me & the twins, & we meet up to c it.

i mean, short of studying & watching vids, there isn't much

else to do. we have screens but most of the internet, apart from encyclopedias, is blocked by some kind of super Company firewall. operational security. really the screens are just for films & vidlinks, & even those are limited to preapproved contacts.

i'm still looking out the porthole when Grandpa's vidlink bongs into the module, *bong bong bong*. i reach over & take my screen & unroll it.

Grandpa's face appears, against a wood-paneled wall that's hung with rugs. it's his living room. behind him is a window, which opens onto the ranch, tho all i can c is bright daylight, making a glare around the frame. i think how weird it must be to spend so long in daylight, a whole 12 hours or more. up here we're orbiting at 17,500 miles an hour & the earth below goes dark every hour & a half.

"hey, Grandpa," i say.

"hey, kid. 2 more moon orbits."

"yeah. i can't wait to c u. i mean, for real."

he takes a breath. "then i get to hug u. would that be ok? if i hugged u. i mean . . . i'm ur grandpa & i've never . . ." he breaks off. "sorry, i'm rambling like an old man."

i smile. "it's ok with me," i say. Grandpa's not been up here since i was born—they say he's too old, his body couldn't deal with the forces. he's a trained astronaut & has been in orbit before tho, of course. working in space: it's pretty much the only thing his daughter, my mother, ever got from him.

she comes up, once a year.

but she is not interested in hugging.

"how's the ranch?" i say.

Grandpa shrugs. "holding on. but they say the aquifer's nearly dry. don't know how long it will last." he shakes his head, then looks up, smiling. "still be here when u come home tho."

i smile back. it's weird to think of Grandpa's ranch as home, when i've never been there. but i am looking forward to seeing it. he has 5,000 acres in Sonoma County in California. cattle mostly, some feed crops. most of the ranchers have left, Grandpa says, because of the drought. but he's still there, & a few others too.

"got a pony for u," he says. "thought u could learn to ride. the Westerson boy was just giving it away. said it ate too much grass."

"oh," i say. i've never thought about riding a horse. but it's never been possible of course. "thanks."

"no problem. lot of things to do when u arrive. take u swimming. teach u to play catch."

"i can catch fine."

"not in 1 g, i bet. gravity is a bitch."

"yeah, u're probably right." i think about this. i'm going to have to learn everything. how to walk. how to sit, when there's a force pulling u down. i don't really want to think about it because i'll only get worried about how much is going to be different, so i say, "what's happening with u?"

"tomorrow i'm driving up to the mountains with Zeke," he says. "we're going to pack a load of snow into barrels. keep it in the cellar. he did it last year. says it kept his sheep alive."

"wow," i say. "sounds amazing."

Grandpa makes a face. "hard work, more like."

"i meant driving. in the mountains. feeling snow. all of those things."

now he grimaces. "shit. sorry, son. always forget, don't i?"

"that i grew up in a tin can in space & haven't seen anything or felt anything?"

"yeah. that."

we laugh then. Grandpa asks me a bunch more questions. am i scared about reentry? am i looking forward to seeing my mother? would i like to choose a puppy when i get there because the ranch dog, Elsa, just had a litter?

(yes. no. of course.)

"hey," i say. "is Mother there?"

he laughs. the word they use in old books is *ruefully.* "what do u think? she's in Nevada at the base. preflight prep, etc. been prepping for the last 10 months, working sims of the cargo container docking."

"u haven't seen her in 10 months?"

"son, u've seen her more recently than i have."

that was a year ago. ouch. "sorry," i say.

"not ur fault," he says. "least she gave me u. & soon i'm going to c u. i mean really c u, face to face."

i take a deep breath. "yeah," i say. it's a yeah that has other words in it, words like: *i can't wait,* & *i'm finally going to hug u & know how u smell,* words i can't say out loud.

it's awkward to carry on the conversation after that, so we soon break it off. i go & train on the ARED exercise machine for a while because we're supposed to do an hour a day of weight resistance, pulling these cables attached to vacuum cylinders to keep our muscle mass up & maintain bone density; Dr. Stearns is always worrying about our muscle mass & bone density.

the whole time, i keep my sweatband around my head. u don't want sweat, or any kind of liquid, spinning around the station. it could get in people's eyes. that's also why i pee in a bag that i have to seal afterward & dispose of in the trash condenser that goes in 1 of the burn-up cargo ships. then they get sent down at an angle deliberately calculated to make them disintegrate when they hit the atmosphere.

afterward i look at my watch & c that it's nearly bedtime, which is of course not something u can tell from looking out the window. i glide along the crossarm of the station toward my bathroom pod & have a space shower, which means i get a little bag of premixed water & soap & squeeze out a tiny amount & rub it over myself & then i dry myself with a towel, being careful not to let any of the liquid fly off because: people's eyes.

it takes a long time.

as i get dressed again, the shutters come down. they do this when we're sleeping, covering the windows, in case a bigger micrometeoroid breaks 1. i don't know why that's not a concern in the day. maybe it's just an old human fear of disaster striking when u're sleeping, the same thing that made people build fires to keep wolves at bay.

this whole ship is basically a machine for keeping us alive, is what i think when the shutters come down. as i said, it's arranged like a plus sign—4 radial tubular sections, made of cylindrical modules held together by hatches. trusses run down all 4 arms, outside, allowing an astronaut doing an EVA to move along, & there are also rails for remote machines & robot arms & so on to run on.

at the end of each arm is a huge solar panel, like a wing, for all our power. & built into each arm orthogonally, at 90 degrees to each other, are 4 moment gyros spinning 6,600 times a minute & generating a momentum storage of 3,500 ft-lb/sec, which can be used to adjust the yaw or roll or pitch of the station, just by turning the gyro within its gimbal.

there is also a rocket in each arm, developing 1,000 ft-lb of thrust, just in case the gyros fail. or, you know, roughly. (sorry, space geek.)

& that's not all. there are:

cooling panels on all the modules, with a simple ammonia heat exchange system, because bodies moving around in a closed system make lots of heat & so does the sun thru the windows & so otherwise we'd all cook.

oxygen candles, burning sodium chlorate & iron powder to make oxygen.

a condensate water processor for sucking up our sweat & breath & turning it into more oxygen via electrolysis.

& as i mentioned already the plants for oxygen too.

(if u're engineering a space station, u worry about oxygen a lot.)

(also the plants are to eat & to admire if u're Libra, of course, but mainly they're for oxygen if u read the manuals, which Libra doesn't but i do.)

a life-support system generating 14.7 lb/sq-in of environmental pressure using oxygen & nitrogen because there's a vacuum outside & it wants us dead, it wants us hollowed out.

sun, star, & horizon sensors for feeding attitude information to the gyros.

VHF transmitters, antennas, satellite dishes.

fire detectors.

gas analyzers.

air pumps.

fire extinguishers.

& on

& on

& on

& all of it there, in essence, to keep us from having our breath pulled out of our bodies, to keep the station's equilibrium so that we don't all die.

the intercom buzzes. "hey, Leo, it's Orion," says Orion redundantly.

"hey," i say. "what's up?"

"death sim," he says.

"now? it's bedtime."

"don't think they care in Nevada. it's all prep time all the time. so get lively. meet us on the bridge, 5 minutes. they want to talk about what happens if we all die."

4
death sim

Libra & Orion & Virginia are already on the bridge when i get there. we're the only people on Moon 2 at the moment. it's 0 g, so we can't exactly sit around a table. instead, the other 3 are holding on to handrails on the command desk. they've spread out a screen on it, & when i float over & grab a handrail myself, i c the boardroom in Nevada.

"Leo, glad u could join us for this simulation," says Commander Boutros. he's the big guy in charge down there. he always wears this shimmery purple eye shadow & matte-effect lipstick.

"hi," i say.

"Leo," says my mother, nodding. she's sitting next to Boutros. she's not wearing any makeup. she doesn't understand the point of it. not that she needs it. skin like polished mahogany. still young. i've seen Orion forget to close his mouth when he's looking at her. not that she cares about that, of course—i mean being beautiful, not Orion's mouth being open.

there's also Dr. Stearns & Flight Officer Brown. i've never met Brown but i've seen him on sims before. he's the 1 who's coming up with my mother, ahead of the arrival of the self-flying cargo unit. Nevada has been planning this space walk for a year now. they're serious about detail.

my mother & Flight Officer Brown will stay for 2 months. till my 16th birthday. then they'll take us all home.

me & Libra & Orion. to earth.

around the boardroom table, there are also several other men & women, & Boutros asks them to introduce themselves.

"Tomlinson. systems."

"Ravzi. engineering."

"Mankiewicz. medical."

"Santiago. PR."

etc.

basically a whole tableful of scientists & astronauts. we can just c the windows & it's dark down there, but the room in the base is lit by bright fluorescent light, & the table is covered with unrolled screens & documents, as well as the green cards for the sim.

at our end, we give our names too, which is redundant really because everyone knows who is up here.

"ok," says Boutros. "so we're launching at dawn. weather seems conducive. orbital trajectory has Flight Officer Brown & Chief Officer Freeman docking with Moon 2 at 09 hundred the day after tomorrow. the unmanned cargo container will arrive 3 hours later, carrying additional fuel for the station & other sundry supplies."

"oh!" says Orion. "is it the kittens i asked for?"

"ur humor is duly noted, Orion." they always use our first names, like we're kids. which we are, but still. "do remember that this is a contingency simulation tho."

"death sim," says Libra.

"we don't call it that," says Boutros.

"literally everyone does," says Libra. me, i keep silent. i usually leave the talking to the twins.

"& we should get on with it," says Orion. "everyone knows no one has died up here for generations. i was watching *Battleship Potemkin*."

i don't know what *Battleship Potemkin* is. but it sounds like exactly the kind of thing Orion would be watching.

"because of our protocols," says Boutros. "so we're all going to take this seriously. is that understood?"

Orion raises his eyes but nods. so does Libra.

"Leo?"

"yes. yes, understood," i say.

"Good," says Boutros. "ok. here's the scenario for the sim. the launch goes smoothly. Flight Officer Brown & Chief Officer Freeman are on Moon 2. then the cargo container successfully docks too. but its momentum throws the station out of correct attitude. the only way to stop it from reentering the atmosphere is to fire the primary booster. Freeman?"

"naturally, i give the order to fire the booster," says my mother.

"Ravzi: green card," says Boutros.

Ravzi—mustache & eyeliner ticked up at the edges to look catlike—picks up 1 of the cards. "fuel line to the booster is shot. only way to fix it is to EVA. immediately."

Mankiewicz from medical stops spinning her pen on her fingers. "procedure is 24 hours in hi-ox before a space walk."

"in 24 hours they're burning up on reentry," says Ravzi.

"but if they get the bends it's going to cause problems later on," counters the medic.

"well then," says my mother, "we use the old Russian system. 1 hour of pure ox & good to go."

"ok," says Boutros. "so u exit the station. u take the new RCV to tow u along the truss to the main booster. Duncan?"

"uh-huh, i monitor on the screens & drive the RCV," says Virginia.

"then we reconnect the fuel supply," says Officer Brown. he

says it confidently, even tho he has never been up here. but then i suppose he has always been elite: as a pilot, as an academic. u have to be to get into the program.

"fine," says Boutros. "green card, Tomlinson."

Tomlinson picks up a card. "fuel is ejecting into space. Duncan can't turn it off from command. what do u do?"

it goes on like this for 15 minutes. all kinds of permutations of things going wrong. until:

"Freeman: green card."

my mother turns 1. "we reconnect the fuel supply & the booster fires without warning, creating a g-force so great that our safety cables are cut & we are thrown away from the station."

"u & Brown are no longer slaved to its momentum & u are quickly lost," says Ravzi.

"yay!" says Orion. "death sim!"

Boutros glares at him. "Freeman & Brown drift until their oxygen runs out," he says. "then they die." he holds Orion's eyes, across the vidlink. "u think that's funny, Orion?"

Orion swallows. he looks at me. his meteor eyes. "no. sorry."

my mother makes an impatient hand gesture. "how do the others on the station get the booster under control? that's the important thing."

"more important than u being dead?" says Boutros.

"yes. we're dead. that's done. but the station needs to reorient." her tone is the way a rock might speak.

"depends on the booster," says Virginia. "is it under control or is it just blasting fuel?"

"it's firing continuously," says Ravzi. "out of control."

"ok," says Virginia. "so i use that. i take any gyros out of law that i don't need & i use the others to complement the torque from the booster, adjusting our pitch & yaw, etc., bringing us farther up & away from the atmosphere & back into most efficient altitude."

"then?"

"then i jettison the booster & go back to full gyro attitude management."

"problem is u've already got 1 gyro putting out 0.2 g of vibration," says Ravzi.

Boutros turns to him.

"that's not in the sim, that's IRL," Ravzi adds.

Boutros raises his eyebrows.

"it's just under 0.2 actually," says Virginia. "not high enough to come out of law."

Boutros is frowning now. "did we know about this?" he says. "will it affect docking? i mean, in real life, not in this sim."

"for Brown & Freeman, definitely not," says Virginia. "for the automated docking of the cargo ship . . . it isn't ideal. but the program can handle it. i figure it's a minor bearing malfunction. long as it stays low, we're ok."

"& if it doesn't?"

"the cargo container arrives after the astronauts, right?" says Virginia. "so Officers Freeman & Brown could install a new gyro. we have 1 on board. we were planning to replace it anyway."

"yes," says Boutros. "but later. that's a big job, & there's no time. we have a narrow window for the cargo container launch. anything else?"

"Leo had an idea about—"

Brown turns to face me, meaning he turns to face the screen. "Leo had an idea? the 15-year-old had an idea?"

"& we're going to listen," says Boutros. "kid's been up there since he was a baby, remember?"

Brown sits back in his chair. to his credit he flashes me a chastened smile. "sure, yes, i was out of line," he says. "go ahead, Leo."

"yeah," i say. "we identify the frequency of the vibration with a Fourier transform & use the other torque generators to modulate the movement of the ship such that we cancel out the vibration from the gyro."

Ravzi thinks for a second, playing with his mustache. "nice in theory," he says. "but we have no models for that."

"what then?" says Boutros.

"boldface says if a gyro is malfunctioning we take it offline & use the boosters instead," says Ravzi. boldface is anything in a manual that's highlighted in bold type. there are a lot of manuals & there is a lot of boldface. Grandpa says boldface is written not in ink but in blood. pretty much everything that's bolded is bolded because it saved someone's life, back in the days of the ISS & before, or because not doing it made someone die.

u always follow the boldface, says Grandpa. u follow it because it's written in the blood of those who went before. so i know already how this is going to go.

"so that's what u do," says Boutros to Virginia. "u follow the boldface."

"but—"

"that's an order, Duncan," says Boutros.

"boldface only says that because it makes sense for a normal situation," says Virginia. she's moved a little closer to me in the command module, defensively. i don't think she realizes she's done it. "where micro disturbances don't matter. docking of an unmanned cargo container is not a normal situation. the boosters would lose me the fine control i need."

Ravzi shrugs. "then we ditch the cargo container," he says. "better than risking the position of the station with an untested idea." he glances at me across the screen, then away.

Virginia reaches out & touches my shoulder. she gives me a "well, we tried" smile. "fine," she says.

my mother sighs. "can we get back to Brown & me being dead?" she says.

"yes, of course," says Boutros. "so, ur oxygen has run out. u're gone. Duncan has saved the station. Tomlinson: green card."

Tomlinson reaches out for 1. but another woman leans forward, young, glasses. she's new & i don't recall who she is. she has a beard that i figure is a gene-mod because over the hi-res connection i can tell it's real.

"wait," she says. "i have 1. Brown's family, or Freeman's family, starts demanding answers. the press gets the story & soon it's on all the apps. 'disaster on Moon 2,' that sort of thing."

"ok," says Boutros slowly. "so we put out a statement. we try to anticipate every scenario but we can't preempt everything, it's a terrible tragedy."

"meanwhile a lot of press attention is focused on Moon 2," says the woman. she has a light Hispanic accent.

Boutros looks over at her. "Santiago, i know u're new here at INDNAS, but—"

Santiago: PR, i remember.

"my job is to contain things. to manage information," says Santiago. "this is relevant."

"so?" says Flight Officer Brown. "everyone knows about Moon 2. it's not a secret."

on the screen, Santiago mimes turning over a green card. "fine. the *New York Times* digs deeper. they interview some ex-employees. start talking about the experiment. then before we know it—"

but we don't find out what happens before we know it because Boutros raises a hand. "yes, yes, we get the—"

"what experiment?" says Orion, from up here.

"the unmanned cargo container," says my mother. "it's still experimental. if we died because of a problem with it—"

"there have been some high-profile cases with self-driving cars," says Boutros. "the public is primed. it could really screw us if they come after us for the automatic cargo program. Santiago's right."

"but—" says Santiago.

"no, listen," says Boutros, his hand up, "everyone, we have to—"

but again we don't find out what we have to because the screen cuts off & Libra & Orion & Virginia & i are standing there looking at a black sheet of roll-LED on the table.

"huh," says Libra. "solar flare?"

Virginia looks out the porthole & shrugs. all we can c is blackness & stars.

a minute later the screen flicks on again.

"sorry for the interruption," says Boutros. "we're back." this seems unnecessary to point out. it's also not, entirely, true. Santiago isn't sitting in her seat anymore.

he sees us looking. "Santiago had to step out," he says. "shall we continue?"

"yes," says my mother. "let's get back to me & Brown being dead. what about notifications?"

let's not, i think. let's go back to the scandal. let's go back to the *New York Times*. because there's something they're not telling us. i look at Orion & Libra, & i can c they're thinking the same thing—but they don't say a word, & neither do i, & i think i know why. because there's an atmosphere in the room down there, u can hear it over the speakers in the station. it's a tension. a vibration, from something being stretched. something we can't c. it feels muscular. full of energy, of potential. like something that could snap.

& hurt people.

an image crosses my mind & i don't know why: Santiago being dragged down a hallway, a suited security officer on either side. i shake my head. what am i thinking?

i focus on the screen again. people have been talking but i missed it.

Flight Officer Brown reaches into his suit pocket & takes out a letter. "i want this delivered to my wife & kids," he says.

Boutros nods, leans over, & takes it. a sim is just a sim but it's also real. it's prep, for if this really happens. "Freeman? any message for ur family?"

"my family is there," she says, pointing to me. "half of it anyway."

pause.

"so? any message for him?"

she turns her hands over, as if surprised to c them connected to her arms. my mother doesn't deal well with this kind of thing: she finds it hard to know what is expected of her. i almost feel sorry for her. "as always," she says. "work hard. focus. that's all."

wow. great, Mother.

even Boutros looks a bit pale, tho that may be his foundation, i don't know. Virginia touches my shoulder again, & Libra floats over & squeezes my hand.

"what about other practicalities. bodies?" says Ravzi. "do we recover them? cremation? burial?"

now Brown looks pale too. "leave me," he says. "space is what i wanted since i was a kid. if i'm gonna be dead anywhere, it might as well be up there."

my mother purses her lips. "fine. me too."

"legal?" says Boutros to someone we can't c.

"Leo's a minor," says this person, a man, it sounds like. "who would take custody?"

"my father," says Mother.

Flight Officer Brown's eyes widen. Grandpa is pretty famous. not Armstrong famous but close. the most flights to the ISS of any living astronaut, etc. appearances on *The Tonight Show.* an autobiography that was on the *New York Times* bestseller list. a children's book. "Bob Freeman?" he almost whispers.

"yes," says my mother. she nods, matter-of-fact. "everything's arranged." in fact this is the first i've officially heard about what is going to happen if my mother dies.

great, i think.

everything is arranged. even me.

5
whoosh

the next day passes slowly. i'm worried about my mother, not that i would ever tell her that. i doubt she's nervous, down there. she doesn't really seem to feel those kinds of emotions.

nerves.

fear.

affection.

love.

instead i imagine she's going thru the manuals, the boldface, before being railed to the rocket on the maglev from base.

Nevada patches us in via vidlink, so Virginia & i can watch the launch on the screen in the bridge. Libra & Orion are doing their own thing. but i know they didn't move from in front of the vidlink last time their mother came up.

i left them alone then, just like they're leaving me alone now.

on the screen, Mother & Flight Officer Brown are 2 specks climbing the outside of the rocket, then they disappear inside. i know they'll be checking all the instruments, making sure their small personal bags are secured. my mother's is extremely small, i imagine. she doesn't even wear any jewelry. she doesn't believe in ornamentation. or sentimental value.

they'll be running thru the manual yet again. every possible variation, every possible problem. checking all the formulas & outputs. fuel. barometric pressure. everything.

Virginia holds my hands when the countdown begins. 10, 9, 8, etc.

then the rocket blasts off. we c the flames & the smoke, smoke like clouds, like the rocket is making its own weather, but the vidlink filters out the shaking of the earth that i know is happening—every action has an equal & opposite reaction—the roar even, it's all muted from up here, & then the rocket is an arrow loosed into the sky, accelerating all the time, full burn, pulling away from gravity's clinging love, into blueness.

we c the back section of the rocket fall to earth, when the fuel is burned out, & i know my mother is feeling maybe 4 g's of force as the secondary rockets kick in &—*zip*—the tiny pencil end of the rocket is gone, into the atmosphere.

"they made it," says Virginia.

"of course," i say. systems do what they're designed to do. it's people who are more complicated.

she smiles. "yes. of course. u want me to sync their updates to ur personal screen?"

"yes please," i say.

i take my screen everywhere with me for the rest of the day. launch out of the atmosphere is only the first stage, since we don't have shuttles anymore. the rocket module has to get into low earth orbit, then fire small nuanced burns, bit by bit, to rise up to meet the space station—all the time very complex calculations being made, so that the 2 ships will meet, so that they will be angled correctly to each other when they do.

i carry the screen into the relaxation module, where Libra & Orion are watching Wile E. Coyote cartoons. well, Libra is watching them. Orion is playing something on his flute, softly, a little refrain over & over. he has a screen propped on his knees—he almost always has, with a book on it, or his flute, or both, like now. i glance at it. the screen, i mean. James Bond. Orion likes old stuff.

Libra too, if by old stuff u mean Wile E. Coyote, which is this show from—i don't know—before the dawn of time. every TV show & movie ever made available to us on the cloud & this is the only thing she watches. she says it's because of the rules. she told me once how Chuck Jones, who made the cartoon, supposedly had some list of rules for the writers to follow, like:

–the Road Runner can only ever say *beep beep*.

–the Road Runner can't ever hurt the coyote.

–the coyote can hurt only himself, as a result of his plans to catch the Road Runner, which must always go wrong.

–the coyote must only use items from Acme Corporation to further his plans & these items must always backfire on him.

etc.

Libra said, *i like that because it's like being up here.* which is kind of true. i mean, our whole life is a list of rules. we're even discouraged from crying, to prevent rogue balls of moisture, same as with the sweat. of course, it's also just because she likes rules. Libra legit looks forward to going to real high school & having a locker & color-coded folders & prom, with all its codes of dress & behavior. i know because she is always telling us.

Orion: well, if they get him to enter the school premises, that would be an achievement.

i hover next to them.

"again?" i say to Libra, indicating the screen.

"always," says Libra. she laughs as the coyote takes out a de-hydrated boulder (Acme Corporation) & it immediately rehydrates into an enormous boulder & crushes him.

"ur mom's launch ok?" says Orion without looking up.

"yeah," i say.

from my screen, my mother's voice: "orbital pattern 1 achieved. programming booster sequence for next shell."

"cool," says Orion. "u'll c her in the morning."

"i will."

he nods. i wonder if he's thinking about his mother. about seeing her. different for him, of course, because his mother hugs him, used to read him stories, that sort of thing.

Libra is still laughing.

"i don't get it," i say. "i mean, i know the rules & all that. but u've seen all the episodes before."

she gestures to the screen. the coyote is running after the Road Runner & then the Road Runner stops & the coyote goes over a cliff. he keeps running for a while, grinning. then he slows, stops. frowns. he is floating in nothing. he looks down, realizes he's in thin air.

then he falls—*whoosh.*

"c?" says Libra. "it's a cartoon but it's got, like, the whole meaning of life in it. i mean, what does it tell u? it tells u that ur body can be broken but it will mend. it tells u that if u do bad things they will rebound on u. it tells u that death is the end. it tells u that u can walk on air, as long as u don't realize u're doing it."

"profound," says Orion, playing a sad mournful tune on his flute. "or it tells u that there's no point chasing road runners."

"like i said," says Libra, "meaning of life, right there."

from my screen: "shell 2 achieved. recalibrating. t minus 14 hours to docking."

"14 hours," says Orion. no inflection. there's something unspoken in the module & it's my mom & what she means. what she means to me.

"i'm going to my quarters," i say.

"sure," says Orion. his eyes are dark as deep space, flecked with stars too. "u know where we are."

"that's kind of the whole problem," i say with a smile.

"yeah, well, a few more days & then we're earthside," says

Libra. "i'm going to drink a milk shake. then watch the sunset. then ride a bike."

this is an old game.

"i'm going to swim in the ocean," i say. "then . . . light a bonfire on the beach. then i'm going to sleep on a real mattress with springs in it & that i don't need to be strapped into."

"i'm going to run in the rain," says Orion. "then watch birds, flying. any birds. then i'm going to go to a concert hall & listen to Jason Mukherjee playing Bach's Well-Tempered Clavier."

this is what he always says, & it's always the end of the game.

"good times," i say.

"good times," they both echo. sometimes it's spooky, the twin thing.

then there's a flicker from the porthole, & i turn. the twins turn too. green fire, over the ocean.

"aurora!" says Libra. she pushes up, floats over, & we join her. there must be a solar storm, a coronal mass ejection, big enough for particles emitted by the sun to make it to these lower latitudes, somewhere over the equator.

to blast atoms of air into light.

i'm going to go ahead & guess the Pacific, from the big blue expanse below us, because that's where we normally are. above it, the aurora neons the atmosphere, making swirling patterns of vivid green, pulsing, thinning, & then expanding, flickering, as if the earth is surrounded by its own ghost. on fire with it. every time i c it, i am amazed that it's only visible to a few people down there, the ones near the poles who c it at night. from here, it's the most obvious thing: a crown of ghost-fire, rippling, holy wind.

Orion takes my hand. he's always been like that, a big hugger & hand-holder, maybe less so now but especially when we were kids. & Libra takes his. except now it's like a circuit being closed, his hand on mine. buzzing. suddenly my body is only my hand;

the aurora electrics thru me, illuminates me from within. i twist inward, a Möbius strip of self-consciousness.

"prom, Paris, seeing a redwood tree," says Libra. 3 things she's looking forward to.

"a Michelin-starred meal," says Orion. "Michelangelo's ceiling of the Sistine Chapel. Jason Mukherjee playing—"

"Bach's Well-Tempered Clavier," i finish for him.

i let go of Orion's hand.

"u?" says Libra.

i shrug. "everything."

"cheating," says Orion.

"please," i say. "u cheated every game of Monopoly we ever played."

he waves a hand loftily. "artists are above commerce."

"u're not an artist," i say.

"not yet," says Orion, with a smile.

i smile back. Libra smiles too. we're not kids anymore, it's true. but we're going home.

nothing will ever be the same—but 1 of the ways it won't be the same is that there'll be ice cream. i smile harder.

6

drone

i torpedo to my quarters, & when i get there, a mountain range is below my window. the Himalayas, i think. or the Karakoram. 1 of those. green-brown valleys lead to glaciers. thin ribbons of river curve, sinuous, down into the lowlands, shining silver in the light.

i vidlink Grandpa. to my surprise, he answers—usually at this time of day he's out on the ranch somewhere, unless we've scheduled a call. calves are always being born; fences always need mending. & always, always, water needs to be found. to be raised, to be given to the grass, to the herd.

"hey," i say.

"hey," he says.

then: weird acoustic effect. thru my screen, which is set to push notifications, & thru the speakers from his end, the same voice. maybe half a second slower on my end.

"Nevada, we're in shell 3. all functions normal. all instruments reading a-ok. t minus 13 hours to docking." my mother's voice.

"they patched u in too, huh?" i say.

"i always listen," she says. "i'm always there."

the unspoken words cross the hundreds of miles between us, cross the atmospheric barrier, into the vacuum, fly thru it. i'm always there for her. if she needs me. which she never does.

"me too," i say.

Grandpa & i lock eyes. precision engineering. human comms. a moment of eternity.

"well," he says, "looks like everything is working."

"yeah."

"i got a new drone," he says. "s'why i'm in here, not outside."

Grandpa uses drones to keep an eye on his property. it's a big ranch. plus, i think he just likes flying them. once a pilot always a pilot.

"u want to c?" he says.

"u need to ask?" i say.

he grins. he looks young when he grins. i mean, not young—his face is still all lined. but younger. full of fire. my grandpa is a sun & my mother is a moon. he reaches down & keys something into another screen, then he makes a swiping gesture, & suddenly i'm looking down, thru my screen, onto brown grass.

"hang on. i'll take u out."

the grass begins to shrink, to grow smaller, more granular, & then a line of fence comes into view & then we're high up, above the broad flat valley, & the drone has a wide-viewing angle, so i can c the mountains in the distance, dark blue against light blue sky, cloud-crowned, topped with snow. & below, groups of cows, dark patches against the grass, moving, & the robot sprinklers that rotate like giant free-rolling wheels across parts of the grass-land, watering.

the drone remains entirely still. defying gravity.

"wow," i say. it's an understatement. i want to be standing in that valley, to feel all that space around me. i mean, i'm sur-rounded by space now, but i'm referring to landscape, real air, moving in currents, birds borne aloft on it, the wide bowl of the valley holding me, holding me up with its firm earth, & the moun-tains beyond, ringing my existence, circumscribing my world.

for a second i glance out the window & c just blackness, forever, & i feel a familiar constriction on my chest & i start breathing harder & harder & my skin goes tight & i feel sweat starting to break out on my forehead &—

"snap out of it, son," says Grandpa. "look."

i look. he brings the drone down, swoops almost, a looping maneuver & then we're above a small stream, & next to it, a mother cow standing with a calf—it must be no more than a day old. it stands on rickety legs, drinking milk from her.

"huh," i say, a kind of spoken sigh. this *huh* contains the words: *marvel, envy, delicacy, strength.*

"beautiful, isn't he?" he says. "i'm calling him Pepper, on account of his markings."

there are indeed little black patches sprinkled on the calf, all over, on the paleness of his coat.

"u'll meet him. just a matter of weeks now, & u'll c ur mother tomorrow," says Grandpa. "focus on that. u've got so much to look forward to."

he's wrong. i know it then. i know it even more later.

7

air lock

i set an alarm on my screen but i wake up at 06:30 anyway, my body's circadian rhythms in co-orbital harmony with my mother's arrival. i un-mute the screen. for a while i lie there strapped into my bunk but then i hear:

"t minus 10 minutes, Moon 2. activating automatic velocity management." my mother's voice.

"10-4," says Virginia. "i have u on my systems."

i hit the button that rolls the coverings up on my windows. we're over, i don't know, Europe maybe? above the pole, the corona wreathes the earth with green flames, but just the ordinary 1, the aurora borealis.

i reach out for a handrail & use it to pull myself thru the hatch out of my quarters, then torpedo thru the station. i pause, floating. i kick over to the nearest intercom terminal.

"Virginia?" i say into it, pushing the button to talk.

"Leo?"

"yeah. which arm?"

"ur mother's hatch?"

"yeah."

"starboard x-axis."

"thanks."

there's an androgynous peripheral assembly on the end of

each of the station's arms, a hatch that pairs with an identical 1 on my mother's docking module—either of them can be active or passive, depending on what's needed, & every ship the Company builds has the same ones, so anything can dock with anything else. it's pretty clever.

"on my way," i say into the intercom.

"figured u would be," says Virginia.

i cut thru the garden, half expecting to c Libra there, working on her plants, but i guess she's still asleep. i roll around a corner & into the starboard side of the x-axis crossarm—i flex my legs to bounce off a wall of bare panels, using my feet to redeploy my momentum in a new direction, the inertia carrying me straight thru a hatch & a spectrometer module. i cross 2 more experimental modules & then i'm at the hatch.

the air lock is closed, waiting. a transparent door secured by a rotating safe-style lock, like when Wile E. Coyote tunnels into a bank vault. beyond it is a space 6 ft. long, full of pumps that can make it a vacuum or a room full of air, depending.

& beyond that is the hatch door, the APA—it just looks like a ring of hooks & latches & attachments, which is precisely what it is.

everything closed, everything waiting.

except me, i realize suddenly. i'm not closed. i'm open, & it's going to get me hurt. so i flush my air lock—suck all the hope out of myself until i'm a vacuum inside, no feelings—& then i'm ready for my mother.

in fact i try not to think of her at all. i focus instead on pretending that i'm going out for another EVA, a real 1 this time. instead of a ship docking, we're using the APA to let me out, so i open the air-lock door & step thru, & when i'm in there i lower the helmet onto my suit & it automatically fastens into place, & i check my air & twist the rotating locks on my gloves & then i raise a hand to the vidlink terminal & give Virginia the command to dump the air, before opening the—

hatch, which at that moment clicks & hisses, on the other side of the air lock, taking me out of my daydream. the station's x-axis is currently facing vertical to the earth, so i'm looking down at the door my mother will come thru.

then the central part opens, radially, like an old-fashioned camera shutter, & i can c right thru the air lock & into the repurposed Soyuz module that has brought my mother & Flight Officer Brown up here. i c them too, but at an odd angle, still strapped into their seats.

"docking successful," says Virginia, over the whole station speaker system. "welcome to Moon 2, officers. welcome back, i should say."

there's movement in the module, & then after what seems like a really long time but is probably minutes, i c the 2 astronauts come clumsily swimming out, like sea creatures in suits of blubber, rising out of the deep. they hold on to the sides of the hatch & 1 by 1 pull themselves into the air lock, where they take hold of handrails & wait, still in their helmets & full EVA gear.

"please wait a moment while i bring atmospheric pressure in line with the station," says Virginia.

"10-4," says 1 of the astronauts, revealing himself to be Flight Officer Brown—it's hard to c into the smooth, shiny visors of the helmets.

there's a loud hiss, & streams of vapor start to pour into the air lock, as it fills with oxygen & nitrogen. i wave thru the door separating us & 1 of the astronauts waves back.

Flight Officer Brown.

it takes time for the air to fill the empty space. try it. breathe out, breathe all the air from ur lungs. then tank them up again. then imagine ur lungs are a space 6 ft. by 6 ft.

hiss.

hiss.

hiss.

then i feel a hand on my shoulder & turn to c Orion, floating behind me. he grabs a handle to pull himself into position next to me.

"hey," i say. "u're up."

"hard not to be, when Virginia's shouting over the speakers," he says. but he's smiling.

"thanks," i say.

he shrugs. "doesn't happen every day," he says. which kind of summarizes our whole childhood experience with our mothers in 1 sentence.

"Libra?" i say.

he shakes his head.

"asleep?"

"no. thinking about Mo— about our mother."

"yeah," i say. "i get it."

i do. i know she wishes her own mother was coming. i know Orion does too, tho he's being nice & generous about it because nice & generous is what he is.

hell, even i wish their mother was coming. or that my mother was a different mother. i don't know.

"14 lb/sq-in environmental pressure achieved," says Virginia over the speakers. "u may step out of ur suits & prepare to board the station."

my mother & Brown start to unclip their gloves & helmets.

"shall we?" says Orion. he yanks on the handle he's holding & the force floats him to the door. he puts his hands on the lock &

i c the veins in them, the tendons, the strength. i am not looking forward to this. at the same time i am looking forward to this because what my mother & Brown are here for, among other things, is to take us home.

to earth.

to gravity.

to birds.

to sky & air & the smell of bonfires & leaves underfoot & the feel of grass against skin & a million other things.

i hit the intercom next to me. "hey, Virginia. Orion's here with me. u want us to open the hatch?"

"sure."

my mother & Brown have taken off their suits now & are facing us in white t-shirts & underwear—it gets hot in a space suit. my mother, of course, is un-self-conscious about it. she would have to have a self to be conscious about, & she has logic gates in place of doors inside her. she just hovers there, watching me & Orion, as if we're interesting species of fish.

not Brown—he is doing a sort of awkward self-hugging thing. cold, maybe, too, i guess.

Orion & i take opposite ends of the wheel lock & spin it counterclockwise, which sounds easy but actually it's pretty hard to turn. muscles raise in his arms. we rotate it 3 full revolutions & there's a *click* & a *shhhh* sound & it sighs open. we reach behind us, grab handrails, & pull ourselves—& the door—back.

it swings open & my mother comes thru, Flight Officer Brown behind her.

"Leo," she says.

"Mother."

she looks the same. no more lines or wrinkles than when i last saw her. smooth dark skin. those big eyes that make her so beautiful in images but so disconcerting in person, because there is nothing behind them; they are like the portals of the station, only u look for stars & u don't c them.

"u've grown." she pauses. "i suppose that's what u do."

"me specifically?" i ask.

"children."

"hmm. i'm not a child anymore tho."

she tilts her head. "technically, yes, u are." she is a very literal person, my mother.

"yes, technically. but that's not—"

"where's Duncan?" she says, interrupting me. "bridge? i want to check on the status of the cargo ship."

"um. yes. Virginia? yes, she's on the bridge."

there's a moment of silence. Orion looks at me. Brown, who is now on our side of the door & pressing himself into the paneled wall, looks at both of us.

"well, come on, then," says my mother. "cargo's due to dock in 3 hours. the first unmanned supply vehicle to leave earth & rendezvous with the station in history. this is a significant moment."

Orion squeezes my forearm. i let the air out of my lungs.

it has been 11 months since i last saw my mother.

"ok, Mother," i say.

"i prefer Chief Officer Freeman when we're on station," she says, deftly slipping past me as if she has been in 0 g all this time, as if she hasn't been down on earth; she swims graceful as a dolphin up the shaft of the crossarm toward the conservatory.

"ok, Chief Officer Freeman," i say to her departing feet.

there's a long pause.

"um, hi," says Flight Officer Brown, looking embarrassed. "nice to meet u."

8

death, not a sim
part 1

i follow my mother, with Orion & Flight Officer Brown keeping up behind me. or Orion keeping up anyway; this is Brown's first time in 0 g, apart from training simulations, & he is bashing against things as he makes his way thru the station.

we stop at 1 of the first modules, where there are bright orange jumpsuits. my mother selects 1 for her & 1 for Brown & they pull them on.

when we reach the bridge Virginia mock salutes, but my mother doesn't understand irony, so she nods in recognition. they've known each other all my life but u wouldn't realize it to look at their interaction. Virginia raises her eyebrows at me & i smile behind my mother's back.

a few minutes later Brown comes in, dragging himself thru the hatch into the module. he is pale & sweating. he looks like he might pass out at any moment. Orion peeled off when we passed thru the garden—Libra was there & he waved to me as they started to talk about some plant she was inspecting.

"first time?" says Virginia.

"yes," Brown manages.

"it gets better," she says. "give it a day or 2. we have some pills too."

"thanks," he says.

"don't take the pills," says my mother. "the quicker ur body realizes u're in 0 g the better."

"oh, i think it realizes," he says.

Virginia asks them how their flight went. my mother dismisses her with a gesture—as if to say, we're here, that's all that needs to be said about the flight. we're not raining down on the Atlantic as shards of debris.

"what's the ETA of the cargo container?" she says.

"2 hours 48," says Virginia.

"ok," says my mother. "let's go thru the manual." pause. "the manual please, Duncan."

pause.

"oh," says Virginia, eventually, as if she's forgotten her surname since yesterday's sim. i mean, me & Libra & Orion don't use it. "yes. of course." she reaches past some screens on a desk & pulls out a folder. inside are sheets & sheets of technical data. mostly print is dead on earth, but on the station, u need it. in case the systems & screens go down. "actually there's kind of a problem i want to talk to u about," says Virginia.

the faulty gyro, i guess. & i frown a question at her.

she ignores me, looking at my mother instead.

"u can go," my mother says to me. she seems to reflect on this. "if u want. u know, play with ur friends."

"i'd like to stay," i say.

she frowns, genuinely puzzled. "why?"

"because . . ." i say. & then i stop, baffled by the size of the question & the impossibility of doing it justice. "because i want to know, & because this is what i want to do," i say.

"what is?"

i point to the blue & green sphere of the earth below us, to the instruments. "this. space."

"u want to do space?"

"yes! i mean, flights. EVAs. the stuff u do."

"u want to be an astronaut?"

"yes."

her frown has diminished marginally. "well, ur math grades are good enough, i suppose. i just didn't think . . . i didn't think of u doing anything. i mean u're just a kid."

"i'm growing up. that's what we do, remember?"

she looks me over. "yes. yes, i suppose u are."

"he's already got the not-feeling-sick part down," says Flight Officer Brown, whom i have decided i like, even if he is turning green now.

"& he did an EVA already," says Virginia. "& he's pretty good when it comes to the computers, that idea he had about the frequencies & taking a Fourier transform, it was really—"

"not an EVA," says my mother. "a 2-minute exfil from the hatch, then reeled back in like a fish."

"it counts!" i say.

"i'm not denigrating u," she says. "in fact i'm pleased u . . . share my interests. it's just a real EVA is a big deal. dangerous. the levels of preparation . . . we've been planning ours for hundreds of hours: the 1 Flight Officer Brown & i are doing tomorrow, to install the new gyro & the new cooling panel motherboard. & even then, something might go wrong. the slightest misstep & we'll be dead."

at this, Brown looks even more queasy, if that's possible.

"so what u're saying is u don't want me to die," i say.

"well, it would be very inconvenient. imagine the paperwork Boutros would want."

is that the ghost of a smile at the corner of her mouth? no. my mother does not joke.

"anyway, let's look at these manuals," my mother says.

she & Virginia pore over the codes & instructions for more than an hour, going over every detail. Brown floats over to the porthole & looks down on South America, then the ocean, then more ocean, then more ocean.

"it's mostly ocean," i say.

"i'm gathering," he says.

then Virginia beckons me over. she points to the screen. "i'm showing ur mother the vibration g graph. look." i'm surprised because she was ignoring me earlier when she went over everything with my mother, but maybe she was just waiting for the right time. she's known my mother years, after all.

i look. the gyro, the 1 that's slightly defective, is putting out 0.9 g now, a faint vibration that is running thru the whole ship. nearly enough to trigger an automatic warning.

"so take it out of law," says my mother. "like we said in the meeting. if it's messing up calibration of the cargo container, just remove it from play."

"i have," says Virginia. "we're on 3 gyros & boosters. & that's fine for macro adjustments, but it's really not fine-tuned enough for the small movements we need."

"then make the cargo container do the small movements. feed it all into ur data."

"i've simmed that too, & it just might work. but ur son here had an idea about ascertaining the precise frequency & then—"

"yes," says my mother. "the Fourier transform he mentioned in the sim. in theory it seems plausible. why don't u run it past ground control?"

so Virginia contacts ground control & tells them the situation.

"vibration is 0.9 g?" says an engineer named Singh.

"yes."

"any fluctuation?"

"well, yes, but never above 2 g."

"i'm running the sims down here too," he says. "& it all looks fine to me. too risky to try something untested."

my mother shrugs. she pats my arm awkwardly. "it was a good idea," she says.

this is in all honesty bewildering to me. usually my mother has only been interested in how i'm doing in my vidlink classes. maybe it's because i'm going back down to earth with her. maybe it's made her think about stuff. about me.

i can always hope.

9
death, not a sim
part 2

20 minutes later, we have eyeballs on the cargo container. well, indirectly: Virginia pulls up an image on 1 of the screens of the big cylindrical object as it slowly climbs up to our altitude.

–3,200 ft.

–2,900 ft.

–2,600 ft.

Virginia is watching code scroll on about 5 different monitors, moving between them & various joysticks & input terminals, typing in data & commands. basically she's controlling the station & the cargo container at the same time, or at least feeding inputs to the cargo container, in addition to its automatic sensors, that help it to make minute changes to its speed & angle in order to meet up with us.

"ok," she says. "slow & steady. velocity is adjusted; trajectory has docking in 4 minutes."

"good work, Duncan," says my mother.

"shit," says Virginia. "shit shit shit." she is looking at a screen where a graph is spiking, black line pulsing high up the y-axis, like a SoundCloud file of a rave song.

"2.5 g," says my mother. "3 g."

Virginia leans on the button that connects us to Nevada. "our outlaw gyro is spinning out," she says into the microphone.

"bearings shot or something, i don't know, but my h-infinity model is at its limits here."

"3.5 g," says my mother. "3.7 g." the vibration is now dramatic enough that we can feel it thru the ship—i put my hand on the metal wall & can detect the humming, like when touching 1 of Orion's tuning forks.

"it'll power down automatically at 4 g," says Singh, from down there on earth, where no one is about to be hit by a giant cargo container the size of a mobile home. in space. with nothing but nothing outside the suddenly flimsy-seeming windows.

i look at the screen showing the container, the thought of it hitting them.

the cargo container is getting closer.

bigger.

−2,000 ft. reads the screen.

−1,600 ft.

"not the point," says Virginia to Singh. "it's throwing the whole control system out of whack. & the cargo container used less fuel than we expected, so the sloshing perturbations are bigger than planned for—i've tweaked for it, but we're compensating for a lot here, & the atmospheric drag is pretty high too, so i don't know if i can bring this thing home, or if it's just going to—"

"so stop the cargo container," says Singh.

"i can't *stop* the cargo container," says Virginia. "do u have any idea of the inertia of—"

"yes," says Singh. "i'm an engineer with INDNAS."

INDNAS: aka the Company. formed by the merger of NASA, the Indian space agency, & a private company owned by a guy who pioneered internet shopping & now basically controls the selling of everything, everywhere.

"ok, ok," says Virginia. "but it's a lot & the boosters on the container are not set up to reverse like a town car; they're set up for small modifications of speed & direction."

"u designed the program," he says. "what do u suggest?"

"i helped design it. there was a whole team. & u designed the container," says Virginia. "i suggest u should have installed boosters that rotated thru 180 degrees."

my mother moves next to Virginia. "this isn't helping. Singh. it is Singh, isn't it? this is a code red, boldface kind of scenario. we need help here & we need it now. cargo container is going to impact in . . . t minus 1 minute."

"so slow it down," says Singh. then he seems to cut off.

we wait for a moment.

he comes back online.

"ok, listen." there are other voices in the background. loud voices, urgent voices. "wait. right. ok. here are some input variables for the cargo container boosters. plug them in. we can't control the container from down here—u have the deck." he reels off numbers & letters.

Virginia moves between terminals, like the Road Runner, typing. she sighs. i don't know if it's fear or relief or both. "ok, t minus 50 minutes to docking now," she says. "that's bought us some time. now what?"

"now power down the loose gyro manually."

"ok."

she floats to the other side of the bridge, flips up a monitor with an attached keyboard, a glowing green background. she presses some keys.

"oh fuck," she says.

no one is pressing the comms button. "what's happening up there?" says Singh.

my mother presses the button. "we seem to have a problem."

"oh god, oh god," says Brown. i had forgotten he was there.

"quiet," says my mother. not angrily. more like: this is business—we don't have time for that.

Virginia pushes off from the other wall & drifts back to us, backward. the cargo container continues to grow on the screen, tho more slowly now.

"it won't shut down," she says. "control is gone. maybe a severed cable, i don't know."

"u've tried—"

"yes," says Virginia. "whatever u're about to say i've tried it."

"vibration's at 4.5 g," says my mother.

"from which we can assume automatic shutdown has also failed," says Singh.

"yes, i deduced that," says Virginia; snaps Virginia, really. she looks at the other screens. "control program can't take it," she says. "the shaking is too great; it's more than the inputs on the container can deal with. i've got all the boosters in law but it's not helping enough." she hits a button. "program output says docking is impossible now. please advise."

"wait there," says Singh.

"well," says Virginia, "it's not like we have anywhere to go."

"unlike that container," says Brown, pointing to the screen where it is gradually growing, like some kind of stop-motion animation.

"what kind of effect is that going to have if it hits us?" asks my mother calmly.

Virginia takes a breath. "an external torque like that? it's going to throw off our attitude, maybe even threaten our orbit; plus, that thing has a mass of, like, 500 tons. it's full of spare fuel for us & equipment & supplies, so it's going to hit us with some serious force, maybe rupture our air supply, or the cooling . . . we could fry. or run out of oxygen."

"oh god, let it be the oxygen," says Brown. he's gripping a handrail on the desk & his fingers are white. "i don't want to cook."

"it's not multiple choice," says my mother. "u don't get to decide ur death."

he blanches even further.

just then Singh comes back online. "ok. so u have nearly 50 minutes, correct?"

"correct," says Virginia.

"the only scenario we can c is that Freeman & Brown EVA from the station & disconnect the gyro by hand," he says. "then ur perturbation is gone & u should be able to control the station's position with the remaining 3 gyros & the boosters, right?"

"right," says Virginia.

"wait," says my mother. "we haven't done any prep. what about camp out? standard prep is 24 hours in 10 lb/sq-in in the low pressure chamber & 30 minutes pure oxygen for any out-of-station activity."

"Russian protocol was 1 hour pure oxygen," says Singh. "u've got . . . 30 minutes. maybe."

"is that enough?" says my mother.

a voice i recognize comes over the intercom—Dr. Stearns. "there's no hard & fast," he says. "but u should avoid the bends. & if u get them . . . u have a chamber on board."

"ok," says my mother.

"*ok?*" says Brown.

"u want to wait here for the cargo container to make impact?" says my mother.

he goes quiet.

there's silence for a moment.

then:

"well," says my mother, turning to Brown again, "it looks like u do get a choice after all. how do u feel about dying on a poorly planned space walk?"

Brown doesn't answer for a long time. well, it feels like a long time, but we don't have a long time so it's probably 10 seconds.

"better than dying in here," he says eventually.

"ok," says my mother. "let's go breathe some oxygen."

10
death, not a sim
part 3

i stay in the command module with Virginia while my mother & Flight Officer Brown go to the end of the portside x-axis—there's an air lock & a hatch at the end of every arm of the space station. this 1 will bring them closest to the faulty gyro. they'll use the external remote control vehicle to move quickly along the truss to get to it.

Libra & Orion both appear a few minutes later. "problem?" says Libra.

Virginia nods. "Leo's mother & Flight Officer Brown are doing an EVA to try to shut down a malfunctioning gyro. u feel that?" she puts her hand on the hull.

Libra & Orion stretch out their fingers. "oh, yeah. it's shivering."

it's shivering, & i'm shivering.

i'm watching my mother on 1 screen, climbing into her liquid cooling suit, then beginning to put on the bulky outer space suit. all the time she is breathing pure oxygen from a tank. she & Brown are in the air lock, where Virginia has dumped some of the pressure to bring them down to about 10 lb/sq-in. soon she'll take it down even farther to 4.7 lb/sq-in, to match the internal pressure system of the suits themselves.

it has to be done gradually, of course, otherwise the astronaut can suffer the bends when going out into space, where the atmospheric pressure is 0 & the pressure inside their suit is a third of that of the space station. tho, as my mother said, 24 hours of prep would be preferable. a space walk is a carefully choreographed thing—not a rush emergency job.

well, in an ideal world.

another expression that feels strange, growing up here. we're not in any world, let alone an ideal 1. we're in a sky.

"that the cargo ship?" asks Orion. he's pointing to another screen, the 1 showing the big cylinder that's slowly moving toward us, the vast moon behind it, shadowed by the earth.

"uh-huh," says Virginia.

"& it's going to dock automatically? cool."

"not if we don't turn off this gyro," says Virginia.

"& if we don't?"

Virginia doesn't answer. Orion gives me a look that says: *oh.* Libra is nervously twisting the vial of earth around her neck.

"still," says Orion. "ur mother is the best, right?"

"yes." this isn't boasting, it's true. she was top gun at the Air Force Academy. PhD at 19.

15 rotations on Moon 2.

the minutes go by slowly. i watch the seconds ticking down on the clocks. meanwhile Singh is constantly on the intercom, checking in for updates, relaying suggestions to Virginia.

on the screen, my mother & Brown snap their golden visors down & my mother floats over to the camera. "ready as we'll ever be," she says.

Virginia checks some readouts. "oxygen ok," she says. "suit pressure ok. no leaks detected. right. u're ready to go outside."

Brown doesn't say anything.

"Freeman. confirm status," says Virginia.

"status ok," says my mother.

"Brown. confirm status."

pause.

"status ok," says Brown finally.

Virginia nods to herself. then she flicks a switch to unlock the hatch. my mother & Brown still need to manually open it—they put their gloves on the wheel & rotate—they're clumsy in their huge suits & it takes some time, but eventually it twists open & they pull back the hatch & head into the air lock.

Virginia tilts & pans the camera—earthrise on the screen, blue ocean below filling the circular aperture of the door onto space. both astronauts lean out, clip their lines to the rail that runs along the station, & then float out into space.

to my shame, the emotion that i feel at that moment is jealousy.

they're out there, in the emptiness, in the inky blackness, & i'm in here. like always. like my whole entire life.

Virginia switches to an external camera & we c my mother & Brown on the surface of Moon 2, their suits very white against the gray of the hull. they make their way inch by inch to the RCV. this is like a flatbed assembly with little wheels that run along the truss. Virginia will control it, driving the astronauts to where they need to be.

Brown holds my mother's arm while she unclips from the rail & on to the vehicle. then she does the same for him. they grab hold of the frame of the RCV—technically it's a translation aid, this little truck. translation as in movement, not as in language, of course.

"ready?" says Virginia into her mic.

"ready," says my mother. "a-ok so far."

Virginia takes a joystick & nudges it gently. the RCV rolls along the truss, taking the 2 astronauts with it. they have boosters on their packs too, little rockets they could use, in theory, to fly around space, but those are really just for emergencies—like if they get separated from the station.

Virginia turns to the monitors & calls up every external camera she can, so we're seeing everything from multiple angles. on 1 screen we can c the cargo container very, very close to the station now. Virginia is constantly adjusting its boosters & speeding up the space station itself, which was a suggestion of Singh's, to keep the 2 apart for as long as possible. the only problem is that speeding us up increases our altitude respective to the earth, because in space, speed equals height, but we're just going to have to readjust our whole attitude when the thing has finally docked.

meanwhile my mother & Brown have reached the site of the gyro, & Virginia zooms in on them. we can actually c the gyro juddering—that whole arm of the station is shaking with the force. the astronauts unclip from the RCV & clip back onto the truss itself; then they approach the cables & circuit boards for the gyro.

"this thing is really bouncing around," says my mother over her mic.

"tell me about it," says Brown. we can c that they are being jolted by the vibrations; it's like they're attached to a building in an earthquake. except that they're surrounded by nothing but empty black space.

"can u still disconnect it?" says Virginia.

"we can try," says my mother.

from the tool station on the translation aid, she takes out a wrench. More than a wrench, really—it's a powered multitool with a built-in electric motor, which astronauts can use for all kinds of tasks. she motions for Brown to do the same & then they start unscrewing bolts on a plate next to the gyro, presumably to get at the electronics controlling the device.

when the panel is unsecured, they lash it to the RCV.

"command, u have a circuit diagram for this thing?" asks my mother.

"yes," says Virginia. "i'm looking at it now. u want to cut the red power line at top left. or pop out the motherboard at bottom right."

my mother selects a different function on her wrench & uses the workstation stanchion to lean over the exposed workings, legs floating in space.

"ready?" she says. "when this powers down, u're going to need to compensate."

Virginia brings up several monitors of code. "boosters & alternate gyros ready," she says.

"10-4," says my mother. "Brown, hold on. this is going to jerk the arm, most likely."

Brown is clipped on but he grips a truss rail anyway, as my mother lowers the wrench.

then . . .

she twists . . .

& . . .

it works.

the shuddering on the image, which has been like a motion blur the whole time, disappears as the gyro shuts off & the spiking g graph that is running on 1 of the screens flattens to 0.

Virginia types furiously, telling every other torque generator on the station to work overtime, keeping the station steady.

my mother & Brown twitch, like marionettes, then get their equilibrium. they high-five each other. "job done," says my mother.

which is when i c something from the corner of my eye. i turn. a flame is spouting from the rear of the cargo container, & i say to Virginia, "Virginia," & Orion says, "oh my god," & Singh is suddenly on the intercom saying, "what is that? what the hell is that?"

& u have to imagine that all of this is happening at the same time, & also simultaneously the cargo container is powering forward, unstoppable, & it was less than 700 ft. from us anyway, almost co-orbiting, held at bay by Virginia's codes & commands that are totally useless at this point because that's a rocket flaming, burning pure fuel, & the massive unmanned cargo container is now a colossal bullet heading tow—

crash!

the station rocks. Libra is thrown into me & i catch her & she buries her head in my chest, as Orion hits the table & clings on to it. Virginia's face slams into the desk & she lifts her hand again, nose & mouth bleeding, but she doesn't seem to notice.

she taps & taps & taps but 2 screens are gone & on 1 of them we c the cargo container rotate about its own axis where it has hit the lower y arm of the station, bits of panel & hull & god knows what else scattering into black space like confetti, the huge metal cylinder turning like a lever, inevitably, & then spinning toward the x arm.

toward my mother & Brown.

broken pieces of the space station, small & large, float silently.

inside, alarms start to go off.

"Moon 2, please come in. Moon 2, please come in," says Singh, over the intercom, but no one is listening to him.

somehow, Virginia is still focusing. she is watching all the screens. monitoring what is going on. "Leo!" she says. "i think it's just the end of the arm. shut the secondary air-lock doors. we have to contain this."

"Duncan!" says my mother.

"yes, so listen—" Virginia starts to speak to the astronauts & waves a hand at me, to say, *u do ur bit.*

"ok," i say. i'm stunned, reeling, in a kind of world where air has been replaced by something thicker & harder to navigate, but her instruction finally breaks thru it.

i bring up the pressure & atmosphere system, & initiate the protocol to close off 1 of the station's 4 arms, the 1 the cargo container hit, which i think is 1 of the infrared array sensors pointing at deep space.

"done," i say.

"pressure normalizing in the rest of the ship?"

i watch the screen.

12 lb/sq-in.

12.5 lb/sq-in.

13 lb/sq-in.

"yes," i say.

words are linear but events don't work like that, so what u have to imagine is that everything that follows is happening simultaneously, all the words superimposed on each other, overlapping, interleaving like playing cards.

from multiple angles, from multiple cameras, a feed comes in of the cargo container, which, now subject to massive rotational force due to the full firing of 1 of its rockets & the fact of hitting the space station, spins thru the gap in the plus sign of Moon 2, &—

the part that i c when i look up from the pressure management system—

bears down on the place where Mother & Brown are clipped on—

"unclip from the station & grab the RCV!" says Virginia into the intercom—

Mother & Brown grab it—

Virginia leans on the joystick, & the vehicle slides down the arm, pulling my mother with it, quickly down toward the middle of the plus sign where we are, inside the heart of the station, & Brown's hand is yanked from it because he left himself clipped to the truss, next to the gyro—

the cargo container scrapes against the truss, with its long end, trailing broken pieces of metal & insulation foam as it goes, & spins on into empty space, & Brown just isn't there anymore, from 1 split second to the next, he's gone. the g-force goes crazy as action & opposite reaction do their thing, & we spin, & for once, as something—a rail?—collides with my back, i feel the truth of our situation: that this is a very, very heavy thing that we're in, lunged by air & buoyed by 0 g but fundamentally, deep down, where the rules are, the rules that keep things together: massive.

the rules that keep things together, & apart.

& then Virginia pulls up another screen & there's the cargo container, rapidly moving away from us, still flipping around & around like a juggler's baton.

& the tiny figure of Brown, arms & legs outstretched, drifting away into blackness, pierced with bright stars.

"Brown!" says Virginia into the intercom. "Brown!"

no answer.

interlude
angels

we're 8, maybe 9.

Libra, Orion, & i are sitting in the cupola, looking down on the arctic ice as it spins below us.

"u think they felt anything?" says Libra.

a rocket blew up on launch the previous day. it was taking 3 astronauts to fix a comms satellite.

"no," says Orion. "probably didn't even know about it."

the explosion was very dramatic. a ball of fire engulfing the launch site. we saw it on a screen, before Virginia turned it off & sent us away to play.

"i wonder what happens if u die without realizing," i say. "i mean, do u know u're dead?"

Orion shrugs. "maybe everything goes black, like when u turn off a screen."

Libra shakes her head. "i think it's the same as dying any other way. i think . . . u just find urself in the next place."

"which is what?" i say. "heaven?"

now it's her turn to shrug—the movement is exactly like her twin's. "Mom said in the old days they thought people turned into angels. that they went up into the sky & looked down on the earth & kept watch over people."

i c ice floes breaking, in the cold blue waters 250 miles below.

we are coming up to the dark line of night. aurora borealis shimmers, crowning the earth, greeny waves, silky.

"like us," i say.

we all shiver.

we huddle up closer together. Libra & Orion put their arms around each other.

we watch the world spin.

we watch over it.

11

suit up

"Brown's gone," says my mother, "Brown's gone," as if now that he is, indeed, gone, someone has to fill his role of stating the self-evident, & i don't know why i have such a mean thought, crossing my mind like a falling star, maybe it's the shock.

"fuck," says Virginia. "fuck. what went wrong with the program? what did i do?" she is crying. i don't know if she realizes. the tears are just leaking out into the 0-g module, forming bubbles, floating around.

"stop crying," i say.

"what? how can u tell me to—"

"no," i say. i point to the spheres, tiny shining teardrops in the light of the moon, drifting like little bright planets.

"oh. shit."

Singh's voice comes thru the intercom. it sounds shaky. "sitrep," he says.

i press the button. "i'm ok . . . um, Leo here. Virginia—i mean, Officer Duncan is ok. my mother appears to be ok."

"i'm . . . ok," says my mother. i can c her on the screen, clinging to the RCV she is clipped to. there are still pieces of metal out there, moving unpredictably—she ducks as a bolt of some kind flies past her. "but Brown—"

"Brown is dead," says Singh. but not flatly, not unkindly. "i . . . his vitals have gone. from our screens."

"i'm sorry," says Virginia. "i'm sorry. i don't know what went wrong. i went over this code a million times, maybe 2 million, i—"

"not u," says Singh. "data says the booster fire was a mechanical issue. it wasn't the software. something . . . some spark ignited the fuel."

"oh my god," says Virginia. "oh my god." she lets out a long breath.

"crew," comes a new voice over the intercom. it's Boutros. the boss. "this is a devastating loss, crew, but we need to focus. Duncan, our screens have u heading for reentry. the impact has knocked u badly off equilibrium attitude. we can help from here but u're going to have to get on it too."

"yes," says Virginia. "yes, of course."

"we also need to get Freeman back inside. right now the perturbations are too great for her to effect reentry."

Virginia looks at me. i know what she's thinking because i am thinking the same thing: it hadn't occurred to me. it hadn't even occurred to me that my mother couldn't get back in.

"ok," says Virginia. she switches comms. "Freeman? are u secure?"

"clipped on & holding on," says my mother. "i'm as secure as i'll ever be." there is something hollow in her voice. i think it's probably seeing her colleague swept off the station by a huge metal cylinder weighing the force equivalent of hundreds of tons.

"nitrox levels?"

"1 hour left," says my mother.

"50 minutes," says Dr. Stearns, over the intercom.

"1 hour," says my mother, in a tone that brooks no argument. "i can turn it down."

Virginia bends over her instruments. "ok, i'm going to use the boosters to try to cancel out most of the external torque, but we don't have a lot of fuel—"

"do it," says my mother. "u'll burn up otherwise."

"shit," says Virginia. "shit. atmos drag is crazy. the gyros are saturating from trying to automatically absorb the momentum . . . i can try to desaturate 1 or 2 of them with a gravity gradient, but . . ."

she works for a long time, firefighting, luckily not literally, but that is about the only thing that is lucky at this moment. she goes from monitor to monitor, pushing between 1 wall & the other.

"can we help?" Orion says.

"no."

"not even Leo?"

"no."

half an hour later, Virginia floats back from a keyboard & blows out a long stream of breath. "attitude reestablished," she says. "Freeman, come back in."

we watch as my mother drives the RCV herself using the hand brake, until she's back at the hatch at the end. Virginia opens the hatch & lets her in, then starts to repressurize the air lock. my mother curls into the fetal position & spins slowly in the tubular space.

"Freeman's safe," says Virginia into the intercom. "but i've got 2 desaturated gyros & i've burned most of our booster fuel. we've also got that 1 gyro off grid, which . . ."

". . . places a reliance on the boosters to maintain attitude," says Singh over the speakers. "because u need 4 gyros for full gyro control."

"yes," says Virginia. "even without a massive torque like that on the whole system."

"shit," says Singh. a pause. "sorry," he says.

"so?" says Orion. he is hanging on to a handrail, a wild look in his eyes. "what does that mean?"

"it means we need more fuel, or we need to get a new gyro online," says Virginia.

"can we get more fuel?" says Libra. "where would we get fuel?"

"from the cargo container," says Virginia.

"oh," says Libra. she looks to be close to tears but she's been up here all her life, she knows about the not crying.

"& the extra gyro?" says Orion. "what about that?"

"we have 1. it's in 1 of the storage hubs. but it's a 2-astronaut job. EVA only. & we've just lost Brown."

"so . . . ," says Libra. "what are the options?"

"i don't know," says Virginia. "fly home? take the module Leo's mother & Brown arrived in & get off the station. but we can't abandon the station. this place cost billions of dollars. it was the life work of so many people. we can't just—"

"or? what's the alternative?"

"or, after an hour or so, we find out what happens to hard objects when they hit the atmosphere at the wrong angle."

silence.

i seize Virginia's hand & pull myself toward her. "i'll do it," i say.

"what?"

"i'll do it. i'll go, now."

"where?"

"i'll EVA. with my mother. she's already suited up, we can install the new gyro. where is it?"

"right by the failed 1, as it happens. x-axis truss. in a storage bay. but—"

"but nothing. come on. i know the protocol. i can do it."

Orion frowns at me. "Leo, i mean, come on . . ."

"u don't have time to prep," says Virginia. "u'll get the bends."

this is the big problem with EVAs. it's a bit like diving. or the opposite of diving maybe, because when u're diving the problem is coming up, transitioning from high pressure to lower pressure. when u're doing an EVA, the problem is going out. u go out into 0 pressure, & u're breathing a mixture of nitrogen & oxygen, which means that if u don't prebreathe oxygen for long enough, & preferably compress too, u get little bubbles of nitrogen in ur blood.

it can make the blood vessels in ur skin burst, in ur eyes too. the bubbles can pop in ur joints, causing excruciating pain, causing immobility. it can make u pass out, even fall into a coma. or suffer long-term neurological damage.

none of which is going to stop me.

"come on, V," i say. "we can cure that. an hour after in the hyperbaric chamber on pure ox & i'll be ok."

she stares at me. "u're going to give urself the bends & then just . . . cure urself?"

"yes. come on, i'm young. i've literally just had a medical. i'm not going to have a heart attack or anything."

"Leo . . . ," says Libra. Virginia starts to say something but Libra puts her hand up, then swims over to me. she puts her hands on my shoulders, her eyes on mine. "Leo. u don't have to do this. u don't have to try to impress ur mother."

i keep a lock on her eyes, genuinely bemused. "i'm not," i say.

"u're not? then what? u want to be the hero?"

i shake my head. "i just want to help. & . . ."

"& what?" she is looking at me with a look that says: *truth, now.*

"& i want to get out there." i point to the window. to the sky beyond.

Orion shrugs. "a wider space," he says.

"exactly," i say.

Libra nods slowly. she turns to Virginia. u can almost c thought processes running behind her eyes, script rolling, like code. "he's right," she says. "not his whole crazy getting-outside-into-space death-wish thing. but about the situation. it's the only option. either Leo EVAs with his mother or we die."

pause.

"unless i do it," says Virginia.

"no," says Libra. "we need u on the programs. on the flight deck."

another pause.

"fuck," says Virginia. she thumbs the button on the intercom. "Boutros? Singh? we have 2 options here. either we all take the landing module & fly home, right now, or Leo EVAs with his mother to install the new gyro. he'll get decompression sickness but we can put him straight into hyperbaric when he comes back in."

she doesn't mention a third option, which is: *we die.*

pause.

"returning is not an option," says Boutros eventually. "we need Moon 2 functioning. u come back, it's coming down behind u in flames. we & NASA & the Russians didn't work 80 years for that."

"u'd prefer we die up here than come back?" says Libra slowly.

silence.

"returning is not an option," says Boutros again. "not until the station is secured & in stable orbit."

"ok," says Orion. "so option 2."

"option 2," i say. i start to move toward the hatch.

"wait," says Virginia. "don't we need to tell ur mother?" she reaches for the comms switch.

"no," i say. "i'll tell her myself."

i torpedo across the station, thru modules & hatches, until i come to the end of the line, to the air-lock door beyond which my mother is waiting, still curled up.

i press the intercom button installed next to the door. "Mother?" i say.

she looks up. i motion to her to float to the intercom on her side.

"yes?"

"u & i are going out. to install a new gyro. we don't have enough fuel to maintain attitude without it."

with my mother, long conversations are a rarity. she is already working out all the angles, is already ten steps ahead. there's no need to talk it all thru.

"who's we?" she says.

"me & u."

she eyes me. "u have no experience."

"i've been out there."

"with Chang?" she says. "yes. for 2 minutes."

ok—FINE—it was 2 minutes. but 2 minutes is more than nothing.

"2 minutes is more than nothing," i say.

for a long moment she just looks at me. "what's the plan?" she says. "compression immediately after? hope u don't get too sick? hope u don't have a stroke?"

i shrug. "yes."

her eyes shift as she calculates. "u're 15," she says eventually. "elastic muscles. good blood pressure. strong veins."

"yes."

"we burn up otherwise?"

"yes. all the spare fuel was on the container."

"installing a gyro is not easy. especially with debris floating everywhere. u do everything i say, when i say it. everything."

"yes sir."

"ok then," she says, apparently not detecting the irony in my address. "suit up."

12
EVA, part 1

so i do.

there's a kind of closet next to the air lock, & i open it & take out the water-cooling suit. it's like a giant set of pajamas, but full of clear plastic tubes that run all around my body, piping cold water to my every extremity. space suits get very hot from the sun & from the lack of moving air to cool them—without the water suit i'd cook in it.

then i put on the bulky space suit. i suppose it's more accurate to say i step into it, into the hard upper torso of it, because it has a kind of door at the back—it's more like an exoskeleton than a suit. mounted to the back is a huge pack that contains my oxygen & nitrogen, the feedwater tank for the cooling suit, which i couple up, a CO_2 removal cartridge to get rid of my waste air, & a dozen other sensors & systems to keep me alive.

Virginia has depressurized the air lock again, & i open the door & float thru to my mother—i say that in 1 sentence but it takes a while, maneuvering in this thing that is more like a vehicle wrapped around me than clothes. every movement has to be deliberate, has to be careful.

my mother takes my hand. or my glove, i should say. not affectionately; just to keep me steady. for a moment we bob, gently, in the air lock.

our umbilicals snake behind us, hooked up to the comms & the power, tethering us to the ship. we are both in the station & outside of it, no longer subject to its pressure. we check our LED displays, making sure our oxygen levels & pressure indicators are reading correctly. a tiny mistake means death out there.

everything is ok.

we check again.

everything is ok.

"open the outside hatch, Duncan," says my mother.

& she does.

there's a hiss & it irises open & we're looking down on arctic tundra, under swirling clouds, on a blackness beyond that goes on forever. now to get out. we lower our golden visors to block the too-bright light of the sun, to save our corneas from being burned from our heads, & worm our way thru the hatch, until we're on the outside of the ship.

"clip on," says my mother, & i clip to the braided cable on the surface of the station. i am focused on this little task, & then i turn around.

i turn around.

& my heart stops.

not because any of my systems have failed, but because of where i am.

it's the beauty.

it's the beauty.

u can grow up inside of a place & know it's right there, on the other side, but it won't prepare u for the height of it, for the scale of what surrounds it, when u're outside. i've been out here before, briefly, with Chang, but even that isn't enough—there are some things that are simply beyond human comprehension, no matter where u are born, & space is 1 of them.

in like 30 minutes it'll be dark again, but now everything is flooded with light, light u can't believe, total & absolute & so bright it seems metaphorical, some kind of revelation.

below us, the earth. perfect & spinning, its curvature clearly visible, lit by the sun. silver threads of river ribboning into dark. & in every direction, space. but *space* is the wrong word, because this is something that goes on forever & is full of worlds, billions of them, pinpricks sparkling in the endless darkness.

for a long moment i am just in shock.

i knew it was coming, but i'm still in shock.

it's like—let me think what i can compare it to. imagine u're in a bathtub & u put ur head under the water & open ur eyes, & instead of seeing the inside of the tub, u're in the deep ocean, the water going light blue to dark blue as u turn ur eyes down, jelly-fish pulsing, a whale swimming by below. that's what open space does to u, even if u've grown up in space.

then i hear a beeping & i focus on the green LEDs on my heads-up display & i c my heart rate spiking.

"Leo. Leo, talk to me." it's Dr. Stearns's voice.

"i'm ok," i say. i check my systems. "systems normal. just . . . just so big."

"we get it, Leo," says Boutros. his tone is like a loving dad's but also like the boss of a huge multibillion-dollar scientific & explorative initiative. "but pull urself together. u have a job to do."

"yes sir," i say, without any irony this time.

"check suit," says my mother.

i look at my HUD—my heads-up display. suit pressure ok. air supply ok. "ok," i say.

"check again."

i check again. EVAs are all checking all the time. a leak in the suit would mean the vacuum outside getting in. which would mean: ruptured lungs, burst eardrums, & our saliva & sweat starting to boil. not a nice way to die.

when she's satisfied, my mother tells me to move my clip over to the RCV & clip onto it. we have to move quickly because nitrogen bubbles will be entering my bloodstream already—the quicker i get back inside & into the hyperbaric chamber, the better.

"Virginia, take us down," says my mother. "& activate the Dextre arm too. get it over to the gyro."

"already done," says Virginia.

"good."

there's a clunk, & then the motored vehicle starts to slide down the truss on the outside of the station. we're clipped to it—Mother's feet are also in the footrests at the front end of the RCV, so she's pointing forward, like the carved figure on the prow of an old ship. i'm drifting behind, 1 hand gripping a handle on the flat truck.

at the moment, the arm we're on is parallel to the earth. so i can c blue ocean turning below, the occasional island. i think it's the Pacific, Japan swinging into view. between us is 250 miles of emptiness. & on the other side of the earth is the moon, some of it visible over the arc of the earth's curvature, gray & pockmarked.

the moon is always there, somewhere, outside the station's portholes. spinning around the earth, endlessly. an orbit of devotion.

nothing in the universe loves like the moon loves the earth.

"focus, Leo," says my mother.

we're coming up to the gyro. it doesn't look like much. a kind of hooded square shape. u can't even c the spinning part or the gimbal—it's all inside a round white cover. to keep it protected from micrometeoroids. tho it seems like something has damaged its bearings anyway.

"clip to the truss," says my mother. & we both hold on with 1 hand, before moving our clips onto the station's cable.

positioned on the other side of the gyro, the portside, is the Dextre robotic arm. "Virginia, u have Dextre control?" says my mother.

"yes," says Virginia, over the radio. she gives a little wave with the end of the arm.

"ok. i want u to lock onto the gyro. Leo & i are going to undo the bolts. then u're going to pull it away from the station. the spare gyro is in bay 3. then we install the new gyro. then u put the old 1 in bay 3 where the new 1 was. got that?"

"sure," says Virginia.

"so repeat it," says my mother.

Virginia repeats it. little mistakes get u killed.

when my mother's happy, Virginia moves the robot arm until it grips on to the external assembly on the gyro. she checks & double-checks that it's secure, by trying to move the arm—gears grind, but it's going nowhere. it's locked on.

"wrenches," says my mother.

i open the tool box on the RCV & take out a motorized wrench & pass it to her. then i take out the second. she beckons me over & shows me the 8 bolts we need to unscrew. "i'll take the ones on this side," she says. "u take that side."

i try to block out what is around us, the stars, the earth, the moon. the endlessness of empty space. i try to shrink the world to what is right in front of my visor: the gyro bolts & the side of the station, gleaming silver in the sunlight. it's hot in the suit, despite the water-cooling undergarment, & i can feel sweat beading on my forehead. all sounds are muffled, apart from the beeping of my heart monitor & the voices coming in thru the radio.

i get my wrench on the first bolt & turn. it's hard. the simplest activities on an EVA become hard because at the same time as twisting the wrench u're trying to maintain ur position vis-à-vis the station, with no gravity to assist & in a bulky suit. all ur muscles are working to keep u straight as u concentrate on the task at hand. not to mention u're manipulating the wrench, with a huge glove over ur hand that makes fine motor control virtually impossible.

twist.

twist.

twist.

i turn the wrench carefully, & eventually the bolt comes loose. before it can float away i catch it in the same glove & transfer it to the tool box on the RCV, which is lined with elastic strips going in orthogonal directions that can be used to secure small objects.

then the next bolt.

then the next.

i glance up at my mother. she's hard at work on her last bolt, way quicker than me. i catch a glimpse of the earth, still rotating below us, the landmass of India now, blue ridges of mountains, brown expanses of desert. the world catches my breath, holds it in the glaciers, in the sprawling cities.

i turn from it & it's still there, the colors, the greens & blues & browns reflected in the shining surface of the space station, in all the planes of metal & glass. a kind of projection of the earth below, shimmering, beautiful, especially because it's so vivid against the deep, deep blackness of space beyond.

"focus," says my mother.

so i turn back to the last bolt, & that's when i c that my visor is misting up.

"uh, Nevada, my visor is . . . i have some kind of condensation," i say. i can c the plate holding the gyro & the last bolt but it's all swimming, blurred.

"condensation or vision problem?" says Boutros, from down there on the earth i've never been to.

"condensation. i think."

"checking vitals," says Dr. Stearns. "heart rate is a little high. but we'd expect that with no prepressurization. incidentally u 2 need to hurry up. i'm concerned about long-term neurological damage."

oh. great.

my mother has swung herself over to me. i c her helmeted head in front of me, smudgy thru my misted visor. now i don't need to worry about the mind-breaking distraction of the view, because i can't c much at all. also there's something in my eye. some kind of grit. "i'm concerned about what's causing his helmet to steam up," my mother says.

"yes, of course," says Dr. Stearns. "technical. over to u."

another voice comes on. a woman. "Leo, are ur eyes sore at all?"

"yes. i mean, not sore. but i have like some grit in there."

"ah," says the woman.

"ah," says Dr. Stearns.

13

EVA, part 2

"ah?" i say. "what does *ah* mean?"

i'm gripping the handle on the station too tightly; my hand is hurting. i try to relax my fingers.

"purification system?" says my mother.

"that's what i'm thinking," says the woman's voice.

"agreed," says Dr. Stearns.

"ok, Leo," says the woman to me. obviously to me. i'm feeling a little hysterical at this point. i'm tethered to the outside of the station & everything on the other side of the suit—which is also nothing—wants to kill me. "ur air is cleaned by a filter that uses lithium hydroxide to remove the carbon dioxide u're breathing out. we think that lithium hydroxide is leaking. it's caustic, so it's irritating ur eyes & causing u to c condensation."

"what do i do?"

"u need to purge ur suit, right now."

"what?" no one ever does this. it's insanity. i'd be purging all the air i have to breathe.

"trust me, Leo. ur suit will be filling with fresh oxygen all the time. try to slow ur breathing, u'll be ok."

"wait, what if—"

"no waiting. now. hit ur purge valve."

"but i—"

"now, Leo." if it's possible for a person to speak in all caps, she is doing it. "NOW, LEO." like that. then she adds: "that's an order."

it's dark now, & not just because my visor is misted; when u orbit at 17,500 miles an hour, the night comes on u like a switch, & now i'm in a total absence of light that feels metaphorical in a much more horrible way.

i c the stars, glinting blurrily, all the magnificence of space, windowed by a small visor: how much beauty it has in it, how much endlessness, & nothing to judge u at all.

& nothing to show u any kindness either. a cold song, with no music to it.

ok, i think. ok, it's up to u, Leo.

i know where the purge valve is, next to my left ear on the helmet, but i never thought i'd use it. it's for dumping my air out into space, after all. but i turn it anyway. the air starts to hiss out of my suit, bubbling out into the vastness of space—i actually c the bubbles, thousands of them, iridescent in the light from the ship, drifting out into the blackness.

i slow my breathing, trying to use as little air as possible while the atmosphere flushes from my suit, constantly reminding myself in a kind of mantra that there is new oxygen coming in, there is new oxygen coming in, there is new oxygen coming in.

i feel light-headed & i only know that i let go of the station when my mother grabs my hand.

slow breaths.

slow breaths.

& then, almost too gradually to discern, the mist starts to lift, & under the beam of my suit lamp i c the truss & the RCV & the robot arm & the gyro again, as if a window is being cleaned in front of me. the pricking in my eye begins to lessen.

i take a deep breath.

"i'm ok," i say. "i'm ok."

"hold on, then," says my mother. i c she's still gripping my gloved hand. i grab the handle on the station with my other hand & let go of her.

"thanks," i say.

u can't shrug in a space suit but i feel her shrug. "we have to move quickly now," she says.

"yes," says Dr. Stearns over the radio. "the leak is still there, so even tho u're filling the suit with fresh ox, the lithium hydroxide is going to start building up again. u have 10 minutes."

"until my vision goes again?"

"until u die."

it's so matter-of-fact, so blunt, that i don't know what to say. "ok," i say eventually.

"here," says my mother. "i'll do the last bolt."

"no," i say. "i've got it."

"u'll need this." she hands me my wrench. i must have let go of it when i was purging.

i nod & turn to the last bolt. i get the wrench on it & turn. nothing. it's stuck. i turn again. nothing. i start to panic.

shit.

shit.

but then my mother puts her hand with mine on the long-handled wrench & we both twist &—

suddenly—

it frees, & then i can turn it until it's off. i stow it in the webbing.

"remove it with Dextre please, Duncan," says my mother. the robot arm lifts the gyro up & away from the station side. she turns to me. "now we have to take out the new 1. robot arm is busy."

it's like a game where u have to move little tiles around to make a picture. Grandpa sent 1 up to me once, at Christmas. old gyro onto the robot arm. new gyro into position, leaving the storage bay free. old gyro into the bay.

we stay clipped onto the cable & move along the ship until we reach bay 3, & my mother undoes the clasps securing it closed. we open it & there's the new gyro. it's heavy—probably a few hundred lbs.—but we're in 0 g, so it's more a case of the bulkiness & the encumbrance of the thing, in terms of its shape.

very carefully, we open the straps that are holding it in place & lever it with a wrench, until it floats out of its storage space. then we each hold on to it with 1 hand, to stop it drifting away from us. it's the size of a bed. not an easy thing to move along, when u're in a space suit & clipped to the side of a space station.

sweating, muscles screaming, i edge along, keeping it steady. my breathing is rapid now. & i don't know how much that's the exertion & how much it's the bends, which i undoubtedly have now—i can visualize the nitrogen bubbling in my veins.

move clip.

move hand.

push gyro along a bit.

move clip.

move hand.

push . . .

repeat.

repeat.

sweat is pouring down into the neck of my space suit by the time we get the gyro roughly into position.

"wait," says Virginia over the radio. "i'll stow the old 1. then i'll help u."

the robot arm has more degrees of freedom than the RCV, which is basically a train that can only go back & forth on the truss. the arm can go round too, so it can move in 2 axes. Virginia drives it round us & over to bay 3, where she gently puts the old gyro away. then she uses the automatic closing function to seal it.

the arm comes back & holds the new gyro still while we adjust its position until the holes line up with the hull.

"there," says my mother.

& then we take all the bolts we removed & screw them back in. simple.

simple—but it takes minutes. i don't know how many minutes, but i do know that as i screw in my last bolt my eyes are starting to feel gritty again, to feel like they have sand in them, not that i know what sand feels like—analogies are a difficult thing when u grow up on a space station. mostly u learn them from books. not from experience.

"new gyro is a go," says my mother. "i repeat, new gyro is a go."

"good work," says Boutros. "now get back inside. right now."

"Duncan, prepare the hyperbaric chamber for Leo," says Dr. Stearns. "immediate compression. 24 hours. pure oxygen."

"already prepared," says Virginia. "Libra & Orion helped."

thanks, Libra, i think. *thanks, Orion.*

we unclip from the cable & clip onto the RCV. then Virginia drives us back to the hatch. my vision is clouding. shit. shit.

"vision is clouding," i say.

"move," says the woman from Nevada. no idea what her name is. "fast."

"how long have i got?"

"2 minutes," says Dr. Stearns. "maximum."

fog erases the earth. the blackness. the moon. the beautiful reflections in the gleaming silver of the station. no vision. no sound, apart from the slight hissing of the RCV wheels & the voices in my radio, increasingly urgent voices.

"get that hatch open."

"move."

"help him thru."

"Duncan, commence repressurization of air lock."

the sun rises.

again.

14
EVA, part 3

& then i'm dimly aware of someone taking the suit off me, easing me out of the cooling garment, pulling me thru the air-lock door & across modules—hatches & panels rolling by, my vision clearing, showing me metal walls, screws, warning signs, all passing me like a vid, scrolling in front of my eyes.

then i'm in a beige chamber, smooth walls curving around me, like a coffin. i feel a squeezing, a pressure on my chest, & then a rushing sensation & a hissing sound as it fills with pure oxygen.

there's bright light to my right, & i turn & c my mother thru a round window in the side of the chamber. she is hovering, face close to the glass.

"how are u feeling?" she says.

i think about this. my joints hurt. my breathing feels shallow. there are stars dancing in front of my eyes, like some part of space has drifted in with me, is encircling me still. my heart is a piston in my chest, pounding, a gyro spinning out of control. "not so good," i say.

"Dr. Stearns is monitoring ur vitals," she says. "he thinks u'll be ok. ur limbs are showing no rashes. ur torso's clean too. so as long as u don't develop neurological deficits . . ."

"is that possible?"

"yes."

i already knew that, but for some reason i wanted her to say it.

"ok," i say. "so now i just wait."

"now u just wait. 24 hours."

i don't know why i say this next part but i do, & then i can't take it back, the sound waves are out in the chamber, in the station, echoing off the module walls. "stay with me?" i say.

"i can't," says my mother. "i need to go to the bridge. we need to follow thru on Brown. notify his family. i asked to be the 1 to do it. i mean . . . i was with him when it happened."

"shit," i say. "i forgot. how could i forget?"

"u had a lot on ur mind," she says.

"oh my god," i say. "his family." i can't imagine the call, how they're going to feel. to know that he was smacked into space by a cargo container because of a dumb-luck accident. i picture them, in a bungalow in California or a suburban house in Atlanta, or wherever they are—i don't know the first thing about Brown other than he was scared, other than he was inexperienced—& i c his family answer a vid call on their screen & their world collapse, the vacuum of space pushing in, crushing it.

a critical leak.

destroying their world. their habitat, their safety.

i feel sick. no one i have met has ever died before, i mean apart from my grandmother, but i only ever saw her on vidlink when i was really little; i can barely picture her now. somehow having been in the same module as Brown only an hour earlier makes it weird in a whole other way. i also feel like it's all my fault. like if i'd pushed for them to use my plan, to use the vibrations . . .

but no. the rocket just misfired, that's all.

i look into my mother's bowl-lens eyes, magnified by the circular window, wondering if she's thinking the same thing as me.

they look back at me, blank as vid screens.

"well," says my mother. "at least he got what he wanted. at least he got his burial in space."

then she's gone.

15

repressurization

i lie in the chamber, for 24 hours.

    nothing to read.

    no vids.

    just lying there, oxygen pumping in to the capsule & to my lungs. pressure at 2x atmos.

    it's dull.

    there's not really a lot more i can say about it.

16
home, part 1

Libra & Orion come to get me when the 24 hours are up.

Dr. Stearns has already checked my vitals, remotely, & declared me healthy. at least until they can do a full functional MRI of my brain down in Nevada, to c if there's any neuro damage from the bends. but my joints feel ok, i have no rashes, & my heart rate & blood pressure are fine.

i made it back just in time.

Libra hands me some new clothes—i was stripped out of the water-cooling suit before going into the hyperbaric chamber & no one much worried about giving me a fresh outfit before saving my life.

"thanks," i say.

"no problem," she says.

"ur mother & Virginia are waiting on the bridge," says Orion. "looks like we're going home early."

"really?"

"yeah. with everything going fubar & all."

"but the station is stabilized?" i ask.

"uh-huh," says Libra. she leads the way thru the station, & i follow, Orion behind me, the 3 of us torpedoing in file. "all 4 gyros working."

"then why take us off station now?"

"u think we were asking questions, once they said we could go down there?" says Libra.

of course she wants to go home. to what INDNAS has called our home anyway. she wants to hold her mother. so does Orion, probably, but he's more inscrutable as usual, is just swimming along behind me, catapulting elegantly off hatches & handles. most likely he just wants to play his flute in a concert hall & hear it echo off the walls.

a simple wish.

simple but impossible.

until now.

when we reach the bridge, my mother & Virginia look up from manuals tied to the table with elastic.

"good; u're up," says my mother. "Nevada wants us in the bus in 1 hour." astronauts like her call the docking & landing module a bus. makes it more ordinary, i suppose. less scary.

"an *hour*?" i say.

"yes. there's a window. conditions are clear at the landing site. they want us down before the next storm front comes in. & they want us off the station anyway."

"why?"

she blinks. "Brown died."

"well, yes, but—"

"& we're low on fuel, even with the gyros back online. with all the people off, they can power down the oxygen & the pressure & the cooling. divert everything into the gyros & the boosters, keep the station in status quo until someone can bring up some more fuel."

this doesn't sound convincing to me & i open my mouth to say so, but she waves a hand.

"listen, Leo. u were going home anyway. after ur birthday. they always said, Dr. Stearns always said, that ur bodies would be strong enough by the time u were 16. well, we're just bringing it forward a little. Dr. Stearns was watching ur vitals when u were in the chamber. he thinks u're definitely robust enough to survive reentry."

"oh good," i say. "he thinks we'll survive." it comes out sarcastic. but then i meant it pretty sarcastic.

"what about us?" says Orion.

"u'll be fine," says my mother.

"how reassuring," says Orion. but he's smiling. Orion doesn't worry about much.

Virginia puts her hands up. "look, we're going. ok? so let's make sure we get down safely. which means me & Freeman going over the manuals. i want to make sure i can take over the bus if . . . if Freeman blacks out or something. u 3: get whatever u need from ur quarters. rendezvous at y arm hatch, portside. 20 minutes. if we're not there, get into ur suits. we'll be along shortly."

well.

i guess that's it.

Libra, Orion, & i dive thru the hatch & swim together for a time, then split up to head to our respective quarters. i don't have much i want to take down with me. it's a space station: there isn't room for a lot in the way of personal effects. i do a somersault over to my cupboard, which is lined with webbing. i take out a photo of Grandpa—an old 1, on actual photo paper.

my watch is already on my wrist. Grandpa's old watch. his Speedmaster.

surely i need something else?

i think.

my life can't be reducible to 2 items.

but it is, i realize.

all my music is online. all my books. all my homework. these are the only possessions that matter to me.

i unroll my screen & press CALL. Grandpa doesn't answer. i

didn't really expect him to. it is—i glance at my watch—3:00 a.m. in California. LEAVE MESSAGE? reads the screen, so i say:

"listen, Grandpa. we're coming down. now. i'm going to c u soon. i . . . um . . . i can't wait. that's . . . i guess that's it. i . . . well. i'll c u soon."

i roll up the screen again. i hate leaving messages. i'm bad at it.

what if i die & that's my last message? my last words?

i unroll the screen & press CALL again.

"i love u, Grandpa," i say. "i . . . that's really it now."

i roll it up & kick off from my bed, floating thru the hatch & toward the y arm, then when i hit the elbow module i fly straight at the wall, bend my elbows when i hit, use the momentum to barrel-roll myself into the entertainment module & then along thru the garden. Libra is still there, putting a plant into a metal & glass tube.

"u're bringing a plant?" i say. "they have tons of those on earth."

she looks at me. "so? it was grown in space. it's a part of here. to take down there."

"um. ok." i don't get it, not really. i mean: either u're up here or u're down there. why would u want to mingle the 2? but she's Libra, & i love her even if she's weird.

"what have u got anyway?" she says.

i look at my watch. "nothing much."

"Orion's taking his flute," she says. "says he doesn't want to change it for a different 1. just wants to hear how it sounds in the air."

silence.

"taste wild strawberries," i say. "go down a slide. ride in an elevator."

she smiles.

"bounce on a trampoline," she says. "hot tub. graduation: throw my cap in the air."

"hot tub. nice call."

"thanks."

"graduation not so much. geek."

she punches my arm.

an awkward moment follows.

"well," she says. she touches my arm more gently now. "time to go, i guess."

after that everything moves fast. we torpedo to the end hatch, thru several modules. by the hatch, there is a cupboard similar to the 1 at the end where i EVA'd from. there are space suits lined up behind transparent doors. Orion is already climbing into his, into the hard-shell torso.

"hey, guys," he says. casually. as if we're not about to descend to the promised land. to gravity.

"hey."

i put my suit on quicker than Libra. but then i have just practiced yesterday. water-cooling suit. torso. close backpack behind me. i leave the visor up, as do Libra & Orion. we're not in the air lock yet.

we tread water there. we don't talk. there doesn't seem to be anything to say. i look out the window. it seems important that i do so. i try to soak in the infinity of blackness, sparkling with stars, to take it into myself. i try to imprint the glowing orb of the earth onto my mind, to never forget it. the gray moon, half in shadow.

space.

my home.

no, i remind myself.

no, i'm going home.

yes.

about 5 minutes later, my mother & Virginia come breaststroking down the tunnel. mother looks us up & down. "ok," she says.

that's it.

then she puts on her suit, & so does Virginia. i feel like there should be some kind of ceremony, some kind of ritual, like we should be breaking a champagne bottle or something. but there isn't. anyway, u can't break champagne bottles in space. the liquid & glass would be a nightmare in the closed-air system.

Orion pats my shoulder. i try to smile at him.

my mother opens the air lock & we go thru, & then the 5 of us are floating in the big chamber.

"close visors. check for leaks," she says.

we close our visors. we check for leaks. everything is fine.

oxygen. heads-up display.

"depressurizing," says my mother. she hits the manual switch beside the door & the room sighs & deflates. i feel the air moving around me.

then we're in space, or as good as, & Mother opens the door to the landing module, the bus. Libra, Orion, & i go first, heads forward, rolling when we get in, to squeeze into the seats at the back. we strap ourselves in. it's a tight fit. Orion & i are next to the side windows; Libra's in the middle.

then my mother & Virginia enter too, & close the hatch opening behind them. they climb into the 2 pilots' seats & commence their checks.

"boosters."

"ok."

"displays."

"ok."

"computers."

"ok."

"comms."

"Nevada?"

"hearing u loud & clear, Navette 3."

"ok."

"temperature."

"still settling. t minus 5 minutes."

"pressure."

"ok."

etc.

etc.

etc.

finally, after what seems like hours, my mother nods to herself. "ok. Nevada, i'm decoupling," she says.

"go ahead," says a voice. it sounds like Singh.

my mother flicks a switch & heavy clunks sound, as the hooks attaching us to the androgynous peripheral assembly open. then there is a kind of pinging, as the springs fire, pushing us gently away from the station.

my mother taps buttons, relays information to Nevada.

minutes pass.

then:

"we're safely away," she says. on a screen in front of her i c Moon 2 come into view—we're already 150 ft. away, maybe more. i have never seen it like this, from far away. it's weird. it's like my whole childhood suddenly shrinks, somehow. like u could fit it in a pocket. i feel my eyelashes fluttering, a sense that something is wrong, that i shouldn't be leaving that small place that seemed so big; but i still my eyes & get ahold of my breathing.

the space station gets smaller. the moon too, behind it. u could reach out & pluck it from the sky. u could spin it on ur knuckles, like a coin, if u had gravity.

gravity.

soon i will be in gravity.

i wonder what it's like. it's impossible to imagine. when u have only known the absence of a thing, how do u construct its feeling in ur mind? i don't know what a kiss will feel like, tho sometimes lately i have looked at Orion, & i have wondered.

i don't know what gravity will feel like either.

"firing engines," says my mother. "10 seconds of thrust."

she flicks another switch. my back presses into the seat as we are ushered suddenly thru space, smooth & silent. "engage orbital dynamics," says my mother, & Virginia taps some buttons.

"wait 2 hours," says Singh—i think it is definitely Singh, from down in Nevada. "fire ur main boosters now & u'll roast Moon 2's solar panels."

"not my first rodeo," says my mother.

"yes. of course."

2 hours pass.

like my time in the compression chamber, it is dull.

Moon 2 gradually shrinks, in the window beside me now, as we orbit away from it, our trajectory calculated to take us ever downward, closer to earth, so that we don't hit it when we come back around.

Virginia takes down notes with pencil & paper, both of them anchored with bungee cords. Nevada is constantly running calculations, figuring out the deorbit burn time, based on the data from our current trajectory. they call out numbers to Virginia to write.

dull.

dull.

& i'm amazed that i can be bored when i'm leaving the space station i have always lived on, to go down to earth, where there are sunsets & smells & animals just walking around, eating grass.

but still dull.

"ok, t minus 1 minute," says Singh eventually.

a pause, as someone coughs down there.

"good luck, all of u," says Boutros, over the radio.

"thank u, sir," says my mother.

Singh comes back on. "deorbit burn 3 minutes 40 seconds," he says.

"10-4," says my mother. "firing main boosters."

she flicks.

& we are flicked, like flies, by a giant hand—a roar, & the spinning plus sign of Moon 2 contracts, quick as a pupil reacting to bright light, like when the sun suddenly rises thru the cupola, as we are thrown toward the earth, & that's really what it feels like: like someone has seized us & is flinging us down.

then we do what thrown things do.

we fall.

17
home, part 2

heat:

that's the first thing u feel when the bus's orbit flattens from circular to elliptical & u hit the low part of the oval, the ship beginning to drag against the envelope of the atmosphere.

i glance over at Libra, next to me, who is sweating too, eyes closed. we can feel & hear the slowing effect of the dense air we're entering, & thru the window i c sparks lighting the darkness; the outside of the landing module on fire.

then the capsule starts to roll, buffeted by the atmosphere. i cling to my straps as we are twisted in every direction, shaken, as if there's still a giant hand outside manipulating us.

"fire explosive bolts," says my mother.

"10-4," says Virginia, & she leans down to jettison the orbital & propulsion modules.

there's a series of bangs & i c something whip past the window as we speed into sunrise, coming down on the curve of the earth, blade-edge planet illuminated against black.

& we keep tumbling. simultaneously the force on us increases—i am being squashed hard into my seat now, my eyeballs feel as tho they're being dragged thru my head, & my whole body is fighting this violent pull from outside.

"3 g's," says Virginia. "4 g's. 5. still climbing."

"hmm," says my mother.

i don't like the sound of that *hmm*. a *hmm* from my mother is like an *oh fucking shit* from anyone else.

the temperature keeps going up.

my t-shirt is soaked with sweat now, sticking to my skin. it's a sensation i'm not used to—in the station the climate was regulated, all the time; it was never allowed to get this hot. i feel like my body is melting.

something drips onto my lap. i look up, & c moisture gathering on the ceiling of the capsule. "um, Moth— officers, the capsule is leaking, or something."

my mother turns back. "what?"

"something dripped on me."

"water or metal?"

metal? i think. if liquid metal is dripping on me, then we are in serious trouble. i move my hand to touch the liquid above me, then lift my fingers to look at them. just raising my arm takes serious effort, as if it's strapped to the walking machine we use in the station. "water, i think."

"good." my mother turns back to Virginia. "ablative shield holding?"

"yes," she says. "but g's are still climbing. 6 . . . 7."

i don't need her to tell us this. i can feel it, & i can c from the look in Libra's eyes, which are now open, that she feels it too— there is nothing to compare it to because i have never lived anything like it before; i've always been on Moon 2, in 0 g. now suddenly there is a pressure on my chest that feels like it will cave it in.

"shit," says my mother.

"what's happening?" says Virginia.

"i don't know. i think 1 of the modules might not have detached."

"Nevada?" says Virginia. "come in, Nevada."

no answer.

out the window, the backlit horizon is spinning giddily.

i can feel the skin on my face, i've never felt the skin on my face before, it's being smushed back, my whole face is being pushed back over my ears, like the capsule thinks it's a mask & is trying to remove it; & i think, *don't remove my face, don't take it off—*

i can't breathe, i can't breathe, the hands are pressing on my chest too, pressing—

i try to lift my arm to push them away, to stop them crushing me, these people, but i can't—

"9 g's," says Virginia.

all sense is gone from my head; the only word i know is *help, help, help.*

"fire drogue chute, right now," says my mother.

"trying to," says Virginia.

& then everything goes black.

18
home, part 3

rolling.

spinning.

a dream of rolling & spinning,

upside is downside & downside is upside &

nothing is still,

a nightmare more than a dream,

the universe uncoupled from its axes, rotating wildly, tumbling thru whatever was there before space exploded outward,

head battered in every direction, straining on seat belts, 1 moment falling out the next moment

PUSHED

into the seat, a seat,

a seat,

yes i'm in a seat i'm in the landing capsule & i open my eyes. outside the window there is just black sky & then

flick

brown earth & then

flick

black sky, red at the side with rising sun & then

flick

brown earth again &

someone is screaming i think it might be me but also maybe

Libra, i would turn to her but i can't; i can't turn my head at all; i can't move anything. what if i'm paralyzed? my lungs are empty my lungs are empty i try,

i try to breathe & i get 1 small wisp of air into me & i try for another,

& another,

& another,

&

"gamma ray altimeter?" says my mother's voice from somewhere in the maelstrom of movement, she is no longer in front of us because in front has no meaning, she is around me, her voice is in me.

Virginia doesn't reply. blacked out like i did? i don't know. i force my eyeballs to turn in their sockets & c my mother frantically pushing buttons, flicking switches, making lights go on & off. i assume she's trying to fire the parachutes, trying to slow our descent, because otherwise we're going to hit the ground & we're going to be annihilated, just so much mangled metal & wetness spread over a mountain or a city street.

then—

snap—

& we're slowing, the crazy gyrations of the capsule beginning to even out, my face starts to creep back onto the front of my head & i can lift my hand, just, to grab Libra's & she squeezes mine back.

"g-force descending," my mother mutters.

we slow even more. stabilize. i look out the window & gasp— farmland is rising quickly straight at us, like a view from 1 of Grandpa's drone cameras, sectioned by fences—there are cows & there's a car on a road &—

"impact in 10 seconds," says my mother, to us maybe, or maybe just to herself.

"brace urselves."

the seconds tick down; it's what they do—u can't ever stop them. no one is calling them out, this isn't a launch, it's the opposite, but i c them in my head:

5

4

3

2

1

bang.

we hit the ground so hard that for a second i black out again, a screech of rending metal, & next thing i know my chin is on my chest & there is something dripping on my hands, something red now, & i realize it's blood, my own blood, from my nose.

for a moment, everything is still.

huh, i think. *so that's what liquid looks like on earth. that's how liquid falls, in 1 g.*

tap. tap. tap.

from my nose. down to my hands.

down.

what a weird idea *down* is. i look out the window. i c only red. i don't know what it is, i don't know how to read it, to parse it. flickering, creeping red, cycling thru shades.

i turn slowly to Libra. "u ok?" i say.

"no," she says. she is cradling 1 arm. i wonder if it's broken.

"Orion?"

"no. i am not ok either."

well, good. they're both alive.

my mother turns to us. "good, u're alive," she says.

then she shakes Virginia. "Duncan. Duncan."

my heart stops in my chest. Virginia can't be dead. not Virginia. Virginia can't be dead she can't be—

Virginia coughs & twists her head wildly. "what's happening—are we in trouble— what's—"

"shh," says my mother, almost tenderly. "we've landed."

"Jesus," says Virginia. "what happened?"

"i don't know," says my mother.

then i c her moving, unclasping herself from her seat & climbing forward to the hatch, & i realize we have landed on our side, which is not usual. the chutes are meant to bring us down gently on the lower end of the capsule so that we're facing up.

how my mother is even able to move i don't know—i feel so weak that i'm not sure if i could unclip my harness.

she opens the hatch a crack & recoils, immediately—& immediately the capsule is filled with an acrid smell, a smell that hurts my nostrils.

she closes the hatch quickly.

"what's that smell?" i say.

she glances at me. "smoke. the orbital module didn't detach. it was on fire & now it seems we're in a cornfield that's on fire."

i look at the redness out the window & now i understand what it is. it's flames. we have landed in a field of corn & we have set fire to it.

fire. that's what that red is, that pulses & flickers outside the portholes.

"'all things, oh priests, are on fire,'" says Orion.

"huh?" says mother.

"Buddha."

"what?"

"he's talking about desire. this fire is more literal of course."

silence.

"so what do we do?" says Libra. always wanting a plan. always practical.

my mother shrugs. "i'm going to try to connect us to Nevada with the emergency radio."

"but about the fire," says Orion.

"wait till it burns itself out, i suppose," says my mother.

"& if we can't get Nevada on the radio?"

my mother sighs. "we have set fire to a field. i think someone will find us."

19
home, part 4

"10-4," says Virginia to Nevada over the radio. "c u soon."

they're on their way. they were tracking us over radar, even tho our systems were down because of the burning orbital module that we didn't know was still stuck to us.

we're in a field somewhere, & Nevada is coming by helicopter, & it shouldn't be long.

outside the window, there is a world of smoke & black stubbly stuff that i assume is burned-down corn. we have been in here a long time, long enough for the fire to consume all the carbon it can, fueling itself on the oxygen that is everywhere here, all around, & i think how crazy it is that a whole field can burn: in space, if anything catches fire, u just cut off the air to that section of the station & there's nothing to sustain it.

here, everything is larger. &, i realize suddenly, in some ways weirdly more dangerous.

"let's try to get out of here," says my mother. she moves forward again & opens the hatch. she tenses, but there is only gray out there. & that stench of burned things.

"all ok," she says.

Libra, Orion, & i unfasten our seat belts. there is something holding me down in my seat & for a moment i think i'm hurt in some terrible way, some broken bone skewering me to the fabric, but then i realize it's just gravity—it's being in 1 g; it's pulling me into the seat.

weird.

i push myself forward—i have to crawl, but i c that the other 2 are having to do the same thing. we crawl over & past my mother's & Virginia's seats & then thru the hatch.

& then my head is thru the hatch, & my mother & Virginia are helping me out, helping me to my feet.

"can u stand?" says Virginia.

i look down. they are holding me up, their hands on my waist & arms & i look around me & the sky is above me & black field is around me & there are mountains in the distance & my feet are on the ground.

my feet.

on the ground.

i feel the earth, the scorched earth, pushing up against the soles of my feet—it's the oddest feeling—& at the same time my whole body is being pulled down, all of it down in 1 direction.

i'm used to living in 3 dimensions: when i'm in the station, up & down are only nominal things & every surface is a surface u can touch, u can use to propel urself . . . & suddenly now i'm in 2, suddenly there's only 1 plane that matters & it's the flat plane of the earth. the sun is coming up on the horizon in front of me, setting fire to the world, like we set fire to this little field.

i try to use my muscles to stand. feeling me tense, Mother & Virginia let go of me.

& gravity lays me down like a doll: the ground rushes up & i hit it, hard, & i'm lying crumpled there, on the burned corn stubble, the suit protecting me at least.

"no," i say.

looking up, i c my mother nod.

she & Virginia reach down & get me propped up against the side of the landing module. then they help Libra & Orion out & do the same with them, so that we're lying against the capsule like injured civilians after a disaster, which i suppose is what we are.

but then Virginia staggers & falls—she puts a hand out, plants it on the wall of the capsule. her head hangs down. she's been in 0 g longer than my mother. weeks. months. my mother helps her down until she's sitting next to us.

"huh," says Virginia. "aren't we a picture."

my mother busies herself with something, walking around the ship, muttering.

even sitting, like this, the earth has hooks in me & it's pulling me down. my legs, my back, my head, they're all being dragged in 1 vector & 1 vector only & nothing about me is floating freely, like before. there is this thing in my nostrils that must be the smell of burning corn, the first thing i have ever smelled outside of the station.

everything is inflected downward. even the burned stalks of corn, they hang down, toward the earth.

i can't understand it.

i can't get my head around it.

but then i hear a clapping rustle & something rises up, a blur of black, vaulted into the sky out of the blackened cornfield on a kind of clattering noise, up into clear air & i c that it's a bird, not something on a vid but a real bird, & the word for what it is doing is flying, black wings beating as it flies flies flies over red sunrise, something alive that exists in every direction, something whose windows open on every side, letting in the world from every angle, & my breath stops for a moment in my chest. i have never seen anything so beautiful.

"did u . . . ?" i say to Libra & Orion.

"yes," they say together, which is something they do sometimes. i c that there are tears running down Orion's cheeks.

down.

everything down.

apart from that bird tho. apart from that bird.

there's almost so much to feel that i can't feel anything—it's so overwhelming. then i force myself to focus, to isolate the sensations, to really appreciate them.

at first, it's all just the force yanking down on my body, sticking me to the earth below me. but then i start to separate the others.

i feel the breeze on my skin. on my face.

the wind carries with it a scent—by definition i don't know what it is because there is little to smell on Moon 2—it's under the smell of burned corn. i think it might be grass?

whatever it is, it is cool & clear & an unspeakable wonder.

& the sound. there is a kind of silence that i have never heard before. the space station is clicking & whirring & turning all the time. & now that it's gone, there's a kind of weird void in its place, a limbo—but no, because as i concentrate, i begin to hear the air around me, the wind itself, & something else. a bird calling? music?

unspeakable wonder.

i press my fingers into the ground. the pads of my fingers sink thru, yielding particulate soil. the feeling is indescribable: it is softness & granularity & separation & surrounding & letting go, & my god if this is what the soil of a burned field in the middle of nowhere feels like, then how will i cope with swimming? how will Orion cope with hearing his flute, echoing around the concert hall?

then, only then, do i look. really look.

the sun is almost risen now, above the mountains in front of us. the mountains are gray & blue & every color in between, rigged to catch clouds as they pass; they are laden with them now, ragged with them. there is an impression of green trees. in between, the field, & i think more fields, stretching a distance that in space would seem tiny but here seems vast; fences & electricity poles rising up.

& the sky.

the sky.

the sky.

skeins of cloud are stretched across the sky; in places fish scales; in places silk. they are pink, & under them, between them & the horizon, is a layer of pale blue—no, not pale, it's the opposite of pale, it's electrified this blue, switched on, lit from within, a couple of stars still hanging on, piercing the blue with sparkling light.

& powering it all is the great ball of the sun, burning, glowing, taking leave now of the mountains & surging into the air above them, burning their tattered clouds to nothing, red-hot flames on the edge of the world, firing the clouds, sending voltage thru that blue.

i watch it & i can't close my mouth.

then more.

more sensation.

i feel something wet on my face. i lift my fingers from the dirt & touch them to my jaw, to my chin, feel moisture there.

my eyes. my eyes are stinging.

it is tears.

tears, pouring down.

always down.

everything in 1 axis, everything following 1 vector.

apart from that bird.

apart from the sun, which is rising.
apart from my heart, which is higher than the stars.
wonder.
wonder.
wonder.

20
oyster

"well, isn't this a shit show," says Boutros.

he covers his head as he walks away from the downdraft of a helicopter. it has landed just next to the capsule, flattening the stalks of corn with the force of the wind created by its rotors.

i am almost incapable of speech, i am all sensorium, a mind full of wonder just feeling wind, wind, wind, hearing the roar of engines, smelling burned corn & earth & green.

"paramedics," he says. "get them onto the gurneys." he gestures to me & Libra & Orion & Virginia. "take their vitals. prep the IVs too." i have never seen him in real life before. he is smaller than i expected, from the vid screens.

other people are spilling out of another helicopter behind him, & there is no transition between them being on the helicopter & them working. they are so fast, so efficient.

some of them have brought folding chairs; they have done this before, i realize, with astronauts like Virginia, who have been up there a long time, but maybe not with anyone as bad as us. Virginia is sitting up. me & Libra & Orion are pretty slumped at this point.

we're pretty out of it too. Orion is just saying *birdsong* over & over again to himself, & Libra has her hands planted in the ground as if they will grow into something, & isn't even saying anything. is just humming, tunelessly.

i can't claim to be much better. i am watching the sun rising in the sky, with my mouth open. it looks so different down here, smaller & yet bigger, bleeding light into the ground.

i feel strong hands under my arms, &—

time skips—

&—

i'm lifted into 1 of the folding chairs. more sensation. a kind of densely woven fabric against my skin—at some point someone has pulled me out of my space suit, & i'm just in a t-shirt & thin space pants. my mother is 1 of the people who helped me into the chair, i realize.

"u ok?" she says.

i stare at her. "i don't know."

she purses her lips. "i . . ." she closes her mouth. "i . . ." she closes her mouth again. then she shakes her head, & walks away. starts talking to 1 of the men in suits—engineers, i guess—pointing to the ship, then making shapes with her hands as she demonstrates something. 1 of them is noting something down on a screen.

there are others walking around the landing module & the orbital module too, which is still attached to it, since my mother has already established that this was the problem that caused us to crash-land miles from where we were supposed to come down. the explosive bolts fired, but it stayed attached, giving us an added downward momentum that my mother described to Virginia as "ballistic."

as in: like a bullet.

we came thru the atmosphere like a bullet, & only the chutes saved us, deploying automatically when the gamma ray altimeter registered 300 ft. from the earth's surface.

even so, we are fortunate to be alive. according to my mother.

i feel . . .

. . . cold, i realize, as the wind passes over me.

yes. this is cold. this is what it feels like. i look down, curiously, c goose bumps on my skin. the temperature on Moon 2 was a constantly regulated 67 degrees.

i shiver.

wonder.

unspeakable wonder.

then a sharp pain in my arm. i twist my head. someone in a green jumpsuit is hooking up a bag of fluid to a tube that snakes into 1 of my veins.

"just sugar," says Boutros, walking past. "for strength."

"wait," i say.

he stops.

"did u c that sunrise?"

he shakes his head. "closed my eyes in the chopper. hate heights. ironic, isn't it?"

pause.

"u liked it?" he says. "the sunrise?" there's a strange expression on his face. guilt? maybe. i don't know why.

"it was the most wonderful thing i have ever seen," i say.

he smiles. a real smile. "oh u just wait," he says. "u're home now. the world is ur oyster."

"my oyster?"

"it's just something people say. means u have a lot to discover."

i nod, feeling the way my head hinges on my neck, the weight as my chin goes down to my chest, which i have to pull up, cantilever back to orthogonal with muscles i have never really used, at least not in this way, where everything is pulling down all the time. "i am realizing that," i say.

he steps away.

just then a vehicle pulls up. it's white, or it was once. now it's mostly dried mud, gray & streaked with waves & whorls. a pickup truck. a man steps out, wearing jeans & an old t-shirt with holes in it. he has brown boots on his feet & a hat on his head. he steps over to Boutros.

"this ur doin'?" he says, looking over the burned cornfield.

"i'm afraid so," says Boutros. "we will of course compensate you for the damage."

the man considers this for a moment. his face is weathered, literally i suppose, lined with cracks like . . . well . . . like the dry dirt below me.

i can do informed analogies now—now that i'm on earth.

"u meant to land here?" he says, eventually, with a frown.

"not in the least," says Boutros. "nor did we intend for the orbital module to stay attached. c it?" he points to the blackened, thick tubular module that is still stuck to our gracefully fluted landing capsule.

"uh-huh," says the farmer, at least that's who i guess it is.

"meant to detach once thru the atmosphere. we estimate the landing capsule reached 12 g's because of the additional momentum. disaster. they should have died, really." now he does an expansive gesture that takes in me, Libra, Orion, Virginia.

"sorry to disappoint u," says Orion.

the farmer chuckles.

Boutros frowns.

then it's as if he realized he's supposed to laugh at jokes, that it's in the rules, in the boldface. he cracks a smile.

"anyway," he says, "landing module has an ablative shield, stops it catching fire with the friction from the atmosphere." he is babbling slightly. i think he's embarrassed, about the field. "the other module doesn't. that's why . . . ahem . . . that's why it set ur . . . ahem . . . field on fire. i'm really very sorry. it was a technical error. a misfiring explosive bolt."

the farmer shrugs. "done me a favor, t'be frank. couldn't afford to keep irrigating it anyway."

Boutros blinks. "oh. yes. of course."

the drought. people on news vids are always talking about the
water shortage.

"well," says the farmer, turning to the 4 of us in our folding
chairs. "welcome back to terra firma. u were lucky, i guess."

he's wrong about that.

he's wrong about us being back, because we've never been
here before, apart from Virginia of course.

but wrong about us being lucky too.

very wrong about that.

21
men in black

strong men & women carry us to the helicopters & load us into 1 of them, strap us into seats that are like those in the module, except now there is an open panel door with air coming in.

they fit headphones over our ears, with mics in them.

the helicopter lifts into the air, & my stomach drops.

i look out & down at the field. the smashed-up module & the parachute lying behind it, half-burned, jellyfish-like, laid flat. the metal of the tube is dented & scorched. it seems amazing that we survived.

the farmer stands by his white pickup, getting smaller.

then a couple of black jeeps pull up. windows tinted. men in black suits get out & walk over to the farmer. they seem to talk.

we power forward, the scene dwindling behind us.

the men lead the farmer toward the cars.

we're drawing away now, air is rushing in, astonishing air, so the scene is small now but i c them touch his arm, direct him, toward—

then someone closes the door, the air stops rushing, & the helicopter speeds even more, & even with the headphones on i can hear nothing but *shhhhhhh* & c nothing but blurred blue out of the window.

going home.

PART 2

earth

1

quarantine

it's earth, but not earth.

the helicopter carried us here, ground rolling below like a satellite image feed, like a dream, fields & houses & roads conveyor-belting below us, fever-fast.

& now we're in quarantine. they're worried about us getting sick: all the viruses we've never been exposed to. it turns out Libra's arm wasn't broken, which is 1 good thing. just sprained.

outside the windows, Nevada scrubland stretches to where the sky & the world meet. just like in the space station, we could c the earth, but we were floating separate from it, always on the other side of glass. it's as if we never left. the view is zoomed in closer, but that's it.

we're at the Nevada base. where all the missions have been coordinated from. where my mother spends most of her time when she's not on Moon 2. the quarantine extends to the internet. they gave us screens but we're restricted to person-to-person comms. no social media, like on the station, but now it goes further: now there's no internet at all.

like they want to keep us in a vacuum.

keep us locked up still. they're worried about us overloading, they say, our brains frying, too much sensory information all at once. they're also concerned about infection, bacteria, viruses. so no one from the outside is allowed to c us, including Grandpa, for now anyway. especially Grandpa because he works with animals, & Dr. Stearns says they have viruses that we're even less protected against than human ones.

it's frustrating, especially because i want a hug from Grandpa like nothing else on earth, which is an expression i can finally use accurately. i've seen him on vidlink a couple of times, have talked to him about the weirdness of being here at last, but i want to c him in real life, in real scale.

yet at the same time . . . it kind of helps, being cut off to some extent. i mean it's too big, the place we live in now.

we have 3 different rooms, me & Libra & Orion. but the first night, i'm lying on the bed—even that is a weird thing to say, to feel—& i can't sleep at all. it's not in any way how i imagined it, not like my fantasies of sinking into a soft bed that i wasn't tethered to. the pillow is pressing up at me, the bed too, & the blanket is weighing down on me, the whole thing feels not right.

i get up, slowly, & put my feet on the floor. it's something i'm still not used to. i put 1 foot in front of the other, concentrating on every movement, every twitch of my muscles. i hit the light; the room glares into brighter being. i walk to the door.

when i say it like that, it sounds simple. but this isn't the treadmill on the station & i'm not secured by straps & the whole process of walking is different. i go 1 step at a time, thinking about it at every point, deliberate.

eventually i reach the hallway & go 1 door down to Libra's room. i knock on the door.

"come in," she says.

i do.

the lights are set dimmer in here, but i c Orion in there too. they are in the corner, they have abandoned the bed. they have sort of piled blankets & pillows there, in the V where the walls meet.

"mind if i join u?"

"not at all," says Orion. "we were kind of expecting u."

"yeah," i say. relief is what i feel tho. i had hoped they'd be missing me too. i mean, that sounds weird—u shouldn't hope for someone to feel a lack of something, of someone . . . but i still did.

"we couldn't sleep either," says Libra.

i go over—simple to say, again—& they make space for me in the nest. Libra holds my hand.

none of us say anything.

the ground presses up against us. i hear their breathing, like the constant *susurrus* of the station. comforting. a background white noise.

eventually, i fall asleep. down thru the blankets, down thru the floor, down thru the air vents & cables & stories below us & all of the earth's hot metal mantle & rock, & down & up into black.

2

walking

here, everything is set up to help us adjust. they call it quarantine, but it's not to protect anyone else; it's to protect us. Virginia's with us, some of the time at least, in the same section of the base, but my mother has gone off somewhere. training people, doing press junkets, helping to develop new equipment. whatever it is she does when she is not in space.

i finish showering & then i stay sitting for a moment. they put a seat in the shower because we can't stand for long. we—Libra & Orion & i—have rubber bands around our chests that measure our heart rates. i've already had an MRI to make sure that the space walk didn't damage my brain in some way. half an hour in a clicking ticking tube. i don't know what the results were. but no one has said they were bad.

after maybe 5 minutes of standing, our pulse rates rise to 140 or more, & we're supposed to sit straight down. hence the seats in the showers.

i have long showers. my fingers go wrinkly at the ends. it's the feeling: the water running over me. & i watch it too: marveling at the way it falls downward, a never-ending stream. then there is cold water & warm water, 2 different entities, & i can switch smoothly from 1 to the other with a turn of a dial; can twist the shower head too, & change it from a mist to a fine rain to a bore of needles that prick my skin. when i rub the soap with my hands it turns by magic into bubbles, into lather that is the smoothest thing i have ever felt.

now i reach over for a towel & dry myself, then get dressed. it's a painful operation. at every moment gravity is pulling down on my feet & the earth is pushing up at me at the same time. i'm not used to it; i'm used to 360 degrees of freedom, like a gyroscope, spinning.

but now i'm anchored. & the effect of it is to feel as if i'm accelerating downward, all the time, as if i'm not standing on the ground but have been fired at it.

damn. i thought about it, & now i feel nauseous. nausea is pretty much constant.

slowly, i put on my bulky g-suit. it's basically a very tight pair of pants. the idea is that it helps the blood to circulate; Dr. Stearns said people wear compression socks that are similar, for long flights; it stops blood from pooling in our ankles & our calves, lowers the chance of a clot—

& now i feel sick again.

dressed, i grab the handrail & walk into the living area. what would take a regular person 15 seconds takes me 3 minutes & 10 seconds—i count it in my head. in theory i know how to walk, i have practiced it a million times on the exercise unit in Moon 2, the elastic tensioners simulating gravity. but real gravity is a whole other story & i don't have the muscles or the coordination for it—i am still as unsteady as a newly walking baby.

in the living area, Orion is playing the piano. he's never played 1 before but he knows how to read music, & he understands how the notes fit together, so it already sounds like something approximating a tune. no, i'm not being accurate. it sounds beautiful. bewildering—like, how is he making that noise? me, i understand the math of it, the frequency ratios, how notes with wavelengths that are regular multiples of each other combine to make pleasing chords, but that's not the same thing.

i watch his fingers, his hands.

"hey," he says, turning but still playing, "u faint?"

"no."

"progress."

the first couple of days we all fainted in the shower a few times—our hearts just not used to pumping blood upward, raising it off the ground. even sitting up.

Libra is sitting on the couch, reading something on her screen, but she looks bored & coiled, mental energy twisted in on itself because of physical restriction. she raises a hand to greet me, like she doesn't have the willpower to talk. figures. it's amazing how many muscles are employed in talking—the diaphragm, the cricothyroid, the geniohyoid, all the little muscles of the chest. when u're using a thousand other muscles just to keep in an upright position, talking feels exhausting.

her screen beeps. she looks at the message, then smiles. "Mom's coming," she says.

Orion holds a chord. "what? now?"

"today. Boutros just sent a message. he also wants us to go to medical. something about another MRI."

"great," says Orion, with a sigh. we've had a battery of tests already. actually 1 of them was literally a battery. they hooked it up to our skin—something about ascertaining whether our electrical conductivity was the same as someone born on earth. every morning there's a blood test, plus blood pressure, ECG, bladder ultrasound.

oh yes: that's an experience, going for a pee, when u've been used to doing it into a suction tube in the side of a space station. the way it arcs downward. the sound. it takes practice. it takes practice not to end up with pee all down ur pants, or on ur shoes, neither of which are fun things for ur friend-siblings to c, or easy to hide from them when it takes u over 3 minutes to move from 1 room to another.

"when are we going?" i say. "to medical?"

there's a knock on the door, & 3 orderlies come in, pushing wheelchairs.

"looks like now," says Orion.

me, i'm still thinking about how their mother is coming. my mother was with me of course when we landed but she's never really with me. i wish my mother would come for me. i mean, not come because she loves being an astronaut. but come *for me*.

Virginia is nowhere to be seen. she recovered ok from the crash landing but she's probably in her room, working on some piece of code or other. the orderlies help us into the wheelchairs & push us down the long white hallways toward medical. from the windows on the other side of the building we can now c rail lines, for carrying shuttles & rockets to the launch site, as well as the launch site itself—a scaffolded column of thin air, over a giant X on the ground. workers are busy all over the site, driving fork-lift trucks, erecting new structures, in 1 corner seemingly taking apart a rocket engine.

i don't know why they didn't give us this view—from our quarters we can only c scrubland, no movement or interest at all. then i realize that's probably exactly why. this view, on this side, shows us everything we can't do: people moving, people fixing things, people making & mending machines that take astronauts to space.

whereas we are children of space & we are so weak we have to be wheeled to medical for our tests.

when we arrive, Dr. Stearns takes us past various people in lab coats standing over centrifuges or checking computers & charts,

& over to a corner of the bay we haven't been to before. there's an antiseptic smell—astringent, sour. Dr. Stearns is wearing blue nail polish that matches his powder-blue shirt, & his cuff links glint in the light from the window. Dr. Stearns is always well presented. he shines his shoes too, or someone does it for him.

"we had this built specially," he says. "General Electric made it for us." he is indicating a round cubicle, like an upright cylinder, on the other side of a glass door. beside us is a bank of desks with screens on them, technicians sitting & tapping at keyboards. "functional full-body MRI—real time. vertical." he opens a door in the structure, revealing a black rolling mat inside. "with a running machine installed. so we can c ur bones & muscles while u're walking."

"we have to walk?" says Libra.

"i'm afraid so. but not for long. just a couple of minutes. don't worry, we'll be monitoring ur heart rate."

"oh good," says Orion.

Dr. Stearns steeples his hands. "i'm sorry. i know this all must seem very frustrating when u have looked forward to earth for so long. but we must take it slowly. there's a lot we can learn from u too. up till now we've been able to study astronauts who come down to earth after a short period in space. now we can investigate the effects on the body of the only humans who have ever grown up out there & then come down here. it's unprecedented."

"glad we can be lab rats for u," i say.

"well," says Dr. Stearns. "it's in ur interests too that we monitor u closely."

"it really feels like it," says Orion sarcastically.

"we do need to carry out some tests," says Dr. Stearns. "to make sure u're strong enough for . . . the next steps. up there we were very limited. it was pretty much ultrasound only."

"next steps?" i say.

"well, leaving here," he says.

leaving here. Grandpa's ranch. wind. sun.

"how lon—" i start to say, but just then a guy walks up & raises a hand to greet Dr. Stearns.

"this the right place, doc?" he says. he is older than us but no more than maybe 18 or 19. he has long blond hair & tanned skin. he looks like a surfer. i mean, like a surfer from a vid or a photo. i've never seen a real surfer of course. his eyes are green & taper gently at the outer corners. part Japanese maybe. Korean.

"it is," says Dr. Stearns. "welcome, Soto." he turns to us. "Soto here is part of . . . um . . . a new program."

"new program?" says Orion.

"ah, yes. the Company wants to send young astronauts up there. 19 years old, max. for 2 years or more. c how the 0 g affects their bodies."

"why?"

Dr. Stearns blinks. "why? why do any of it? to prepare for . . . travel."

Libra cocks her head. "to other planets?"

"possibly," he says. "or some kind of staging post. an artificial moon? we're really only at the beginning of the project. of the mission."

"the mission to explore space," i say. "like the old days of NASA, right?"

"& to live maybe," says Soto, the new guy, & when he says it i c that he has a stud thru his tongue—a flash of silver in his mouth. Dr. Stearns raises a hand to stop him. Soto shrugs. "what? it's true isn't it? we're running out of space down here. out of water."

"well, there's a lot of space up there," says Orion. i laugh, & so does Soto. i c his eyes wrinkle. he has dimples. i look away.

i also stop laughing: it hurts.

"anyway," says Dr. Stearns, looking uncomfortable. "Soto is going in the MRI too. after he's been on Moon 2, we'll scan him again. c if his bones have . . . deteriorated. his muscles too. he'll also provide a useful baseline for ur results. a control."

"i've always wanted to be a control," says Soto, with a wink to me.

my breath catches, just for a second.

Dr. Stearns opens the glass door & motions for Soto to enter. "u first," he says. "2 minutes walking please. it will be very loud. here." he takes a pair of headphones from a table next to him. "wear these. & please remove any piercings."

Soto does a mock-outraged pose, & then smiles & unscrews the bolt thru his tongue. he drops it on the table with a *clink*.

"watch? jewelry?"

Soto shakes his head. Dr. Stearns takes him thru the door, closes him inside the machine, & then comes to stand on the other side of the glass room with us. technicians bend over screens just to our left, & i realize they're operating the MRI.

the noise is unbelievable. some of it is like music: there are beats, sometimes surfacing in the stream of sound, & i can c Orion listening intently to every click & whirr & pulse. the machine runs thru various different cycles. i don't know what they are but i can tell they are different because the rhythm & tone of the noise changes: sometimes it's harsh white noise, fuzzy; sometimes it's bleeps; sometimes it's a kind of percussion.

after 2 minutes, the door opens & Soto steps out.

"Leo, u're up next," says Dr. Stearns. he accompanies me thru the glass door & then into the cubicle, which is thick plastic on the outside, & inside feels like a module in the space station, circular, smooth. he positions me on the black track.

"the conveyor will start at the same time as the MRI," he says. "slow walking pace. just keep moving."

i look around. "are there any handholds?"

"no. we need to c a natural gait."

ha-ha. the idea that my gait might be natural when i have only ever known 0 g, have only ever known swimming from one hatch to another, is laughable. but i don't laugh.

"ready?" he says.

"i don't know," i say.

"good enough."

he hands me my ear protectors & then steps outside & closes the door & i don't hear him go thru the glass door, the sound is muffled by the cubicle & the headphones over my ears.

then the noise begins.

the noise begins, & the track underneath me starts to roll, & i concentrate on the orchestration & agglomeration of muscles & tendons required to make me move, 1 step at a time—i am in a stage that Virginia calls conscious competence, we all are, which means that i just about know how to walk but only if i focus on it.

whirr. buzz.

click click click.

boom boom boom.

the MRI roars & beats & hums around me, & i walk, & i keep my eyes on the inside of the cubicle—it's so smooth, it's just like a module on Moon 2, enclosing me in a tube, & the track is like our exerciser, & i turn around—

where's the window?—

& stumble, no, i'm in an MRI machine; just focus on the cream wall of the cubicle, keep moving, my legs are burning, my lungs are burning, i am being shot at the ground, why am i still falling?

i thought we landed already. i thought we hit the earth

already, but i'm still racing down toward it, still being pulled thru the air, & i'm still in some kind of landing capsule, smooth around me, encircling me, enclosing me—

& i hear a beeping—

& my belt is buzzing around my chest—

& when is this thing going to land? i brace for impact & curl myself into a ball &—

i fall, & finally i hit the ground, finally we're down, but the ground is slippery, is moving, & it rolls me into a wall where i come to a stop, & the floor keeps creeping below me, rubbing against my side, against my skin.

then the wall opens, falls away, & i tumble out into brightness & my headphones come loose & unimaginable weight of sound lands in my brain & i look up to c Dr. Stearns & some guy in a green medical outfit, holding a kind of technical suitcase & defibrillator.

"check his heart," says Dr. Stearns, as if from far away, maybe he is still up in space, maybe it's only me on the ground.

the guy in green starts to check me over & gradually the room resolves. i'm in the glass antechamber outside the MRI machine. Soto is in there too, looking down at me, concerned. i don't think he should be there but i think Dr. Stearns is focusing on making sure that i'm not having a coronary.

which i'm not. i don't think.

Dr. Stearns puts a device on the end of my finger that measures my oxygen saturation levels. Libra & Orion are also standing there in the room, looking even more concerned than Soto, which seems natural, since they haven't been in the machine yet.

Dr. Stearns finally rocks back on his heels. he waves at the guy in green—a paramedic?—to dismiss him. "u're going to be ok, Leo," he says. "u gave us a fright there. we thought u guys would adjust more quickly but this is all useful data. useful data." it's as if he's talking to himself. "what happened?" he says, addressing me now. "u lose ur balance?"

"no," i say. "no. i . . . i thought i was back in the capsule. i think. i didn't trip, or anything . . . i just freaked out."

"interesting," says the Dr. "i had not considered psychological parameters. we should invite Dr. Santat to future tests." he's talking to himself again. Dr. Santat is the psych who interviews us every morning. *is earth what u expected? what is home to u?* that kind of thing.

"what now, doc?" says Soto.

Dr. Stearns rubs his chin. "let's get him up." they put hands under my armpits & hoist me into a standing position. Dr. Stearns keeps an eye on the graphs coming from his screen. my belt has stopped buzzing on my chest.

they help me out of the glass room & into a wheelchair. Libra & Orion sit down again too. & it strikes me that they got out of their chairs when i fell, that they stood for me, & it gives me a warm feeling in the pit of my stomach. they're what feels like home, here on earth, those twins.

nothing else fits & i don't fit. like someone who walks on their hands.

"let's reduce the time protocol," says Dr. Stearns to 1 of the technicians at a screen. "1 minute each for the other 2."

"u're doing this again?" says Soto.

"have to," says Dr. Stearns. "we need to know what's going on inside their bodies. their stress points. if they're ever going to leave this place, we need to know they can take it."

Soto shakes his head but doesn't say anything.

"just 1 minute," says Dr. Stearns, as if justifying it to himself. "then we pull them out." he taps a technician on the shoulder. "i want to c joint operation particularly. keep an eye on the knees & ankles." then he turns to us. "ok, let's get this done."

Orion puts up his hand. "oh, Dr. Stearns. pick me. pick me. i can't wait."

"ha-ha," says Libra.

Soto catches my eye & winks again, not jokingly now, more sympathetically. but my heart doesn't flicker this time. my heart has had more than it can take already.

3
rooftop

when Libra & Orion are both out of the MRI machine, we are wheeled back to our rooms. Soto comes along too—he doesn't say anything, it isn't discussed, he just kind of ambles along. Dr. Stearns doesn't do anything to stop it but he doesn't look thrilled either.

if i was paranoid, i would think he was worried about Soto hanging out with us.

but i'm not paranoid.

i don't think anyway.

when we arrive at our quarters, Libra says she wants to get ready for their mom. she lives in Florida, their mom, that's how come it's taken her a couple of days to get here. she's not as big in the organization as my mom but she did a few tours: she was on the team who installed Canadarm 2 on the space station, which was the robot arm before the current 1.

Orion mumbles something about wanting to get ready too, & they both disappear into their rooms. Soto looks at me for a moment.

"want to get out of here?" he says. he smiles. when he does it's like he makes his own light.

i stare at him. "i can't," i say.

"oh i don't mean off the base," he says. "i just mean out."

"out?"

"like on the roof."

i'm still staring. "we can go out on the roof?"

"no. not technically. in terms of the rules. but, i mean, actually? yes."

i shrug. "yeah. of course. yeah." i try to sound casual but this is amazing to me, this idea that we can just . . . go outside, & onto the roof. on the station, that kind of freedom simply doesn't exist. there are the modules, & outside the modules, there is nothing.

he nods & takes hold of my wheelchair & wheels me back out into the hallway. he takes me down a couple of long stretches, around a couple of corners, & then stops at a nondescript gray service door. it reads: FIRE EXIT.

"we have to lose the chair here," he says.

"uh-huh."

"u want to lean on me?"

"please."

he stands still while i get up, & i put a hand on his shoulder. i feel the strength of his muscles thru his shirt. a little electric current goes thru me. i feel something happen, in the center of me. blood, rushing inward. a tingle. it is something i felt once before, in space, when i hugged Orion.

"ok?"

"ok." i wonder if my cheeks are red, if my nerves are visible, jangling under my skin.

he opens the door & then leads me up a flight of steps. every step is torture. the ground is still attacking me, still rearing up at me, & i am still being pressed down into it. every coordination of muscle & joint is conscious & planned. i am sweating from the physical exertion as well as the mental concentration on each component of each movement.

slowly,

slowly,

slowly,

we stagger up the stairs. there are corners too where we double back on ourselves. i never thought, i never thought up there on Moon 2 about stairs & how they would be my nemesis.

my undoing.

i am panting for air now as we climb, sweat dripping from my eyebrows, wondering if i can simply give up. it's not just that it's physically exhausting; mentally too, i am focusing so much on each movement, merely to not fall over. i could sit down here. just say "sorry, i can't make it" & sit down on the stairs & get him to go for help.

but then i look up & we're 2 steps from the top.

"u did it," he says. he is still by me, still propping me up. the upright easy power of him.

knees & ankles screeching like poorly oiled parts—it seems like he must hear them too—& muscles on fire, i push myself up those last 2 steps. there's another gray door in front of us with a picture of a man running from a fire, only this door is framed by a keyline of bright white light.

"that's it," says Soto. "the door to outside."

he supports me as i limp over to it, then opens it. sunshine blinds my eyes to begin with. i blink & glowing circles fill my vision, then gradually clear.

i c an expanse of asphalt, or bitumen, or something: i'm not good with earth substances. i'm still learning.

the roof is flat & punctuated by covered shapes that i assume are some kind of air outlet, or AC inlet. beyond them, the blue sky unfurls like a bolt of silk. & below, small vehicles & cars move around.

"wow," i say. i'd forgotten the feeling, even in the few days since i was in that cornfield. the air on my skin. the smell. complicated: dry grass maybe? & something oily & mechanical, & a sharp tone that might be ozone; a storm coming, perhaps? the wind is up, i can c it smoothing the long grass beyond the perimeter fence into shapes & whorls.

a bird wheels past, cawing, tumbling in the sky, a black scrap of fabric plucked up by the wind & falling down again. i think of vids i have seen & realize that this is a crow, rising up on a thermal i guess, & then plummeting down over & over.

as if it's playing, almost.

do crows play? i nearly say it out loud but don't. Soto points to a spot to our left & then helps me over to it. when we arrive he motions for us to sit, & aids me in getting down onto the roof.

the surface presses up, as i lower myself onto it. pressure on my tailbone. i was never aware i had a tailbone, on Moon 2. now i feel it every time i sit down.

"look," he says.

i look. we're on the edge of the roof. the eastern edge? i'm not sure. facing away from the center's busy test facilities, it's almost the same view as from our rooms, but it's not filtered anymore, not mediated by glass—it's a little like when i stepped out of the space station—swam out, more like—& i was suddenly in openness & even tho it looked superficially the same it felt entirely different.

i'm outside.

in the air.

& the view is amazing: grass rolling away over gently undulating earth all the way to the sharp horizon, where the earth gives way to that shining blue-silk sky; & i feel the sharpness of the horizon too, it does something to me, it hinges open something inside me, like the blade of a knife, it shucks me, like an oyster.

the world isn't my oyster, i think.

the world is a knife.

i am the oyster.

"u're an oyster?" says Soto, & i realize i must have said that out loud.

"oh. nothing. sorry."

"don't apologize. u're in a pretty weird situation." he leans back on the rooftop & puts his hands behind his head. i'm tempted to do the same. but i would not match his casualness, & i might not be able to get up again. but the roof is warm beneath me, & it does look appealing.

he looks up at the sky. it's bright daylight, the sun a hot disk behind a few tatters of cloud, but there's a crescent moon, pale against the blue.

"i can't believe u were up there for so long," he says. "it must have been . . . amazing."

i shrug. "it was just where we lived." i wave at the general everythingness around us. air, grass, the few thin leafless trees or cacti or something in the distance. "*this* is amazing."

"it's Nevada, honey."

"well, it's amazing to me." i breathe in slow thru my nostrils. something tingly & fresh on the air.

"rain," says Soto, seeing me do it.

"yeah?"

"yeah. on its way. a storm." he points to dark clouds on the horizon.

a comfortable silence.

"u haven't been up then?" i say eventually. the answer is pretty obvious but it's not like i've had a lot of conversational training.

"nope. only just got my doctorate."

"u're, what, 18 & u have a doctorate?"

he half smiles, not boasting, but not embarrassed either. "well, yeah. it's a young-astronauts program. a PhD & some serious flying qualifications are the basic entry requirements."

"so u fly too?"

"air cadets, then air force, yes."

"impressive. i feel almost bad. i got to live up there & i didn't have to do anything to qualify for it."

he nudges my arm. "come on. u're space *born*. a native. i heard about that EVA u pulled off. to replace the gyro."

i try to mimic his half smile. i don't think it's very successful. i think i probably look like i'm passing gas. "there wasn't really much choice."

"spoken like a true astronaut."

a pause again. the sun warm on my face. when i close my eyes i still c it, glowing red thru my eyelids.

"u want to go back up?" he says.

i cover my eyes with my hand, turn to look at him. "to Moon 2?"

"yeah."

"i don't know. i don't really know anything about earth, yet."

"i can c that."

"i mean," i say, "they always call it home. but we've never been here, u know?"

"but u wanted to come down?"

"yeah! of course. i mean, to experience it. to meet people who aren't astronauts or Libra or Orion. i mean, not that i don't love them. but . . . to have friends! play sports! & to know what earth feels like. there are so many things. waterfalls. swimming. the ocean. throwing a baseball. roller coasters! walking in long grass. snow. sand. everything. i want to feel *everything.*"

he is nodding. "me too. that's why i want to go up there. feel what 0 g is like."

then we both nod, because i guess we realize in that moment that we are mirror images, we are inverse people.

"when do u go?" i say.

"a couple of months, i think," he says. "there's a ton of prep but there's so much pressure to keep the program moving, with the drought, u know, & all the overcrowding & stuff."

i stare at him blankly.

"what?" he says.

pause.

"they don't talk to u about this stuff?" he says.

i shake my head. "i mean, we hear about the drought, from my grandpa & on the news vids & stuff. but . . ."

"but they didn't, like, share the whole imperative of the mission?"

"i guess . . . i mean, i knew the goal was to prep for life in space. but i didn't think—"

"—that the time frame was so urgent?" he asks.

i shake my head.

he shakes his head too, but with a whole different connotation. "man. so the fresh water is running out, basically. it's the carbon levels. hundreds of tons of glacial ice have melted over the last couple of decades, so the ocean levels rose too & flooded a lot of land with salt & . . . long story short, the whole planet is thirsty. at the same time there are way more people than ever. 10 billion. it's unsustainable in the medium to long term. hence: me & the other candidates."

"what are u supposed to do about it?"

"we're astronauts, right? pilots & also certified geniuses." he says this with no trace of arrogance. "math prodigies, eidetic memories, capable of committing endless numbers & coordinates & rules to our brains. but we're also physically weird, or unusual, or whatever. big lung capacities. strong hearts. low resting-pulse rates. there were the obvious tests to get in but also a lot of medical screening."

"so?"

"so the idea is to send us up there for a long time. 2 years. & monitor us medically & test us when we get back down, like in that MRI machine. c if we can handle it."

i look up at the faint sickle of moon in the sky, floating there. always there, even when u can't c it. orbiting. never leaving the earth's side. "why?"

"because they're also building long-range ships. exploratory vehicles. this is, like, a 50-year plan BTW. but they want to travel to other planets. c if we can colonize them."

"seriously?"

"oh very seriously. whole teams of astronomers around the world have been spending decades identifying possible host planets." he turns his head, as if scanning the sky. then he points, behind us. "Kepler-186f, for example," he says. "it's over that way. 2.9 quadrillion miles away, so not a good fit from the distance perspective, but it's around the same size as earth & in the same habitable orbital shell around its sun. could have water & oxygen."

"huh," i say.

"they find weird stuff too. there's this planet, 55 Cancri e. about a third of it is made of diamond. liquid & solid diamond."

"doesn't sound very livable."

"no but it's awesome, isn't it? i mean literally. up there"—he points up at the blue sky—"there's a planet made of diamond. i think about that sometimes, when i'm going to sleep, or whatever. about all the stars, the sheer number of them. & a planet made of diamond. it makes me feel . . . i know this is stupid, because there are 100 billion times 100 billion stars, so it should make me feel small, but it makes me feel . . . less lonely, somehow."

i look at him. my pulse has jumped, the blood shushing in my ears.

"sorry, that makes me sound stupid. i shouldn't talk like this, i should—"

"no," i say. "i do that, but with the moon. like, the way it circles & circles the earth?" i feel stupid now, i'm the stupid 1, but i keep on, like a projectile careering forward. "i mean . . . it feels to me like a kind of love, u know? always there, no matter what. locked together, co-orbiting."

his eyes narrow. but not in a bad way. "yeah," he says. "i know."

silence.

then i hear Libra's voice. & Orion's laughter. something golden & shimmering in the air dissipates.

"help me up," i say.

he hauls me to my feet & i sway for a moment & then he is my crutch as i hobble over to the front side of the building, the north side, i think. i look down. it's a parking lot, & i guess the entrance lobby of the building because there's a circular drive where a car can pull up in front. there is a Mexican-American flag, fluttering on a pole.

1 car is parked in the little half-moon drive, a German sports hatch made for hugging corners & i think that's a car an astronaut would rent, & sure enough: as i lean forward i c Libra & Orion's mother standing by it, then stooping, to embrace Libra, who is sitting in her wheelchair, an attendant standing behind it.

she hugs her daughter, for the longest time. Cheryl is their mother's name. then she breaks away & hugs Orion too, holding him tight; i can almost feel it from up here, almost feel the tears that i can c glistening on her face in the light.

i wish . . .

i wish my mother would do that, sometime.

then i tell myself not to be stupid. it's like wishing to land on Kepler-186f to make it ur own little kingdom; it's like wishing u could harness Cancri e, or whatever the other 1 was called, & bring it into orbit, have ur own spinning diamond mine with most of the diamond in the universe.

my mother is my mother. & there's no use wishing otherwise.

i straighten up, & take in breath, sharply, partly the wish popping like a delicate bubble under the blade of the sun, partly the pain that shoots thru my knees.

"ur mother's here, isn't she?" he says.

"somewhere," i say. "i haven't really seen her."

he holds my gaze. "i've met her. did some of my training with her. i can . . . i can imagine."

"yeah," i say.

"u have any other family?"

"my grandpa," i say. "but i'm not allowed to c him yet. quarantine."

"but the twins can c their mom?"

"she doesn't handle cows. cows have bad germs apparently."

"that sucks," he says.

pause.

"u said there are a whole lot of things u want to experience, right?" says Soto.

"uh-huh."

"well, let's check a small 1 off the list."

"like what?"

he shakes his head. "wait here," he says. "i won't be long." he propels me over to 1 of the duct-intake-outtake things & leans me against it, like a prop to come back to—an umbrella, a stick, but not like that because he does it with care. then he disappears thru the door.

i stand & just let the sensations course thru me. the gritty texture of the rooftop beneath my feet. the breeze. the light. the scent of a coming storm. i didn't know there were so many scents to the world, so many textures. in space most everything is smooth, & smells of sweat or disinfectant.

after maybe 5 minutes or longer, Soto reappears. there's a

cardboard box in his hand & he pops it open as he walks over, tilts it so i can c in.

i look. little white balls, nestled together.

"Ping-Pong balls," he says.

"Ping-Pong balls? where did u get those?"

"there's a table. down in the rec room. i kind of stole them."

"& what are we going to do with them?"

"we're going to throw them. come on."

he marches me back over to the east side of the roof. immediately below is a strip of concrete, cracked, & then a fence & then a kind of moat of grass & then a bigger fence, topped with rolled barbed wire. i shade my eyes with my hand—the sun hurts them.

he takes a ball from the box & holds my hand, so that i remain stable. then he swings his other arm back & throws the ball—it arcs up, up, up & then when it reaches the apex of its curve thru the air—its invisible curve but i c it anyway, the inviolable formulae of mass & force & angle & velocity that govern its flight—it begins to fall, the indescribable beauty of it, glistening math written on the surface of the air, & it falls & it falls but still following that flattened curve &

bounces,

with a

ping,

& bounces again, ripples described vertically, little arches as it hops along, decreasing bridges, *plink plink plink,*

& stops.

"wow." i say. "it might sound stupid but that was amazing."

he smiles. a full smile this time, lights going on. flash. "when u were up there u could make a ball from water & float it around. i'm trying to turn that around, to c thru ur eyes, & no, i don't think it sounds stupid."

something turns inside me. no one has tried to c thru my eyes before. maybe Libra & Orion, i suppose, but they're ... family. they're not friends. & Grandpa. but he doesn't need to try. he gets me already.

anyway, the point is it unlocks something, it turns a key.

"thanks," i say.

"de nada," he says. & he offers me the box.

i take a ball. i wind my hand back & throw, not nearly as well as him, not nearly as far. i have had precisely 0 practice, but it arcs up & falls just the same, & bounces on the pavement below.

& he throws 1.

& i throw 1.

& we throw all the balls, 1 after another, & they go *ping ping ping ping ping* on the ground, they rain down, & they're all white & the ground is gray & the grass is brown & the sky is blue & it's a moment i can still c, all these beautiful colors & sounds, whenever i close my eyes. i'm alive, in that moment, i'm on earth, & i'm taking it all in, all this sensation. i can hear birdsong: high, clear, stitched invisibly on the air.

then suddenly i think of Brown, how he can't take anything in now, how he's floating up there even now, like i was. i think of his family. how they'll be sitting around now, getting used to him not being there. to his empty chair at dinner.

the ball stutters from my hand, falls short.

"let's go in," i say.

4

freeze

Soto helps me down the stairs. it's slightly easier than going up.
only slightly.

as we descend the steps he turns to me. "what have u eaten so
far?" he says.

"i don't know," i say. "they bring us food on trays."

"that stuff," he says. it's kind of a question. "can't be that different from what u ate on the station."

"no, not really," i say.

"u had any ice cream yet?" he asks.

"no."

"come on then. we're going to the canteen."

"i don't think that's allowed," i say.

"nor is going on the roof," he says.

which is a fair point.

we collect the chair at the bottom of the stairs, & Soto wheels
me down the hallway & then down in an elevator to a wide, busy,
noisy room where people sit in rows on benches & eat & talk.
clash of cutlery, a sea-sound of conversation. i have never seen so
many people in 1 place.

it's overwhelming, but then everything is overwhelming.

Soto wheels me to a space. there is no one else at the table
right now. "BRB," he says.

i sit & wait.

soon Soto returns with 2 bowls. he sets 1 in front of me. there is a ball of white, a ball of pink, a ball of brown.

"vanilla, strawberry, chocolate," he says. "holy trinity."

i look around at the staff, the hundreds of people in this big hall. i wonder if i should be recognizing anyone. i glance around to c if my mom & Virginia are here but am not surprised they're not: those 2 are not sociable canteen types. they'll be working on something, somewhere. there's no one else i know. actually, it strikes me, there are very few people i know, period. Libra & Orion, a few astronauts. plus the core ground team: Boutros, Stearns, Ravzi, Santiago . . .

people keep looking at me, then looking quickly away.

that name makes me wonder what became of Santiago. i'd never known that before: someone being taken out of a sim & not coming back. the Company doesn't operate like that: sims are important, especially death sims, & everyone knows it.

"u hear of someone in PR called Santiago?" i say to Soto.

he shakes his head. "nope. lot of employees here tho."

hmm. i wonder about this. are there that many people who—

"Leo?" says Soto.

i snap back.

i pick up the spoon & take a mouthful of chocolate.

my brain explodes.

seriously: here is a thought experiment. imagine that u have never eaten anything that didn't come out of a packet or a can. imagine that everything u have ever eaten has been dried or preserved.

now imagine putting ice cream into ur mouth.

the coldness.

the sweetness, the freeze, the way the whole thing is shot thru with air, little bubbles, as if inflated. then the way it melts into liquid.

cold, sweet, air, liquid, the state of being frozen: these are all things that existed on the station. but never together, never combined in this . . . this . . .

"oh my god," i say eventually. then the taste hits me: i've had chocolate before but this is different, this is coating every taste bud on my tongue & it's like an explosion, a detonation, but everywhere, lighting sparks in my head.

"right?" says Soto.

i lift the spoon again, take too much, &—

"aargh!" i clutch my head, where a spike of ice has just been driven into my cerebral cortex.

"ha," says Soto. "brain freeze."

the sensation dims. "that's a thing?" i say.

"yeah."

"but u still eat it?"

he laughs. "it's kind of worth it, isn't it?"

"yes," i admit, taking another mouthful. but slower this time.

i feel a hand on my shoulder. i turn & look up & there's Dr. Stearns, stern look on his face. i almost laugh: stern Dr. Stearns.

"Leo," he says. "u're meant to be in quarantine. back to ur quarters."

"oh come on," says Soto. "what's the worst that could happen?"

5

the worst that could happen

here's another thought experiment:

imagine that u have never, ever been sick. imagine that u grew up in a hermetically sealed environment & no one was allowed to enter it without being entirely, completely free of viruses & bacteria.

now imagine that u get a cold.

imagine that ur head is aching, ur throat is a bag of knives, ur nose is apparently now something like a faucet, ur limbs are aching, & u don't know where the ache from learning to walk ends & the ache from the virus begins.

i lie in bed for 3 days. or rather in a corner of the room. Libra & Orion try to keep away but it doesn't help—they get it too, & then we sleep together. their mother brings them soup, hot tea with lemon, that kind of thing.

my mother brings me nothing.

Orion sulks. "u weren't even as excited as us about coming down here," he says. "u & ur astronaut obsession. but u're the 1 who breaks quarantine & gets us sick?" he sighs. "couldn't u have just stayed in the quarters?"

"u guys went outside to meet ur mom, i noticed," i say.

"shh, both of u," says Libra. "this isn't helping."

she sneezes.

at times we wonder if we might be dying.

totally worth it tho.

6

routine

at first, once we recover from our colds, they check us every hour. heart rate. blood pressure. CAT scans.

then twice a day.

then once a day.

then every other day

the time passes very slowly.

1 morning, just casually, i unroll my screen & call the switchboard on vidlink, which is 1 of the numbers preprogrammed into it. a woman answers, or at least i think it's a woman. i don't c her. the camera is switched off: operational security, i guess.

i ask to speak to Santiago in PR.

"we don't have anyone working here by that name," says the woman on the other end of the line.

7

provisional

Libra & Orion's mother stays for another week or so. my own mother is still testing flight suits or running sims, whatever it is she does—sometimes i c her, when we go down for meals, or when we're in the medical bay, being tested.

the rest of the time is pretty boring. we watch vids on a screen—films, sitcoms. i try to check the news on the screen but it's blocked; we still need time to adjust to the here & now, to the world. it's like they think we have PTSD or something. maybe we do, i mean, it's all pretty hard to adjust to.

every morning we take our pills: stuff to keep our bone density up as much as possible. to maintain adequate blood pressure. iron supplements. potassium. lots of them, all different colors & shapes.

sometimes we read. sometimes we wander the hallways, tho wandering makes it sound very casual & actually there is often a crutch or a wheelchair involved.

we're getting stronger tho. with every step we take we are less shocked by gravity's force, less weighed down by it. our movements are becoming smoother, more fluid. they are happy to check us every 3 days now.

no one really speaks to us. we pass people in the hallways & they lower their heads & go about their business. i haven't seen Soto since the day on the roof—it's as if he's avoiding me. & we're not allowed outside, or at least they discourage it for more than a minute or 2; they say the sunlight is still too much for us.

then, maybe 3 weeks after our first walking MRI scans, Dr. Stearns comes to our common area. Libra & Orion's mother is with him, my mother too.

"Leo," she says.

"Mother."

she gives a businesslike nod.

Stearns comes forward. "so!" he says. "today is a big day."

"it is?" says Orion. "do we get 2 blood tests? oh please say yes."

"very funny, Orion," says Libra.

"no, we want to try u in a new environment," Stearns says.

"a new environment like . . . ?" says Orion.

Dr. Stearns looks at the mothers. Libra & Orion's mother has wet eyes. she's wearing a suit today, & makeup. she looks like it's a special occasion. "well," he says. "we were thinking of . . . discharging u. provisionally. with lots of safety checks in place."

"oh," says Libra.

"as in . . . we're leaving?" says Orion. i feel the same surprise that i c on his face. i think i had started to believe we were going to live in these gray rooms forever.

"yes," says Dr. Stearns. "for a month, initially. we need to keep monitoring u. u will each be given blood-testing kits, & will have to upload ur results once a week. u'll have to keep taking ur meds of course. we'll also be sending a nurse every week to take scans, plus lung-capacity measurements, that sort of thing. after that month we'll need u back here for bone scans, to test the density. but for now . . . u're free to go."

"we weren't free to go before?" i say.

"it's an expression," says my mother. neutral.

"personally i would have preferred a longer supervision period," says Dr. Stearns. "u 3 have physiologies entirely different from anyone on earth & it behooves me as a doctor to make sure u're safe"—he glances at my mother, at Libra & Orion's mother—"but i have been persuaded that the best thing for u is to be in a home space. for now. with monitoring."

a home space.

whatever that means.

"so . . . where do we go?" says Libra.

"u 2 will come with me," says their mother. tho her cheeks are wet, she is smiling. "back to Miami."

Libra grins & goes & hugs her. it makes me wince inside. even Orion is smiling.

"& u'll be living with Grandpa," says my mother.

"u're not coming too?" i ask.

"i'll join u. in a week or 2. i have some things to take care of here."

"oh. ok."

this is all so weird. all presented so stiffly & awkwardly, like protocol has been suspended & no one is quite sure who is making the decisions. on Moon 2, everything was logical, everything followed rules, everything followed the manual. now it seems like no one quite knows what to do with us. i look over at the window, at the scrubland beyond.

getting out. going to the ranch.

being a real person.

i feel weightless for a moment, an instant of 0 g—i reach out a hand & grab a chair arm to steady myself. i hadn't realized, until this instant, how much i have been feeling like a prisoner, how much i wanted to get out of this building, this compound.

to actually visit earth. where we have been, but not been, for over a month.

"u should wear sunglasses any time u go outside," says Dr. Stearns. we have been given special prescription sunglasses to limit the light hitting our eyes because our retinas developed entirely indoors, in artificial light, no outside light. "& factor 50 on ur skin of course."

"sure," says Orion. "but do u think we could get, like, a more stylish frame for those glasses, because really . . ."

his mother laughs. i laugh too. the glasses are terrible: round, blocky, made of thick black plastic.

Dr. Stearns does not laugh.

pause.

"when?" i say. "when do we go?"

"today, if u like," says Dr. Stearns. "ur grandfather flew in yesterday & is arriving by helicopter within the next hour. he'll take u back to the ranch. he has been fully briefed on ur medical needs."

"to the ranch," i say.

"sorry?" says Dr. Stearns.

"u said *back* to the ranch. but i've never been there. so it's *to* the ranch."

"oh, yes," says Dr. Stearns. "of course. to the ranch."

"& then what?" says Libra. "he goes to the ranch, we go to Miami, & then . . . what happens then?"

Dr. Stearns blinks. "what?"

"what do we do after that?" says Orion.

"well . . . u live. i suppose. ur mother"—he turns to me—"ur mothers will have to enroll u in school, i imagine; i'm not clear on the legalities. i'm sure Boutros or his office will advise. as for the rest . . . that's really up to u."

"oh," says Orion. it's becoming a catchphrase of ours.

for some reason, i had always thought that at some point we would go back up to Moon 2. i don't know why i thought that. i mean, earth was the promised land. we were always told: when u're strong enough u'll go down to earth. so that was clearly the end point, the goal, & yet somehow . . . somehow i saw it as a circle. saw myself back up there.

"a problem, Leo?" says my mother.

"no, nothing," i say. "i just . . . i guess i always thought i'd go back up, 1 day."

she nods. "i c."

"&?"

now she shrugs. "i guess u will have to apply urself, & try to become an astronaut."

yes. yes, i suppose that makes sense. we are not astronauts. we are people who happen to have been born in space.

Libra & Orion & their mother go to start getting things ready, but my mother walks off with Dr. Stearns, which i suppose i should have expected, & i am left to prepare to leave the base.

to go home. to a home i have never known.

8
flight

so i:

   –pack. this does not take a long time. i don't have anything.
   just a watch. some Company-issue clothes. i do have to go
   down to medical & pick up a kit: it contains home blood
   tests, a pair of crutches, a foldable wheelchair. it all goes in a
   trunk thing so when i say pick up i do not literally pick it up.
   someone checks all the stuff & then it is put on a cart & 1 of
   the orderlies wheels it to my room.
   –wait.
   –wait.
   –say goodbye to Libra & Orion. this takes longer than
   packing. tho much of the time is taken up with awkwardly
   standing there & not really knowing what to say. we try to
   find Virginia, to say goodbye, but she must be working still,
   & Boutros doesn't know where exactly.

   "i don't really know what to say," says Libra.
   we are standing in our living area. i have just had a message on
my screen that Grandpa is here, that his helicopter has landed—
they told me he could come down to the rooms but i said i would
rather go up to meet him.
   i want to meet him for the first time in real air. outside air. i

haven't spoken to him since i got sick. they've now disabled calls on our screens too—said that it was better for us to not have too much direct contact with the outside world until we were settled. to help with the transition. a quarantine for the mind as well as the body.

"nor me," i say.

"nor me," says Orion.

"i just thought we'd always be together, u know?" says Libra. she is twisting her little bottle of earth. she still wears it, even tho she's on earth now. tho maybe she's like me. maybe it won't feel real for her till we're out of here. out of the base. "it seems stupid now," she says.

"no," i say. "i get it." i always thought that too, without thinking it. a premise. an assumption of togetherness, like something axiomatic, like the moon orbiting the earth.

but now, it seems it was never a rule. just . . . a circumstance. i feel a prickling in the corner of my eyes & i tell it to go away.

"what are u going to do?" says Orion.

"do?"

"at the ranch."

"i don't know," i say. "what are u going to do? in Miami?"

"go listen to a symphony, dude," he says.

"oh come on," i say. "u're not going to check out McDonald's first?"

he smiles. "well, yeah, maybe."

"Mom says i can have a corner of the backyard for a garden," says Libra.

i smile. i can c her in it. i can c Orion listening to his symphony, closing his eyes, the music washing over him.

"i'll go c Grandpa's cattle," i say. "the puppies. he says there are puppies. & he has a horse for me, i think. & learn to fly & study physics & . . . i don't know. everything." suddenly i feel nervous.

everything is a lot of things. that's a stupid thing to say. but hopefully they know what i mean.

Orion raises his hand to pause me, then goes & picks up 3 water bottles from the table. he hands them out & we clink them together.

"to everything," he says.

"to everything."

"to everything."

then we step forward, awkwardly, & hug. Libra first—she pulls me close & i smell the shampoo in her hair, & it's a new scent, an earth scent, a scent u'd never get on the station.

then Orion. all my nerve endings are dancing. i feel the muscles under his skin, less developed than Soto's but still strong, still Orion who i have known since i knew what it was to be alive, & i try not to hold on too long, not too short either, & now i'm self-conscious but then—he winces, & i step back.

"what's wrong?"

he grimaces, twisting his shoulder, like he's working out a kink. "just . . . stiff," he says. he breathes in deep.

i frown. "since when?"

"since . . . it's not a big deal. adjusting, that's all."

"does Dr. Stearns know?"

"Christ!" says Orion. "Dr. Stearns has x-ray, MRI, & CAT scans of my whole body. he knows things i don't know."

Libra & i exchange a concerned look but Orion is already crutching off down the hallway—the orderlies have gone ahead with my trunk of medical stuff. "come on," she says. "don't u want to meet ur grandpa?"

& i do.

of course i do.

it's something i have looked forward to all my life, so i follow Orion, not using crutches myself: i can manage the walk to the elevator, i think. Boutros said it was just up to the 8th floor & the helicopter would be on the roof.

we press the button & the elevator rises, a light flicking from 1 number to the next, chiming each time: 2 *ching* 3 *ching* 4 *ching* 5 *ching* 6 *ching* 7 *ching* . . .

8.

the elevator doors open & i curse as the sun fills the oblong space; i hold the door with my shoulder & take my glasses from my jeans pocket & put them on. the light dials down a notch. the helicopter is still on the roof, maybe 20 yards away, its blades spinning slowly.

&

& there is a man standing in front of me, with a worn leather hat on his head, a checked shirt, jeans. boots. he tips his hat at me.

i would like to say i run forward but i can't run, so i walk gingerly forward instead, needing to concentrate less now on every component of walking, but still not quite a native.

he walks forward too, & i c the crinkles around his eyes, because he's smiling, & i c that his eyes are wet too.

we stop, & just stand there, for a long moment.

then he puts his arms around me & hugs me tight. i hear Dr. Stearns, who is over to the left, give a little cough, & Grandpa eases his hold, instantly, like he hadn't even thought of my physical fragility, & of course he probably hadn't, in that moment, he just wanted to hug me.

"hi, Grandpa," i say. "nice to meet u."

he laughs. a choking sort of laugh. "nice to meet u too, Leo," he says.

he holds me at arm's length, hands on my shoulders, examining me. his eyes are a paler hazel than i realized. not gene-modded, just washed by the Californian sun, which has also constellated his face with freckles. then he nods. "landing didn't take too much out of u then," he says.

"oh u should have seen me on Moon 2," i say. "i was like a bodybuilder."

he smiles. "well, they do say the camera adds 10 lbs."

"yeah." i smile back.

people are moving around us & i c Boutros, as well as my mother, among them. i glance over & c Libra & Orion too—they lift their hands & wave, coordinated.

"take good care of him, sir," says Boutros, stepping forward. he shakes Grandpa's hand.

"of course i will," says Grandpa. a complicated look passes between them.

Grandpa nods to my mother. i assume they've spoken since he landed. caught up. tho i don't know what catching up with my mother looks like. i can't imagine the 2 of them hugging.

Dr. Stearns runs Grandpa thru the medical stuff again. it's not very interesting.

eventually, we make our way to the helicopter & Grandpa helps me up into it. we take our seats & he hands me a set of headphones—he has 1 too—& we can talk to each other using the attached microphone, over the din of the rotors.

slowly, the helicopter lifts into the air. then it banks forward, & we move away from the building, over the compound. we speed up—a fence goes past below, then the outer 1, topped with wire, & then after brown grass has crossed below us for a minute we pass another fence, lower this time but with some kind of guard tower standing over a gray road.

on the road, i c a group of people holding signs of some kind. there are tents—they must live there. but then they're gone, behind us.

"who were they?" i ask Grandpa.

"who were who?"

"those people. with the signs."

he shrugs. "i don't know. anywhere the Company has a site, there are protesters. Area 51 crazies. alien conspiracists."

"isn't that all finished? since the Company took over the base?"

he shrugs again. "not for them."

soon i am not thinking about those people anymore because for a while we pass thru banks of cloud, or fog, i'm not sure. i've only ever seen this stuff from above before. it surrounds us like the beginning of a dream, on a vid, when the scene dissolves, & i watch it swirling, shades of gray & white.

the helicopter thrums with a rhythmical hum, vibrates. i close my eyes. i think i must fall asleep, i don't know how long for, but i know it's sleep because for a moment i'm a salmon, swimming thru roiling white water, bubbles so dense it's like foam, like cloud, pushing upstream, over smooth stones in every shade of gray, leaping over rocks where the water sheets down in milky ribbons u'd think were ice, always struggling, always straining my body to rise, to rise up into the mountains &—

"oh, hey."

it's Grandpa. i look up at him. i'm in the helicopter, leaning against him, my headphones are in an uncomfortable position, pressing my ear flat. i am drooling a little. i sit up.

& watching the earth going by, far below us, the fields & roads & poles & little towns. the cars, driving who knows where. the rivers, their water low & brown. the lakes, some of them little more than dried-up beds, but some of them sparkling in the sun still, even now.

"it's so beautiful," i say.

"yes," says Grandpa.

i look out, at the sky, towering with clouds, whole superstructures of white, tumbling into the distance.

i think: how people used to call the sky the heavens.

i think: how if the heavens were the counterpoint to the earth, the thing that people looked up at, which made them think of infinity, of promise, then if i was born in the sky, then the earth is my heaven.

& people are not meant to live in heaven.

but then we tilt down, toward the earth.

"here it comes," says Grandpa. "Sonoma."

we have been crossing a wide plateau, an expanse of grassland, & now in front of us is a wall of mountains, & before the mountains a sudden rise in the earth, & then—

then i c it, a storybook valley, wide & low & green, or mostly green, framed to the east by mountains, a few thin rivers ribboning thru it, sectioned into different farms. clusters of buildings. barns. big metal things—pylons? or something else. they seem to be on wheels.

it's beautiful.

we get closer. the valley grows: it fills the windows.

we fly down lower & lower toward it.

we flee toward it.

9

guns & money

we land on a square of concrete, surrounded by low prefabricated buildings.

"the local school," says Grandpa. "but it had to close a few years ago."

"why?"

"not enough kids. too hard to make a living up here, so most families have moved north."

i look at the basketball hoop, its tattered net swinging lightly in the breeze. the white lines painted on the asphalt. i feel almost sad. like . . . now i won't get to play here, to have a locker, do all those normal school things.

i don't know what the plan is for school actually: will Grandpa teach me at home? will i still have vidlink tutors? i make a note to ask Grandpa later. i should have asked Boutros, i guess, but everything is so new, so different, it's hard to know what to concentrate on first.

i blink, & focus—right now—on right now. i follow Grandpa, who has paused to wait for me, & we cross the yard, buffeted by the wind from the helicopter.

guys from the Company carry my crate to a pickup, which is parked on the street outside. Grandpa puts a hand under my arm, helps me walk.

they hoist the crate up onto the back, & Grandpa climbs into the truck bed—i notice that he winces when he raises his knee—& ratchets straps to hold the crate in place.

then we say goodbye to the Company men. Grandpa opens the pickup door for me & takes some of my weight as i lever myself into the passenger seat. i am breathing heavily at this point, conscious of my diaphragm expanding & contracting. my spine feels compressed, from sitting in the helicopter & now sitting again—it's as if i'm in a vise, squeezing me from above & below.

Grandpa starts the engine & pulls out onto an empty road. we pass a few houses & then halt at a stop sign. i c more buildings ahead, rising 3, maybe 4 stories.

"this is what passes for the town round here," says Grandpa.

he puts the truck in drive & we roll forward, past a row of what look like Victorian houses, like something from a western movie, followed by a few stores. there are a handful of people on the street, all wearing hats & leather boots. it's a kind of time travel.

i crack open my window. cool air winnows into the car.

"fall's coming," says Grandpa. "u can smell it on the air."

i draw it in. something rich—grass? & something clean & cold—something that is perhaps the scent of rocks & white streams running down mountains, if those things had a scent.

then we pass a tall store of some kind where people are in a line outside; no one young, i notice. "what's that?" i say.

"bank," says Grandpa.

a block later we pass another store with a line; this time maybe 10 people all waiting patiently.

"bank?"

"gun store," says Grandpa.

more stores flick past, flipbook style. all empty, no lines outside.

"why those stores?" i ask.

"why what?"

"why the lines?"

Grandpa shrugs. he has 1 hand on the wheel. the other is resting on the side of his door. "hard to make a living these days. so people want to keep their money liquid. & they want guns to protect it."

i frown. "huh."

Grandpa doesn't say anything more tho, so i fall silent too, as the buildings peter out, & then are gone. we are on a wide road that runs thru the center of the valley. even if i wanted to say anything, i don't think i would now because my attention is all on the landscape around me.

i know this valley, from satellite imagery. it's 17 miles long, a few miles wide. below it lies an aquifer, an underground lake, that at its height in the 19th century was 300 ft. from top to bottom in places. at its depth, i should say, i guess. but then every farmer in the valley sank wells into it & the rain stopped coming, & there was only 1 way that equation was going.

i know all this, i know the geography & the history, but to c it is another thing. the sun is midway between vertical & the horizon; the whole land is white with it, bleached with the brightness of it—if i wasn't wearing my special-issue sunglasses it would blind me, i'm sure. around us is grassland, sectioned by fences. some of it is green but most is brown.

soft hills rise in what i know is the west. in the east, a ridge of mountains, snowcapped, deep-shadowed. there are few trees. the sky hangs above, seeming bigger than space, bigger than the endless blackness that used to surround me, pale blue & dusted with white clouds.

& it's all so beautiful.

it's all so beautiful it cinches my heart in my chest, belts it around & squeezes, tho that might be the atmosphere too, we're 2,000 ft. up & there is less oxygen than i'm used to.

we pass rows of huge metal structures on wheels, tho they are still, not moving. i think they're the pylon-like things i saw from the helicopter. they are triangular, rising up to a point, made of a kind of steel scaffolding, set on black rubber wheels. they stretch across the fields in chains, like the backbone of some enormous dinosaur.

"what are those?" i say.

"center pivot irrigators," says Grandpa. "they roll along, spray water as they go. means u can evenly distribute."

"they're not moving."

"no."

but as we drive along, the grass becomes greener, & i c more of them, moving this time. at the top of the triangle is a bar that rocks back & forth, & water mists from it, sparkling in the flat, absolute sunshine. the moving structures cast short, sharp shadows & they seem a little like birds, pecking.

"these ones are moving," i say.

"Harrison's land," says Grandpa. "good farmer. when the summer pumping ban came in 20 years ago, to preserve the aquifer, he'd already started collecting rainwater."

"u did that too," i say.

he nods.

"so does that make u a good farmer?"

a ghost of a smile. "i try my best."

the fields scroll past, the grass, the light. after maybe a half hour Grandpa points ahead & to the right. "our land," he says. i like that. how he calls it ours.

we have been driving slowly toward the mountain range, on a road that bisects the valley. ahead, there's a track that branches off, & a heavy metal gate a little farther on, as tall as the tall fence that borders the road. no way u could climb it.

"here we are," says Grandpa.

there are tatters of colored fabric or rubber or something tied to a fence post by the turning where we come off the road, fluttering in the breeze.

Grandpa sees me looking.

"balloons," he says. "ur grandmother tied them for ur mother's 16th. to show everyone where to come. i don't know why. there's no one in this valley doesn't know us & where we live. but i've never been able to take them down."

i don't say anything. my grandmother died when i was young. i don't remember her very well, & Grandpa never really talks about her. i don't ask either. i get that he doesn't want me to, & it's ok. he'll talk when he's ready, maybe.

Grandpa slows even more as we approach the big gate; presses a button on the dash. the gate begins to swing open, & Grandpa crawls until it's fully open, then drives thru. he presses the button & it swings shut behind us with a solid clunk.

serious security, i think.

we bump along for a mile or 2. there are no irrigators here, at least not now, but the grass is greener than most i have seen, & there are Black Angus cattle grazing on it, not that i recognize them as such, i mean, i'm not an expert on cows, but Grandpa has told me enough times on vid what they're called. i also know that Grandpa has 210 head of cattle—that's what he calls them, heads, like they just go around without bodies, floating above the ground.

actually, in the haze of light, some of them do seem to be floating. they're much bigger than i expected—1 or 2, close to the road, fully as tall as the pickup truck, which scares me a little, tho there's a fence running beside the track with red balls threaded on its wires, making me think it's electric.

we turn a corner & the ranch comes into view. my heart lifts. i have imagined this moment so many times, so many nights when going to sleep, i have pictured myself pulling up here. i lower the window further, & something animal enters the car on the wind, something earthy & full, with notes of grass under it, at least i think it must be grass; it makes my head spin.

the ranch house is entirely constructed of wood. my grandpa built it with his own hands, in between space missions. it's not only my mother who is driven, who is dedicated. it's a trait she inherited from him.

"welcome to Big Sky Ranch," says Grandpa.

"thanks," i say. & i mean it. i am so grateful, in that moment.

we turn a slow corner & stop in front of the house. Grandpa turns off the engine & there is silence, & i realize that i went from the helicopter to the truck & the helicopter's rotors were still turning at that point, & this is 1 of the first times—apart from the cornfield or the roof with Soto—that i have heard the world without air conditioners pumping or pistons rising & falling, drowning it with white noise.

i listen.

in the distance, i hear a sharp cry. a hawk? i remember Grandpa mentioning them. & around us, the rustling of grass. somewhere i hear a chirp & i wonder if i'm right to guess that it's a cricket calling—they will be gone, the crickets, when the weather gets colder. this is something else i have learned from vids.

"u ok?" says Grandpa.

"yes. just listening."

he nods. "i get it."

of course he does. he is 1 of the only people who would, along with Libra & Orion. my mother would ask what we were doing & shouldn't we be working on something productive.

Grandpa waits, while i soak in the sun thru the window, the sound of the grasses blowing in the breeze, the feel of air into my lungs. then he opens his door, comes round, & opens mine. "we'll get ur stuff later," he says.

he anchors me, places my hand on his shoulder, & walks me up to the porch. the air is cool on my skin. the ranch house is gently curved like a crescent moon. its windows are small & low to the ground, which makes it seem like its eyes are hooded, or half-shut, but not in an unfriendly way.

to the right is a covered area, a porch, with a rocking chair & a checked blanket folded on it. the door when we reach it is blue, but the paint is fading & peeling. i touch it with my hand as Grandpa opens it for me; feel the roughness with my fingers.

"it's the light & the wind," says Grandpa. "they take the color from everything, leach it out. got so i couldn't c the point of repainting it anymore."

"i like it," i say.

i do. it is a color that has years in it, & weather, & the air itself.

we step inside & i'm about to take off my protective UV-blocking sunglasses but am then surprised by how light it is, because the windows are so small. daylight seems to hang everywhere, suspending motes of dust in it, as if thicker than air, as if glowing water.

"it's light," i say.

"low windows," says Grandpa. "for light in the morning & afternoon, but not at midday when it's hot. & so that the sun shines in during the winter, but not too much in summer."

"huh," i say. there is so much thought that has gone into this house, so much time & effort—i look around me at the doorframes, the windows, the floors worn smooth by the passage of feet. all of it made by Grandpa. it's a humbling thought. i listen: the birds speak a different language here than the ones in Nevada, i notice.

Grandpa takes me thru a door & leads me to a living room. there are rugs hung on the wooden walls, brightly colored. a couple of sofas & armchairs, sinking to the ground with age. i recognize the 1 Grandpa would usually sit in when we would vidlink, & i smile to myself.

i'm here. i'm finally here.

next, Grandpa leads me to a cast-iron stove in the corner. it's on: i feel the warmth from it as i approach even tho there's no chill in the air yet, & there's a blanket on the floor, folded over, & lying on it, curled up—

"ur puppy," says Grandpa. "think of him as a welcome-home present."

i stand & stare, just stare, at this little black-&-white shape, knotted on itself, only 1 ear visible, chest rising & falling as it breathes. it makes me think of the word *compact* & it makes me think of the word *perfect* & it makes me think of the word *life*.

i can't say anything. my mouth is not working.

"do u . . . like him?" says Grandpa.

i dig my nails into my palms. i can only manage to nod. i don't want to start crying again: i have done too much crying since i landed on earth.

pause.

"can i . . . can i touch him?" i say.

"'course u can touch him," says Grandpa. "he's urs. u should probably name him too, i guess."

i take a step forward. i feel a little weak. Grandpa catches my arm. "help me down?" i say.

he pulls over a chair, then lowers me into it. it's a little chair, maybe my mother's from when she was small? i don't know. but it works well for my purposes, & it strikes me that Grandpa has anticipated this, has had it waiting for me.

i lean down, Grandpa holding a hand on my chest, & i put my palm on the rolled-up ball of fur. the word that is in my head is *quick,* like the old meaning of quick, something i learned in a vid class—how quick used to mean alive; the quick & the dead, & so on. warm. rising & falling, on waves of breath. the softness of it.

then the ball lets out a little yip & rolls under my touch, & sits up, unwrapping itself into a perfect blinking puppy. it presses its head against my hand, pushing up against me, against gravity, to be stroked, & i stroke it & then it lifts its paws & brings its face up to mine—its bright eyes, shining in its head—& its nose all moist against mine, the feel of it a kind of crushed smoothness that has roughness in it too, a sensation i imagine people must mean when they talk about things being as soft as velvet, & it barks excitedly & licks me.

the word that is in my head is *love.*

the dog spins on the spot, still barking, & then comes & licks my nose again.

"he likes u," says Grandpa.

i like him too. i look at his fur, the spots of dark & light. he looks like the surface of a meteor & there's a streak of white on his face like the tail of a comet, so i decide that will be his name.

"i'll call him Comet," i say.

"Comet. a good name. for a good cattle dog. he's a border collie—fast. i figure we'll train him together. then 1 day it'll be u & him, bringing the cows in."

i grin. "i'd like that."

the puppy, Comet, is kind of bouncing on the spot now.

"he needs a walk," says Grandpa. "u want to take him out?"

"really?"

"of course really."

"u coming?"

he shakes his head. "going to have a little sit-down. old men need their rest." he sits on 1 of the armchairs.

it's a challenge. i know it. it's like 1 of the tests at the base, only it's Grandpa doing it, so he's smiling. can i walk on my own? can i take the dog outside?

"ok," i say.

"it's farmland all round," says Grandpa. "no cars. he'll be safe."

u'll be safe, is what he means.

i nod. i turn to the door & walk. "come on, Comet," i say. i beckon to him. he bounds forward, nearly trips me up, & i hear my grandpa's intake of breath, but i regain my balance & put a hand on the wall, to ease myself along to the front door.

step. step. step.

down the hallway.

step. step.

to the door—haloed with light.

there is a rail at the side of the steps. it doesn't look worn. i wonder if Grandpa installed it for me. i didn't notice it on the way in. now i put my hand on it gratefully & use it to go carefully down to the ground. eddies of dust swirl in the light wind. there is still that smell—the musky tones that i guess are cows, tho more distant now, & indeed the cows are small spots in the distance—& grass & trees & flowers & whatever else.

Comet barrels down the steps & out into the yard. there is a field right in front of us, no fence or anything, just a field stretching away to a small hill, & then farther to the mountains. fall flowers are dotted all over it; i would have to ask Grandpa the names. clouds move quickly overhead, ferried from the mountains, it seems, over the low lands, by the wind.

i walk toward the field. my balance is unsteady. i am fighting for breath, panting, but i don't care. the dark ground is warm underfoot, from the sun.

"run, Comet," i say, & Comet either understands or he doesn't, but he does streak over the yard & out into the field, fluid on his little legs, flowing like water.

he runs, & he runs, & sometimes he loops back to me & pushes his muzzle into my hand, & shivers with delight as i pet him & say my Comet my Comet hello my Comet.

then he runs again, over the earth, over the grass, over the flowers, a missile flying low, unbelievable in his energy, in his perfection, the perfect rhyme of his movements with the land.

he catches my breath.

10

we can help u

light wakes me.

Grandpa doesn't believe in curtains. he thinks a farmer should rise with the sun, & it's not yet October, so the sun is still rising early.

it shafts thru my window, the sunlight, gilds the floorboards where it lands. it brings with it the sound of birds singing, a weightless, liquid sound; i will have to ask Grandpa the names of the birds.

it's bright enough, even in the house, that the first thing i do, after moving Comet off my feet, where he is lying like a hot pillow, is to put on my sunglasses.

i get up, pull a shirt on, & leave my room. only, in the night, someone as usual has dismantled the house, taken its constituent elements & rebuilt them in a slightly different configuration, so that i stumble on a small step, & bang my shoulder on a doorframe, & nearly fall on a rug. this isn't like Moon 2, where every movement, every transition from 1 module to another, was smooth: this is all jump cuts; that was all dissolves, all fades.

eventually i make it to the kitchen, which along with the living room is the heart of the house. i look at my watch: it took me 6 minutes & i've been here a little less than a week. maybe after a month i'll do it in under 5.

as soon as he hears my steps on the wood floor, Comet wakes

up too & i hear him barrel out of the room, then he skitters & slides along the wooden floor in front of me.

i'm on the ground floor so i don't have to contend with stairs. despite my clumsiness i'm getting stronger all the time, & my balance is better. i take out my blood-testing kit from the cupboard: a smooth, sleek metal tube that i press against my skin, which automatically fires & draws in a tiny amount of blood, unseen. i plug it into a screen & it begins testing the sample right away, uploading results straight to the Company servers.

in a couple of weeks, the nurse is coming with a portable CAT scan machine & lung-capacity measuring devices. surreal.

while i'm there, i look thru the cupboard. old tea sets. some bottles of whiskey & gin, etc., half-empty. i make a mental note to try some when Grandpa isn't around. at the back, there's a faded box that reads THE GAME OF LIFE on it, & next to it is another: PICTIONARY.

wow: real, old-school board games. i try to imagine Grandpa, Grandma, & Mother playing 1 together, & i just can't. my mother, sitting at a table, rolling dice? no.

i slide out the Pictionary box. inside are cue cards, little pads of actual paper to draw on, pencils worn down to stubs. i remember playing this game with Orion & Libra & Lakshmi, who was babysitting at the time. on our screens, of course—but the same rules.

Orion draws beautifully but he & Lakshmi still lost: he spent too long trying to capture everything just so—dragon; out of this world (expression); vegetarian; jazz—& it slowed us down. Libra draws like shit, as do i, but she understood that it was more important to convey something clearly & quickly. she got the strategy.

i wonder what they're doing now. maybe they're playing Pictionary with their mom in Florida. i go over to Grandpa's screen & unroll it & ping them.

nothing happens.

bong bong bong bong—still nothing. Grandpa doesn't get good service out here.

i flick to the browser & search "news."

—U ARE CURRENTLY DISCONNECTED—

i look at the wi-fi bars: full signal. but i haven't been able to connect since i've been here. it sucks. maybe someone at the base didn't unlock my screen before i left. i'd like to talk to Libra & Orion. i'd like to talk to my mother. find out when she's coming. on the station there was a routine, there were protocols. even when we needed some alone time, we always knew we'd c each other again soon, for tests, for debriefs, for class. now there's no structure: no rules.

good smells are coming from the kitchen tho, so i go in, not even catching myself on anything as i do.

Grandpa is cooking bacon. i sit down—this is a bit more of an involved process than it sounds; & Grandpa helps a little before returning to the pan. he fries the bacon first. i didn't c any food being prepared at the base, & i can't get used to it now: the sound of it, the smell, that incandescent aroma of bacon, which somehow contains sunlight in it; the spit of the grease.

Grandpa takes out eggs next, & i marvel as i have done before at the perfect ellipse of every 1, a shape that is engineered by nature to give maximum strength, to avoid rolling; something more perfect than any Company tech could create, speckled & hard. & then it cracks into the pan, & the white, which isn't white at all—it's translucent—slowly comes into its name, slowly turns opaque, crackles into being, the transformation like transubstantiation, like something holy.

i mean, it's just bacon & eggs. but still.

Grandpa smiles at me watching. then he heaps my plate with 3 slices, before sliding a fried egg on top.

"screen's down still," i say.

"huh," says Grandpa. "getting less & less reliable. i'll call the company."

i don't know if he means the internet company. or means the Company. it may well be—it is probably—the same thing.

i inhale the steam rising from the food, draw it into me, its molecules into mine. when all ur food has been freeze-dried or grown in the garden module, bacon becomes 1 of the wonders of the world. Grandpa doesn't raise pigs, but he trades some of his beef every year for bacon & ham from the Harrison guy he mentioned the day we arrived.

he keeps preserved meat in a storeroom at the back, because there's too much for the fridge, & anyway all his electricity comes from the solar panels on the roof & the windmill in the rear field & he likes to conserve it. before he cooks the bacon, he cuts off the fuzzy mold that grows on it. he says it's cured, that it can't go bad. i don't care anyway. when it smells & tastes like this i would happily eat the mold too.

"eat up," he says. "busy day."

Comet looks up at him imploringly with those enormous bright eyes of his; he is sitting down by my chair. Grandpa chuckles & drops a piece of bacon straight into his open mouth.

"yeah?" i say.

"yep. i've been fattening the 2-year-olds on the summer pastures," he says. "but the cover crops are getting low. today we weigh the cows & send them to slaughter."

i swallow. "really?"

"yes."

his eyes are on mine. it's another challenge.

"ok," i say.

"some hired hands are coming. between us we'll get u to the

field. figure u need to get to know about the cattle season, the round-ups." he keeps dropping hints like this, that the ranch will be mine 1 day. i haven't had the heart yet to tell him what i want to do; how i want to train, like my mother, to go back to space.

not forever. just to learn. to EVA. to work.

anyway. i don't say anything. i eat my bacon & eggs.

"now remember what we talked about," says Grandpa. "u grew up in & out of the hospital. u were sick. that's how come u've never been here before."

i nod. "i remember."

the Company doesn't want attention, about us. Grandpa's the same. he thinks people will get too curious. too involved. he wants to keep me safe, he says. "u don't know what it's like, being a celebrity," he says.

i don't, that's true. i know what it looks like, from vids, & it looks fun. but i don't say that; i mean, he loves me, & there's all the time in the world to disagree about things later. i can tell people i grew up in a hospital if that's what he thinks is best.

we sit & wait.

a half hour later the hired hands turn up. 3 of them, in a pickup truck. it's even more faded & battered than Grandpa's; i think it might have been red once. Grandpa said the light & wind take the color out of everything but that's obviously excepting people's faces, because even tho they're not black like Grandpa—most of them are a mix like most people are—these guys are all deep brown from the sun, & their skin is lined as if scoured by the wind, tho the eyes set in those faces are younger than Grandpa's.

"Kyle," says 1 of them. the others stay quiet. they are chewing something—tobacco maybe.

Kyle's eyes lock onto mine. he's even younger than the others, not much older than me. his eyes are as blue as the sky, & his mascara is not black but dark purple. he lifts his hat in greeting. he smiles, & i smile back.

"Leo," i say.

"pleasure to meet u, Leo," he says. he holds out his hand to shake mine, but Grandpa steps forward, blocks it.

"Leo was very sick," he says. "pretty much spent his whole life in a lab." kind of true. "he's very delicate. his bones . . . think of him like . . . like a deep-sea fish out of its depth."

Kyle lowers his hand. "like an alien," he says.

Grandpa frowns. "i guess."

a complicated look crosses Kyle's eyes. "i never met an alien before." he smiles then, & the skin around his eyes crinkles.

Comet boings over, an animated spring, soft-furred. he stops at my feet, as if to guard me.

"& this is Comet," i say.

"well," says Kyle. "an alien & a Comet in 1 day."

1 of the other men rolls his eyes. "come on, Kyle," he says.

they pile into their pickup & i get into Grandpa's & we drive maybe ten minutes up a succession of gradually rising dirt tracks until we reach a field that abuts the foothills of the mountain range. a thin, silvery stream zigzags down the nearest hill, white where it crests over hidden rocks.

i turn back & the ranch is far away & below us, a toy ranch. the valley stretches away beyond it, toward the ocean, which on clear days u can c, according to Grandpa, tho i haven't yet. maybe it's my glasses, maybe it's my eyes. at the base they said we were a little nearsighted, from the confinement of the space station.

i turn away from the ranch & the downward sweep of the valley.

the field that lies before us is like the 1 in front of the ranch, tho the grass is shorter. there are also some kind of cabbage-like things, & bright yellow flowers.

Kyle steps up next to me. "ur grandpa was 1 of the first to rotate his fields & plant cover crops again," he says. "it's 1 of the reasons his ranch has kept going."

Grandpa & the other men are standing a little distance away—they have a number of dogs with them, & they are pointing at the grazing cattle, making gestures, talking.

"rotate?" i say.

"c, water is a big problem here," says Kyle. "but so's erosion. the soil blows away in the wind."

"ok," i say. like: so what?

"so there's this old idea, & ur Grandpa went back to it before anyone else: u keep ur cattle down on ur lower fields most of the year, while u let ur upper fields grow. & u plant them with cover crops, stuff with strong roots. collard. rye. clover. then, right at the end of summer, u move ur cattle up to the upper fields & u let the cows eat those cover crops till they're almost gone, before u send the cattle to slaughter or back down to the low fields, if they're still too young or they're too old or too light or whatever. u move the cattle around, never letting them graze the land completely. & u plant carefully. & that way u keep ur soil."

i feel proud of Grandpa, in that moment. who am i kidding. i feel proud of Grandpa most of the time. "thanks," i say. "for explaining."

Grandpa explains a bit—but i think he is also 1 of those "learn from doing" kind of people. he is all about doing, really. look at the ranch he built.

Kyle tips his hat to me again. "any time."

Grandpa & 1 of the other men—i think his name is Alonzo & he has a mustache & green nail polish—come over & nod to Kyle.

no, not Alonzo. Lorenzo. "we're going to drive them down the west chute"—Grandpa indicates a direction—"& into the corral there. there's a race: we can separate the 2-year-olds from the rest of the herd. then u can do the ultrasounds. ok?"

"ok," says Kyle.

"ultrasounds?" i ask. it's a weird after-echo of the base, like something of it has stayed lingering in the world around me, a mirage. i think of the nurse. maybe they don't need to send him. her. whoever. maybe Kyle could do it instead. scan me.

"i'm a vet," says Kyle. "at least i worked with 1 for a while. i ultrasound the cattle. check the marbling of the meat. it's all quality & provenance now. well, i guess since quantity became impossible anyway. only rich people can afford beef & they only want the best." he says this as if the words taste bad, bitter, & i wonder if he's the son of 1 of the farmers whose ranch has failed, with the drought, or if he just doesn't like people buying top meat when most can't buy any at all, but i don't say anything. Kyle tips his hat to me again & goes to plan with the others.

i stand for a moment, just looking at the land & the cattle, so many of them, dozens & dozens, that are scattered around—over maybe a hundred acres. i know the dogs will round them up, but it seems like a difficult task.

i look down at my own dog. he is twisting around my feet. i say, "sit," & he keeps twisting around. i say, "sit," again, & he still runs. again—& finally he sits down, in the grass. i have kept some pieces of bacon in my pocket & i bend to give it to him. he licks it from my hand with his leathery tongue—the sensation of it when i first felt it on my skin was so startling i almost cried out.

i'm training him. Grandpa told me how. i want him to be the best cattle dog in the valley, 1 day.

i pick up a stick & throw it for Comet—tell him to fetch it. that one's easy. fetching is hardwired. dogs just do it naturally. then i start slowly walking in the direction of the cows; the ground is uneven, so i step with care. i tell Comet to heel, & repeat it until he shadows my movements, as if tacked to me.

Grandpa talks to the others for a while, then comes over to me. "good dog, that," he says.

"i figure that's why u chose him for me," i say.

Grandpa winks. "he can watch the others round up the cows," he says. "he'll hear the whistles. start to learn."

"ok," i say. "& what do i do?"

"u stay right here," says Grandpa. "don't get too close to the cattle. u can move along with us to the west if u like. when we have them corralled u can come & sit on the fence. ok?"

"ok."

"keep Comet close. u don't want him getting trampled."

"ok."

"ur crutches are in the truck, if u need them."

eyes on mine. challenge 3.

"i won't," i say.

challenge accepted.

he walks off with the others, & Kyle tips his hat to me from afar as they start to work.

i watch. it is like a ballet, a performance, it is orchestrated & almost mute, the men just occasionally shouting some instruction to one another that makes no sense to me. they whistle to the dogs too—all border collies, 3 of them Grandpa's & the others belonging to the men. the dogs circle groups of cows that huddle, scared, & then move when the dogs yip & nip at them, responding to high-pitched commands from the men.

i purse my lips, try to whistle. nothing but the sound of air escaping a vent. i will learn. like Comet. the puppy is dancing at my feet—occasionally he runs toward the cows but i call him back, & to my amazement he comes, each time, fleet over the clumped ground, "fleet" the only word for it, because it's a word for fast but it has that *L* in it, has liquid in it, & his speed is something more of water than of flesh.

we make our way steadily westward, as the sun climbs in the sky. we are working early—even at this time of year it gets hot at midday, & Grandpa wanted it done before then, that's what he said in the truck.

as i walk, i c something smooth & white on the ground in front of me, paper of some kind. i glance around: a few ft. away i c another, bent against a tuft of grass.

carefully, i bend down & pick it up. it's a small sheet of shiny paper. on it is printed a short message:

SPACE BOY

we can help u.

call vidlink 598.9xt.87##

i swallow.

i look around again. in the distance i think i c another sheet, half-pressed into the ground. did someone drop these from a drone? from a crop-dusting plane? the fence is a long way away but they're here, these pieces of old-school paper, & they seem to be meant for me.

space boy.

i think of Kyle calling me an alien. but he said it nicely, & of course he doesn't know the truth, whereas this feels . . . not threatening exactly, but scary. assuming this is meant for me, why would anyone think i need help? why would anyone know where i really came from? it's meant to be a secret.

i wish Libra & Orion were here, or i could vid them, so i could talk to them about it.

Grandpa turns, a few hundred ft. ahead. "come on, Leo," he says.

the sheet of paper is kind of folded in my hand & from there he can't c it, at least i don't think so. i wave, to say, *yes, i'm coming.*

then i fold it again & put it in my pocket.

something is going on: i know it. & i need to find out what it is.

11

witness

choosing my steps, i cover the grassy ground, trying not to fall. heart hammering; chest rhythmically rising. i fight gravity. i fight it with every step. Comet meanwhile seems only half subject to it; seems a creature of permanently coiled & potential energy, a spring always ready to bounce off the ground, Hooke's law in action with a k value of stiffness immeasurably smaller than mine, a thing of rubber, not flesh & bone.

he skips, & gambols, & runs; i stagger.

but we mirror the movement of the cows & the men as they gradually head to the chute, which turns out to be a smooth silvery tapering pen, made of walls of thin steel, leading to a long fenced section of ground, enclosed by wooden posts on either side. this must be the race, i guess.

i stop, my muscles aching. the sun is nearly at its zenith & i am sweating too, the liquid running down my skin, a sensation i am still getting used to. i can put out my tongue & taste it—salt, on my lips.

space boy, i think.

why would a boy from space need help? how would anyone know i was a space boy in the first place? i'm in a wide-open field, my grandpa is here, these men he trusts. yet i feel vulnerable, small, scared in a way i didn't on the station.

the other men drive the cows forward, until they enter the

chute & hurry down it, then into the track of grass beyond. i c that Grandpa has moved to the far end, where he is operating a gate that can swing 1 way or the other, like a tongue in a mouth, sending the cattle either into a round fenced corral or out into another field.

finally there are no more cows entering the race, & Grandpa shuts the gate he has been manipulating to close off the corral. he sees me watching & beckons me over.

i make my way to him, Comet running ahead. there's a weird moment—i am about to take a step when Comet jumps at me, barking, & i fall back but catch myself & don't go down. i sway for a second. then i c: in front of me is a hole in the ground, maybe there was a rock there or something or it's a small sinkhole, & i was about to step into it.

it's as if Comet saw it & warned me—& maybe that's exactly what happened. i bend to him—which still hurts—& put my arms around him & hold him close. i feel his breath hot against me & he makes a low growling sound that sounds like happiness.

then we walk again, to Grandpa. i wonder if he's seen them, the flyers. i passed a couple more, in the grass. from the condition of the paper i think they were dropped there recently. but he doesn't say anything & nor do i.

he waves over Kyle, & the 2 of them catch me under the legs & lift me up onto the flat-topped, wide fence of the race, so i can c into the corral but without my legs dangling into it. then they stoop & pick up Comet & put him into my arms, where he squirms at first, & then settles, pressing into me.

"now, we weigh & scan," says Kyle.

between them, the men work to separate single cows, or bulls, & i suddenly realize. meat herd—they're all bulls. the dogs push them into a little area within the corral, fenced, where they stand on a metal plate that i suppose is for weighing them. meanwhile

Kyle is next to them with a handheld wand that is connected to a machine running off a generator, & displaying images on a screen that is too far away for me to work out. they must have brought the equipment here before they came to the ranch.

i can smell the fuel from the generator tho, the exhaust. i can smell the animals—i feel like i can even smell their nervousness. when they pass close by i feel the air move & i c the beauty of their big dark eyes, framed by lashes—when i look into those eyes it seems almost as if there is something being communicated, some bond; it's weird, & it makes me feel sad, because this is all about choosing which ones are going to die.

sometimes Kyle shakes his head, & then Grandpa or Lorenzo or 1 of the others takes the cow away to the field, where the too-small remaining cattle were thinned out. but most of the time he nods, & they go thru a gate in the little channel where he is working & into yet another field—the field of slaughter, i think to myself, & then chide myself for thinking something so melodramatic.

the day wears on.

my tailbone aches. the wood presses splinters into the backs of my thighs. flies from the cows buzz about my face. incredibly annoying: in space there are no small things with wings that zip about u, emitting low drones, tickling ur hair & skin. but i won't complain, not to Grandpa.

Comet goes to sleep on my lap.

the smell is always in my nostrils: dung, sweat, hide.

the sun arcs across the sky.

the clouds continue their endless journey from the mountains where they are made.

& finally, the herds begin to thin. occasionally Kyle presses his hand to his back—he is sore, i think, from bending to ultrasound the cows' flanks. i swat flies from my eyes.

then a trail of dust, rising like smoke, resolves itself into a truck—no, 2 trucks—driving up a road hidden from me by a crest of land. they pull up beyond the field the best 2-year-olds have been sorted into, & i realize they have come to take them to the slaughterhouse.

Grandpa comes over to me. as he passes 1 of the few remaining bulls, he stops, looks into its eyes, whispers something in its ear, & then pats its nose before slapping its rump, so that it hurries toward Kyle & the other men.

he leans against the fence next to me.

i c that he is crying—either that or he is sweating in a really strange way, from his eyes.

"u're crying," i say.

"yes," he says.

"why?"

he forces a smile. "because i am killing my cattle."

"but . . ." i look around me. i think of the vids i have seen. the books i have read. "i thought ranching was all about being . . . tough. i mean, u *grow* them to kill them. or u rear them. whatever."

"yes."

"but u're still upset."

"yes."

i shake my head. i don't understand.

"have u looked into their eyes?" he says.

i have. i have seen into them. the blackness. like looking into deep space.

i nod.

"so have i," he says. "farming is not about being tough. it's about looking after them as best u can. & then bearing witness, when they go. not closing ur eyes."

as he says this, the men begin to herd the cattle into the

trucks, maybe a hundred yards from us—i can't c the wheels, but i can c the heads of the cattle, disappearing up into the vehicles.

Grandpa watches the whole time. he never looks away. finally the trucks drive off, swirling with dust.

"well," says Grandpa. "home." he sets off toward the pickup. Lorenzo & the other guy whose name i don't know are doing the same, making their way from where the cattle were being loaded into the truck, their dogs following.

i realize i am meant to get down from the fence & follow them. challenge 4.

i sit there for a while. then Kyle passes.

"u're crying," he says. "are u ok?"

i am thinking of the eyes of the cattle. of their gentleness, the flicking of their tails, the flickering of light in those eyes—stars, distant.

"yes," i say. "just witnessing."

"ah, yep," says Kyle. "the old man is a romantic all right."

i nod.

"u want a hand down from that fence?"

"yes please," i say.

challenge 4: accepted.

Comet stirs in my arms as Kyle puts a hand under my knees, the other under my arm. he lifts me & i feel his strength, the perfect assembly of his muscles & tendons, so effortless, so efficient. things i have never felt in space: the engineering of another body, the gravity-fighting mechanics of levers & springs. when he eases me down & steps away i feel relieved but also like my body has been hit by a very mild stun gun.

i take a step. instantly awake, Comet leaps from my arms & bolts off ahead of me.

"heel," i call.

he turns & flashes back, something of light & movement, not even physical, & then he is at my feet.

"u're training him well," says Kyle.

"thanks," i say.

& we walk.

we pass another of those sheets of paper. i can just c the letters ACE B— the rest is hidden. by the way it's been trampled into the earth, i'm guessing by a cow.

Kyle doesn't look at it or say anything. so i don't either.

interlude
but not right now

Grandpa has his screen on his lap. Comet is on *my* lap, snoring.

the stove is sending a glowing, pulsing heat into the room.

Grandpa is talking in Russian to a man on the screen. for once the internet is working.

the man Grandpa's talking to has very white skin, whiter than i've ever seen. he has long, bushy, pale eyebrows, & glasses, & looks like a retired university professor but actually he's a cosmonaut named Yuri; at least, that's what Grandpa said when the call came thru on the screen.

Yuri laughs a lot. he gestures a lot too, & Grandpa laughs, talking to him. i get the sense they have known each other a long time. they must have flown together. or were up on the station together.

then Yuri looks sad. he dabs at his eyes. Grandpa's tone goes low & sympathetic. they talk like that for a bit longer until Grandpa says goodbye & cuts off the call.

"what was that?" i say. "why did he cry?"

"they're an emotional people," says Grandpa. "he was talking about the end of the Russian space program."

"ah," i say. "end of an era."

"yeah. now it's all INDNAS. no Russia. no USA."

"uh-huh," i say.

"now it's all just gathering dust," says Grandpa. "the Russian equipment."

"yeah?"

"yeah. Yuri said he'd been out to Baikonur recently & they've got a big hangar there full of old Buran shuttles, rusting. they just shelved them. fully operational spaceships, abandoned."

"oh," i say.

"yeah," says Grandpa. "shame. used to be it was all of us together. now it's just the Company. the Russians helped to build the first station, u know? actually they were kind of instrumental in the early stages."

"yeah," i say. i'm Mr. Monosyllable today.

"now Yuri's just sitting around in his father's cabin by the Black Sea, telling anyone who will listen, which is mostly me, anecdotes about his time in space. looking after his woodland." he pauses. "he misses space a lot."

"sounds like u do too," i say.

Grandpa gives me a slow, sad smile. "sometimes," he says. then his smile grows brighter, & he indicates the fire, the dog, me. "but not right now," he says.

12
4,000 volts

it's a cool day when it happens.

fall is well named, & when it comes falling like a rock in these parts, i'll know it. that's what Grandpa says. 1 day it's summer & then 1 morning there's a thin film of ice on the puddles. there aren't many trees to speak of, so we don't c leaves turning orange & dropping, but every morning when i wake, it's cooler, until my breath smokes above me, as i lie under several blankets—& Comet.

always Comet. curled over my feet, or nestled into my side, hot as a hot-water bottle—that's a comparison i can use now. the space station robs u of most similes—u have never experienced anything but space, so it is hard to hold 1 event or thing against another & say *these are alike.*

another morning we wake & there is a filigree of frost on the inside of my window; delicate as fern leaves—something else i have now seen, in the fields. the seasons are turning. it's to do with the earth's precession. the earth wobbles up & down in a slow wave, as it circles the sun, tilting the northern hemisphere closer & then farther from the sun, close-far, close-far, close-far. & when the earth leans to the sun in the summer months, the sun is higher in the sky, & when it leans away in winter, the sun is lower & hits the horizon sooner in the evening.

i can picture it, the orbit of the object, the tilt, the spin—the sine wave of the sun's height in the sky relative to a person standing on the northern hemisphere.

only now i am a person standing on the northern hemisphere & i can *feel* it too.

the seasons, turning.

it makes me wonder when my mother is coming. summer is giving way to fall, a whole shift is happening, & i have not seen her since that day on the rooftop. i don't miss her or anything. but it's weird. i'm her son. doesn't she want to come home & c me? i do miss Orion & Libra, but whenever i try to vid them i can't—the internet is down, or they're not answering. i don't get it. they must want to speak to me too.

the piece of paper, meanwhile, i have hidden in the dresser in my room. *SPACE BOY. we can help u.*

sometimes i think i'm being blocked from speaking to the twins. like maybe that's what i need help with, according to the mysterious flyer people.

i wonder who could be trying to communicate with me. someone from the base? it doesn't make sense tho. wouldn't they have done it when i was there? then who? thinking of the base makes me think of Santiago, how she raised the possibility of some kind of PR leak. at the time, i thought she meant about the cargo mission, like she was exploring the scenario of something going wrong & the media finding out.

now, i ask myself: was the leak she feared the story of me & Orion & Libra? us growing up out there? i've never really thought about it before, but from what Grandpa has said about avoiding celebrity, i get the impression . . . that people don't know about us. don't know that we were up there. & came down here.

maybe whoever left that flyer *does* know tho. maybe they know & they want to help me.

but that thought circles me back to: why? help me with what? i'm ok here. i'm happy.

so mostly i think i'm being paranoid. the Company wouldn't cut me off from Libra & Orion. what would be the point? i'm with my grandpa. he loves me. i have my puppy. i also, for some reason i can't explain, don't believe that whoever printed those sheets actually wanted to help me, not really. i sense . . . a threat behind it. & anyway, they may not have been for me.

no. they were for me.

i shake my head. too much worrying. i need to enjoy this. to enjoy earth.

i go downstairs, Comet at my feet. in the living room Grandpa is lighting a fire in the woodstove & i help him. every time i do something like this i increase my flexibility but i add to my bank of experiences too, the things i can hold against 1 another in my mind.

i'd read books: i knew that there were sounds described as dry twigs snapping, or logs crackling. but i had never heard a dry twig snapping, or logs crackling in a fire.

now i have.

mutely, i hand Grandpa a bundle of twigs. he snaps them until they are the right size—*pop, pop, pop;* this is the sound of a dry twig snapping—& then pyramids them over the dry moss & leaves he has gathered as tinder, in the bottom of the fire grate. he lights it & when the flames are whooshing up, blue & green & every color in between, he begins to add in compressed pellets of turf.

they crackle.

fire, talking low to itself, about how it feels to burn.

Grandpa nods, satisfied. i still say nothing. Comet too sits below me, looking up at me; the mute adoration of a puppy. his eyes dance in the light of the fire. i have discovered that Grandpa is not big on talking, not like over vidscreen—when there is no news to relate, he'd prefer silence. it's fine by me.

we go to the kitchen & have breakfast.

"what jobs today?" i say, when we have eaten our bacon. there are other foods, but i feel like i haven't exhausted the appeal of bacon yet.

"no jobs," says Grandpa. this is unusual. every day there is some fence to be mended, or hoof to be fixed, or snakebite to c to, or irrigation device to mend, or drone to pilot over the calves, checking they're all ok.

or immunizations.

or booster feed.

or . . .

or . . .

"thought we'd tour the perimeter," says Grandpa.

i look at him questioningly.

"i do it with the drones, mostly," he says. "but i also like to walk the perimeters as much as i can too. study the land. check the fences. u know?"

i don't, but i nod. "ok."

all the time he's talking, there's a screen in front of him, & a flip device is projecting a keyboard onto the table. "what are u doing with that?" i ask.

he turns it round. i c a field from above, a tall fence like the l alongside the road we drove in on, some cows in the distance.

"preflying the route," he says. "checking if there's anything we should be looking out for."

"& is there?"

he turns the screen, taps on the keyboard. the image jumps closer, a saccadic zoom—*snap*—& when he pivots the screen i'm looking at a hole in the fence. the drone is hovering, preternaturally still in the air.

"who would make a hole in the fence?" i say. i'm thinking: maybe whoever dropped those flyers.

"could be wild dogs," he says. "but it's an electric fence. we'll check it out. maybe get Randy down with his crew to patch it up. voltage is still running thru the upper part at least." he taps the screen where the higher section of the fence is.

i drop a dog biscuit to Comet. he eats it noisily, then barks.

"we're supposed to be fattening the cows, not the dogs," says Grandpa. only half joking.

i only half salute, in return, & he raises his eyes to the sky.

then we start heading out. before we leave the house Grandpa goes to a cupboard on the wall in the living room & opens it with a key he takes from his pocket. from a rack inside he lifts a shotgun & a pistol. he puts the pistol in his pocket & carries the shotgun out to the pickup truck. i think of the people lining up in the town. for money they're short on & guns to protect it.

i follow Grandpa. Comet runs ahead of me. when i climb into the passenger seat—i can do it myself now; the running board Grandpa installed helps—he jumps in after me & turns a couple of times before settling on my lap.

Grandpa leans the gun in the footwell by his feet & starts the engine & we bump across the field & drive straight for a few minutes before we reach the tall perimeter fence. i think again how no one could climb over it. i think of the line at the gun store. i think how the fence height is probably deliberate.

i think of the gun, propped against Grandpa's leg. & the other in his pocket.

we drive, following the line of the fence, & slowly warm up. we're wearing thick clothes & also Grandpa is blasting the heater on the old pickup truck, which doesn't work very well. i mean this thing is from the early 2000s or something. the sun's climbing too tho.

every so often he stops & we get out & Comet catapults around, chasing shadows, as Grandpa examines a calf or some invisible defect in the fence. at 1 point we come across a cow that is lying on the ground, dead. it looks like she got her foot caught & then something wild got to her. mountain lion. coyotes.

Grandpa kneels beside the cow & puts his hand on her side.

"goodbye, Matilda," he says.

"u recognize them all?" i say.

"of course," he says. he pulls out his portable screen, unrolls it, & calls a number. "yeah, Murat? i got a cow that's died on me. tomorrow morning? great."

he hangs up.

strange that we still use that language. no one has hung a phone on a hook since about 1930, when everything was made of Bakelite. no one has "dialed" a number since 1960.

we get back in the truck & drive on.

the sun rises.

clouds scud. only clouds & ships scud—i mean dogs don't do it. cars. nothing else that moves. another weird thing about language.

that's what happens when u're in a pickup truck driving around a big ranch as light slowly floods the day—ur mind wanders.

we pass a small cow or bull. "that's Pepper," says Grandpa. "u saw him on the drone cam?"

wow. i marvel at his already-tallness, how quickly his rickety legs have grown.

eventually we reach the hole. we stop & get out. Grandpa goes over to it & crouches down. crouching is still tricky for me but i follow him & stand there, looking. the gap is roughly circular. it's like it's been cut, but i don't know what by. the thick wires, thru which electricity courses, are just gone.

"what could have done that?" i say.

Grandpa touches the ground. there's a smudge of black on the grass.

"blowtorch?" he says.

i glance around. i suddenly feel vulnerable. just the 2 of us standing by a fence in a field, with a wide valley all around us, stretching all the way to the mountains in 1 direction & the fields in another—no other person to be seen, & i don't know if that's reassuring or not.

"are u serious?" i say.

"yes. or bolt cutters. my guess is blowtorch because of the 4,000 volts in the fence."

"why?"

he looks around now too. there is a hawk circling far above us. "cattle rustling would be my guess. used to be a big thing. tho now there aren't so many other ranches or markets to take them to. also it used to be u could cut the tags out but now we earmark the cows, or put the tags in randomly. to help stop thieves."

that word: *help*.

it echoes in me.

i take a breath. "Grandpa," i say. "is there anyone . . . i mean . . . would anyone think i needed help?"

he leans his head to 1 side. "help?"

"yes."

"with what?"

"i don't know," i say.

he purses his lips. "i don't really understand what u're asking."

"i don't really either," i say. "but i feel like there's something . . ." i think of the things i don't understand. of why i can't get thru to Orion & Libra but Grandpa can call Yuri. of why Santiago was there 1 second & gone the next. i even think of the farmer & the guys in the suits who descended on him as we took off; of the flyers. "i feel like there's something i don't know."

"there are a lot of things u don't know," says Grandpa. he smiles. a half smile—sort of sad too.

then he is frowning. he looks up.

i look up too. i realize it isn't a hawk. it's the drone, circling. i don't know why i thought it was a hawk actually. the 2 wings are superficially similar, but the drones have spinning rotors, i can c the blur of them from down here.

"well, i'll keep that looping the perimeter," he says. "set it to motion sense & infrared."

"ok," i say. what else can i say?

we get back in the truck—Grandpa is even quieter than usual. even Comet seems subdued, slipping off into a fitful sleep almost right away as we bump over mounds of grass.

we pass a familiar shape to our right, which i c is the corral where we gathered the bulls for slaughter. i say *we* but i mean Grandpa & the men. but i walked on my own, without crutches, & when we got back to the truck—i had been distracted by following the cows on the way—i was surprised to c that we had covered maybe 3 miles in each direction.

he's sneaky like that, Grandpa. he gets u doing work, gets u making progress, without u realizing. i wonder how much that contributed to my mother: to her being top gun so young, getting her first doctorate at 19, that stuff. if it did, i wonder if she even realizes.

maybe she does. maybe that's part of the problem.

maybe he made her what she is.

i blink this thought away. the hole in the fence has made me feel unsafe. visible. i understand what prey have felt like, all thru history.

i shake the feeling away, & Comet shakes too, in his sleep.

we drive a little farther & then Grandpa stops. we are at the edge of the pasture where we collected the 2-year-olds. above us, the mound of the first hill that eventually turns into the Sierra Nevada Mountains. we get out & i look up & c their snowy peaks. then i feel something, & raise my hand, palm up.

a tiny sensation of cold—sharp against my skin, yet somehow soft too.

i turn my head, watching. snow is falling—not much of it, but fat flakes, drifting slowly down. amazing, in their softness & size, like interference, like the signal of the whole scene i can c is being disrupted. no 2 are alike; we can't know that absolutely, of course, but scientists have extrapolated it, from observing sufficient quantities. i think about that: all these snowflakes falling, every 1 different, every crystalline structure a different pattern.

Grandpa raises his hand too. "wait. this is ur first snow, isn't it?"

"yes."

he smiles. "stick out ur tongue."

i do. i have to wait a while—whole minutes—but then a flake lands there, nestles, feathery cold. it's like . . . i don't know. similes, & all that. it's like a charge, thru me, the shock of the icy feeling, then the melting, & then a tiny drop of water, that i swallow.

"wow," i say.

Comet is going crazy with it. yapping & running in circles, trying to catch the snowflakes, & i am catching them too, my palms & tongue extended—i must look like a crazy person, to anyone watching, to anyone with binoculars.

i stop.

the snow continues to fall, lightly. not much of it. but a sign, all the same. of winter coming. ice. the precession of the earth, casting us into darkness.

13

dry twig

Grandpa points up the hill. "c something strange about the fence?" he says.

i look.

it takes me a while, but then i c it. the fence goes up the hill, disappears from sight. then far to our right, it appears again, & snakes back downhill. it frames the hill, a curve, embracing it almost.

"c anything else?"

i look.

i c the stream that runs down—& as he traces his finger over the land i c how it channels into his land, into our land as he would call it, & then disappears behind a rise to our right.

"i bought this land in 2018," he says. "people thought i was just expanding the ranch—it was contiguous with my existing parcel after all."

"contiguous?"

"bordering." he narrows his eyes. "we need to think about school for u, boy. ur brilliance is a little inconsistent."

i shiver, & not just with the morning chill. but it's a passing moment, & Grandpa is focused again on the ranch, as he usually is. school frightens me. all the people: i am not used to crowds, to busy hallways. apart from the canteen, i have never been in a space with more than 4 or 5 people in my life.

but still. i need to go. i know that. i need a math degree, or physics, if i'm ever going to be an astronaut.

"anyway," he says. "i didn't buy it to extend my land. or at least i did, but not so i could have more head of cattle, which is what the others assumed. or high ground for summer grazing, because i was already an advocate for rotation in those days. no. can u guess why i bought it?"

well, there's only 1 thing that i can c.

"for the stream."

he nods approvingly. "yes. i bought the stream. & the source of the stream. now u know why my irrigators can still run. a lot of the others, they got banned from pumping, or had half their land turned over to forced fallow. they got by a few years, on subsidies mostly, but they were finished when the aquifer dried up."

"but u had the stream."

"yes. at the right time, & in the right place. precipitation's been falling, but the ice on the mountains has been melting too. of course that's not sustainable; it'll run out eventually, all the snow, but that's ur problem, not mine." he winks at me.

"u kept the farm alive," i say. i look at the land, stretching back below us, the whole strip of it, from the stream down to the valley floor, dotted with cows. on 1 of the lower fields the rows of irrigators are slowly rolling. i can c the ranch, small as a toy set.

"yes. it was just a question of opportunity. & money."

money & guns, i think.

i shiver again.

i c movement out of the corner of my eye. i turn & c a calf, a small 1, picking its way across the uneven land. i'm not yet a rancher & even i can c that it isn't meant to be here. it must have gotten separated from its mother. Grandpa sees it too & frowns, starts to walk toward it.

"grab him," says Grandpa.

"what?" i say.

then i clock that he is looking down at Comet, who is taut as a slingshot stretched, but too late.

because just then, Comet bolts away from me. this is an event without transition. he is at my feet, frantic but keeping by me, & then he is a streak of black & white across the grass, & i track ahead of him & c the calf, & that Comet is going for it. i don't know if it's just a hunting instinct—it's a small calf—or if he has some idea of herding it, or what, but he is fast, & the calf sees him, panics & starts to run, slipping & sliding.

it takes a while to get its balance & Comet is on it, his muscles have thickened & he has grown & he is a projectile fired at the running animal, at the prey, which has nowhere to hide on the sparse, treeless ground.

"no!" i call.

Grandpa starts to run & turns, his face a mask of anger. "come on!" he says. "ur dog. u stop him."

i run forward, catch up with Grandpa, calling. "no! Comet! no!"

Grandpa speeds up, waves at me, urging me on.

"faster!" he shouts, over his shoulder.

i run.

i run, & i am not looking down at my feet, & i feel a jolt as i go down into 1 of those deep holes in the ground—maybe it's a rabbit's hole, i think even in the moment that i'm falling forward, my momentum carrying me on like the cargo container that hit Moon 2—& the lower part of my leg hits the layers of rock & loam while my knee continues at maybe 30 mph in its previous trajectory, following a vector defined by my mass, my direction—

—& something in my shin snaps—

pop.

i hit the soft grass-cushioned ground but even so it knocks the breath from me for a second, which is the only moment when i'm not screaming, my screaming otherwise populating the air with sound, tearing it, rending it.

i lie there, & i scream.

i hear Grandpa skidding to a halt beside me, calling my name. i hear Comet barking with frustration, as the calf gets away from him, at least i assume. all i can c is the blue sky above me, a few snowflakes drifting down, landing cold on my face.

i have metaphors now, i think, & my thoughts have the tone & color of screaming.

i have metaphors & i have similes.

i am no longer a space man.

i know what it sounded like when my lower leg broke, pouring lava of pain into the whole limb, seeming to crack not just a part of me but my whole world, & i suppose in the end the world is what i experience, so that makes sense; i exist phenomenologically & now both i & the world have broken—

with the sound—

the *exact* sound—

of a dry twig, snapping.

interlude
shooting star

it's 1 of my first nights at the ranch.

Grandpa wakes me—it's full dark outside, no moon.

"what's up?" i say.

"come on," he says. "meteor shower."

he takes me out onto the porch, then lowers me into the rocking chair. there is a little table & on it he has already put 2 steaming mugs of hot chocolate, with marshmallows floating in them.

he drags over a kitchen chair & sits in it, next to me.

we look up at the sky. as my eyes adjust, stars start to appear in the gaps between brighter stars, until the sky is a milky profusion of millions of stars, shining ice-bright in the darkness.

"there," says Grandpa. he points.

i look. a streak of light across the sky.

"there."

another.

another.

little sparking bolts across the darkness, as meteorites burn up in the atmosphere.

"make a wish," says Grandpa.

i do.

we sit in silence for a while, watching. every few minutes a shooting star gleams into being, the movement making us turn to it. the air is cold: Grandpa gets a blanket & spreads it over my legs.

i drink the hot chocolate. it is warm & sweet & the marshmallows have half melted into it: it is 1 of the many wonders of the earth.

so why is it that when i c the planets & stars above me, the glowing firmament, the heavens, it makes me feel something tight in my chest, something that feels like homesickness?

i lean back & rock slightly in the chair. i am looking up at that incalculable expanse of stars.

"u ever wanted to go back up there?" i say to Grandpa.

he shakes his head. "no. & u?"

"no," i lie.

& i don't tell him what i wished for.

i don't know why not.

i just don't think he'd like it—i don't think he wants me to do what he & my mom did. i think he wants me to do what he's doing now—take the ranch, keep it going. he doesn't want me doing flight training, reading up on astrophysics, entering the air force.

anyway. i think about that night, as i close my eyes & the pain of my broken leg soaks me, immerses me.

because now i'm not going to be learning to fly any time soon, am i?

14

x-ray

there's no point calling an ambulance to the ranch, so Grandpa drives me to the hospital in the pickup.

it goes:

noise of engine

pain from leg

frames of sky thru the window

pain from leg

jolting of ruts & bumps

pain from leg

with always the pain underneath everything: i can feel the bone pressing into my flesh, from the inside. things are not where they are meant to be, within my body, & it is awful.

Comet, barking in alarm.

pain from leg.

i sit a little, & find that i'm lying across the rear bench seat of the truck, not strapped in. i'm still wearing my jeans but i make the mistake of looking down & c that my ankle & foot are jutting up at an obscene angle. i don't remember getting here. Comet is standing in the footwell below me, scrabbling for balance as the car bounces along the road. Grandpa must have gotten him back from the trail of the calf.

"i'm sorry," says Grandpa. "i'm so sorry."

"why?" i gasp.

"my fault," he says. "i wasn't thinking. just freaked out about the calf. i'm sorry. i'm sorry."

i'm confused & mixed up & i don't really understand what he's apologizing for. i tune it out.

i reach down & get my hands under Comet's front legs & lift him onto me. he quiets immediately, his barking fading to a low whine, & he presses himself into me.

i hold on to his warmth, his beating heart.

after some unknowable time we arrive, & Grandpa leaves the car to get the paramedics, who come out & lift me onto a gurney. they try to take Comet away but i won't let them & he won't either for that matter; he bares his teeth & growls, low.

so Comet rides with me on the gurney, & Grandpa walks beside us, into a low brick building & a succession of cool hallways, uniformly white, smelling of something strong that i presume is for disinfecting, an acrid smell that gets into my nostrils. the men in green push me into a waiting room, lots of green plastic chairs in rows, bolted to the floor.

there are a few people, scattered on the chairs, trying to sit as far away from each other as they can, it seems. some ashen-faced. some with bandages.

there's a big screen on the wall. a ticker tape runs along the bottom. some kind of news show. i do a double take.

there, on the screen: it looks like Dr. Stearns, in a studio, talking to a man in a suit. on the crawling banner at the bottom the words:

CONSPIRACY THEORISTS CONTINUE TO QU—

but then i hear Grandpa's voice & notice that he is over at a little counter with a sliding glass partition; there's a sign next to it saying WAIT HERE FOR TRIAGE. he says something i can't hear.

i turn back to the screen & it's off, just black—an image of deep space.

huh.

maybe it wasn't Dr. Stearns, i think. just someone who looks like him.

yeah, i think. that's likely. there's something going on & it increasingly looks like it involves me & Libra & Orion, but the pain in my leg is kind of more in the foreground of my mind right now.

we roll to a room with an x-ray machine & a curtain on rings that they can pull around to give privacy. first the paramedics check me over: they take my blood pressure, my heart rate, my oxygen saturation levels. they make notes on a screen.

then a few minutes later a Dr. in a white coat comes & leans down to me. he is not old but not young, maybe 30.

"i'm Dr. Kohli," he says. "& u're Leo, right?"

i nod.

"& this is ur dog?"

another nod.

"he's cute."

he's a cattle dog in training, i think. he's smart & can turn on a whistle & fetch a wayward calf in from the back field. at least he will be able to.

the Dr. turns to Grandpa. "what happened?"

"the dog bolted after a calf. Leo here ran after him . . . i made him do it, i guess . . . & his foot went in a rabbit hole."

oh. so it was the rabbit hole.

"ouch," says the Dr. "that'll do it. any existing medical conditions i should know about? allergies, blood pressure, heart disease?"

"no," i say.

"he—" starts Grandpa. then he falls silent.

"what's that?" says the Dr.

"nothing," says Grandpa.

"ok, well," says Dr. Kohli. "i'm going to need to do an external examination first, ok?" he doesn't wait for an answer, just calls for a nurse, & a short woman with a kind smile comes over & they cut open my jeans & i feel a pressing on my leg as he moves his fingers down it.

i gasp.

"sorry. nearly done."

he hums to himself. he says things to the nurse like *closed fracture; minimal swelling; circulation appears normal.* she is making notes all the time on a screen.

Dr. Kohli moves up to my head level again & looks down at me. "i'm going to x-ray ur leg now, ok? it's pretty clearly fractured but i want to assess the damage accurately so we can identify the next steps."

"ok," i say.

"we're also going to get u some pain relief," he says.

"that . . . would be good."

"i'm sure."

he instructs the nurse on what amount of painkiller to inject into me & i'm not really paying attention because i just want it & i want it now.

then she leans down & i feel a scratch on my arm & almost immediately warm water seems to flood my body, a bath inside me, filling me to the brim, & the raging pain in my leg lessens, as if by some magic trick. Comet kind of sighs & softens into me: it's like he has felt the pain go out of me & is glad.

i realize he is snoring.

the Dr. swings the screen of the x-ray around on its white elbowed arm & takes images of my leg, occasionally saying things like *oblique fracture, tibia, & fibula* to the nurse, who is taking notes.

i notice that he is looking at the screen for quite a long time.

he is sucking in air thru his teeth, like people do without know-ing, when they're thinking. he turns to Grandpa.

"ur son—"

"grandson," corrects Grandpa.

"sorry, grandson. u said he had no medical conditions?"

"no," says Grandpa.

"because this bone density . . ." he trails off. "i want to do some more tests."

i am fuzzy from the drugs, & my body is not entirely confined in space. i blur at the edges. but i catch his tone. "what's wrong with me?" i say.

"i don't know that there's anything wrong . . ." says the Dr. "it's just . . ."

Grandpa is standing, staring at him.

"ur bones are more fragile than i would expect in someone ur age . . . like i say, i would want to do some more tests. bring in a specialist."

"& the break?" says Grandpa. it's as if he wants to change the subject.

the Dr. nods. "that's more straightforward. simple fracture of both bones, should mend pretty easily if we inject stem cells & cell-signaling proteins as well as splinting. the quicker we start & get Leo's leg stabilized, the better; i don't want any swelling to damage the muscle."

"but u're confident about setting the break?" says Grandpa.

"yes," says Dr. Kohli. "it's amazing what the cell injections can do. & without wishing to brag, i'm 1 of the best at this kind of injury." he smiles. "a lot of skiers in these parts. i'm going to have to be careful given the . . . weakness . . . of the bones. but the good news is that we can have him patched up pretty quickly. then . . ."

"then what?" says Grandpa.

the Dr. kind of inclines his head toward me & then walks a little distance away with Grandpa, twitching aside the curtain that surrounds me so that they leave my little cocoon. i hear Grandpa & the Dr. talking in hushed tones.

"ok," says the Dr. "let's go."

he opens the curtain again. he takes a screen from the nurse & hands it over to my grandpa. "consent form," he says. "it's pro forma. the usual risks, painkiller prescriptions, etc." he indicates some places on the screen. "sign here. & here."

Grandpa signs.

"the dog is going to have to go with u, Mr. Freeman, i'm afraid," says the Dr. Comet is still curled up asleep on top of me.

"oh," i say. "can't he stay with me?" the words come out a little squished, as if the drugs have softened them inside me, soaked them, & now they are crumbling.

"i'm sorry," says Dr. Kohli. "it's a sterile environment."

i sigh.

Grandpa lifts Comet gently—he wakes, & yips.

"bye, Comet," i say.

he barks. i know i was chasing him. but it wasn't his fault.

Dr. Kohli is looking thoughtful. "wait," he says, turning to Grandpa. "*the* Robert Freeman?"

Grandpa nods.

"the Robert Freeman who was the last man on the moon? wait. yes. i recognize u! but u had a beard then."

"yes."

Dr. Kohli whistles. "i had a photo of u on my wall when i was a kid," he says. "u were on *The Tonight Show*! & u signed my book at the stage door. i always wanted to be an astronaut. but i ended up fixing bones instead."

"well," says Grandpa. "if u're as good as u say u are, then i'm glad."

men in green reappear, & the nurse is alongside me & Dr. Kohli too, & we go down white hallways with a green channel running along the middle of the wall & thru swinging doors & into a very bright room with lights in the ceiling & big white machines & stands with implements on them. the metal smell of disinfectant is even stronger in here.

there's another Dr. already there, an oldish man with a white beard & piercings all up 1 ear & thru 1 eyebrow. he is wearing green eye shadow that matches his eyes—Dr. Kohli isn't wearing any makeup at all, i realize.

Dr. Kohli greets the other Dr. & they discuss something together; Dr. Kohli mentions my painkiller, & then the 1 with the beard comes up to the head end of my gurney & smiles down at me. "i'm going to put a mask over ur face, Leo," he says. "& i want u to count down from 10 for me. can u do that?"

"yes," i say. i notice he has a bolt thru his tongue too.

the Dr. presses, gently, a plastic thing over my face.

i count down.

10.

9.

8.

then i feel sleep fire its rockets & propel me: inverse launch, not into the sky, not into the ceiling but downward; it fires me into the bed. i accelerate down, & i understand for the first time why it is called falling asleep. on the space station, sleep is all around & u can access it in any direction; on earth, sleep is something that is below u.

i fall . . .

& i'm in the blackness of space.

i have fallen off the earth.

15

nails & screws

the room coalesces around me.

i c light coming thru windows, slanted, bright, sliced by blinds. the walls are green. on 1 of them is that famous painting of sunflowers. i'm on a bed & there's a chair in the corner—Grandpa is sitting on it. my mother is standing over him, talking to him. he is moving his hands a lot. i realize it was their voices that woke me.

i don't move.

". . . thought u'd have learned ur lesson about pushing people too hard," says my mother.

"i said i was sorry," says Grandpa. "told him that too."

"anything else u told him?"

"no," says Grandpa.

"good. i don't want u going too fast with anything else. rushing anything."

"u don't think he should know?" says Grandpa.

"oh, & how do u propose telling him?" replies my mother.

"we won't need to, if this Dr.—"

then he looks at me, & this is a man whose eyes have been honed by years as a pilot & astronaut, & just as many years scanning distant horizons for cattle. he falls silent & stands, then walks over to my bedside.

"hey, champ," he says.

"hey," i say. what am i meant to do, say, *what were u just talk-*

ing about? & why did the Dr. want to know if i have a condition when he examined me? why did he trail off when he mentioned my bone density?

& by the way, what were those flyers about & what happened to Santiago?

but i don't say any of that. there are things u sense u can't say.

"u want me to raise the bed so u can sit?" asks Grandpa.

"sure."

he picks up a remote control & presses a button on it: the end of the bed where my head is rises, pushing me into a sitting position. i realize that i haven't even thought about the gravity yanking me down: i'm really getting used to it. what i am thinking about is my leg, which is dully throbbing.

i look down. my lower leg is covered with a brace or wrapping that looks like it's made of Kevlar or something.

"i'll call the Dr.," says my mother.

"hi," i say.

she turns. her eyes squint slightly. "yes. hi."

it's the best i'm going to get.

she steps out of the room & Grandpa pats my shoulder, & a moment later Dr. Kohli enters with my mother.

he comes to stand by the bed. he has a screen in his hand.

"Leo," he says. "how are u feeling?"

"bit woozy," i say. "but fine."

"great. that's great. & ur mother's here. she flew in from Nevada as soon as she heard."

i look at her. "u did?"

she shrugs.

"2 astronauts," says Dr. Kohli. "12-year-old me would not believe this. to meet 1 person who's been in space, that's incredible. but 2 . . ."

"actually—" i begin.

"—what's the plan now?" says my mother, cutting me off.

"the plan?" says the Dr.

"with the leg."

"oh. yes. um." he unrolls the screen. "basically, Leo," he says, "we've put long nails down ur fibula & tibia. right inside the bone. they're made of a special fiber with . . . a sort of honeycomb that ur bone grows into, with the help of the stimulating cells we've injected." he sketches the long bones on his screen, the nails running thru them. "the nails hold ur bones together—they were both split at an angle. then we put screws thru transversally"—he draws the screws, passing at right angles thru the bones & sticking out of my leg on either side.

he taps the shell encasing my leg. "the cast—we call it that even tho it's not a cast anymore—is ballistic-grade material. actually i think they use it on satellites. that is going to keep ur leg nice & still. u won't be doing any running for 4, maybe 5 weeks. in the old days that would have been months. & ur bones will knit together nicely." he glances at my mother & Grandpa. "he really needs to be seen by a specialist tho, about the . . . more general issue. i've encountered osteoporosis in people of all ages, but his bone density is—"

"is fine as long as he doesn't run into rabbit holes," says my mother.

"but—"

"we'll be taking him home today," says my mother. "i'll stay at my father's house with him for 7 weeks. help out. do u have any objection to that?"

"w-well . . . ," stammers Dr. Kohli. his forehead is creased. "he's not in mortal danger, so if u want to discharge him, then that's up to u; the leg is seen to. but i would really rather—"

"that's good then," says my mother.

"we can take him home today?" says Grandpa.

Dr. Kohli looks at him. "yes."

"good." Grandpa smiles at me.

something about that smile reminds me of my first day at his house, & i remember Comet, & i can't believe i haven't thought of him until now. his gleaming eyes. his energy. the way he seems permanently wound up, a spring inside him.

"Comet?" i say.

Grandpa smiles wider. "in the truck. he was running around the hallways, terrorizing the nurses."

i grin back. i can imagine it.

"then i guess we can say—" the Dr. says.

"goodbye," says my mother. "i'll come with u to complete the paperwork. my father will take Leo. a wheelchair can be arranged, to the car, i assume?"

"y-y-yes, of course." Dr. Kohli presses something on his screen & there's a *bing* & then he says, "wheelchair to room 202 please." he turns to my mother. "we'll need to give u some crutches too, of course," he says.

"oh, we have some," says my mother.

"right. ok," says Dr. Kohli. i can c he is thinking he's going to have to write this up somehow; i can c he is worrying that something is wrong.

he is not the only 1, i have to say.

things move quickly. an aide comes & helps me into a wheelchair—my mother goes off with Dr. Kohli—& Grandpa walks beside us as the aide wheels me thru the white hallways toward the door & then out into the blinding sunshine—i don't have my glasses—& across the wide dusty parking lot, to Grandpa's battered & faded pickup.

once there, the aide silently helps Grandpa maneuver me into the rear seat. they prop my leg between the 2 front seats.

Comet is there, in the back, waiting. he leaps up at me,

slobbers on me, rubs his wet nose against mine. i pull him hard against me, & he squirms & then licks me again.

"hello, Comet," i say.

bark, he says.

he jumps into the footwell & settles down over my good foot, warming it instantly, a pulsing blanket.

we sit & wait in the truck. Grandpa puts on the heating—it's chilly. after a while, the car starts to warm up & the insides of the windows fog, rubbing out some of the concrete parking lot around us, the weather-beaten cars.

my mother turns up maybe 15 minutes later. she has a determined expression on her face—more determined than usual, anyway. she is putting her wallet into her bag—when i say her bag, i mean a practical shoulder bag, not a purse.

she climbs into the passenger seat & points forward, like, *go.*

"so," Grandpa says to her. "u're coming home."

"just to help out for a short while," she says.

neither of them say anything else.

16
gray dust

Grandpa drives back to the ranch. the sun is bright, hanging low in the sky, like a floodlight for tracking fugitives.

& as we turn off the road & thru the heavy security gate, i c the tatters of the birthday party balloons, fluttering multicolored. then we're on the bumpy path leading to the ranch, & Grandpa drives slowly so as not to shake my leg too much, i assume. Comet grumbles a little in his sleep as the car shudders.

Grandpa parks in front of the house, & i shake Comet awake & open the door for him: he jumps out, then waits for me on the earth by the car.

Grandpa & my mother get me out of the truck & onto my crutches: i make it into the house fairly easily, i mean, i have been accustomed for weeks to discomfort & the pressure of the world's weight; ever since i landed on earth i have been like a beached creature plucked from buoyancy; the broken leg is just an expansion of a theme.

i walk, & Comet walks close beside me, sticking to my heel, like he knows to do.

i sit in the living room, & Comet jumps up beside me & waits for me to lift my arm to accommodate him, then lowers himself onto the sofa—my arm, which fits him perfectly underneath it, like he was made for me to rest on, goes down & we are a unit of 2 bodies.

Grandpa starts to light a fire: i feel echoing snaps inside me when the twigs break; i feel my bone giving way again. *pop. pop. pop.*

"i'm going to my room," says my mother. "i have some work to do."

"don't u always," says Grandpa.

"well, i wonder who i learned that from."

he looks up, from the fire—he has his pyramid of kindling now, neatly stacked. "i was always there when u needed me," he says.

"& i am here for Leo," says my mother. "Leo, call me if u need help walking or with the bath. ok?"

"ok," i say. i feel like i am in the middle of an old fight.

she turns.

"why 7 weeks?" says Grandpa.

"what?" she replies.

"u said to the Dr. u'd be here 7 weeks. it seemed very specific."

she blinks at him. "i'm going back up." she looks at me. "with Soto. u met him, i think. he talks about u a lot." she pauses, as if the concept of talking about people is something alien to her. "he's been flight cleared. my job is to get him up there, then fly back."

"u're delivering the boy to space," says Grandpa.

she doesn't answer. she just looks at him.

"very well," says Grandpa. "u'd better go & check in with base."

she nods & disappears, & i hear her footsteps on the stairs—i know her room is up there, but i've never been in there. i don't know why. maybe i'm not so curious about her. maybe i'm a little scared of her. it's ok. it doesn't bother me. i know she doesn't c me the way other mothers c their children: i'm her shadow, not her reflection.

but still.

at least she came when i was hurt.

Grandpa lights the kindling & soon the fire is burning in the stove. he shuts the door & comes & sits on the sofa on the other side of Comet.

"Grandpa," i say. "what was it like on the moon?" i'm thinking of the Dr., of how starstruck he was.

Grandpa shifts in his seat. "u asking idly or u really want to know?"

"i really want to know."

"there was a lot of gray dust," he says. "& u could bounce around, if u wanted. i didn't have any kind of epiphany, if that's what u mean." he rubs his eyes. "i'd already been in orbit. i'd already seen the earth as a globe, from afar. the moon . . . that's just a ball of rock."

but it's a ball of rock that never leaves the earth, i think. that circles it all the time. it's love.

"oh," i say. it's an *oh* that contains all the wide horizon of my disappointment in my mother & now my grandpa, for seeing the universe as something merely mechanical.

"anyway," says Grandpa. "it wasn't what i was doing it for. u know, being an astronaut. i wasn't 1 of the romantics."

"romantics?"

"the ones who read science fiction. who want to reach space, to enlarge their minds."

"so what were u?" i ask.

he thinks for a second. "i was someone who wanted to be the best. the best pilot, the best astrophysicist, the best astronaut."

i nod. i can c that. i would like to be the best. i would like to be the 1 they call when the EVA is too difficult for anyone else to do. but there was an inflection on the word *was,* i noticed.

"& now?" i say.

"now what?"

"now what do u want?"

again he takes some time to think. "to look after my land & my loved ones," he says, at last.

i smile at him. i feel Comet's heart beating, under my palm. Grandpa pats my hand. my leg is beginning to burn, i realize. i look into his eyes & i c only love there, only security, only things i can trust.

"Grandpa . . . ," i start to say. i want to ask him about the men in black, Santiago, everything. but what would i say? *Grandpa, there's a secret & i want to know what it is.* i'd sound like a child.

"yes?" he says.

"i think i need some of that painkiller," i say.

he looks at his watch. it's a civilian 1. i'm wearing his old 1, after all, his Speedmaster, the 1 he wore over his suit when he space-walked. "u're right," he says. he gets up with a creak & a slightly exaggerated groan & goes & gets a glass of water & the pills.

i swallow them.

we sit, in the warmth. Grandpa doesn't like to watch shows or movies.

after a while, i reach out for my screen, which is on the little table by the sofa.

i unroll the screen & tap Orion's name & hit CALL.

bong. bong. bong.

but no answer.

i tap Libra's name & then CALL.

bong. bong. bong.

no answer.

i smack the screen down on the couch. this is getting old. then i look up to make sure Grandpa didn't c me. i close my eyes & take a breath. pull calm into my lungs; breathe out frustration. i guess they're both busy, doing something with their mother.

i wonder what. waterskiing? i don't really know much about Florida. maybe Orion is in a concert hall somewhere, letting Bach's harmonies wash over him. maybe Libra is in her mother's garden, digging up carrots.

the room is getting warmer.

Comet snuggles closer to me & whimpers, then paddles his front paws against me. chasing calves maybe. which is good, chasing them in his sleep is altogether safer, i think.

my eyelids are getting heavy.

they're closing.

red flickering of the fire flames thru my eyelids.

glow.

i breathe it in.

breathe out frustration. breathe out pain. breathe out everything.

17
ALARM. INTRUDER.

i sleep, for i don't know how long.

then: *bing. bing. bing. bing.*

i blink.

i grab for my screen, thinking it's Orion or Libra, calling me back. but it's dark, & rolled up. then i notice that Grandpa's screen is on the table too & the tube of it is flashing red, vibrating, with the *bing bing bing* tone.

Grandpa is snoring on the sofa next to me, head back, mouth open, eyes closed.

i have to stand to get his screen: i prop myself on my crutches & get myself into an upright position. i hook the screen with a hand & unroll it in 1 smooth motion.

on it:

an image of silhouetted people seen from above, shining red in the darkness, moving thru what looks—tho the image is dark & grainy—like the big hole in the fence. infrared footage, i realize. from the drone. 2 men. maybe 3. carrying long, thin things that might be guns.

bing bing bing is not a ringtone at all but an alarm tone; how did i mistake it for a ringtone?

ALARM, INTRUDER reads a warning on the screen.

ALARM. INTRUDER. ALARM. INTRUDER.

18
boldface

"wake up, Grandpa," i say.

i shake him. he sits up, blinking. "what is it?"

i show him the screen.

"dammit," he says. "how many?"

"2, i think? or 3."

"armed?"

"yes."

"dammit," he says again. then he stands & walks over to the cupboard on the wall while taking the key from his pocket. he opens it. lifts out a shotgun that he racks with 1 hand—*kerchuk*—& a pistol that he hands to me.

"what do i do with this?" i say. it's cold & heavy in my hand.

he reaches over & thumbs a switch on the side. "safety's off," he says. "point the barrel end at ur target. then pull the trigger."

great, i think. something like the feeling of putting ur tongue on a battery terminal is running thru me, but i feel it everywhere—in my mouth, in my stomach, in my legs.

my leg. shit.

Grandpa hauls me up to my feet. Comet jumps down to the floor & looks up at me, wondering what all the commotion is, presumably. his eyes are big & wide.

"can u get upstairs?" Grandpa says. "with the crutches?"

"i don't think so," i say.

a pause. "they're on foot?"

"yes."

"ok, so we have maybe 5 minutes. i'll help u upstairs." he pulls another shotgun from the rack & puts it under his arm with the other weapon. "come on."

we pick up my crutches & i wonder what to do about the pistol. Grandpa takes it back from me, flicks the switch on the side, & tucks it into my waistband. "turn that safety off again if they get to the second floor. hopefully they won't."

yeah, i think. *hopefully.* my heart is colossal in my chest, battering, going *ba-dum ba-dum ba-dum* to a crazy rhythm, like it's on a different tempo from the rest of my body.

Grandpa takes my weight on my weak side & carries 1 of the crutches as well as the 2 shotguns. together we manage to hoist me up the stairs, 1 by 1. halfway, my muscles are flooded with lactic acid & burning—near the top, i feel that my lungs might collapse.

Comet bounds ahead of us, then waits at the top, as if mocking me.

but we make it, & i lean against the wall for a moment, gasping.

"come on," says Grandpa. "no time."

he bangs on my mother's door. then bangs again. she opens it, frowning. a screen on the desk shows a view of some kind of lab at the base.

"what?" she says.

"intruders," says Grandpa. "on the way."

she doesn't say anything else, just nods, & he hands her the spare shotgun. "u 2 stay up here," he says. "i'll try to stop them from getting up the stairs."

i think of the hole in the fence.

i think of Grandpa, talking to me about the stream. *just a question of opportunity. & money.*

i think of the lines in the town, outside of those 2 stores. *guns & money.*

opportunity.

guns.

money.

i am shaking, i realize, when my mother puts a hand on my forearm. "it's going to be ok," she says.

"u don't know that," i say.

"no," she agrees.

oh. great. sometimes i don't think she really understands this mothering thing.

we follow Grandpa to the stairs & he runs down, surprisingly nimble & quiet. the front door opens right onto the hall & faces the staircase & we can c it from up here. Grandpa stands on the side where the hinges are. he motions up to us for us to go, for us to hide.

but i don't move.

my mother pulls on my arm. "to the room," she whispers.

i shake my head. i want to watch Grandpa. i want to c that he doesn't get hurt. my mother has put some kind of cream on her face. i can smell it: lightly floral, lightly mineral. moonlight is coming in thru a window in the landing, slanting bluely down at us.

she sighs. "ok."

unnecessarily, she puts a finger to her lips. we shuffle a little into the shadow, away from the glow of the moon.

"stay," i whisper to Comet, at my feet. he sits down on the floorboards, head on his paws.

a minute passes.

2 minutes. i'm still watching Grandpa as he stands by the door.

then the door handle—it's round & brass—jiggles. rotates from side to side, someone trying to open it, to turn it. the sound is furtive, rodent-like. a crepitation. the door doesn't move.

an even fainter sound now, metallic. something is being fitted into the lock, it sounds like.

schhh. schhh.

& the handle turns again & the door opens slowly inward, & because of the side Grandpa is standing on he is hidden by it. a man in black with a mask over his face steps thru, holding what looks like a long pistol, & Grandpa levels the shotgun at chest height & fires, straight thru the door, the sound is monumental, epochal:

BLAM—

& the guy sort of falls to the side & drops to 1 knee, screaming. at least i think he's screaming—it might just be the high-pitched sound in my ears that has followed the gunshot. Grandpa steps around the door & kicks the man's wrist, knocking his gun to the floor, then takes another step & kicks the pistol—it skids, spinning, down the hallway & out of my & my mother's sightline.

the guy reaches out & grabs at Grandpa's leg, but Grandpa clubs his hand away with his shotgun & then:

pew—

& Grandpa ducks & runs out of sight as something hits the stairs, splinters them, & my mother pulls me back, down the hallway. but at the same time there's a smashing sound, followed by a tinkling—the unmistakable noise of a breaking window.

we move quickly, me on my crutches, to Mother's room & there: glass is gleaming on the floor & a man in a ski mask is leaning in, knocking more sharp shards from the window frame onto the floorboards. i feel the cool night air, rushing in from outside.

my mother runs forward, shotgun held in front of her. she lifts it to her shoulder as she gets closer, but several things happen in extremely quick succession:

the man in the window—he must have climbed up a ladder taken from 1 of the barns maybe—leans forward, legs still outside, & my mother doesn't stop soon enough:

he grabs the end of the shotgun:

yanks, hard:

& simultaneously kind of twists to the side:

& my mother is pulled thru the window & falls, with a surprised yelp, & then:

a thump,

which resonates thru my bones & mind.

briefly, the man fills the window—all moonlight is blocked out, all stars. the room is shadows, pooling, looming shapes. then he is thru, landing catlike on both feet, & light shafts in again & i am a statue, turned to stone by it, unable to move, unable to do anything.

he still has the shotgun in his hand, but he's holding it by the barrels. he grabs it with his other hand & turns it, as he takes a step toward me.

& almost without my expressly deciding to, my hands push the crutches to either side; they topple away from me, slowly falling trees:

my right hand moves to the pistol in my waistband,

takes it out,

my other hand rises to flick off the safety,

& i aim, roughly, & maybe it's growing up in space where u have to be good with ur hands, u get used to needing to be dexterous, or small things float away from u, & u get used to tapping commands into multiple instrument panels or washing with dry soap or whatever—to spotting handholds as u float thru the

modules & seizing them, quick, & turning or deflecting ur momentum—

maybe it's that—

or maybe it's seeing & hearing my mother fall out of the
window—

but it takes me a lot less time than it takes him to turn the
gun &:

to my surprise i am pointing the gun at someone who is in no
position to fire in return because he's still getting his hand onto
the grip of the shotgun, & right at that moment a border collie
puppy comes flying at him, claws skittering on the floorboards, &
jumps up & bites the man's leg—

& he sort of jumps around, trying to kick Comet off him—

& so i fire.

the gun kicks in my hand, but less than i thought it would—
what shocks me is the devastating noise of it, the thunder filling
the room, & the guy seems shocked too because he staggers back,
but then i realize that's because:

he's bleeding from his shoulder.

he drops the shotgun & sits down.

"fuck," he says. "fuck."

i take a step, but i have forgotten my cast & i step onto it &
lose my balance—i fall, putting my hands out & the butt of the
gun strikes the floor with a hammer sound & there's pain in there
too: my wrist breaking? i wonder, looking at my arm. i lie there
winded, before awkwardly shifting myself into a sitting position,
bad leg out in front of me.

my wrist isn't hurting, but it's bent in a way it shouldn't be &
i'm sure the pain is not far away. i move the gun to my other hand.
like that's going to do any good.

i mean, i was aiming at the guy's arm & i hit his shoulder.

& that was with my dominant hand. i'm just glad i didn't

shoot Comet, who runs over to me yapping, at least i think he's yapping, it's hard to tell with the ringing in my ears, & he shivers with delight when i rub behind his ears.

"thank u, Comet," i say.

"we're trying to fucking help u," says the guy. he reaches out his hand for the shotgun. draws it toward him. begins to lift it. "get u out of here."

"get me out of here?" i echo.

he's staring at me. "Kyle said u looked human. didn't figure it'd be so spooky tho."

"human?" i say.

he points the shotgun at me. "whole thing is screwed now tho. catastrophe protocol."

"what?"

"if u can't take the alien, kill the alien. i'm sorry." he sights down the barrel at me. i am too stunned to do anything with my gun.

then Grandpa walks in. he enters the doorway, shotgun out in front of him. when he sees the guy pointing the gun at me he doesn't hesitate for a moment he fires as easy as breathing & the man is thrown back against the wall, a spray of blood, an arc of it, his head hitting the wood with a thud.

interlude
space boy

it's the same moment.

   i'm there, bone a tuning fork of pain in my arm, in my wrist, singing from within its song of agony.

   blood splatters the wall, the spray of it, mathematically curved.

   i think:

   space boy.

   we can help u.

   i think:

   we're trying to fucking help u. get u out of here.

   i think of Grandpa saying:

   Area 51 crazies. alien conspiracists.

   i think these things, & i don't like where they might lead.

19
window

Grandpa sucks in breath & rushes over to me, keeping the shotgun trained on the man on the floor by the window.

"i'm ok," i say. my own voice comes out cotton-wooled. "think i hurt my wrist tho."

Grandpa glances at my arm. "dammit."

then he looks at the man, walks over, nudges his body with his foot, & kicks away the gun. just in case. which seems crazy because that man is very clearly dead.

"should have taken out the drone," Grandpa says to the dead man. then he turns to me. "where's ur mother?"

i point to the window. "she fell out," i say.

"oh," says Grandpa. "shit."

20
safe

"stay here," says Grandpa. "i'm going down to check on ur mother."

"ok," i say. he obviously isn't going to tell me anything. not right now anyway. & i do care about my mother too—i want her to be ok. even if she only cares about me in the abstract.

"keep the gun on him," he says, pointing to the intruder.

"he's dead," i say.

"better safe than sorry."

Grandpa shifts me into a slightly more comfortable sitting position. i lift the gun in my left hand & point it at the man who broke in. he is sitting in a little pool of moonlight & blood, & his eyes are pure blankness, like empty space.

Grandpa takes a deep breath. he puts a hand on my shoulder. "Leo," he says. "cops are going to come. we tell them these men were looking for my safe, ok? i keep a lot of cash in it."

i stare at him.

"please, Leo," he says, "trust me. i'll explain later."

a moment passes. our eyes are on orbital lock.

"ok," i say eventually.

he nods. seems only then to let out his breath. & heads downstairs.

my leg & wrist are killing me but i try to drown out the signal from my nerve endings.

i fill my head with a mantra instead: *be ok; be ok; be ok.*

"stay with me, Comet," i say. Comet licks my hand & settles himself next to me.

Grandpa moves to the stairs & goes down. i don't hear anyone else. maybe they're dead, i realize. the ones downstairs. Grandpa was in the air force before he was an astronaut. he wasn't just testing planes; he saw actual combat. in the Iraqi state. & other stuff. i forget that sometimes. but i saw the way he took out this man, moving as smooth & no-thought as water.

the clock on the wall taps out the time, measuring it into ticking increments.

then Grandpa calls up from outside.

"she's all right," he says. "might have dislocated her shoulder in the fall, but she'll be just fine. i've called 911."

she's ok, she's ok, i think. i'm surprised by how much i wanted her to be ok.

"thanks," i call down. "tell her . . ."

"what?"

"tell her i'm all right too."

there's a pause.

"she says good," says Grandpa.

oh well. that's probably the best i can hope for.

i stay sitting.

the clock keeps dividing out the time, *tick tick tick*. the minute hand moves around, in little jumps. like something imbued with some kind of life.

after it has turned a few times around the clockface, i hear sirens approaching. i can tell they're approaching because of the Doppler effect: the frequency of the pulses of sound seems elevated, to my ears.

that, & they are getting louder.

there are at least 2 kinds of sirens outside, weaving into 1 another: police & ambulance, i guess. soon there is red & blue light washing rhythmically thru the window, illuminating the room, waves of it, making the window a bright rectangle, framing the man sitting on the ground, a little slumped now. the sirens wail, loudly.

cops in uniform enter the room, their guns out. paramedics follow. i put my hands in the air; surrender my pistol. the paramedics realize they're going to need a stretcher for me & call down to someone to bring 1 up.

"that man was breaking in," i say, pointing to the burglar.

"yep," says an older cop with a mustache. "i know ur Grandpa."

"i think . . . he wanted to kidnap me. he said he was here to take me." i catch myself: i wasn't supposed to say anything. "i mean, i don't know," i say. "it was hard to make out; he was kind of babbling."

"uh-huh," says the cop. he doesn't seem too interested, which is strange.

he walks over to the man & crouches down & puts a hand to his neck. he shakes his head at the paramedics.

a woman in her greens sits on her heels next to me. "ur grandfather said ur wrist was hurt?"

i lift my right arm. she takes 1 look at it & nods. "ok. we're going to get u into the ambulance & across to the ER. we'll need to do x-rays. but i guess u know all that." she is looking at the cast on my leg.

"yep," i say. "bit accident prone lately."

she smiles. she has a pretty smile. green eyes.

the stretcher has arrived. she helps 2 men to lift me onto it. when Comet sees what's happening he starts leaping up & down, yipping.

"can he ride with me?" i ask.

"don't c why not," says the woman.

"thanks." i lean down to him. "Comet," i say. "jump up."

Comet jumps up onto the stretcher & sits on me, like he owns me. maybe he does. he has a narrow look in his eye. like *i saved his life, & u'd better know it. he's my human.*

"hi, Comet," says the woman, doing a little bow to him. he likes that. he yaps back. "i'm Shirley," she says.

"Leo," i say.

"Leo," she agrees. "well, let's check u out & then get u to the hospital, Leo."

& that's what they do.

first they check me out.

they examine my wrist, palpate it slightly—i scream & Comet bristles, nearly bites 1 of the paramedics—& make notes on their screens. they conclude that it's a sprain, & i don't seem to have cut off the blood supply to my hand or ruptured an artery or any of the really bad things that could happen.

then they take me downstairs. it's not a comfortable journey, bumping down the steps on the stretcher.

we ride in the ambulance. i'm on a gurney secured to 1 side of the vehicle; my mother is on 1 on the opposite side. they attach various machines to both of us. keeping track of our oxygen levels, our heart rates, all that stuff.

they frown when they c my readouts, & whisper to each other.

shock, i guess. i'm in shock & it's screwing up my heart rate & stuff.

anyway, it doesn't matter because they also put me on some IV pain medication, which makes everything all floaty & less important.

i don't know where Grandpa is. talking to the police back at the ranch maybe.

it's cold in the ambulance. there's a smell of blood & anti-septic.

my mother is only barely conscious. she turns to me at 1 point, nods slightly when she sees me.

"Leo," she says.

"Mother," i say.

that's it. our greeting. the only greeting we've ever had for each other.

drugs in my veins, the ambulance spins, rotates like a space station, its siren an alarm, sounding a breach, sounding a disaster.

"Mother," i say. "am i an alien?"

21
promise

Mother looks at me for a long time.

"Mother, did u hear me?"

she sighs. thinks for a moment. "Leo, if there's 1 thing i can promise u, it's that u're not an alien."

it's weird the way she phrases it. the way she considers it before speaking.

i narrow my eyes.

"so what can't u promise me then?" i say.

she turns away. she doesn't answer.

the ambulance spins off into space.

22

feds

i come in & out of consciousness, sunrise & darkness flipping & flipping thru the cupola of the station, which is also an ambulance on a road, in California.

we ride, sirens going. no Doppler effect this time. true frequency. we are the source, moving. the epicenter of the sound waves. we travel, making ripples of noise across the valley; i imagine them spreading out, like from pebbles dropped into a pond, rolling over the dark fields, thru the odd trees, thru gates, like they're not even there; like water coasting away from us in circles, fading, breaking eventually onto the grass & dying away to dew, just the after-echo of a siren, sounding.

i hear Grandpa on the phone with someone, arranging for the hole in the fence to be patched, & then—talking to someone else i think—paying with a payment code for a guard to patrol the perimeter.

we blur thru the night, blaring.

i imagine a rabbit sitting up: what was that?

it was an ambulance passing.

how would u explain such a thing to a rabbit?

i think thoughts like that.

not-quite-coherent thoughts.

when we reach the hospital, we back into a bay with wide

doors like an aircraft hangar & the doors are opening as we back up. they roll us straight out & into a wide hallway that funnels down into the busy ER department.

then we split up: the guys—& Shirley—pushing me into a windowless examination room & my mother into another.

a Dr. comes to c me. she has gray hair & a slightly tired air. she doesn't introduce herself & i can't quite make our her name tag. Dr. Reynolds? something like that.

"that dog can't be in here" is the first thing she says. not angry. just sort of weary.

"he's staying," i say. Comet presses down against me, flattening himself on top of me, as if to underline my words.

she lifts a hand & lets it flop down again. "fine. fine."

she asks me some questions about my leg:

"u broke it very recently?

"does it hurt?

"are you on any blood-thinning medication?"

(yes. yes. no.)

she glances down at some notes on her screen. "& i c Dr. Kohli wanted to do some additional tests," she says.

"yes," i say.

then she frowns. she taps the screen.

"what?" i say.

she purses her lips. "odd. ur notes end there. he doesn't say why he wanted more scans."

"he said something about my bone density," i say. the drugs are wearing off now. reality is bleeding back in, gray in color. gray with pain.

"hmm." she taps her fingernail on the screen thoughtfully. "i don't have any x-ray images here either. i can c that he set ur leg. but i can't c any visuals." she sighs. "this hospital needs a new

IT department. mind u, this hospital needs more doctors too. then i wouldn't be working 60-hour shifts & inheriting patients with incomplete records."

"u could ask him," i say. "Dr. Kohli, i mean."

"nope," she says. "he quit yesterday. walked out at the end of the shift. that's what the hospital manager says anyway."

oh.

weird.

"well, let's look at this new injury," she says. she says it almost like a reproach, like i've been careless. "u sustained this in an altercation, i understand." she tucks her gray hair behind her ear, in a move that looks to me like a habitual tic. she is younger than i first thought, i realize.

"no," i say. "i fell."

"down some stairs?"

"no. just . . . forward. on the floor."

her eyebrows come together again. "running?"

"no."

she lifts the screen & taps something. pulling up the paramedics' notes, i assume. "u got a bad sprain like this from just falling over?"

i do my best at shrugging—lying down, it's difficult. from outside, there's a sound like rotors spinning, the hush of downdraft. it's a sound i know from movies. an emergency helicopter, i presume, landing on the roof.

"huh."

pause.

"ok, well, let's x-ray u & take it from there. best to be sure."

she calls a nurse on her screen & soon a guy in a white hospital uniform rolls in an x-ray machine & they set it up & scan my arm.

"as i thought," she said. "simple sprain, no need for—"

then she stops.

"what?" i say.

"but these bones . . ."

"what?" i say. "what about my bones?"

"this is not . . . i mean . . ." another tuck of the hair behind the ear. she is wearing small diamond studs in her earlobes. the kind u wear if u're a modest person & u don't want to wear anything that could catch on stuff, or be a health risk in a hospital—but u're still someone who cares. who takes care, of ur appearance. & now i c that she's probably beautiful, when she's not tired. which is probably never.

pause.

"i just . . ." she halts again. "do u have any preexisting conditions? osteoporosis? leukemia? any kind of immune deficiency?"

"what?" i say. "no."

can't take the alien, kill the alien.

she taps her fingernails on the screen again. the ends have sparkling nail polish on them. but it's flaking off. being pushed to the edge. i feel like i need more painkillers, i feel like my leg & wrist are filled with nails, poking into me.

"um, Dr.?" i say.

she looks at me. it is the first time our eyes have really met.

yes, beautiful, i think, looking into her rain-cloud eyes.

"sorry, Leo, yes," she says. "i think . . . i think Dr. Kohli was right to suggest more tests. ur mother is in room C3, i understand?"

"um, i don't know. but she's here. at the hospital, i mean."

she nods. "i would like to talk to her. when she's ready. . . . then i will arrange some scans." she does a little shake of her head, like she's telling herself off. "i mean, we'll splint ur wrist first of course. make sure u're comfortable." but she says it almost distantly, like her mind isn't really on it.

Comet wants to get down. he doesn't understand why he's just sitting on me, why we're in this place again. he is restless, & i put a hand on him, & feel him go still, feel his heart beating, the pulse against my fingers. his quickness.

he gives a little bark.

"it's ok, Comet," i say.

but it's not ok.

it's not ok because then the door opens & Boutros walks in. he's wearing a pin-striped suit & flanking him are 2 men in black, with earpieces in their ears, coiling, white. it's a look i know from movies.

it's a look that says: feds.

it's a look that says: trouble.

for u.

not for them.

because their look also says: competence.

their look says: hardness.

the men hold their hands in a strange way. then i realize it's a ready-to-draw-a-weapon way.

the Dr. stares at them. "who are u?" she says.

Boutros waves this away like a wasp, or something lesser maybe—a fly. "we'll take over from here," he says.

& then the men escort the Dr. from the room.

Comet barks & barks in alarm. the epicenter. waves of sound pond-rippling away from us, echoing off the walls of the little windowless room.

23
jet

Boutros requisitions a wheelchair from somewhere, & they sit me in it & push me down the hallway until we reach the exit. then we go thru a sliding door & into the cool night air. above, thin clouds drift past the stars.

they wheel me along the pavement a short way until we reach a convoy of big cars with blacked-out windows. Comet is agitated: i keep my good hand on him, stroking him, reassuring him.

he whines, low.

we reach a van. black like the others. chrome bumpers. ahead, there's an identical 1, & i c my mother being wheeled up a ramp at the back, her arm & shoulder bandaged. i call out.

"Mother."

she turns, looks at me.

unspoken questions flow thru the air from me to her, waves of them.

then she looks away again. they push her into the van & close the doors.

the doors of the closest van are opened. the men in black roll me up the ramp & secure the wheelchair with straps. it's as if they have planned for this. 1 of the men in black sits in a seat just in front of the space where i'm secured. doors open & shut.

then the engine vibrates into life, & the van pulls away.

"u going to tell me what's going on?" i say to the man.

he keeps looking straight ahead.

"thought not," i say.

we drive for no more than ten minutes. then we stop. the doors open & artificial light pours in. i blink. the man in black undoes my fastenings & presses a button to lower the ramp. then he wheels me out.

we're on a landing strip. big arc lights on poles illuminate the scene, banishing the stars. a hangar of some kind stands to the right. there are other low buildings in the distance, some stationary vehicles scattered about: forklift trucks, small flatbeds. i c a red-&-white-striped wind sock hanging slack in the slight breeze. on the runway is a small plane, also black.

the goon pushes me toward it. Boutros walks ahead, with other suited men. i hear an engine buzz & cut out, tires coming to a stop. i look behind. the doors of a van open, & my mother is rolled out. now we are both being pushed across the wide-open tarmac to the jet. steps lead up to it.

when we reach the steps, 2 men lift me up from the wheelchair. i glance back & c that my mother is being lifted from her chair too.

"wait," i say, as Comet digs his claws into me in alarm. i sort of scoop him up with my 1 good arm, hold him tight against my chest.

he doesn't like it, but he doesn't resist.

surprisingly gently, the men carry me to the steps & start climbing them.

i don't know why it surprises me actually. gentleness is 1 of those strange things: the stronger u are, almost the easier it is.

but that's not important.

what is important is that i am taken into the cabin & placed in a big leather seat. it's not like planes i've seen on vids. it's an open space, with seats more like armchairs, facing each other. the side walls of the aircraft are white. there is a lot of wood detailing: panels, accents. it's like a luxury apartment. on the floor is a thick carpet.

what is even more important is that Grandpa is sitting in 1 of those seats already. at his feet is a gray duffel bag, zipped up.

gently—again—they lower my mother into another seat. she blanches, & i c sweat beading on her forehead. *why's she allowing this to happen?* i wonder.

what's going on? i think.

because i know something is going on.

i have known for some time that something was going on. but maybe . . . i didn't want to know.

at the same time.

then Boutros comes & stands between us, hands clasped together.

i let go of Comet. he jumps down to stand at my feet, as if guarding me. i realize that he is growling, quietly, at Boutros, the hair stiff on his neck.

Boutros glances down at him. "he'd better not shit on the carpet," he says.

Grandpa makes a tutting noise. "he's house-trained, but i guess it depends on how long the flight is," he says.

Boutros nods. "u have a lot of questions. i understand."

Grandpa smiles. "oh, u do, do u?"

"events have overtaken us," says Boutros.

"no shit," says Grandpa.

"we knew the nutjobs were getting bolder. we didn't think they'd actually . . ." he trails off.

actually: break into the house.

actually: try to kidnap or kill me.

"to answer ur indirect question," says Boutros, "we'll be flying for around 5 hours. we're going to Mountain Dome." he says it like that. with capitals on the *M* & the *D*.

"oh," says Grandpa.

my mother's eyelids are half-closed. she forces them open a little more. "why?" she says. her voice sounds dry. croaky. a crow mimicking human language.

"like i said," says Boutros. "events have overtaken us. clearly the wider world is not safe for Leo. too many people want him."

"how did they even know where we were?" says Grandpa.

"we've had . . . a leak," says Boutros.

Grandpa nods. "i assumed."

silence.

"but . . . why?" i say. "why do they want me?"

Boutros makes a gesture with his hands that might mean: that's too big a question for me to answer right now. "*X-Files* loonies," he says. i know that's a TV show from decades ago. "twisting the information. convinced u're something u're not."

"an alien," i say.

he nods.

pause.

"am i?" i say.

"Leo, i told u," says my mother.

"u haven't told me anything," i say, smacking the armrest of my seat. "i want answers." & i do. no more waiting. no more bullshit. it's time to get the truth.

"& u'll get them. at Mountain Dome," says Boutros. his tone is final. his tone says: don't ask again.

"i still don't c why we're going there of all places," says my mother.

"we also have some . . . medical issues," says Boutros. "the other 2 subjects. there are . . . complications. we are hoping the high altitude will help."

"we have some of those here too," says Grandpa. he cuts his eyes to me. my leg in its cast. my wrist.

my mother says nothing, she just looks back & forth between the 2 of them.

"yes," says Boutros. "the doctors at the hospital assured me that there was no immediate risk. we can administer pain medication on the flight. when we arrive, of course, Dr. Hendricks & the medics at the facility will take it from there: get Freeman's shoulder fixed; check the boy's wrist."

"Dr. Stearns is unavailable, i suppose," says Grandpa. there is something in his voice. a knowing tone. an implication.

"Dr. Stearns is no longer with us," says Boutros.

"i know," says Grandpa. still that undercurrent of belligerence in his voice.

Boutros claps his hands together, softly. "well," he says. "i will be aft, for the voyage. if u need anything—painkillers, a drink, whatever—just press the button on ur armrest."

"have a good flight," says Grandpa, sarcastically, it seems to me.

Boutros turns on his heel & walks away & thru a door at the end of the cabin.

"what's happening?" i say to Grandpa.

he shakes his head. "it's not for me to say," he says. "i apologize." it sounds like he finds these words difficult, his mouth unused to them.

huh.

"it's not for u to say, or u don't want to?"

he smiles at me, a sad smile. "both," he says.

"Mother?" i say. but she doesn't answer. her eyes are closed. she's asleep, or pretending to be.

Grandpa sits back in his seat. i feel the plane begin to move, & we taxi for a moment, before the engines power up fully & the thrust pushes me back. it reminds me of when i first landed & the days afterward. that impression of being catapulted into the ground; into a bed; into a chair.

the plane rushes forward, & i rush backward, into my seat.

& then we're in the air—

i feel it, i feel it deep inside me, the sudden divorce from gravity, the leap up, the springing into another dimension, into weightlessness or near it—

i feel it with every atom in my body, every spinning particle orbiting around nothingness, feel the beauty of all the heavy material, the thick mantle of earth falling away, below us.

flight:

the noun for flying.

& the noun for fleeing.

we flee the earth, & my heart pounds with the joy of it. what's wrong with me? all i ever wanted was this place. the ranch. the feeling of the ground beneath my feet.

but when we take off, into the sky, my body sings with it.

24
coming down

we rise & rise, & my ears pop, again & again. i swallow, to clear them. Comet turns in circles, barking excitedly. he doesn't know what this is, this strange kind of motion, this lifting up. he runs over to Grandpa & jumps into his lap & twists there a moment, then jumps down again & runs over to me.

"it's ok, Comet," i say. i lower my hand & rub behind his ears.

he calms a little.

eventually we level out.

minutes pass.

more.

hours.

i close my eyes & i think i fall asleep.

when i wake, nothing has moved, & no one. like a slice of time has just been elided, like my sleep was a bracketed clause, & the sentence just goes on, full of commas, full of &s, never reaching any conclusion—& the plane moved, & they sat there, silent.

i watch my mother, her eyes closed. Grandpa looking out of the window, as if the clouds can tell him something.

then finally a period, & a new line:

.

my mother's eyes open. she winces.

"he said u could press the button in the seat arm for pain-killers," says Grandpa.

Mother nods. she pushes the button, & a moment later a guy in a black suit appears.

"drugs," she says.

"uh-huh," he says. he goes away & comes back with a plastic cup of water & some white pills. my mother knocks them back. the guy disappears.

Comet walks over to her & winds around her foot.

"hello, Comet," she says.

bark.

"hello, Mother," i say. "what's going on?"

she shakes her head.

great.

she squints at Grandpa. her eyes are clearer now, her eyelids drooping less. "after the fence, u should have got him out of there. taken him to the base." her tone is accusatory.

"the base isn't safe either, Marie," he says. "u know that. pro-testers all around. they'd c our car a mile off."

it's the first time i've heard that: Grandpa calling her Marie.

"the advantage of the base . . ." she sucks in air thru her teeth, adjusts her leg. ". . . is that it doesn't bring armed men to ur house. on the base, the armed men are on the perimeters. guarding it."

he doesn't say anything to that. he closes his eyes for a moment. "i'm sorry," he says, a little later.

she flicks this away with a hand.

pause.

"why are u here?" says my mother. "with us? why didn't u stay on ur precious ranch?"

he blinks, like it's a ridiculous question. "i'm here for Leo. i'm here for u."

she does that laugh that has been carved out, just empty bones, rattling. "first time for everything," she says.

i feel like i'm watching a vid in a foreign language, without subtitles. or like i have entered a room & missed the first part of the conversation, even tho i have been here all the time.

i close my eyes.

time passes.

after a while, Grandpa clears his throat, low & quiet.

"are u going to tell him, then?" he says, in an almost-whisper.

"not here," says Mother. "not now."

Grandpa shrugs. "soon he will know anyway."

silence.

the plane begins to descend, i feel it, it's a feeling a little like sadness. coming down. i think how those words convey loss, convey the end of a dream. coming down to earth. coming down with a bump.

Grandpa unbuckles his seat belt & goes over to the windows. he opens the blinds & the plane banks & i c snowy mountains below, glittering in the pale light of dawn. the plane lowers & lowers in the air & i realize we're circling, going round & round a high-up valley in the mountains. they stretch almost to the horizon, this range—i can c green trees, but a long way away.

i can't get out of my seat but i'm quite close to the window. i watch. there is a building of some kind at the top of the valley, a semisphere, rising from the snow, glassy it looks like. panels of translucent curving wall, a sort of biodome shape. below it is a landing strip, lit up by twinkling blue & red lights.

Mountain Dome, i presume.

"where is this place?" i say.

"Mountain Dome," says my mother.

"i guessed that."

Grandpa stirs in his seat. "it's a high-altitude, low-pressure training facility. i haven't been here since before the moon trip."

"oh." i think for a moment. hope for a moment. "we're training for something?" it's so obviously not the case, but sometimes it's nice to say something, to act like it might be true.

"i don't think so, Leo," says Grandpa sadly. the plane roars as it goes into a landing pattern. i hear the wheels deploy. "i think this is more of a permanent arrangement."

mother gives him a look but doesn't say anything.

the door opens & Boutros comes in. he puts a hand on my mother's headrest to steady himself. he looks at Grandpa & at Mother, her eyes more alert now. "u discussed the Constellation Mission yet?" he says. something in his tone tells me he already knows the answer. maybe he's had a camera on us this whole time.

actually, he has definitely had a camera on us this whole time.

"no," says my mother. "treatment first."

Grandpa gives her a look. i don't know what it means.

"fine," says Boutros. "i would like to be present, if that's all right with u."

my mother inclines her head. but it wasn't really a question.

"right," says Boutros. "seat belts on for landing please. we'll take u straight to medical."

we fasten our seat belts.

he goes away, thru the door.

in my head: *what is happening? what is happening? what is happening?* Comet poises, then pounces up onto my lap. he curls up. i scratch under his chin—he loves that. he growls quietly, a satisfied-but-still-a-little-frightened growl. a what-is-happening growl.

i know how he feels.

coming down.

wheels squealing.

coming down to earth.

air brakes flip up: thrown forward into seat belt, digging into my waist.

coming down with a bump.

25

the truth

the cold hits me like a wall when they carry me down the stairs & out of the plane, unlike anything i've felt before on Moon 2, where every temperature is controlled. this is like loneliness; like death; made into weather.

they put me into a wheelchair that is waiting. my mother too.

Comet walks alongside as they push us. i c him stumble a little, then regain his balance. he seems unsteady on his feet. disorientation from the flight, i assume.

we cross a snowy runway, Grandpa insisting on pushing my wheelchair, the scent of what i assume is pine somewhere, thinly, on the air. i am conscious of being at a great height—in the distance, i c hills, giving way to woody expanses, but they are a long way down. a mountain peak rises above, rock & ice lit by the rising sun.

the dome is huge ahead of us. a hill in its own right.

they push us across the runway & ahead, thru glass doors, into the dome. immediately, warm air embraces us. a vast atrium rises around us, curving into the distance, gangways & lights & scaffolding. there is a sense of much greater depth than we can c. in front of us is a semicircular wall, as high as the dome, which is maybe 100 ft. tall, with doors set into it.

Boutros walks up alongside us, his heels clicking on the concrete floor. one of the doors in front of us opens & we move toward it, then thru, & into a hallway. fluorescent lights are set in bars overhead.

to my surprise, Comet chooses to walk alongside my mother's wheelchair, behind me.

"hello, Comet," says my mother.

bark.

then he runs up & bounces along next to me, as the men push me. i reach down my hand & pat his head, & he yaps. to him this is some kind of adventure, i guess.

the hallway turns, once, twice, & we go thru a couple of doors, & then we're in what is clearly a medical bay. a man in a white shirt comes over. there are nurses too, & people at computers, & others pushing equipment around.

"Dr. Hendricks," he says, & reaches out his hand to shake mine, but Comet jumps up at him & barks.

"sorry," i say.

Dr. Hendricks smiles & the smile pulls his eyes in too; they crinkle at the corners. "no problem. he's cute," he says. he takes a step back. Comet sits back on his hind legs, looking up at him. "u must be Leo." he turns to my mother. "& u're Flight Officer Freeman."

"yes," says my mother the conversationalist.

Dr. Hendricks nods. "right." he lifts a screen. "i have Leo's x-rays here & his new injury is straightforward. so my registrar"— he indicates a guy in a turban standing close by—"will take care of a better cast for that, actually we just use a kind of special wristband, while we get u seen to, Flight Officer. ur shoulder has been reset as i understand it? but i'd like to give it a second look all the same."

"ok," says my mother.

they wheel her off & Dr. Hendricks follows. so does Boutros. they go thru a white door & out into some other hallway probably.

meanwhile the Dr. in the turban takes me & Grandpa & Comet to another room. he doesn't say much. he just puts a rod along my forearm & then bandages it up. then he puts on a long carbon fiber glove that goes over my thumb & covers most of my arm up to my elbow. he secures it with Velcro. "try not to move it too much," he tells me.

"that's it?" i say.

"that's it," he says. "no lateral movement. it'll heal itself, mostly. just needs to be immobile for a while. waterproof of course. tell us if u need more painkillers."

then he starts to walk out.

"wait," i say.

"yes?"

"what about moving around?"

he looks at me blankly.

"my leg, it's broken too. i was using crutches, but now . . ." i lift my injured wrist.

the Dr. scratches his chin. "u'll have to stay in the chair," he says.

"i have to have someone push me around? how long for?"

he does a side-to-side head wobble thing. "6 weeks?"

i think back to the base. how we couldn't ever really go anywhere. how trapped i had felt. & that was just a month.

"i'm not going to rely on other people pushing me for another 6 weeks," i say.

the Dr. is looking me in the eye. i c him soften. "i get it," he says. "we'll find u an electric chair."

"thanks," i say. & then he does leave.

Grandpa opens the door & pushes me back into the main medical hall. we c Boutros walking over to us. he puts up a hand in greeting when he gets close. Comet growls at him. Boutros's face registers a flicker of annoyance.

"ur mother will be done in an hour or so," he says. "we have state-of-the-art facilities up here. she'll need rest for a few days. but then she'll be fine."

"um," i say, "good."

"in the meantime, we have a comfortable room overlooking the glacier. u can wait there for her."

"ok," i say.

i notice that the men in black suits seem to have melted away. i didn't really c it happen. it's just me, Grandpa, & Boutros. & Comet, head cocked to 1 side, who is up on a chair next to a lab worker. the young woman with her hair in a net, standing over a microscope, looks at him with an amused expression. she sees Boutros turn to her, then lowers her head down to her work.

Comet barks, & she flicks her eyes over to him, trying to stifle a smile.

"come on, Comet," i say. "heel."

strange thing to say, when u're in a wheelchair, but he bounds over all the same & follows as Grandpa pushes me behind Boutros, who leads us thru another door to the 1 we came in thru & down a hallway until we reach a door that he opens with a keycard he takes from his pocket.

we go into a room on the outside of the dome. that is: it's in the outer section, so the wall to our left is just a sheet of glass from floor to ceiling. at the moment, the glass is black & electric lights shine brightly. the room itself is kind of pie-slice-shaped, which makes sense, i suppose, when u're in an enormous dome. there are sofas & armchairs & personal screens on tables & a big screen on the wall.

Boutros goes over to the wall & taps something on a small keypad there & the glass wall turns frosty, a kind of jeweled icy-opaque effect, then that dissolves & it's just clear glass. i take a breath. below, the glacier stretches out, racing away down the mountain, riven with cracks. it glows blue in the early-morning light. & below *that,* smaller mountains & then hills roll downward, lowering all the time, to an undulating brown wilderness, threaded with ribbons of river, that goes all the way to the horizon.

Comet barks like crazy, turning round & round. he goes over to the wall-window & looks out. he barks at the glacier loudly.

"impressive place, isn't it?" says Grandpa.

"yes," i say.

"a nice place for a visit. bit far away from the rest of the world tho." he looks at Boutros as he says this.

"hmm," says Boutros.

pause.

"of course, u can stay as long as u like, Mr. Freeman," says Boutros. "u are an honored guest here. an ex-astronaut such as urself. 1 of the last men on the moon."

Grandpa raises his eyebrows.

again i sense an unspoken conversation.

Boutros clears his throat & moves toward the door. "i'll bring ur mother to u soon," he says.

then he goes.

Grandpa rolls me over to the wall, so that i can look out more easily. i c a hawk—maybe even an eagle—circling far, far below. we must be 8,000, maybe 10,000 ft. up here. nearly at the peak of the mountain.

"what is this?" i say to Grandpa. "why are we here?"

he stands beside me. Comet stands between us, head high. we are all looking out at the snow & ice, the impossible drop. the far horizon. "wait for ur mother," he says.

"i want u to tell me."

he shakes his head slowly. "i'm just ur grandfather. we'll wait." his voice strains. like the words are hard to say, resisting the effort of his vocal cords to shake them from the air.

"u might not want to work with Kyle anymore," i say. a quick slick twist of bitterness on my tongue. i liked Kyle.

he frowns a question at me.

"i'm pretty sure he told them where to find me. the men with guns. maybe cut the fence for them. they mentioned his name."

"goddammit," says Grandpa.

i fall silent.

time passes.

the eagle circles.

the sun moves across the sky, making different parts of the glacier shine & shimmer as it passes.

finally, the door opens & Boutros comes in, pushing my mother ahead of him in her wheelchair, her arm now in a sling. he brings her alongside & we are all there, looking out.

Boutros turns my mother toward me. Grandpa turns my chair too.

"ur electric chair is on its way," says Boutros.

"thanks," i say.

silence.

my mother is not looking at the view. she is looking down at her hands.

"go on," says Grandpa.

she glares at him. then she takes a deep breath. she looks at me, then cuts her eyes down again. "it's time u knew the truth, Leo," she says. she pauses, as if expecting me to say something.

"yes," i say.

another breath. "17 years ago i was working as an astronaut already. i had just done 2 tours in space. i was 28. then the Company called me in for a meeting. they were more closely tied to the government in those days. but it was essentially the same organization as now. we all knew of course that the ultimate goal was to colonize space. i mean, there were teams around the world looking for earthlike planets. & every mission was going a little farther into the solar system."

pause.

"the water was running out already," says Grandpa. "the planet was warming up."

"yes," says my mother. "the problem was that, for generations, the scientists had been astronomers & physicists. they were interested in slingshotting around planets, that kind of thing. the mechanics of space travel. they didn't spend a lot of time thinking about the mechanics of reproduction."

something pings tinnily inside my mind.

she meets my eyes & sighs. "then it occurred to various people. what if we get to some other planet, & we terraform it, & all of that stuff, but we can't actually have babies."

jangling, now.

jangling.

i focus on the glacier. its white coldness. its smoothness.

"the Russians sent some geckos up, in a satellite," she says. "male & female. they all died."

pause, again.

"they wanted u to have a baby in space," i say, surprised to hear the words come out of my own mouth.

"yes," says my mother. "& not just me. there were 2 other women." she closes her eyes & rubs them for a second. "we would spend at least a year in orbit. on Moon 2. they used . . . um . . . IVF." another breath. "that was administered in space too, in 0 g. everything about reproduction had to be simulated as closely as possible. to c if it worked. implantation, pregnancy, birth."

i stare at her.

at the cold hard glacier behind her, flowing in geological time.

"i'm an experiment," i say. it comes out flat. words stripped of their music, false notes from a broken instrument.

"yes," she says.

this comes out with a twang, painful, jarring.

a string breaking.

26

Constellation Mission

i am thinking, all this time. mind racing. that's a cliché, of course. as if minds could race.

"the names," i say.

"what?" says my mother.

"Leo. Orion. Libra. all constellations." how could i have been so stupid? how could i have believed that the docs would miss my mother being pregnant before she flew up to the space station? i mean, how could i have been so naïve?

or maybe i just didn't want to believe.

"uh-huh," says my mother. "the Company picked the names. it was part of the thing . . . the mission. it was called the Constellation Mission. only i & Libra & Orion's mother became pregnant. & i took longer than her . . . as for the other woman . . . it never worked."

the air seems to wait around us, vibrating, every atom of oxygen & hydrogen a struck tuning fork.

"i'm a fucking experiment," i say. my voice doesn't sound like my voice.

"i wouldn't—" my mother starts.

"yes," says Grandpa.

Boutros clears his throat. "u have to understand, it was a different administration then, & there was a lot of pressure, with climate change &—"

"is that even legal?" i say, ignoring him.

Boutros makes a gesture that says, maybe not.

"& u," i say to my mother. "they ask u to do this, & u say yes, ok, i'll have a baby in space just to c if it's possible?"

she closes her eyes again. "i was loyal to the Company. i was loyal to my job."

Grandpa kneels next to my chair. "she didn't know it would be u," he says. "we didn't know u then. she didn't know how she'd feel when u came along."

"i don't think she feels anything," i say.

but a single tear is tracking soundlessly down her cheek.

i don't care.

i am the ice of that glacier, cracked, in the bare raw sunlight.

"did Virginia know? Lakshmi?" i say. pretty much everyone must have been in on it, i realize. everyone i know. even fucking Santiago, who i only saw on vid for, like, 2 minutes.

"yes," says Boutros.

simple. straightforward.

i think of them both, making us meals, teaching us, reading to us. & lying all the time.

i look down at Comet. "up here, Comet," i say, & click my fingers. he jumps up onto my lap. i lift him up, bury my face in his fur, the soft warmth of it. he squirms until i let him go to sit on me, then he licks my hand.

"& what am i doing here?" i say. "in the dome?"

Boutros takes a step forward. "there is . . . a media problem. Dr. Stearns was . . . uncomfortable about ur . . . physical status, when u came down. u & the twins. he wasn't happy about letting u go. but others . . . other board members wanted to c how u would accommodate to ordinary life on earth."

"others including u," i say.

he doesn't answer, which is an answer.

"anyway," he says. "now Dr. Stearns has left us & is talking to the media about the experiment. the people who authorized it are no longer with the Company but . . . we decided to move the 3 of u here."

"Libra & Orion are here?"

tiny pause. "yes."

"so u brought us up here to hide us away," i say. "so u can sweep the whole thing under the rug. wait for the news to move on to the next scandal."

"not exactly," says Boutros.

pause.

"tell him," says Grandpa.

Boutros blows out air thru his nose. "u're all . . . that is . . . ur physiologies are adapted to space. in that respect the . . . um . . . experiment as u call it . . . was a staggering success. but on earth . . . ur lung capacities . . . ur bone densities . . . it all developed in 0 g. u are better than the others but the doctors when u broke ur leg . . . they were surprised it was the first bone u had fractured. theoretically u could bump into something & crack a bone."

"oh," i say.

"u're better off than the other 2," he says again. there's a tension in his voice. "they have . . . not fared so well. but all of u . . . u're all having to wear eyewear to protect ur corneas." he points to my sunglasses. i had forgotten about them. they have become second nature now. "ur tendons, ur joints . . . none of it is built for 1 g. none of it is built for strain. for impact."

"so . . ."

"so we brought u here. Dr. Hendricks is of the opinion that the lower pressure, the higher altitude . . . it might be beneficial. in the long term."

"in the long term, like . . . living here?"

he nods.

"but what about school? jobs?"

Boutros makes a face. "let's cross that bridge when we come to it. the people who dreamed up this idea . . . they didn't think very far ahead. no one really envisioned this scenario."

"what, no one thought we'd still be alive?"

it's a deliberately provocative question but he considers it. "maybe. i'd like to be clear, i would not have approved Constellation Mission if it was mooted when i was in charge. it predates my employment."

"that's a real comfort," i say.

he has the grace to wince.

then i think about an intonation, a weird tonal pattern in his earlier sentence, about crossing bridges. "we're not going to live for very long, are we?" i say.

he looks away. "i can't say," he says.

wow.

silence.

"how long?" i say.

"no one knows," says Grandpa. "but ur . . . skeleton isn't going to get any better adapted. ur heart either."

oh my god.

i was an experiment, & now i'm dying here. like a fish, flipping on the shore, uselessly.

no one says anything for what feels like a long time.

"so," says Boutros. "what do u want to happen now?"

i laugh at this, on the inside anyway. as if i can make anything happen that i want. as if i'm in control of anything. i look at my mother & suddenly i don't want to be looking at her, maybe ever again. "i want u to go away, Mother," i say. "just . . . go."

"but—" she begins.

Grandpa puts a hand up to her. "let's go," he says.

"yes, u too," i say to him.

he kind of inclines his head at this, but takes Mother's wheel-chair & starts pushing her toward the door. Comet follows them for a moment, shadowing my mother's wheelchair, & Grandpa looks down at him & says, "no, Comet; stay with Leo." Comet turns in confusion, then trots back to me. i lower my hand & stroke his head. he makes a sad little whine.

Grandpa keeps pushing my mother toward the door. partway there he stops & turns. "i want u to know," he says, "i opposed this, in the beginning. but when u came . . . u were the greatest gift. the greatest of my life. i want u to know that." then he turns & walks away, taking my mother with him. the door soft-closes behind them, with a *shhh*.

i turn to Boutros.

"u want me to leave u alone?" he says.

"no," i say. "i want u to take me to Libra & Orion."

he straightens. "all right," he says. "i thought that might . . . i thought u might want to. u should, um, prepare urself."

"how?"

he doesn't answer.

he takes the handles of my wheelchair & pushes me thru the same door my mother & grandpa went thru, then down a succession of hallways.

we come to a door that he opens with his card & then we are in a long, narrow room that is darker toward the end, with a glow coming from some kind of tent. he wheels me forward. we're back in the medical bay, i realize. there are plug sockets along the walls for medical devices & beds, tho they're empty, & rails for curtains that aren't there.

just that glow from the end of the room.

we keep moving.

i c an old lady in front of us, leaning on a walker.

we get closer.

we get closer still.

it's Libra.

she is clinging on to this structure on wheels that is holding her up & attached to it is an oxygen tank with a tube leading to a mask that hangs around her neck. she is as pale as the moon & i can c her bones thru her skin.

i stare at her, mouth open.

"hi, Leo," she says. "u look good."

"u . . . ," i stammer.

"i know," she says. "i look smoking, don't i?" she tries a smile; the effect is ghastly. she coughs & bends over her walker. then she lifts her head again.

"what happened?"

she shrugs, or gives an impression of 1. "gravity," she says.

i take in the blank walls. the empty beds. the glowing tent that i somehow don't quite want to look at. "what are u doing in here?" i say.

"visiting my brother," she says. her voice is raspy. dry. the voice of paper. of papyrus.

i am looking past her now, & i c that what i thought was a tent *is* in fact some kind of tent, erected over a bed. i point & gesture to show that i want to approach & Boutros rolls me a little closer & i look thru the puffed-out plastic material, like an inflated wall, a transparent bouncy castle, & on the bed inside is a body, lying, the chest rising & falling very slightly, very gently. wires & drips run into the body's arms.

Boutros rolls me on.

the head turns.

Orion opens his eyes & looks at me.

his cheeks are sunken. his eye sockets are black bruises; collapsed stars.

"oh my god," i say. "oh my god, Orion."

i lean back, in my wheelchair.

i feel dizzy.

so dizzy.

& the world falls away below me, & i'm floating in darkness again, where i was born.

26.1
later

i lie in bed.
    i feel like i'm losing my mind.
    i cry my eyes out.
    i cry myself blind.

26.2
even later

funny, how we fall back on clichés when things go wrong.

all these things we say that can't possibly ever be real.

as if u could really lose ur mind.

if only.

as if u could really cry ur eyes out.

as if tears could stop u from seeing what's in front of u, what's real.

interlude

1 of me falls, & dies, & a new me rises in his stead.
i am a tree, i am a mushroom, i replace myself.
i am not who i thought i was.
but maybe that's not true.
maybe i always knew.
maybe i just didn't want to know.

P^RT 3
moon

1

Eden

"this way," says Libra.

we're walking Comet, a few days later. we're both in electric wheelchairs, with little stick remote controls like the ones that manipulate the robot arm on the space station. we're also on our way to c Orion, who has his own room now. i don't know where Grandpa & my mother are.

Comet meanders along beside us, slower than usual to accommodate our pace in our chairs, sniffing at fire extinguishers & water fountains as we go.

"Comet, jump," i say. he turns at the sound of my voice, almost smiles. then he jumps up, & his nose touches my outstretched hand. "good boy," i say. i take a doggy treat from the bag on my lap & throw it to him—he catches it in his mouth. that's 1 advantage of being the virtually imprisoned subjects of an unethical scientific experiment: u ask for something, like doggy treats, & u get it.

"where is it we're going?" i say to Libra.

"u'll c," she says.

we cross a wide hallway & turn a corner, then Libra waves her pass at a scanner next to a door in front of us. with a *shhh,* it slides open, & we drive thru & into—

a garden.

& not just a garden: we're on a kind of viewing platform with a walkway that slopes down into a vast, circular, tropical rain forest, landscaped—with small hills & a waterfall & a bridge—& moving, with colorful birds flitting between the branches, butterflies hovering in front of us. Comet leaps at them, jaws spanning, ineffectual. it's warm too, & humid—i can c a thin mist in the air, & even as we sit there, small jets in the walls fire steam into the room. enormous lamps hang from sections of truss along the curving glass that is both walls & roof. some of them are lit, but there is daylight flooding in too.

it's the central section of the dome, i realize—it must be the length of a football field or more in each direction, & the glass ceiling is maybe 10 stories above us. crazy i didn't even know it was here: i was so focused on the experiment, on what i'd learned, that i didn't think about the layout of the base. some of the trees are taller than houses. 1 side of the dome faces right onto the glacier; the other side is abbreviated by a wall, & that's the side we entered from—the offices & rooms of the building.

Comet sits down beside us. he is panting, his breath coming heavy & labored.

"wow," i say.

"yeah," says Libra. "welcome to another of their experiments."

i look around. "into . . . ?"

"creating Eden."

i watch a monkey scale a tree trunk, then jump smoothly to another tree. "as in . . . ?"

"as in perfecting biodomes for construction on earthlike planets."

"ah," i say. "i c."

"slightly simpler from an ethical point of view than making children in space, of course," she says.

i smile. a pained smile.

"u really never suspected?" she says.

"no. but u did?"

"well, Orion did, at first. we never really believed it tho. until . . . well, until it turned out to be true."

i shake my head. "how did u not . . . lose it? break stuff?"

"u're assuming i didn't."

"i know u didn't."

"ok, i didn't. only"—she looks around—"i don't like it, but i'm glad i'm alive. can u understand that?"

"yes," i say. because i can. even if i don't feel it, not yet anyway.

she turns her chair & starts descending the ramp. i follow her, & Comet follows both of us. when we reach the bottom, i c that a path runs all the way round the outside of the garden—little tributary paths snaking off into the undergrowth. bright flowers bloom in every corner of the rich, dark soil.

Libra drives to the edge, where the path gives way to vegetation, & stops. i look for Comet, & realize he's still on the slope—he notices me looking & speeds up, still breathing hard. he sits down again when he reaches us.

Libra locks her chair & slowly pushes herself up & into a standing position. she doesn't have any broken limbs & is able to move under her own power for short times—gravity has mostly affected her core strength & her muscular system, as well as the density of her bones; her body finds it difficult to get the oxygen it needs to sustain prolonged activity in 1 g.

that's why there's an oxygen tank strapped to her wheelchair, tho she hasn't had to use it yet since we left her room.

she slowly bends down & touches the soil, lifts it, lets it fall thru her fingers. i think of her in the small hydroponic suite on the space station; think how marvelous this must seem to her, even with her physical weakness. she points to a small, unremarkable leafy plant.

"that's the 1 i brought down from space," she says. "remember?"

"uh-huh," i say. "a piece of there. to bring down here."

"yep, & now it's in their weird Eden project. as am i. seems fitting, doesn't it?"

"yeah," i say. still Mr. Monosyllable apparently.

now she indicates another plant with a long, elaborate, delicate flower. "i planted that orchid," she says.

"really?" it's tall—a foot maybe.

"yes."

"um, how long have u been here?"

she brushes 1 of the leaves with her hand. "almost since the beginning," she says. "we got sick very quickly."

"what happened?"

"fainting. falls. that kind of thing. Mom didn't seem very surprised. then . . . then Orion bumped into a table & broke his leg. we went to the hospital & he was ok to start with & then . . . he just went out, like a lightbulb, & they had to resuscitate him & . . . well, anyway. it was awful. he had lots of tests. they kept him overnight. then . . ."

pause.

"the next day, we went to c him. he was on IV fluids, oxygen, everything. they'd operated on his leg but they said his lungs were in danger of collapse. i . . . i've never liked . . . hospitals anyway. blood. i fainted—hit my head on the floor."

"ow," i say.

"yes. when i woke up i was in a hospital bed too. a different room, on my own, just a window & a bedside table with nothing on it. i freaked out. then a Dr. came in. they'd taken blood & i had a dangerously low red cell count, she said, liver function warning signs . . . a bunch of stuff. i passed out again. when i woke up . . . Mom was there. she said they wanted to do tests. that they thought it might be cancer."

"Jesus."

"it's not," she says hurriedly. she walks back to her chair & lowers herself into it. her breathing is shallow & fast. she lifts the cup end of the tube leading to her oxygen tank & takes a hissing hit. she breathes a little easier. "my mom leaned in close & said, *it's just gravity, i'll fix this, don't worry.* then she went away."

"& called Boutros."

"i guess. i guess. the nurses brought me a screen so i could watch stuff. i saw Dr. Stearns on the news, talking about something terrible the Company had done, but i didn't catch enough of it to add 2 & 2, not then anyway. the next day, Mom came back & suddenly none of the usual doctors & nurses were around but Boutros was, & others. & they brought us here. in a private jet. Dr. Hendricks had a bed for Orion."

i think of how Dr. Kohli wasn't there the second time we went to the hospital. "they took over."

she nods.

"men in black suits?"

she nods again.

"they're pretty powerful, huh?" i say.

"yes."

"& now what? what happens now?"

"what do u mean?" she says.

"to us. what happens to us?"

she shrugs. "the doctors are not sure. this has never happened before, so there's no data. it's possible we might . . . get stronger. they've increased our vitamin D & A dosages, calcium, potassium. but it's possible we might not. it's possible we might get worse."

silence.

"i didn't mean that," i say. "i meant, what do we *do*?"

"oh." she leans back in her chair. "we stay here. it's not so bad. there's the garden." she looks at it, at the trees towering above, & i c real love in her eyes. of course she loves this place, this part of it, at least. Comet snores next to us. napping. it must be the heat. "they're going to get me a tutor. i'll take the SATs. maybe even study to be a botanist."

"& then what?"

she looks at me. "what?"

"when u're a botanist. if we say u are, 1 day. then what?"

"then i work in the garden. do experiments, maybe i even get strong enough to leave. study other places."

i shake my head.

i can't stay here. i can't do it. i look at the dome around me, the mountain. the oppressive closeness of everything. gravity always there, an unseen enemy, grasping, reaching up with its hands, like the denizens of hell in those old paintings, clawed fingers pushing up thru the earth, trying to yank everyone down with them. i can't live down here. i feel close to panic. the world should be something far below me, curving, viewed thru a window, & i should be in orbit, spinning.

if i stay here, i won't really be alive. i will be a person existing entirely in the present, a person living in the country of now, & tomorrow will be something i don't understand & can't stand, & i will only ever want to escape today. to be slingshotted again, thru the blackness, thru the space between the earth & the stars.

i don't know how to say a single atom of that to Libra.

"b-b-but . . . ," i stammer instead. "the gravity, the weight, how can u stand it?"

she grimaces. "i'm getting used to it."

"not me," i say.

she shrugs.

"but . . . ," i start, then stop. i take a breath. "but . . . how can u stay here with these *people*?"

"what people?"

"the people who *made* us. Boutros."

"it's not them," she says.

"it's . . . ?"

"it wasn't their idea," she says. "it was 16 years ago. everyone has changed. it was an experiment that failed. we're all sick. but they're not just abandoning us. they're trying their best."

"by imprisoning us here."

"it's for the altitude," she says. "the pressure."

"hmm," i say. it's not like the pressure variation is dramatic, & if anything the oxygen saturation levels are lower here at altitude. tho i guess it's true that there may be fractionally less strain on our skeletons.

pause.

"& ur mom?" i say. "where is she?"

"i don't know."

"u don't know?"

"no."

"u didn't want her here?"

our eyes meet. she says yes with hers.

silence.

"tho i don't think she liked it anyway," she says eventually. "i mean, seeing Orion like that. me."

sadness fills me—like filling a balloon with something heavier than air, with nitrogen, seeing it fall. i think of how jealous i always was of their relationship with their mother. of their hug outside the base. now they're here, & their mother is not.

"sorry," i say.

"not ur fault," says Libra.

she starts her wheelchair, & i prod Comet with my foot. he wakes with a snuffle & stands unsteadily, then follows us around the wide curve of the path.

"Orion's room is this way," she says. "he's always there. at least when he's not in the oxygen tent or having a transfusion."

2

oxygen

we quarter-circle the garden, sticking to the side where the wall is, the glacier over to our left.

Libra opens a door with her card & we go thru. she's ahead of me—2 wheelchairs don't fit thru a door at the same time. "come on, Comet," i say, because he is dawdling behind us. Libra waves her card at the sensor to make sure that the door stays open for him.

we go down the hallway &—after knocking, which is less easy from a wheelchair than it sounds—into Orion's room, which is at the end farthest from the entrance, its high glass wall facing the cliff side, scree & stone, every shade of gray, dotted with snow. it's a generous-size room, chairs by the glass side, a low table with old-fashioned printed books & magazines on it, a chest of drawers against 1 of the concrete walls, a lamp by the bed.

the bed is angled to the glass side too, so Orion can c out.

he has a remote control in his hand that i guess operates the bed. it's raised almost into a seat, & he is sitting in it, a screen in his other hand, which he lowers as we enter & he turns to us. he takes off heavy, high-quality headphones. his handsome face is gray, thin, as if someone has suctioned some of what makes him him out of it.

he is wearing pajamas & a bathrobe. he wears a mask that connects, via a tube, to the wall. there's a row of sockets next to where the 2 meet, & a little sign reading OXYGEN & a lever switch below it that says ← OFF & → ON.

the chairs are in the way but Libra shunts them aside & we drive round so that we're all huddled together, like the worst sports team in history, in any sport.

light from outside floods the room, hard & mineral as the rocks. i'm glad i have my sunglasses on & i wonder why Orion doesn't darken the glass, but then i remember: he's Orion.

"hey, Leo," says Orion.

"hey, Orion," i say.

pause.

"sorry about ur mom," i say.

"sorry about urs."

"uh-huh."

silence.

"well, this sucks ass, doesn't it?" says Orion.

& i laugh & Libra laughs & it's like no time has passed.

"i tried to vid u both," i say. "lots of times. never worked."

Orion nods. "we tried to call u too," he says. "the Company was blocking it."

"they didn't want u to know how sick we were, i guess," says Libra. "maybe they thought u might . . . make it. in the real world."

silence for a moment.

"well, i'm glad we're together again," i say.

"us too," they say together, in that way they sometimes do.

"who's the dog?" says Orion as Comet turns in circles.

i pat my lap, & Comet jumps up & then kind of collapses onto his side, tongue lolling.

"Comet," i say. "usually he's a lot more bouncy than this."

Orion nods. "me too."

this time we don't laugh.

pause.

"i saw real snow," i say, thinking of our game on the station. "falling from the sky, i mean. i caught a flake on my tongue. i shot someone. it's a long story. i ate bacon. oh my god, did u guys eat bacon?"

"like, a metric ton of it," says Orion.

"what else?" i say. "did u do any of ur 3 things?"

"i swam in a lake," says Libra. "that's about it."

i turn to Orion. "u? did u run in the rain? did u go to a concert hall & hear Jason Mukherjee play Bach's Well Tempered Clavier?"

"no," says Orion. "i saw birds flying tho. i had a bath. i threw a ball against a wall."

i nod.

"i'm . . ." i don't really know what to say. "i'm sorry. about u being sick."

he waves a hand dismissively. "i don't know if i'd even call it that. i'm not sick. i'm just not made for this place."

that hangs in the air a moment, silvery, almost chiming. none of us are made for this place.

"so . . . what happens to u?" i say. "i mean, next."

"i don't know," he says. "they keep giving me blood, iron infusions, oxygen, vitamins. it's all meant to make me stronger. & some days i do feel stronger. but . . . i don't know what the end game is. do u?"

"no," i say.

"so i listen to my music," he says. "& i look at the snow & sometimes i go to the hospital bay & sometimes they take me to the other side so i can c the glacier & the land below. it makes me feel a bit like i'm at home. looking down. u know?"

that hangs too. shimmering, ringing on the air, a memory of a note.

home.

"ur dog doesn't seem to have much energy, for a young dog," says Orion. he is frowning at Comet.

i look down.

i c Comet's chest rising & falling, rapidly, his tongue still hanging out. i raise my hand & put it on his side & feel his heart beating skippety skip, fast & light, like fingers nervously drumming.

i think of his slowness, down the slope.

i think of his panting.

"oh no," i say. "NO."

2.1

i unroll my screen & call Grandpa.

i haven't spoken to him since i learned, since i heard, since i knew, since i don't know what the word is for when u find out u are a human petri dish & everyone u love is a liar.

but i don't know what else to do.

3
goodbye

i wake up, but i don't get up.

there's no reason to get up.

Comet lies at my feet, curled over my toes. i'm in a room just down the hallway from Libra's & Orion's. it faces the mountainside too. it's like they thought that if we had a wider view, a view of all that land falling to the horizon, it might hurt us, all the distance that we can't go out into. maybe they're right.

Comet has altitude sickness. Grandpa came & helped take him to the medical bay.

i didn't know dogs could get altitude sickness, but apparently they can. the good news is that he's not dying, or anything like that. the bad news is that he isn't up to doing very much. he spends most of his time lying at the bottom of the bed, looking miserable. his ears still prick up when i tickle behind them tho, when i stroke them.

apparently altitude sickness doesn't get better either. that is: most people who have it, they just have it. there isn't really much they can do about it. there's a drug but a lot of people get bad side effects. they find out when they trek to Everest base camp or what have u. that's what the doctors told me. & basically then some just have to go back down—it's something u're either born with or not.

the same is presumably true of dogs.

which means as long as he's here with me, Comet is condemned to feel dizzy. nauseous.

i don't like that thought.

but i don't like the thought of being without Comet either. & anyway, where is he going to go?

(to the ranch, i answer myself. to the ranch.)

most of the time i watch movies on my screen. the screens here have their connectivity limited too, even tho we know why now. i don't think they want us watching news stories. there's a lot that might upset us, apparently. as if being in this place is not upsetting enough.

it's a little like being back on the space station, i suppose. cut off from the world. in it but not of it. looking thru glass, at things we can't touch.

only, on the station, while we were limited in scope & scale & the ability to go outside because outside would kill us in a heartbeat, we were free in every plane. we could float up & down & to the sides & our world was a sphere all around us.

the earth, meanwhile, looks like a sphere from above, but when u're on it it's just 1 plane, the 1 below u, the 1 that sucks at u, anchoring u to the ground.

it is a place of endless down.

& now we're trapped here, having been born as part of an experiment that no one today thinks should have happened, but no one really knows what to do about since it has. & our mothers chose to have us as some kind of employment contract not because they wanted to be mothers, & basically no one wants us, really.

these are the cheerful thoughts i fill my day with.

sometimes i go to the garden with Libra. i find that even with my wrist brace i can use crutches a little, pivot my weight about the axis of their handles, walk for short distances without putting too much strain on my broken leg.

sometimes i watch vids with Orion. or we listen to audiobooks. there is 1 about a Stradivarius violin & the different people who owned it over the centuries, which Orion likes.

we sit together, on his bed. closer than i mostly wanted to get, on Moon 2, after we hugged on his & Libra's birthday & our bodies got weird with each other, magnets turned to push each other away.

it's something i would have panicked about, back then. the proximity of his body. his arm, next to mine, his hand near enough to touch.

here at Mountain Dome it doesn't feel like that, doesn't affect me in the same way, because of his frailty. because of his sickness.

right now, tho, i'm lying on my own with Comet, not wanting to get up.

then there's a knock on the door.

"come in," i say.

the door opens & Grandpa enters. his hair looks a little grayer than the last time i saw him, tho it's barely been a week. he seems to have acquired new lines in his face, like there are harsh winds that only he can feel. maybe it's just my imagination. he walks over to my bedside & sits down, doesn't wait for an invitation.

"hi," he says.

"hi."

he sighs. "ur mother."

"what about her?"

he rubs at his stubble. another new thing: he was always clean-shaven before. "she didn't mean to hurt u, u know," he says.

"well, of course not," i say coldly. "she didn't know me. when she decided to be part of the experiment, i didn't exist. i was just supposed to be a scientific outcome."

"ok."

"she didn't mean to hurt me. but she didn't want me, did she? i mean, not really."

he touches my hand briefly. "first," he says. "i don't know how much choice she had. u didn't belong to her, she wasn't allowed to . . . mother u. not really. second. ur mother. she . . . she's different. u must know that. she doesn't . . . experience things in the same way as u & me. but that doesn't mean she doesn't care about u."

silence, on my part.

outside the glass, the shadow of a cloud moves over the mountainside before us.

"ur mother loves u," he says. "in her way. & i love u. when u came along . . . when i saw u, on the screen, from down on the ranch . . . u know i saw u when u were 1 hour old? they held u up to the camera. i felt my heart lurch, like u put it into a new rhythm."

pause.

"i knew what she was doing. i didn't like it. we fell out & she left & went to Nevada & then up there to the station. but when u arrived . . . u were the best thing. the best thing. & i have loved u since the moment i saw ur little face, ur hands, opening & closing like stars. u were small enough that when ur mother held u in her arms, u almost disappeared. a conjuring trick."

pause.

"& all i wanted, for nearly 16 years, was to meet u."

i don't say anything. still. there is a tear on my cheek & i wipe it away.

"& then i did, & u were even more amazing than i imagined. stronger. braver."

"not so strong now," i say.

"oh, i don't know," he says.

pause.

"u know i wasn't the best dad to ur mother either," he says, after a while. "i was always working. always at the base. or in space. on a mission. remind u of anyone? & when i was home . . . i was stressed. angry. some people . . . some men . . . i don't know. it takes our testosterone a few decades to calm down."

i think of him testing me. challenging me. leaving me on that fence. i imagine it x 5, x 10, x whatever factor it must have been when he was younger, when he hadn't had time to mellow.

huh.

"well," he says. "i didn't come to chat. not just, anyway." he reaches out a hand & pets Comet. Comet lifts his head & rumbles a little & curls up tighter.

"what else did u come for then?" i say.

"ur mother's here."

"here where?" i ask. i look around me.

"here, as in outside the room," he says. "waiting to come in. if u will let her."

"i don't have anything to say to her," i say.

"i figured as much," says Grandpa. "but she has something to say to u."

he stands there just looking at me until i say, "ok, fine." then he goes over to the door & opens it, & my mother comes in.

mother.

even the word now seems like some kind of cruel joke.

she's beautiful, as always, beautiful & empty.

like where i grew up.

like most of the universe.

"hello, Mother," i say, ironic.

"hello, Leo," she says. because she doesn't do irony.

4
go

my mother walks over to the bed & stands next to it, not looking at me, but instead out, onto the snow & rocks.

Comet yaps with joy, at least as close to it as he can manage, when he sees her & lifts his muzzle to her, & she reaches down & pats him. he licks her hand.

"i would say i was sorry," she says. still not looking at me. "but i don't think it would adequately cover it."

"no," i say.

"but i am," she says. "sorry. i . . . i didn't mean for any of this to happen. they asked me to do something. it was an honor, i thought. a mission. i didn't think . . . i didn't think past the birth. what it would mean. having a real person."

"like me."

"yes, like u."

pause.

"i . . . i am very proud of u," she says.

i stare at her, surprised.

"i am," she says. she meets my eyes & then looks away. "the space walk. ur math. ur physics. u are . . . u are a lot like me, when i was younger."

huh.

i don't know if that's a good thing to be.

she sees that in my eyes, that thought, & looks down, her

eyelashes fine, sweeping her cheeks. on another person her features would be delicate. but delicate is not a word you'd associate with my mother.

i sit up a little straighter in the bed. i want to seem strong. capable. "if u think i'm just going to be ok with this because we've had some kind of mother & son bonding session, then u're wrong," i say. "we're not going to be playing happy families."

"no," says mother. "i c that."

pause.

"so what, then?" i say. because i can tell she's there for something.

"i'm going to go back to the ranch," she says. "i've talked to ur grandfather about it. someone needs to fix the fence. look after the cattle. ur grandpa could go . . . but of the 2 of us, he's the 1 who's . . . who's better staying here. with u. i mean . . . he knows how to . . . how to be with u. look after u. better than i do."

there's a sadness in her eyes that i have never seen before & i wish that i could tell her that none of this is true, that she's my mother, she's the 1 who should be with me, but that would be a lie.

& we both know it.

so instead i say, "oh."

it hangs there in the air, a small sound, a fractional sentence.

"but," says Grandpa. i kind of forgot he was there. he steps forward.

"yes, but," says Mother, suddenly brisk & business again. "i've spoken to the doctors & to ur grandfather. & i thought i could help with something. maybe."

"help with what?"

she reaches forward & strokes Comet again. "i thought i could take him. Comet. back down to the ranch."

a pause in which the mountain rises from the ground, trailing tree roots & crumbling earth & rocks, snow dusting into the air, creaking & groaning with epochal, earth-shaking sounds that vibrate thru us, send all the lights crashing down from the ceilings, as we lift into the sky, birds cawing & wheeling away from this landmass taking into the air, the peak breaking thru clouds.

& then crashes down again, & is in the same place, birds settled on their stones & branches, as if the mountain never moved at all.

"no," i say.

Grandpa puts a hand on my shoulder. "Dr. Hendricks says the altitude sickness is most likely not going to improve," he says. "it's cruel to keep him here."

"i know but—"

"Leo," says my mother softly. surprisingly softly.

i turn to her.

she moves her hand toward the bed. Comet struggles his head up again & nuzzles it.

"he likes me," she says. "u must have noticed that."

i have. i have noticed that.

"yes," i say.

"i promise i'll keep him safe," she says. "he knows the ranch. his mother is still there. i'll take him for walks. keep training him, like Grandpa says u've been doing."

i notice she's calling him Grandpa now.

"& we can vid call," she continues. "u'll c him all the time, & 1 day u'll come down from here & he'll still be ur dog. this will just be like . . . dog-sitting. temporary."

i look at Comet. feel his warmth on my legs. the coiled energy of him. he is a spring disguised as a living being. i remember him jumping up at the man who broke into the house. running ahead of me, his paws hardly seeming to hit the ground, as if he were something liquid flowing across it. i remember when i first felt his heart beating thru him, drumming his rhythm thru his little body.

i sigh.

"ok ok ok," i say. "i get it. he's sick. he can't live here."

"it's for the best, Leo," says my mother.

"u don't get to say that," i say, a little petulantly. "that's for me to decide. but yes, i think he should go down. i don't want him to suffer."

she nods. "i'll leave as soon as i can arrange things with Boutros. & ur grandfather. u'll want a bit of time to say goodbye, of course."

"no," i say.

"sorry?"

"no," i say again. "take him now. just do it. just take him now."

i turn away from her, so she can't c me crying.

"what about . . . i mean, u were training him, weren't u? i don't want to get it wrong, to . . ."

"it's easy," i say. "sit, heel, stay. a puppy could learn it. u'll pick it up."

my voice comes out too sharp. she takes a tiny step back.

i ignore her.

i lean forward, lean my face down toward Comet & press it into his fur. he makes a little growl deep inside, resonating inside the chamber of his chest. i hug him tight.

"goodbye, Comet," i say.

bark.

then i lift him, & hand him to my mother, into her arms. she cradles him like a baby, & i get a flash of her holding me as a baby, my grandpa seeing me over the vid screen, as she floats in 0 g, & i can't imagine it ever happened & yet at the same time it did. it did happen.

i turn to the snow & the rocks, & i feel like my hot salt tears would melt them away if they touched them, to nothingness.

"go," i say.

5

what a planet feels like when the small thing orbiting it, always there, is suddenly gone

i am untethered.

unmoored.

an object in space with nothing to orient me, nothing to tell me which way to spin, & why. things lose their gravity; the center fails. everything is edges & outsides.

i don't c Grandpa for a few days. i guess he is with my mother, making preparations. maybe he even goes with her, to the ranch, to help get her set up, & then flies back. i don't know & i don't ask. we're not really in a position to know things about the outside world, here.

i pass the time, when i'm not watching vids or reading books, with Libra & Orion. right now we are in the garden. it's night, & the great dome that covers most of the room—until it ends at the wall leading to the hallway—has dissolved into the darkness, the glass liquefying into black, pinpricked with stars. it is as if we are beneath the canopy of the heavens—earth's counterpart rises above us; something for us to aspire to.

for me to aspire to.

Libra is pruning something or taking a cutting or something. i was not really listening when she explained. she is standing with small shears by a plant, bending over it. even tho i'm missing Comet, now that i'm over the shock of seeing Libra &

Orion so sick, it's good to be with them again. they're my family, i realize.

Orion is in a chair with an oxygen mask strapped to his face. he is conducting with his hands, but gently, very gently. from hidden speakers in the walls, Vivaldi is playing.

we don't lack for luxuries. only freedom.

he pushes his mask aside for a moment. "i'm not a fan of the romantics," he says, "but in the present context it seems appropriate. the garden."

he covers his mouth again, takes a deep breath.

Libra will have to return to her chair soon. she can't manage standing for too long. i meanwhile am on my crutches. it is as if we are on an EVA from the world itself. reliant on oxygen to support us. devices made of metal & plastic, to which we are tied.

i am not on oxygen yet. but it's only a matter of time, i imagine.

Libra snips a leaf & it flutters to the ground. around us, moths or butterflies fly, clumsy & soft.

"what are we going to do?" i say.

Libra turns to me. "what do u mean?"

i make a gesture that takes in the garden, the dome, all of it. "this. our lives. what are we going to do with them?"

"well, it doesn't seem like we have much choice, does it?" says Libra. she returns to her chair & sits. sweat is beading on her forehead. i can smell the intensity of flowers, all around us. a smell that is made of night colors: velvet in texture. "we're staying here."

"till when?"

Orion moves his mask. "till we die."

i shake my head.

"what are u shaking ur head for?" says Libra.

"what do u think?"

"u have some other idea of what we should be doing, i suppose," she says. "u have some kind of dream." she throws the shears & they disappear in the undergrowth, in the darkness beyond 1 of the round lights at our feet.

i shrug. "everyone has dreams."

Orion shakes his head now, lifts his mask. "i don't think ur mother dreams."

i smile. then i picture her, on the field in front of the house, shouting to Comet as he moves fleet over the earth, over the clumps of grass. "i don't know," i say. "she's revealing unexpected dimensions."

Orion nods slowly. his hands are still moving to the time signature of the music.

clouds move, & the moon appears above us, bright & shining. Libra indicates a point just off to our right. "night-flowering jasmine," she says. "c?"

i do c. little flowers, white, stars in the bushes near us, fallen from the sky.

fallen.

pause.

"what do u want to do then?" says Libra to me.

"isn't it obvious?" i say. my heart tap tap taps in my chest.

she looks at me, as if to say, *no*.

i point up. past the dome. at the vault of light-splattered dark, the endless night sky. "i want to go back up there," i say.

Libra opens her mouth, then shuts it again.

Orion presses the joystick on the left arm of his chair, & it whirs as it turns to face me. he withdraws his mask. clear plastic, a tube running into it—secured by a green rubber strap that circles his head. the hiss of oxygen. "why?" he says.

i didn't know i was going to say it till i said it. but still. it *is* obvious.

"because it's home," i say.

he is breathing shallowly. "no. it's space. it's empty. hostile."

"& the place i grew up. where we grew up."

he frowns. "& . . . what? u'd just stay up there forever?"

"i guess," i say, having given it precisely no thought until this moment.

"they'd never let u," he says. "u're not an astronaut. u're a kid. an experiment."

"i know 0 g better than any of those astronauts," i say. "better than Soto. better than my own mother."

"yes," says Libra. "but u don't know how to pilot a rocket. they only send qualified people up. pilot & copilot. people who know what they're doing."

Orion removes his mask again. a bit of color has returned to his ashen face. "anyway, u'd be stuck there," he says. "all we ever wanted was to come down."

"maybe," i say. "or maybe that was what everyone always told us we wanted."

Libra frowns. "come on, Leo. u'd be floating around in a tin can, till the end of ur days."

i think of the view of space, the earth below, turning fast. the moon. "yes," i say.

"u wouldn't be able to have kids," says Libra. "i mean, unless some crazy woman astronaut went up there with u or—"

"i don't think i'm going to have kids," i say. the room seems to take a breath. "not . . . in the conventional manner anyway. so that's not an issue."

silence.

i meet Orion's eyes. & for once i don't turn away. he doesn't either. something that has never been said has stepped onto the path in the scented night of the dome, is a presence in the space we occupy, almost standing between us, face in shadow.

Libra is peering at me as if confused.

"come on, this isn't news to u," i say.

mask off. "no," says Orion.

"there's still love, tho," says Libra. "settling down. family."

"there's love up there too," i say.

"ok," says Libra, "what about a career? ambitions? u can't just be in a space station till u die."

"other people train for decades to get the chance to go to the space station," i say. "& anyway, what kind of career are u going to have, living in this dome?"

she doesn't answer.

"sorry," i say. "that was mean."

she shrugs. "it's ok. i get it."

"we're just as trapped here as we were up there," i say. "only we're trapped far away from home."

she fingers her locket, the earth she keeps there. "no," she says. "this is home." she stands, & then slowly kneels & touches her hand to the dirt. "this. here. the earth. where we're meant to be."

pause.

she turns to Orion. "& u?" she says.

he inhales, then lifts the mask. "home is where u are," he says. another whir as the chair spins. "& u," he adds.

but not quick enough.

silence.

"they still won't let u," says Libra. as if that settles it.

"who says? have u asked them?"

"no," she says. "have u?"

a moth lands on her wheelchair. she smiles at it, reaches her index finger & gently brushes it.

huh.

6
asking

i walk into 1 of the conference rooms. anonymous seating around an anonymous table.

Grandpa is standing with Boutros. they have been looking at blueprints, mission plans, or something. Grandpa seems to be getting back into the astronaut thing, here.

"what is it u need?" says Boutros, focusing his attention on me.

"i need u to send me back up there," i say.

he blinks. "where?"

"to the space station. to Moon 2."

silence.

"u want to train to be an astronaut? it's a noble ambition but with ur health—"

"no," i say. "i want to go back now. i don't want to stay here. i want to be up there."

"Leo . . . ," says my grandpa. but then he doesn't seem to know how to follow it.

Boutros doesn't look sorry tho. he looks tired. "no," he says.

pause.

i wait for him to add something, to qualify, to soften.

he doesn't.

"just . . . no?" i say.

he gives a curt nod. "just no. that's my answer."

"but . . ."

"u want reasons?"

"yes."

he holds out his hand, taps his fingers as he counts them. "1/ it's expensive—millions of dollars expensive; 2/ u have no training; 3/ u're a kid & i'm not sending a kid into space; 4/ it would be a PR fucking disaster; & 5/ u're a kid. did i mention u're a kid?"

"i was a kid when i was up there before," i say.

"that was different," he says.

pause.

"listen," says Boutros. "u want me to keep counting?" he holds out his other hand. "6/ it's not a holiday camp up there—we need the space for astronauts, scientists, experiments; 7/ . . ." but he has realized his mistake. his mouth closes.

"i'm an experiment," i say for him. "so there must be room for me."

Boutros raises his hands in a placating gesture. "no one's calling u an—"

"experiment? but it's what i am."

he sighs. "Leo, look. we're all trying our best here. but we can't send u back up to the space station. it's just . . . it's just impossible. do u understand?"

i turn away. i take my crutches & plant them & use them to carry myself over the floor & out of the room.

i don't say anything.

that's my answer.

interlude

i am sitting with Libra in Orion's room overlooking the valley. Orion is sleeping. it's night: moonlight is reflecting on the snow of the glacier; glowing blue. clouds cover the moon, race past it, unveiling it again & again, an aperture thru the dark sky & into a universe of light.

Libra & i are watching the Road Runner on her screen. it's not even from this century & u'd think she'd have found something new by now but no. we are on a sofa that we have turned to the window, but we're not looking out of the window; we're looking at the vid.

the coyote opens a box from Acme. it says BAT-MAN'S OUT-FIT on it. maybe this is before Batman or before trademark law, i don't know.

he puts on the suit & it has wings that open out in ridged elegance on either side of him, a mask too. he looks rakish, like he might be going to a cocktail party—admittedly a strange kind of cocktail party.

then he steps off the cliff—he wants to swoop down on the Road Runner, catch it. he folds his wings & drops, fast.

he starts to flap his wings.

nothing happens.

he flaps more—desperate now. beating at the air, trying to get a degree of purchase on it.

he keeps dropping.

now we c sharp rocks beneath him, their triangular shapes like teeth.

he drops . . .

& then his wings catch, & he skims over the rocks & lofts up, into the sky. he folds his wings again, swooping upward, his downward fall revealed as merely the first part of a perfect arc, as he shoots up up up into the blue sky.

he relaxes.

he dances, on the air.

he lifts up, hanging on it, reveling in the buoyancy, & then lets himself drop, then rises again. then he begins to fly in a leisurely way forward, slowly bringing his wings down & back, down & back, as he raises his head in a smug way, closing his eyes.

he drifts, in a casual rhythm of wing beats, folding the air beneath himself, *swish, swish, swish.*

then he hits a cliff face:

smash.

he sticks there for a moment.

then he falls, & the camera pans up & over him, & we c that he is a tiny body falling into a huge, deep, exaggerated canyon.

he dwindles.

time seems to stretch.

then a puff of dust, as he hits the ground, far, far below.

"all of life," says Libra. "just like i told u. all of life is in this."

"jeez," i say. "i might go out & sit in the snow till i die. it would be less depressing than being in here."

she looks at me.

pause.

my mouth cracks, at the side, into a smile.

then she starts laughing, & i start laughing, & we laugh till our stomachs hurt.

"next 1?" says Libra.

"yes," i say. "of course."

"he always gets back up again," says Libra. "that's life too."

i look at Orion. i look at her.

now we're not laughing.

"i hope so," i say.

7

fire bombs

"open windows," i say.

the glass slides away, & the snow field directly outside is drawn into the room, almost; along with icy air, which rushes over my shoulders, making me shiver.

i lower myself a little farther into the hot tub. a marvel, in 1 g. the simple miracle of being immersed in water.

they say it's good for us too. suspension: it takes the strain off our bones & joints. this is spring water from lower down the mountain, piped up here. they mix salt into it, to make us float even more, to make our bodies feel less dense to us. in the past it was used for astronauts who were in training, who needed to rest their muscles.

it's a relief actually: to hang in it for a while, in the enveloping warmth of the water, to feel some of that constant weight, that constant pull, fall away.

i close my eyes.

i am thinking that this is 1 of the small blessings of life on earth but then another thought chases it away, like a curtain opening, dispelling shadows: what makes this amazing is that it is something of space, here on earth.

it is floating.

it is weightlessness.

the water is different on the skin but the fundamental

sensation is 0 g: it's hovering; it's being pulled in no direction, being a still point in the universe.

god. i miss space. a few days have passed since my conversation with Boutros & i'm still seething.

"mind if i join u?"

i look up. it's Grandpa. he's standing by the hot tub, dressed as always in boots & jeans & a button-down shirt.

"in here?" i say.

"yes."

"u're not exactly dressed for it."

he shrugs. "they have plenty of clothes here," he says. "& plenty of towels."

he takes off his boots. then he puts a hand down & crouches & lowers himself into the hot tub, all his clothes still on. i blow air thru my nose in amusement: ha.

he stretches out, his arm almost going around me, almost but not quite.

we sit there in silence for a while.

sunlight sparkles on the snow outside. a long, long, long way away, & a long, long, long way down, smoke drifts over a forest.

"he's a glorified bureaucrat, u know," says Grandpa. "Boutros. he doesn't mean to be cruel. he's just . . . trying to make the most of a difficult situation."

"i know," i say. "he can still keep me here."

Grandpa nods.

"i'm still a failed experiment. something to be hidden."

more silence.

"how's Comet?" i ask.

"doing well, according to ur mother. much livelier, down there. eating properly again. running."

"oh," i say. "good." livelier down there, without me.

"i didn't mean . . . i mean, i'm sure he misses u."

more silence.

then:

"u ever hear about the discovery of the jet stream?" says Grandpa. he's not looking at me; he's looking out at the valley, the great sweep of it down to the hills & lowlands.

i let my feet float up, lie my head back. "no."

"u know what it is?"

i roll my eyes. "very fast channel of air, high altitude, runs west to east around the world."

he nods. "Japanese guy found out about it first. i forget the name. it doesn't matter anyway. he sent pilot balloons up, from near Mount Fuji, noticed that they were moving faster than he expected. he published his results too—in a journal of meteorology. he wrote his paper in Esperanto. figured that way everyone would be able to read it."

"Esperanto?"

"an invented language. the idea was that it would unite the world. simple to learn, etc. but no one ever really bothered with it. except this guy. result: no one read his paper. & no one outside Japan had any idea the jet stream existed."

pause.

"so?" i say.

"so a while later it's WW2. the Japanese try to use the jet stream because they know about it & no one else does. they send helium balloons loaded with explosives over the Pacific to America, with the idea that they'll land & explode here."

"huh."

"1 of them actually does explode. by accident really. it lands in Washington State, i think, somewhere in the woods. some hikers stumble on it & set it off, or some Boy Scouts, something like that. it kills a couple of people. the only fatalities on the American mainland in the war."

"wow," i say.

"anyway. the war goes on. toward the end, the Americans start to bomb Japan. we're trying to make them surrender. my own grandfather was 1 of the bomber pilots. u know that?"

"no."

"well, he was. flew a B-29. it was mostly because of him i wanted to be a pilot myself. he never dropped 1 of the nuclears, but he was part of the firebombing of Tokyo. & that's when the jet stream comes in again. u c, our Bomber Command planned the bombing. November 1945. they worked out the altitudes, everything. 30,000 ft. they assigned targets: munitions factories, cottage industries making guns, that kind of thing. they wanted to destroy the ability of the Japanese to make sophisticated modern weapons."

pause.

he takes in a lungful of mountain air.

"but here's the thing. the pilots go up—including my grandfather—& they fly to their designated targets & they open their bomb hatches & . . . the bombs miss, by miles. part of it's the cloud cover messing with their accuracy but there's also something weird going on with their speed. no one gets it. the instruments on the planes are saying 400, 500 miles an hour. but the bombs are landing way off target, like the planes were going 600, 700 miles an hour. none of it makes sense."

"it's the jet stream," i say.

"yes. that's what they eventually work out—there's a current of air, or something like that—& it's throwing off their calculations by a huge margin. which is 1 reason they change tactic—i mean, it's war, there's no time to spend months figuring out new equations, adapting the Norden bomb aimers they use. so

320

this new guy LeMay comes in to lead the bombers & he decides they're not going to go in at 30,000 ft.; they're going to go in at 7,000."

silence.

"&?"

"& that's what they do. they switch their bombs to M-69s, incendiary devices. low-altitude. they go in fast—there's a much higher risk of flak, much higher risk of attack by enemy planes, much higher risk of being shot down—but on the other hand they can do a lot of damage, very quickly, & the Japanese fighters are waiting for them at 30,000 ft., so the Americans have the element of surprise."

pause.

"they hit the major munitions factories, the cottage fabrication plants—they destroy 16 square miles of Tokyo. but a lot of Tokyo is made of wood. fires combine, create firestorms. hundreds of thousands of civilians are killed. burned to death. my grandfather would wake up screaming, & he never even saw it; he was up there in the clouds. he never really forgave himself, for what they did."

pause.

"u c?" he says.

i shake my head.

"if the Japanese scientist had published in English, or even Japanese, everyone would have known about the jet stream. the US Air Force would have known. they'd have factored it into all their plans, from the beginning. would have known how to hit those military targets more accurately."

pause.

"unintended consequences," he says. "who could have predicted that the discovery going unnoticed could result in such tragedy for Tokyo? so many innocent civilians killed. all because someone decided to write in Esperanto. or partly because anyway. i mean, the Americans might have decided to firebomb no matter what happened. those civilian deaths were not good for enemy morale, which was good for the Allies in the long run."

i sit up in the hot tub. a cloud has gone over the sun. i splash water on my face. "why do i have the feeling this is meant to relate to me?"

he shrugs. "unintended consequences. the Company wasn't like that Japanese scientist: the mistake they made was a moral 1, not a bad choice of language. only here's the thing. they did something terrible, an experiment that never should have happened. but the consequence? the unintended consequence?"

he looks at me.

"yes?" i say.

"the consequence was something beautiful."

pause.

"the consequence was u."

his arm goes around me now.

& i let it.

"here he is," says my mother. she is in the field in front of the house. on our screen, the world tilts & rushes at us, & then the view is down at grass level & Comet's face fills the screen, his big shining eyes, his muzzle.

"Comet!" i say.

he barks back at me ecstatically, turning on the spot, then comes forward, & his tongue, huge & pink, licks the screen.

"it's nice to c u too, Comet," i say. inside me is sunshine & rain, all mixed together; which is what makes things grow; i am Libra's dome, made flesh.

yap.

my mother lifts the screen again & holds it at arm's length, & i c that she's wearing a thin sweater. there's a clarity to the air around her, a crispness to the ranchhouse in the background, that also suggests cold. smoke is rising from the chimney into a pale blue sky & her hair is tied back & she looks . . . peaceful.

weirdly, it's quite nice to c her as well as Comet. Grandpa & i are sitting on the sofa in my room, morning painting the walls with its flat clear light. in the mountains u can almost tell the time of the day by the light; it's not like light in space, which when it's there is constant & colorless; here it gets thicker & warmer as the afternoon turns, goes buttery & almost liquid.

"here," she says. "watch."

she sets the screen down, & for a moment Grandpa & i are just looking at clover & blades of grass. then she picks it up again & her hand covers it, does a swiping multi-finger gesture & the picture goes black before a new view appears. now we're looking down at the field from maybe 50 ft. up, my mother is a foreshortened figure below us & Comet is a dense patch of movement, circling her feet. the angle is wide enough that we can c the misty mountains in the distance, purple in the low, sideways, early-morning light.

we're seeing thru a drone's camera.

my mother picks something up, something circular. Comet goes still, ears pricked. she throws the object & it flashes fast over the gray-green of the planted land, spinning—a Frisbee of some kind. Comet follows it as if attached to it by some invisible thread, no interval between his stillness & his streaking across the ground, simply missiling after the Frisbee.

his mind is an h-infinity model & a better 1 than any computer; it calculates vectors & velocity & the down drag of gravity & friction & his own momentum, a perfect system for making sure that 2 airborne bodies meet in the right place, & it sends him leaping into the air a fraction of a second later & he catches the Frisbee in his mouth, brings it down, he & the toy rolling together, sliding to a stop.

black—

& then my mother's face reappears. "getting good, isn't he?" she says.

"yes," i say. a little choked up. "thank u."

she doesn't smile but she does nod, & even that's progress. "i thought u'd like it," she says.

Grandpa leans in beside me. "show me the drone view again," he says.

"ok," says my mother. her fingers manipulate the screen &

it flicks over to the bird's-eye view—she gives a functional little almost-wave at us, from down there.

Grandpa peers at the screen. "turn the cam toward the mountains," he says.

the image rotates & we're looking at the rocky range, the clouds above it pink, the peaks whiter than when i was there. i watch Grandpa's face. the focus of it. the intensity. i'm sure he's not aware of it but a smile is gently lifting the corners of his mouth.

he loves it. the ranch.

"thanks," he says. "i thought so."

click back to my mother's face. "what?"

"looks like snow's coming soon," says Grandpa. "those clouds . . . u should get the wire frames. put some hay out in the cattle fields."

Mother nods. "sure," she says. "but snow? i don't know when it last really snowed here. a dusting, sure, but—"

"put out the hay all the same," says Grandpa. "as a favor to ur old man."

she rolls her eyes now. "yes, of course."

"u brought in the cover crops?" he asks.

"yes," says my mother.

"moved the cows with twins to the lowest pastures so they can fatten up?"

"yes, everything u told me."

"good girl."

my mother raises her eyebrows at me. it's an unexpected confidence. a little moment, a connection, laughing together at my grandpa. i laugh & she smiles too, faintly.

i c it a little more all the time. how who he is shaped who she is. how things might have been before, when she was younger. i think of Grandpa, the way he pushed me to chase after Comet, when the little dog went for the calf. the way he didn't even think about it. i think of him 30 years younger, with the hormones of a young man.

his drive. his desire to be the best. the way he might have channeled that, projected it. onto his daughter.

maybe he pushed her, i think. he pushed her out into life, into his career, into following him, the way he pushed me after Comet. & she broke something, just like i did.

but he's mellowed, with the years. he's mellowed & i love him.

which is not to say that i don't c, a bit more, what my mother came from. what made her.

i have not forgiven her. maybe i never will, entirely. but i feel like i c her more clearly than i ever have before. her sense of duty. her hard work. her drive.

i hear barking & she angles the screen so that i c Comet jumping on the spot.

"he wants me to throw the Frisbee again," she says. the view lurches as she picks up the Frisbee & flings it—then she turns her screen so that we watch Comet's tail as he fires himself after the departing projectile, muscles flying him over the grass, neurons fizzing with equations.

my mother turns the screen back to herself. "i should be going," she says. "Lorenzo is coming to help me get the barns ready for winter."

"good," says Grandpa. "well, we'll be here, whenever u want to talk."

"i know," says my mother.

pause.

she reaches her hand out.

"wait," i say, thinking.

another pause.

"if they asked u again . . . if u could go back in time . . ." i don't know how to ask this. she frowns & i c the faint lines she is developing on her face. "i mean . . . do u regret it, having me?"

she looks at me for a long moment. "if u're asking whether i'm sorry . . . then yes. u know that. i'm sorry. & i'm sorry i didn't tell u sooner. & i'm sorry for . . . for how it happened. i was young. i signed up for an experiment that i was told was for the good of humankind. just an experiment. but when u came . . . i felt . . . something. i promise u i felt something. & i was . . . i was ashamed. & proud. & . . . i don't know. but i . . . i was happy. when u were born."

"u had a weird way of showing it."

"they told me u weren't really my child, that u belonged to them. that u were not mine. they didn't let me keep u very long. they had formula, to feed to u . . . everything . . . they took care of it all. managed it. that's what companies do, isn't it?"

"doesn't seem like u fought them very hard," i say.

"no." she closes her eyes. "that's another thing i'm sorry about."

"yeah," i say. "u're sorry. u wish it had never happened. u wish i had never been born. i get it."

now her eyes open & go wide. "no!" she says. "i never knew how to make it right, & i never knew how to tell u. i closed a door on you, somewhere inside. but do i regret having u? never for a second. i may not be . . . an affectionate person. but i think u are rather remarkable, Leo."

"um," i say, looking at the sadness in her eyes. "thanks." it seems like a lame response.

"are u studying?" she says. "aeronautics, astrophysics?"

"no," i say. Grandpa shifts beside me.

"why not?"

"i'm stuck in this place," i say.

"but u wanted to be an astronaut."

i rub my chin. "my bones. i'm not strong enough. not smart enough. not . . . i'm not like Soto. i'm not from here. i'm not built for—"

"Leo," she says. "u performed an EVA with no training & helped me to swap out a malfunctioning gyro. most astronauts haven't done that. u're a third-generation space pilot, Leo. i thought u had more ambition."

"i do!" i say. "but there's not much i can do here."

she shakes her head ruefully. then the world as seen on the screen pivots around the axis of her hand as she stoops to pick up the Frisbee again & sends it arcing thru the air, Comet bounding after it.

"oh i don't know," she says. she seems to be looking at Grandpa. "i think u're like Comet there." he is already a dwindling dark spot. "i think u will go far."

9

unintended consequences

"u ever think the experiment might have been a success after all?" says Grandpa.

i frown at him. "what?"

it's dinnertime. we're eating meatballs in the dining hall, pushing them around on our plates. outside the windows, black sky studded with stars. some kind of glow up high, like they're working with arc lights, farther up the mountain.

"the Company," continues Grandpa. "Boutros. they all act like it's something to be ashamed of."

"it is," i say.

"i know, i know, but let me finish. what i am trying to say is . . . they treat it like something that went wrong. i mean, u're right, it was wrong, ethically speaking, that's categorical. but . . . not necessarily a failure within the objectives & the parameters of the experiment."

"u've lost me," i say.

"they wanted to c if people could reproduce in space, right? with the long-term goal being to colonize another planet, 1 whose climate hasn't been screwed up yet."

"right."

"& it turned out people *could* reproduce in space. that's success number 1."

"but look at me now," i say. i gesture, a wide gesture that takes in my hunched frame, my crutches leaning on the chair next to me.

"yes. u came down to earth & ur body couldn't adapt & u got sick. people can reproduce in space. but the . . . offspring are not suited to gravity."

i tap my crutches. wave my bandaged wrist. "i know."

"which is bad," says Grandpa, "if u want to colonize worlds. big orbiting bodies of rock, with big gravitational pulls. but there's still the same problems here on earth: global warming, rising sea levels, flooding, drought, hurricanes, a growing population, & shrinking resources. so now they've got their new program, & they're looking for strong kids like Soto to send on long-distance missions. they think those kids are the future. but what if the future is still u?"

"i don't understand."

"it's the assumption," he says. "that that's the goal—to colonize *planets*."

i start to c. i nod, slightly.

"adjust the assumption tho," he says. "the parameters. look at it as an experiment into whether it's possible to conceive & give birth to children who are perfectly suited to drifting in space in a space ship. then, the experiment becomes a resounding success."

"but they don't want people drifting thru space in a space ship," i say. "u heard Boutros. they say they don't even have room for me. why would they want to make a lot of people who could do that?"

he shrugs. "i don't know. a station colony orbiting at 1 of the moon Lagrange points maybe? why would we need to know about the jet stream? it turns out it's very useful for saving on fuel when flying from west to east. unintended consequences."

something hangs in the air, silvery. a thread of an idea.

"unintended consequences," i say.

pause.

i am thinking about something Grandpa told me once, about rockets, rusting away in Kazakhstan.

"u know ur friend who lives on the Black Sea?" i say.

Grandpa nods. "Yuri."

"u told me he said there were still some shuttles. in a hangar somewhere."

the thread turns, an aurora, glowing.

"yes," says Grandpa slowly. "the old Burans. in Baikonur."

"u think any of them can still fly?"

pause.

"please," i say. "i can't stay here."

Grandpa looks at me for a long time. he pushes a meatball around on his plate.

"well," he says finally. "well, i could ask him, couldn't i?"

the possibility hangs between us.

then there's a voice behind me. "Leo?"

i turn.

it's Virginia.

10

aurora

"i, um, had better go & make that call we were talking about," says Grandpa. he stands.

"uh-huh," i say.

he walks away.

going back to space. it's a nice idea. but it somehow feels distant now, with Virginia in front of me. she looks smaller than she did on the station, or even back at the base. here in 1 g. as if the gravity has pressed her into a more compact shape.

"they didn't want me to come," she says. her eyes are puffy. i think she has been crying. "but i came anyway. as soon as i heard u were hurt."

"hmm," i say. this is a *hmm* that contains the words *what really hurts is everything u have done & said & most especially not said for the last nearly 16 years.*

she pulls up a chair. "do u mind if i sit?"

"will it make a difference?"

she draws in a breath—not loud, but i hear it.

"listen, Leo," she says.

pause.

"i've been thinking about what i could say to u. what might make it better. but i don't think there is anything."

"no," i say.

u lied to me all my life.

she smiles a sad smile. "i did what i was paid for. i kept the secrets i was paid to keep. but not everything was a job. i think that's all i can tell u."

i frown a question.

"i mean . . . looking after u. it was more than . . . it was . . ." she closes her eyes. opens them again. "i held u. i fed u from a bottle. i sat with u for hours on end when u were crawling on the treadmill, the 3 of u. straps holding u in place—u would not believe how long those took to fasten. & can u imagine, the time all of it took? on earth, a baby just learns to crawl. up there, i had to set aside hours for it. encourage u. weigh u down. play games with u to get u to move. & that's not even counting when u were learning to walk."

that, i remember, or i remember it from watching vids anyway. the 3 of us strapped, pulleys holding us down, the carpet rolling beneath us.

"i changed ur diapers, Leo," she says. she makes a face. "can u picture what it's like to change a diaper in 0 g?"

despite myself, i laugh a little.

"& all the time . . ." she pauses again. "here's the thing, Leo. i can't have children. it's just . . . it's not something i can do. but with u 3. up there. i . . ."

pause.

"there's something Boutros said to me once," she continues. "he said that when he & his wife had a baby, he finally got it, that thing people say about dying for someone. he held his daughter in his arms, & he was, like, *i would step in front of a bus to protect u.*"

long pause now.

"& that's . . . that's how i feel about u. & Libra & Orion. i kept something from u, & i shouldn't have done that. it was weak of me. but i would die for u. to keep u safe. if there's anything . . . anything i can do for u, i will do it."

silence.

more silence.

more more silence.

"Boutros really said that?" i say eventually.

she smiles. "yes."

"wow. still waters," i say.

"get him drunk, he's a whole different person," she says.

another silence, but a more comfortable 1 now. then movement outside catches my eye, & i c that what i thought was artificial light, up there, is moving, is green, is diaphanous across the black, drifting.

"aurora," i say.

"what?"

i point out the window. she turns & looks. "oh! yeah."

i look at her. "there is something u can do," i say.

11

ghosts

we sit outside the dome.

well, Libra & i sit, & Virginia too, on a folding chair. Orion lies, propped on pillows on his bed on wheels.

they didn't want us to come out here, but Virginia has influence, it seems. authority. we are all bundled up, warm, wrapped in silvery reflective thermal blankets.

the aurora dances above us, green curtains across the sky. the lights are beautiful, no less so than up in the station, but in a whole different way—we are looking up now, into blackness, & they glow against it. they seem something of space & the sky, where from up there they seemed something mantling the earth, wrapping it.

they seem, literally, otherworldly, rippling in the dark. ghosts. intimations of some existence beyond this 1, maybe another life where this hasn't happened to us & we just get to be normal. even tho i know of course the lights are in reality just molecules of the atmosphere, exploding, blasted apart by energy from the sun.

Virginia talks. she talks & talks & talks, tells Libra & Orion everything she told me, everything she feels, her regrets, her love.

they talk too.

there is hugging.

& the northern lights swirl above us & we're together again, seeing them, the 4 of us, just like up there, just like nothing has changed, & we talk & talk & there's more hugging & it's morning.

the lights are gone from the sky; the sun, a burning convex on the horizon, above the low hills.

"oh!" says Virginia. "that's another reason i came. happy birthday, Leo."

12
1 good thing about earth

1 good thing about earth, it turns out, is candles.

　　i hadn't realized.

　　i mean, up there, when Virginia would turn out the ersatz, LED versions—a white stick with a flickering light in the end—i thought that was a reasonable facsimile. but it doesn't capture the whoosh of air, the bend of the flame away from ur breath, before it sputters out, the whole physical aerodynamic flow of the thing, the satisfaction of blowing & the candle bowing to that, allowing itself to go out.

　　"again," i say, when the 16 candles are out.

　　Grandpa lights them again. the cake is round & white, like the moon. Virginia & Libra & Orion sing "Happy Birthday."

　　i blow them out—or rather i blow about half of them out.

　　then my breath catches in my chest.

　　i try to get it moving again. it won't.

　　pinpricks of black appear in my vision. inverse stars.

　　i start to pant. to panic. i fall back on my bed, which i have been sitting on, so i'm lying on my back.

　　Grandpa hits a red button in my room, & soon medical staff arrive. they extinguish the candles with no ceremony, pull an oxygen tank from the wall, get the mask over my face. i draw it in, the sweetness of it, feel it rush around my blood, tiny bubbles.

　　i lie there, looking up at the ceiling.

eventually, i motion to the medics & they take the mask away.

"not how i imagined my 16th," i say.

Grandpa smiles.

"i mean, u could at least have gotten a DJ," i say. "or a band. so we could dance."

Virginia laughs. "u don't want to c me dance."

we all laugh. the medics look at us like we're crazy.

13
ready

a couple of days later, i'm in the hot tub. it's my favorite place to be: floating, pretending gravity is not there. Virginia has gone back down to Nevada, needs to work on some project.

Grandpa walks into the room.

"tomorrow," he says. "18 hundred hours. after dinner. be ready."

"ready for what?"

"to go."

"go where?" i ask.

"where do u think?" says Grandpa. "come to my room after u're done in the tub. we can discuss it more."

he walks out.

14
set

"can i say goodbye to the others?" i say to Grandpa, in his room.

he's talked me thru his plan, the bare bones of it: fly to Kazakhstan; get on a shuttle; fly to the space station.

it sounds so simple, when put like that.

"to Libra & Orion?" he says.

"yes."

"depends," he says. "u think they'll tell anyone?"

i blink. "what? no."

"ok then. but i want to be there. i need to monitor all angles."

"right. so . . . when?"

"no time like the present," says Grandpa. "tomorrow things are going to move fast. the plan is . . . changeable. u may not get the chance."

i'm on my crutches, & we head down the hallway to Orion's room, where i know Libra will be as well. i feel like i should get used to the crutches. Grandpa said i won't be able to take my wheelchair.

it hurts my wrist, still, but i'm getting used to it, finding a technique, a way to balance myself & to move without twisting it too much. & then the brace helps, of course.

"5 minutes for goodbyes," says Grandpa. "then we're out of here."

"how are we even leaving?" i say. "we're on a mountain."

he taps his nose. "i have a plan. but we don't have much time."

i knock on the door, & Libra's voice answers. "come in."

when i go in it's dark in there, tho there's still a purplish tinge to the sky thru the huge windows. the sun has just set outside & there's a lamp on by Orion's bed, which is semi-raised so that he's sitting up, holding Libra's hand. music swells, from the speakers in the walls. Rachmaninoff, i think.

Grandpa stays at the doorway & i hobble in, making my way over to the bed. but when i arrive i don't know what to say.

"Leo?" says Libra.

"huh?" i say.

"u're looking really strange."

i am watching them, illuminated by a circle of warm lamplight. they have been a fixture in my life, all my life. not friends, exactly, not family, exactly, but always there. i c the way they're holding hands & i c the way the light cradles them, & i wish i could be inside it with them, inside that circle, but i have to go.

"i'm . . ." my voice cracks. i look at Orion's face, his cheekbones, his mouth. i always thought he would be the first person i would kiss.

that's not true.

i always *hoped*.

i never thought.

his eyes are on mine, concerned. "what is it, Leo?" he says.

"i'm leaving," i say, all on 1 downdraft of breath, the words themselves like an exhalation.

they stare at me. "leaving to go where?" says Libra.

"back up there." i point at the ceiling. beyond it. at space.

"they're letting u go back?"

"um, not exactly."

"u're breaking out?" says Orion. "but how are u going to fly back up there?"

Libra is looking at the doorway thoughtfully. "ur grandfather," she says.

"yeah," i say.

Orion tilts his head. "this is insane," he says.

"i agree," i say, sweeping my hand in a gesture that takes in his bed, his gaunt hollow face, his bloodshot eyes. the oxygen mask that he lifts & holds to his mouth & nose again. "or did u mean me going back?"

he removes the mask. "ha-ha, Leo," he says.

at the door, Grandpa clears his throat.

"listen," i say. "i'll vid u, ok? i'll vid u as soon as i'm home."

Libra's eyes fill with tears. "*home?* u're serious, aren't u?"

"yes," i say.

she wipes her eyes, the arch of her nose, roughly, with the back of her hand. "what if something happens? what if u die?"

"i'm going to die here," i say. "maybe not soon. but eventually. i can't do it. i can't be trapped in this place."

"u'll be trapped up there."

i think of the cupola. i think of the windows. i think of the earth below, its colors, the sphere of it traced with glassy clouds, like a paperweight. "no," i say. "i'm more at home on Moon 2 than i could ever be here."

Grandpa clears his throat again.

i put my hands on Libra's shoulders. "u could come," i say suddenly.

she shakes her head. "no. i . . ." a pause. "i like it here, Leo. i know u don't understand it. but i have my garden. u know?"

i nod. "i know. but, Libra, what about other people? what about the world? u can't engage with anyone here, with anything."

she sucks in air. "our mother called," she says. "she said . . . she said she was sorry. she's arranged things, with Boutros. she's going to come & live here, with us, 6 months of the year. we're going to be together."

"ah," i say.

silence.

"don't go, Leo," she says.

Orion just looks at me, with those sunken eyes.

"i need to," i say. "u have ur garden. ur mother."

"ur mother is down here on earth too."

"it's not the same & u know it," i say.

"does she even know what u're planning? ur mother? doesn't she deserve to?"

i blink. it hasn't crossed my mind. i glance at Grandpa. he shakes his head. "um, i don't think so. & no."

no, she doesn't deserve to.

Libra looks up at the ceiling. "this is crazy."

"no," i say. "this is what i have to do. this is what i always had to do." & it's true. i fell, but i didn't fall from Eden, i fell to Eden, & now i need to be back in the heavens.

pause.

"i know," she says at last.

then she pulls me into a fierce hug, squeezes me tight, i'm almost worried another of my bones might break.

after an eternity i pull away. "goodbye," i say.

"goodbye, Leo," she says.

nothing else needs to be said.

i love her. i love Grandpa, & Libra, & even my mother. i love them all. i love, like the moon loves the earth.

& i need to be up there, like the moon too.

i step back & then look at Orion. "bye," i say.

"no," says Orion, thru his mask.

"what?"

he takes the mask off. "no, u can't leave."

i stare at him. "i'm sorry, Orion, i have to—"

"i don't mean that. i mean u can't leave yet."

he takes a deep breath of his oxygen, then lowers the mask again. "i haven't seen a concert," he says. "u think Boutros is going to take me? no. it has to be u. u & ur grandfather."

"a . . . concert?"

he taps his screen & the Rachmaninoff stops. he swipes up the net & types something, then turns the screen so i can c. "tomorrow night," he says. "Deer Lake Park in Vancouver. it's free. the Northern Symphony Orchestra. they're playing Mozart's Symphony Number 39."

Libra is staring at him too. "u want us to take u to Vancouver? tomorrow?"

but he doesn't smile, or otherwise show that he's joking. "it is 1 of the greatest pieces of music ever composed. i'm dying, Leo. & Vancouver is nearby, i think."

"we're in Alaska," i say. "Vancouver is not nearby."

"it's all relative," he says.

he puts his mask back in place, lets his head sink into the pillow. breathes deeply. the constant hiss of the oxygen tank.

i turn to Libra. "what . . . i mean . . ."

she shakes her head. "this is crazy."

Orion lifts his mask. "please," he says. & then he replaces it. *hiss. hiss.*

please.

the same thing i said to Grandpa.

"what do u think?" i say to Libra.

she closes her eyes & takes a long, slow breath. "i think he's dying," she says. "& i think if he's going anywhere, i'm going too. so i guess . . . i think . . . we're coming with u."

"but . . . ," i say, "how would we . . . i mean, he can't even walk."

"he has a wheelchair," says Libra.

"& what about getting back here?" i say. "i presume u are planning on coming back here? i mean, Grandpa & i, we're going to Kazakhstan. u can't be thinking of coming with us."

Orion shakes his head. "after the concert, u just leave us with a screen. we wait till u're safely clear. then we call Boutros. there'll be a helicopter touching down within half an hour, guaranteed."

"hmm," i say.

i think of Grandpa telling me not to bring mine. i don't even know if we can get to Vancouver, or how we're getting out of this place in the first instance.

"wait here," i say to Libra.

i walk over to the door.

"i gather we have a bit of a problem," says Grandpa.

15
(hold all systems)

the next day is as long as a life.

i walk the hallways.

i eat in the cafeteria.

Grandpa makes calls in his room, hustles. adjusting plans to have Libra & Orion there too. to stop off in Vancouver. which means putting off our departure by a day. it's crazy, the whole thing, but we seem to be doing it. he can't argue with the logic either: if they make some kind of distress call from there, then for sure the Company will turn up. they won't want the twins being taken by what Boutros calls the nutjobs.

there is 1 thing i need to do, but i keep putting it off. then, the following day, i just do it, without thinking. i open my screen & punch in my mother's number & when she answers it's sunny in California, & she's on the porch, holding wires. it looks like she's installing some kind of alarm. extra security?

"hey," i say.

"hello, Leo," she says. & nothing else. some things never change.

"can i c Comet?" i say.

she seems distracted. "um. yes. hang on." she puts down the wires next to some pliers—i get a brief angled view of a tool box—& then she is walking in thru the door & she flips the screen so i c Comet curled up on the sofa, in the place i always sat.

i wonder if he chooses that place because of my smell. i feel my eyes well up.

"hi, Comet!" i say. he pricks up his ears, then sits up. Mother brings the screen closer to him & he comes in close, eyes & nose filling the camera. he yaps at me.

yap, yap.

"hello, hello," i say. "i'm so glad to c u."

yap, yap.

his nose snuffles the screen; he tries to lick me.

"ugh," says Mother, pulling the screen away. "anything in particular u wanted to say to him?" she says.

goodbye, Comet. i love u. i wish i could be with u, but i need to go far away. to somewhere u wouldn't be able to live. so that i can live.

"no," i say.

"ok, well, i'd better get back to this wiring."

"yes. yes, sure, Mother. speak to u soon."

"yes. goodbye, Leo."

goodbye, Mother.

END CALL.

16
& finally: go

we cross the lobby, the enormous doors in front of us.

Libra is using her walker. i am on my crutches. Grandpa has a couple of bags slung over his shoulder. he is also pushing Orion's wheelchair, the oxygen tank strapped to the side of it. & sliding along, the IV pole that holds Orion's drip. none of us knew exactly what was in it, so we figured we should bring it.

the thing that is not being said is that we might not need it for long. Orion's skin is almost a gray color, a concrete color, a color leached of life.

Grandpa said, when we huddled at the door, whispering, that i should prepare myself for the worst. & i can c from Libra's expression that she is steeling herself too.

but how do u prepare urself for something like that? how do u possibly?

right now tho, there are bigger things on my mind. like: the doors. the fact that we're at a secret Company training facility on a snowy mountain in Alaska, in the tallest mountain range in North America. the seeming impossibility of escape. Grandpa joked that he had been thinking of stopping in Vancouver anyway, at an airfield some friend of his owns, to switch to a jet to take us to Kazakhstan. i don't know if that's true, but i am going with it.

i mean, i don't know if the Vancouver part is true, tho actually i don't really know if any of it is true.

Grandpa keeps on heading toward the glass wall, however. a bag is slung over his shoulder, which i guess holds clothes, supplies, his passport maybe? i don't have a passport, for obvious reasons.

there's no one in reception & no one seems to have noticed or paid any attention to our movements so far. i know Boutros is still here somewhere, & a few doctors & scientists, but there aren't actually that many staff. i get the sense this place had lain fallow for years, like 1 of Grandpa's fields, that most of the activity was at the base in Nevada.

Grandpa doesn't head for the big doors. he turns & pushes the wheelchair toward a service door that i wouldn't have spotted otherwise. he waves his card at the scanner next to it & the door opens with a soft click.

he goes thru first & i follow. the cold hits me immediately, the icy air in my nose, my lungs. snow has been cleared from the tarmac outside the door & my crutches don't seem to slip, tho i plant them cautiously as i follow Grandpa, testing their hold. there's a *sooosh* sound as Libra lets the door shut behind her, & i turn & glance at her as she slowly walks behind me.

"this way," says Grandpa. he points toward the runway just below, where we landed when we came here. it's maybe 150 ft. away, not far. tho far enough with crutches or a walker.

"there's no plane," i say.

he turns & keeps going. "there will be," he says.

just then a dark silhouette unpeels itself from the night & steps out in front of us, an assault rifle in his hand. a guard. "excuse me," he says. "where are u going?"

Grandpa stops.

i stop.

Libra stops.

mountain breeze sighs around us, sharp & shiny with snow. u could imagine that if it stopped blowing, if the air stopped moving, all the ice in it would fall to the ground, sparkling, like tiny crushed jewels, tinkling.

my breath is loud & hot, steaming into the night. my eyelashes stick when i blink, the moisture on the outside of my eyes freezing.

Grandpa shrugs the bags aside & reaches into his inside coat pocket & takes out a wallet & flips it open. hooking the wheelchair with the crook of his elbow he slides out a card & shows it to the man. "Dr. Mahoney," he says. "the kid's taken a turn for the worse. i'm medevacing him to Vancouver Coastal hospital." he lets impatience creep into his voice. "every second counts here."

the guard peers down at the card. Grandpa goes just fractionally stiff.

oh no, i think.

then Orion starts coughing & doesn't stop—kind of slumps forward in his wheelchair, & when the guard looks over to him Grandpa palms the card & rushes to Orion's side. he lifts Orion's chin, says something low & urgent to him, then looks up & back at us.

"we have to go right now," he says. "the kid is critical." he puts the card back in the wallet, which he returns to his pocket.

the guard steps back. "of course. good . . . good luck."

Grandpa nods curtly & keeps moving, pushing Orion. Libra & i follow.

"where's . . . where's ur aircraft?" the guard calls after us.

"on its way," Grandpa shouts back.

Orion removes his mask & winks. "my heart could do without that kind of thing," he says. then he reconnects his oxygen.

when we're a few ft. from the runway, there's a buzz from Grandpa's pocket & he takes out his screen & unrolls it with a flick of his wrist. "coming in," says a voice. "little light would be appreciated."

"roger," says Grandpa.

he stops the wheelchair & puts on the brake. drops a bag from his shoulder to the ground & unzips it. inside are clothes, as i expected. then he moves the clothes & takes something heavy & pistol-like from where it was hidden between them. he aims it up, toward the far end of the airstrip, & fires, & a red star goes streaking up into the sky, arcing, glowing bright, trailing sparks as it goes. it lands somewhere in the snow on the other side of the runway & keeps burning, a hot crater surrounded by whiteness.

Grandpa stoops, picks up a cylinder, which he racks into the barrel before firing again, this time illuminating the near end of the runway.

"where the hell did u get a flare gun?" i say.

"let's just say i did a bit of breaking & entering," says Grandpa.

"seriously?"

he smiles. "i'm trying to make it sound more dramatic than it is," he says. "i trained here, remember? i've even flown in & out. there's a supply hut down at the far end of the landing strip. simple padlock. i broke in yesterday."

from behind us, a voice—shouting, but still a good distance back. "hey! u can't just use the lights?"

"sorry!" Grandpa calls. "emergency!"

at the same time, there's a whine of engines from above & i look up to c the outline of a twin-prop plane, coming down fast. the mountains form a black triangle, rising above us; there's only a thin crescent moon & the dark is deep.

"here we go," says Grandpa.

"who is that?" i say.

"Rick," he replies. "sprays my crops every year. i give him some of my water too. figure he owes me a favor."

"pretty big favor," i say. "he must have been flying all day."

"oh easily," says Grandpa. "with refueling stops. but he's ex-military. this is an adventure for him."

the plane banks, adjusts, starts descending to the runway, coming in on the side farthest from us. the hum of the propellers runs thru me.

"how long till the guard realizes something is wrong?" says Libra.

as she says it, lights click on inside the dome. lots & lots of lights.

"not very long, it seems," says Grandpa. "ok. this might get interesting."

17
belt up

the plane touches down & bumps & slides for a moment, rocking, before its wheels find purchase. the ailerons go up & it slows with a *shhh* sound of rubber on tarmac, the engine roar loud now in our ears, & finally comes to a stop only a few ft. from us.

"go go go," says Grandpa. i hear the joy in his voice. i hear the astronaut in him, still there, a man in a silver space suit who lives inside my grandpa's skin.

we go.

i hobble. Libra pushes, the little wheels of her walker squeaking over the ground. Grandpa hustles Orion forward, making sure the IV bag on its pole doesn't drag behind, doesn't snag.

the door of the plane opens & a man in a baseball cap peers out, shielding his eyes from the cold air, then hits an unseen lever & stairs unfold onto the tarmac with a pneumatic hush.

"stop!" says a voice behind us. i turn & c several doctors hustling out of the dome. the guard confers with them for a moment, then starts half running toward us, as if careful not to slip on the cold ground.

"stop!" he shouts. "i'll shoot!"

"he won't," says Grandpa.

bang.

i glance back & c the muzzle-flare out of the corner of my

eye—there's a whistling sound & the sense of something passing above us.

"he's firing over our heads," says Grandpa. "just a warning."

1 of the doctors starts shouting at the guard, & he holds his hands up, like, *what?* but then another Dr. yells at the first 1 & no one seems sure what they're doing.

meanwhile we are at the stairs of the plane.

"what the hell, Freeman?" says the man, Rick, from the aircraft door. icy wind snatches his words half away. "u didn't say there'd be guns." then Grandpa is gently picking up Orion from his chair, a fireman's lift, holding him over his shoulder while tucking the drip under his arm, balancing the oxygen tank.

"i said it was a rescue," says Grandpa. "what did u expect? anyway, quit whining. a little help here please."

Rick hops down the steps. he's short—maybe 5'6"—but muscly, wiry. he has a twirly mustache that curls in loops at the side of his mouth. he nods at me & Libra. "hey," he says. then he gets hold of Orion with Grandpa & they start carrying him up the short flight of steps.

they disappear from view.

i hear running footsteps behind. i turn. the guard is 100 ft. away.

80.

70.

he pauses, shoulders his gun. fires once more over our heads. "stop right now!" he says. "those kids are Company property."

"oh *screw* u," shouts Orion from the door of the plane.

"hurry," i say.

Grandpa comes out again & holds the handrails, just slides down, feet at the sides of the steps, *whoosh*. he lands in a crouch on the runway. Rick runs down behind him & picks up Libra while Grandpa grabs her walker.

"Leo, u're on ur own," he says. "throw the crutches in first."

i look at the steps. they seem very high, somehow, even tho there are only 3 of them, maybe 4.

i turn.

the guard is 20 ft. away. if he jumped now, like a football player going for a touchdown, he could almost reach me.

i c Grandpa enter the plane with the walker & i move quickly. at the bottom of the steps i hoist each crutch & then throw them like javelins, thru the hole of the door. then i hold on to the railings & try to put most of my weight on my good wrist, on my good leg, as i climb.

1 step.

2 steps.

it's the first time i've been up steps since i was at Grandpa's house, i realize, & then i remember the first time i did it at the base, the pain of it, the feeling of wrongness. now that feeling is made worse by my blood pounding in my ears. i can hear my heartbeat so loud, & it seems like even the guard will be able to hear it as he closes on me; i hear the crisp sibilant sound as the soles of his shoes skid to a halt on the tarmac, right behind me.

"last chance, stop now," he calls.

but i'm thru the door. Rick is beside me. he pulls me in, almost pulls me off balance. i kind of dance awkwardly into a seat that's just opposite. he yanks on a metal lever & the stairs fold up with a breath of pumps, & then he hits another button & the door snicks shut.

click.

outside, the guard shouts. "do not even think about taking off. if u try, i will shoot, i will—"

everyone ignores him.

Rick gestures at my seat. "belt up," he says.

i look behind me. Orion & Libra are already strapped into

seats, on opposite sides of the plane. Orion's drip is lashed to his armrest with some kind of canvas strap & i wonder how they managed that so quickly. he is terribly pale, breathing deeply from his oxygen tank, which is strapped into the seat next to him—2 seats on each side, 2 rows.

i turn back to the front of the plane & c Grandpa leaning back from the cockpit. "ready?" he says.

"er, yeah," i say.

there's more shouting from outside.

"where'd u get this plane from anyway?" i hear Grandpa say. "this isn't ur crop sprayer."

"borrowed it from the flying club," says Rick, pulling on headphones as the plane turns. "don't think they expected me to take it to Alaska."

"well, thanks," says Grandpa.

"any time," says Rick.

he throttles down. the plane accelerates, going back along the runway the way it came. i look out the window, c snow & rock blurring past. i tense, waiting for gunfire, but it doesn't come.

a sudden pull on my stomach, & a lurch, & then the plane is in the air, climbing. gravity fights: i feel it pulling down on every fiber of my body. but we're leaving, we're going, we're letting the ground fall away from us, & i hear a whooping sound & realize it's me, yelling with happiness.

i think again how the word *flight* is the noun that relates to flying & also the noun that relates to fleeing.

fleeing the mountain. fleeing Boutros. fleeing the earth.

fleeing my mother, even.

i stop thinking about that.

we rise, & rise, & rise, & the mountaintop is beside us & then it too falls away, & we are just in blackness, in space, as we begin to level out.

Grandpa sighs heavily, a kind of happy sigh, & comes out of the cockpit. he steadies himself with his hands as he walks down to us & stops, checking us all over.

"u guys all right?" he says.

Orion nods. Libra puts her thumb up. "yeah," i say.

he smiles. "told u i had a plan," he says.

i rub my eyes. "i thought he might shoot us down," i say.

"never," says Grandpa. "they're all about PR, these people. how would they explain that?"

i nod. yeah. that makes sense. "lucky u stole that medical ID card," i say.

he looks at me blankly. "what?"

"the 1 u showed the guard. when u said it was a medevac."

Grandpa laughs. "that? no. that was just my Farmers Union card. good thing Orion pulled that coughing fit."

18

hardcore

6 hours later, i know we're descending because i feel the buildup in my ears & swallow to pop them, to clear the pressure.

i look out the window, pressing my forehead against the cool of the plastic glass. Vancouver reveals itself as a network of light below, the ocean & the land varying patches of darkness. we fly over it & out to sea, then double back, losing altitude all the time. the propellers make a keening sound, over the rushing of the air.

"buckle up," shouts Grandpa from the front.

i look at Orion & Libra, their expressions unknowable, then click my belt so it's locked.

the plane dives steeper still, & i feel my organs rise toward my throat, feel almost as if my body wants to lift up, up, up into the sky, into space, wants to untether itself already & go floating up there, without even the aid of a rocket.

but the ground is getting closer & closer, the buildings too, big shiny office blocks all made of windows, with lights flashing on their roofs. it's as if we're flying right into the city & for a moment i wonder if Rick is going to land on a street, just come down to rest in the middle of some Vancouver avenue, stopping traffic, but then i c the green dots of a runway just ahead & to the right, & we swing down toward it.

it's about a mile from the high-rises of the financial district, the runway, & it's a big 1, like a commercial airport—a couple of low white hangar buildings over to our left as we come in to land & vehicles parked everywhere—a big control tower with a tall mast on top that must have cleared us for landing, & i wonder how Grandpa has managed to pull strings this big.

coming in close to the ground, we almost seem to stop for an instant, to hover, to remain for seconds between earth & sky, hanging. then the wheels touch the ground & we bump along, & i feel the force of the brakes as we slow dramatically.

then we stop.

Grandpa gets up & comes back to us. "Rick's opening the door. there's going to be a car waiting. we'll carry u down & into the car & it will take us to Deer Lake Park. by the time we get back, there'll be a private jet ready for us."

"another private jet?" says Libra.

"yes," says Grandpa.

Libra is speechless for once, for a moment. then: "cool," she says.

Rick appears, & he & Grandpa go to Orion first. he winces as they lift him up & carry him down the stairs, being slow & careful, because of his IV. they prop him against a wheel. then they come back for Orion's wheelchair, then for Libra, & finally Grandpa comes up on his own. he moves up the plane, leans into the cock-pit, & snags his 2 bags. he drops 1 at Rick's feet. Rick glances down at it & nods.

i realize this must be payment of some sort, cash that Grandpa has somehow gathered together.

i can't ask him. i don't know the words.

i feel tears stinging my eyes & i blink them away.

Grandpa sees me looking at the bag & shrugs & smiles, & it breaks whatever spell is on me. "grabbed everything in the safe before we left the ranch," he says. he offers me his arm, to help me down the steps. he holds my crutches.

Rick leans against the wall of the plane. "well," he says. "this is as far as i go. i'd better get this baby back to California before the week is out or the club will start wondering." he gives a little salute. "good luck, Leo."

i salute back. "thanks, Rick. thanks for coming for us."

he shrugs. "best night i've had in a long time," he says. then he turns & heads to the cockpit. he stops. looks at Grandpa. "actually, if ur friend could c his way to refueling me, i'd be grateful."

"consider it done," says Grandpa.

"all right then. i'll c u on the other side."

"i'll call u," says Grandpa.

"u better," says Rick. "i'll be needing some water for my horses pretty soon."

"sure thing," says Grandpa.

& that's that.

we go outside, & start down the steps.

the air is less cold than at the mountain but still cool, with a salty tang in it that i assume drifts in off the sea, the very breeze tasting of it. at the bottom of the steps, a dark limousine waits, its windows blacked out. a door at the back stands open, & Libra & Orion must be inside.

for just an instant, i think of the men in black suits & their black cars, back in that farmer's field where we landed all that time ago, but then the front door of the limo opens & a guy in a very different kind of suit—pinstriped, gray—leaps out. he has neat white hair & a white beard & is wearing a red tie against a white shirt, matching his red pocket square.

he walks over briskly & waits at the bottom of the steps. & when we get down he claps Grandpa on the shoulder.

"Freeman!" he says. "welcome to Pearson Field."

"thanks," says Grandpa. "& thanks for ur help."

the man waves this away. "this ur grandson?" he says.

"yes," says Grandpa. "Leo, meet Jonas Lindsen. Jonas is the CEO of Lindair. they make planes—private jets mostly—which they test right here. Jonas: Leo."

"good to meet u," i say.

"so u're the 1 who wants to go back to space." it's mostly not a question but there's a hint of a question in it.

"yeah," i say.

he nods. "closest i got was high-altitude test flying. high enough to c the curve of the earth, u know? man, i'd love to get back up there. sadly none of our planes can fly that high."

"u could always come with us," says Grandpa, smiling. some private joke is being had, i think.

"& ruin this suit?" says Jonas. "this is Italian herringbone."

Grandpa grins. "well, we're grateful," he says. "without u this wouldn't even get off the ground. literally."

Jonas shrugs. "it's nothing for me. a car. a plane. i have lots of them." there's a thread of irony in his voice that makes me smile. like, he's rich but he also knows it's ridiculous to be rich. even tho it's something useful, or something like that. it's hard to describe.

"well, it means a lot," says Grandpa. "the car u'll have back in an hour, maybe a bit more. the plane . . . it might take me a bit of time to return it."

"u're flying to Kazakhstan?" says Jonas.

"yes."

"u're going to go up in 1 of those old Burans they've got stashed away there?"

"u know about that?" says Grandpa.

"i know a lot of things," says Jonas. "so?"

"i couldn't possibly comment," says Grandpa.

Jonas laughs. "ok. well, just bring the plane back whenever u're ready."

i stare at him. at the crinkles around his eyes. the wry smile.

the silver pin thru his tie. "u're not worried about, i don't know, losing ur plane?" i say.

he looks at me. bends down a little, so we're on an even level. "listen," he says. "ur grandpa & i were in the air force together. actually, he was my commanding officer. he asks for something, he gets it." pause. "plus, 30 years ago, i had a contract with NASA. supplying engines. the Company came in, took over, & they canceled the project. i had to let 200 people go. in the air force, they used to say, *no man left behind.* i do not like leaving people behind."

he straightens, & puts out his hand, then shakes mine—his grip is strong.

"well, thanks," i say.

"any time," he says. "altho in this context that does not seem very appropriate."

another black car pulls up behind & he points to it. "that one's me. the limo will take u to the park. the concert starts in"—he looks at his watch, an old Speedmaster like Grandpa's, i notice—"10 minutes. u will miss the beginning. but with Mozart, it's the endings that matter."

he strides over to his car & Grandpa & i go to ours & Grandpa helps me in, to a seat next to Libra & opposite Orion. i c that Orion's wheelchair is parked in a space that has been made by removing some of the seats, & i wonder if Jonas arranged that, before we arrived, if it's all been planned.

yes, & in great detail, i suspect, are the answers, if i know Grandpa at all. to be honest, i don't even believe he didn't steal a medical ID card. i think he really did. i think that thing he said, in the plane, about the Farmers Union, is just the type of joke he would make.

i think . . . i think my grandpa might be kind of hardcore.

"u have a lot of friends who owe u favors, huh?" i say to Grandpa.

he nods. "it's a good life strategy."

the car pulls away & we drive down the runway, then off onto a path marked by cones, which leads past some airport buildings to a security gate that opens automatically, rolling smoothly on bearings. we drive out onto the street.

to a concert.

on earth.

with Libra & Orion. & those are things that even two days ago i wouldn't have thought i would be saying. ever.

19
symphony

we cruise thru a land of wide streets & strip malls, which quickly gives way to bigger buildings. streetlights wash over us, faces illuminated & plunged into shadow in turn as we pass them, the red glow of Somali food stores, neon signs in Arabic, the riotous multicolored logos of Jamaican cafés.

people hurry down the sidewalks, not looking up, hunched over. intersections flick past, & the tick of the indicator as we turn, as we roll thru dark Vancouver, windows leaking light, makes me feel sleepy, makes me feel like maybe we should just stop here & forget this whole thing, forget going back.

lights flash on hard surfaces of glass & metal.

we slide thru the night.

it's almost like being back on Moon 2 & it makes me feel sleepy . . .

but just as my head is nodding forward we pull to a stop in a parking lot.

the partition window lowers. "this is the park," says a deep voice from the front seat. "head thru that gate in front of us. can't miss the concert. they put out chairs right in the main space." pause. "oh, wait." a hand appears, holding a thick wedge of blankets. "u'll be needing these," he says.

"Jonas think of that?" says Grandpa.

"yes sir," says the driver.

the door pops open & Grandpa helps me out, then Libra, who leans on the side of the car, then Orion's wheelchair & finally Orion.

we stop, & sit there for a moment.

Orion takes off his mask.

"i can hear it," he says. his voice is quiet, weak. "i can hear the violins."

i listen. & sure enough, i hear them, their thin tremolo, like the air itself is vibrating.

"come on," says Libra. "let's go."

Grandpa tucks a blanket over Orion, then starts pushing him, & Libra props herself on her walker & follows, & i crutch along after them, thinking what a strange group we must look like, the 4 of us. we go thru the gate & down a path that turns, & then we're in a wide-open space. a low building made of glass walls is on the far side, & all around are carefully arranged gardens, borders planted with flowers whose colors shine under fairy lights strung up everywhere above. a lake is ahead of us, gleaming dully.

there are rows & rows of seats placed in the central open area in front of the lake, & on a stage at the foot of the building, an orchestra is seated, dressed in white shirts & black jackets & trousers, holding their instruments, & playing.

some of the seats at the back are empty, & Grandpa leads us to a row where he & Libra & i can sit, & Orion can park in the center aisle. an old lady, wrapped in furs, turns & tuts as we rasp into our seats, then looks aghast when she sees the walker, the crutches, the wheelchair. "sorry," she whispers, & turns back to face the orchestra.

i look around. trees & shrubs are planted artfully, & the scent of pine rides the waves of music, from a stand of trees nearby.

or maple, maybe. does maple have a smell? i don't know. i don't know trees, for obvious reasons. Libra would know, but i can't ask her.

to either side, the park flows out into the darkness, & we are in an island of light, the audience & the plants illuminated by a million points of brightness, little LED bulbs strung in every direction in a kind of web above us.

& everywhere, the music.

it swells, it grows, it builds.

sharp cymbals & timpani, the vibration of the strings, the hum of the woodwinds, & the metallic sheen of the brass flow around & thru me, & they sound like the stars might sound if u could hear them, all of them, all the billions & billions of them, singing their song, & if this is how it makes me feel i don't know what Orion is thinking.

what i do know, apparently, is what the different instruments are, & that's all thanks to Orion, & i look over at him & smile as i realize how much i've inadvertently picked up from living with him.

still, i have never really appreciated Mozart properly, just pretended to care about it when Orion would play us vids of famous performances. but what amazes me now as i listen to the symphony in real air & in real time is that i hear feelings in it, i hear thoughts, which appear deliberate—it seems to be music about longing, about anticipation, & it is leading to something, to some great revelation, to some event, & my heart seems to inflate in my chest, as if it might burst.

i look over at Orion, & c the tears running down his cheeks.

he makes no attempt to brush them away.

& the music builds.

& it builds.

it is almost as if the music is alive, as if it possesses some kind of intelligence, & maybe that's why it sounds like the song of the stars to me, like the heavenly bodies joining in a chorus, because it seems almost that there is a voice there, saying something, if only i could understand.

but whenever i think i understand, it slides from my grasp, quick, like water.

the violins are getting faster, & the percussion drops, & now the music is rain, falling on us, & i feel the cold & the wet of it, & how is it that u can feel music?

i didn't know. i didn't know about this.

but Orion knew. he always knew what it would be like, he could imagine its contours, even as he'd never heard it, & i c the smile on his face as he cries, as he cries.

the rain falls but there is no rain. it is a clean & crisp & cold night. i clutch my blanket to me.

the music swells, & swells, & the meaning of it is just there, just almost in reach—& then the melody comes, gently, to an end.

the audience erupts into applause.

i am dizzy, i am breathless, i am floating in the air. i am weightless, & yet i'm tied to my chair, gravity is holding me down.

i turn to Orion.

i smile.

he smiles.

he closes his eyes. i can almost c his eyeballs thru his eyelids: they are translucent, like something made by a wasp from chewed-up wood.

he's d—

starts a voice inside me.

i clamp down on it, make it stop.

"ok," says Grandpa. "we need to move. i don't want to stay in 1 place for too long." people are glancing back at us. others are getting up, starting to leave, squeezing past Orion's chair. "we're very recognizable," he adds.

he stands, & goes to Orion's wheelchair, & takes the handles at the back.

"no," says Orion. he has pushed his blanket away & it lies puddled in front of the wheelchair, like something collapsed, like something dead.

i get up, hold on to the back of my chair. i take Libra's hand & help her stand too & back out of the row, till she can catch hold of her walker. Orion is still sitting there in his wheelchair, & Grandpa is looking down at him, puzzled.

"what do u mean, no?" i say to him.

Orion looks up at me. his eyes are half-closed, his skin is paper thin, is lit from within, like the moon. the mask is dangling, hanging on his ribs, which i can c even thru his loose gray Company sweater. he lifts the mask & takes a halfhearted pull of oxygen & then holds it loosely by his mouth.

"this is the end of the road for me," he says.

"no," i say. i look at Libra & i c that she is crying, that she has already understood, maybe a long time ago, maybe back in the dome even. but it's a wave, that understanding, & i don't want it to break over me yet, i don't want it to break me yet.

"yes," he says. his chest is rising & falling rapidly, his hands are so small, his fingers are so slim, he has the bones of birds in them. "u knew that," he says. "u must have known."

Grandpa lets out a long, low sigh; the music it makes, the sound of a soul whistling thru a person's mouth.

people keep moving past us, endless people, some in jeans & parkas & some in suits & ties & long evening coats, & they barge past, a river of them, & some of them look at us curiously but no one stops, no one asks, they just keep on leaving, & soon it will be just us, all alone here, under the million little lights, with the echoes of the symphony dying around us, & the scrapes as the musicians clear away their instruments.

& i did know, i knew it like i knew my mother did not sail thru preflight medical checks with a fetus already inside her; i knew it when Orion laid out that ridiculous scheme about screens & calling Boutros on them & what kind of an idea was that anyway, what kind of fairy tale was that?

i knew it in the music.

i heard it in the tingling anticipation of the strings, in the crescendo as it rose & rose & rose.

it is what the music was trying to tell me.

20

love

"i want to talk to Libra . . . for a moment," says Orion. he has abandoned any pretense of putting his mask back on; it hangs down on his chest, shiny in the artificial light, some kind of sea creature, a squid maybe.

Grandpa & i back away. what else can we do? Libra remains by his side, sinking into a chair next to him so they can lean together, so he can speak. they whisper, he & Libra, for a long time, their heads together. then she stands, & comes over to where i wait, her cheeks wet with tears.

"he wants to talk to u," she says.

gravity is pulling me even more than usual, my feet are leaden on the ground. i move slowly.

i look down at him.

he is so very pale now, under the many-pointed light. everything else has fallen away; we're on our own asteroid, floating thru space.

"in the back pocket," he says. "of my chair. get it."

i go to the chair & take out what's in there. It's the book of e. e. cummings poetry, the 1 i gave him.

"for u," he says. "take it back up there."

"really?"

"cummings belongs in space, i think," he says.

i feel myself starting to cry. i stop myself. this isn't about me.

"i'm sorry," he says. "& i'm sorry for . . . u know. for who i am. for who u are. i always knew, u know? but i could never . . . i could never have been what u wanted me to be."

"i know," i say. his eyes are filled with distance. galaxies, eons. blackness stretching to infinity. he's slipping.

he closes them.

"no," i say. & that's when i do start to cry, the hot tears spilling out of me like they will never stop. i had no idea there was so much liquid in my body, & it's churning, making waves inside me, & i might never make myself solid again. i try to speak & choke & then try again. "no, i don't want u to go. i just want u to stay, just please stay, that's all i want."

his eyelids flutter. "sorry," he says again.

my tears are falling on him, on his skin. i barely thought about him when i was on the ranch, not much—how could i not have thought about him? i should have been talking to him all the time, all the time i should have been on the screen to him, seeing him. & now i'm hating the Company for blocking the screens & everything i c is blurred; i don't even c him now, when i need to.

"don't," i say. "don't go please don't go. come on." i'm pleading now, babbling, almost delirious. "u can't go anyway u can't," i'm shaking him, "u can't because i always thought my first kiss would be with u i always dreamed of it anyway & u can't go because i haven't had my first kiss so u can't go u can't go u can't go."

silence.

then a whisper, silken on the air between us, so faint & smooth, so quiet. i don't hear what he said.

"what?" i say.

a breeze, passing between his lips, no more. i can't understand.

i lean closer. "what are u saying?"

& he lifts his head just for a moment & puts his hand on mine

& kisses me, on the cheek, & his lips are dry as parchment, & it's not at all how i imagined, how i dreamed, but at the same time the world stops just for an instant & the moon too, because it's all held together by love—the moon is tied to the earth by love.

he lowers his head again.

"there," he says.

"thank u," i say.

the shadow of a smile on his lips. "i imagined u were ur mother," he says.

i laugh, & then i feel bad that i laughed.

"very beautiful woman, u know, ur mother," he says. then he smiles. "thank u, Leo," he says. "for most this amazing day."

he's unraveling, even his words are not in the right order.

& he doesn't speak anymore.

i am bearing witness, & i don't close my eyes.

i keep looking into his.

galaxies, black foreverness, all the everywhere depth of yes.

yes.

& then he dies.

i feel it happen. i c his chest stop rising & falling, c a slackness fall over his face, his features, & he's gone.

"no," i say. "no no no no no."

& Libra comes back.

& we hold each other.

& we don't let go.

because we're held together by love.

21
earth

Libra lowers herself into the seat next to Orion's wheelchair. she pulls her blanket over herself, then holds out her hand, as if for us to give her something.

"what?" i say.

"give me a screen," she says.

"what?"

"a screen. so i can call Boutros. like Orion planned."

"but Orion's dead," i say. the words sound surreal coming out of my mouth. like they can't be true. but they are.

"exactly," she says. "& u're not. which means u need to go & u don't need me getting in the way, & anyway i don't want to go with u. i want to go to my garden. so give me a screen. then leave. i'll wait for 15 minutes before i call."

"& if they ask where we've gone?" says Grandpa.

"i'll say i don't know," she says.

"they might . . . pressure u," he says.

she indicates the walker nearby, the oxygen tank strapped to it. "what can they do to me that they haven't already done?" she says.

i hesitate for a moment.

"please," says Libra. "go. vid me when u get up there."

"she's right," says Grandpa. "we need to get moving."

"ok ok," i say. i lean down & give Libra a kiss on the cheek—her skin is softer than Orion's, warmer. "i love u," i say.

"i love u too," she says. "i hope . . . i hope u get there." she hugs me, deft & quick, & then lets go, & wraps herself more tightly in the blanket. then she lifts a hand. "wait." she adjusts the blanket, puts her hand down inside her gown & lifts out the locket with the thimbleful of earth in it, the 1 her mother gave her. she passes the silver chain over her head & holds out the necklace.

"for me?" i say, dumbfounded.

"yes." she lowers it; the chain pools in my cupped palm like cool water. "a piece of earth," she says. "wear it & remember us. wear it for luck."

i nod, gravely. i slip it over my head, feel its coldness against my skin, then push it down under my sweater, under my t-shirt. "always," i say.

she lifts her hand, shows me her finger with the ring on it, the 1 i gave her with the sunflower seed inside. she smiles.

i touch the bump of the locket, under the fabric of my shirt. i smile too.

i remember when she wanted to take that plant down, to have something from up there down here, & i think how i'll be doing the opposite, taking this piece of earth from her, taking it with me up in the sky, & i get it now.

i get why u would want to mingle the 2.

"ok," she says, after clearing her throat. "now fuck off back to space."

i laugh, shocked, & she turns away, laughing too, but crying now also, i c.

"do it for me," i say. "graduate high school. become a botanist. have kids. all of it."

"u know i'll try," she says.

& yes, i do.

"let's go," says Grandpa. but not unsoftly.

& so we go.

we:

–walk back to the car.

–drive thru the streets of Vancouver, lights swishing past stores, sidewalks.

–reach the security gate where a big sign reads PEARSON FIELD—LINDAIR FLIGHT CREW & EMPLOYEES ONLY.

–drive into the airfield, as the gate rolls open on little wheels.

–pull up to a sleek private jet that is sitting on the runway in a dark lake of its own shadow, the silhouette of 2 pilots at the front, wearing hats, the stairs already down & waiting for us.

"this is ur ride," says the driver. he reaches a hand thru the partition, shakes ours. "good luck," he adds.

"thanks," we say.

then we climb the steps, Grandpa assisting me, air rushing thru our hair, floodlights banishing the darkness, little colored dots marking the geometrical shapes on the ground of runways & access routes & paths to the terminals.

there's no crew, so we just take a seat in 1 of the plush leather chairs, & buckle up. "welcome aboard," comes a voice over the intercom. "i'm Captain Angelos & my copilot is Flight Lieutenant Lanlokun, & we'll be flying u to Baikonur tonight. cruising altitude will be 35,000 ft. we'll be stopping for fuel & not arriving at our destination until well into tomorrow, so make urselves comfortable. there's a fridge back there with snacks & drinks— unfortunately we couldn't provide any air crew on such short notice. but we hope u have a pleasant journey."

click. the intercom goes off.

a man in a uniform, presumably Flight Lieutenant Lanlokun, comes back & closes the door.

then:

we taxi to the runway.

we accelerate, & lift up into the sky.

& all the while i'm thinking of Libra, sitting there on her own next to her dead brother, wrapped in her blanket, & all the while i'm squeezing the locket in my grip, her gift to me, squeezing it tight, holding on to the earth with that hand & that 1 hand only, as the rest of me rises into the sky.

22
tranquility

we fly for hours & hours. it's like being home: black sky lightening slowly as the sunrise chases us.

we land somewhere on the far eastern end of the Russian landmass, i guess—an anonymous airfield where unseen people refuel the plane. then we take off again, as the sun peels away from the horizon behind us, lofts up into lightening blue.

i must sleep a little, then, because when i wake we're descending again, my ears popping, & soon we're touching down on a scrub-lined runway, the sun high in the sky, desert stretching away in every direction, a few low buildings the only evidence of any kind of airport or infrastructure.

the intercom crackles.

"Baikonur," says the pilot. "air temp is 30 Fahrenheit, according to my instruments. i hope u brought warm clothes."

click.

Flight Lieutenant Lanlokun comes aft & nods at us, then waits by the door. for steps of some kind, i imagine. eventually he cranks it open & light tunnels in, tubular, framing him, making his edges glow fuzzily.

we get up & go over to the door. Lanlokun is a middle-aged guy with a very short haircut, his hair gray & his skin dark. "i'm not asking any questions," he says. "but i'll be watching the news."

Grandpa smiles. "we'll try to make sure it's not unpleasant viewing."

Lanlokun nods, & shakes our hands before we leave the plane. "say thank u again to Jonas for us," says Grandpa.

Lanlokun salutes. "will do."

then we're out in the blink-making brightness. Grandpa ferries my crutches down before coming back up for me, & then helps me down the steps. i look around. we're in the middle of nowhere, just a few hangars & what looks like 1 administrative building. low, flat land, mostly scrub & sand & red earth, surrounds the airport. the air ices my skin, & i shiver in my sweater & jacket.

"Kazakhstan," says Grandpa. "it's a bit of a shithole, to be honest. now where's Yuri?"

as he says it i c an old military jeep driving toward us, battered, its green paint faded. the car pulls to a stop just short of us on the runway, & a barrel-shaped man descends from it, beaming from ear to ear. his mustache quivers in the wind. "Freeman!" he shouts. "Freeman!"

he sort of waddles over, still smiling, & pulls my grandpa into a huge bear hug, lifting him off his feet. "hello, Yuri," says Grandpa.

Yuri puts him down, then bends a little to look at me—he's tall, maybe 6'5". inconveniently tall for an astronaut; a lot of his career would have involved crouching, stooping, i realize.

"& u must be the little astronaut," he says—it could sound patronizing but somehow it's not. "the 1 we are shooting into space."

"um, yes," i say. "i'm Leo, hi." i put out my hand to shake his.

he laughs, & swats my hand away like it's a fly, then he picks me up, just lifts me off the ground & squeezes me tight.

"watch it," says Grandpa. "his bone mass is—"

"damn, i forgot," says Yuri. he releases his hold & lowers me gently to the ground. he claps Grandpa on the back. "it's shit-good to c u, Freeman," he says. "i thought i would not c u in body again. just on screen."

"u too," says Grandpa. "u haven't changed at all."

Yuri grabs a handful of his belly. he's wearing a thin shirt & a furry hat & no jacket; i can't believe he's not freezing. "nonsense," he says. "i am becoming fat & wobbly like blammidge."

"blammidge?" says Grandpa.

"blammage. blammanch?" says Yuri. "dessert. wobble wobble."

"oh, blancmange!" says Grandpa.

Yuri pulls an expression. "u are saying i look like blanc-mange?"

"no, no, i was—"

Yuri roars with laughter. "i fuck with u," he says. he produces an e-cig from his pants pocket & puts it in his mouth. then he turns to me. "ur grandfather & i, we had many missions together. many months in space. when u are like this with another person, pissing in suction tubes next to each other, for samples, it makes u close."

"um, yeah," i say. it's true tho. i think for a second of Orion, of Libra, then i chase the thought from my mind.

"me & Freeman," says Yuri. "piss brothers. for life."

"piss brothers?" says Grandpa. "wonderful."

Yuri rolls his eyes. "now, we go to cosmodrome, yes? it is maybe 1 hour drive. i will take u in my car."

Grandpa eyes the jeep. significant portions of the bodywork are missing. 1 tire looks very flat. there is rust all down the sides. "this thing?" he says.

"Russian engineering," says Yuri. "in better shape than it looks. same with our old rockets."

"well, i really hope so," says Grandpa.

Yuri shakes his head. "i don't need hope," he says. "i have luck. always." he winks at me. "ask ur grandfather. i am lucky. lucky charm."

Grandpa smiles at me. "he's pretty lucky," he says.

"the most lucky," says Yuri. "& now u are here again. even luckier! so. let's ride." he opens the door & ushers us in, the 2 of them lifting me in to the backseat, then slinging the crutches into the rear of the car. Grandpa gets into the front next to his old friend, & Yuri puts the car in gear & drives jerkily off.

soon we leave the runway behind. there's a guard post & a gate topped with barbed wire, but the men with Kalashnikovs who guard it seem to know Yuri & wave him thru. we bump onto a rough road that leads away from the airport, into the blank land that lies around it. i feel alternately sweaty & shivery—my body doesn't seem to be able to adjust to the cold.

i look out the window as we drive. i feel dislocated, discombobulated, disorientated, disarmed. everything i feel begins with *dis*. less than 48 hours ago i was in a facility on a mountain in Alaska & now i'm in Kazakhstan, in an old Russian jeep, on a road that is barely a road, in a landscape wiped clean by wind & snow, pockets of which lie whitely & thickly here & there in the sand.

we drive, & it is as if we are not driving, because nothing about the world around us changes—there are mountains somewhere in the distance, a gray smudge on the skyline, but we come no closer to them, only rattle across desert.

minutes pass.

more.

finally a space begins to open up in front of us, an impression of the land dropping away, & the road starts to curve, gently at first & then more steeply, & i realize that we're following the course of a river that is below us & to the left, in a shallow ravine. on the other side of the river, the desert continues, as if the river was only a brief distraction in its endless story of sand & low bushes & patches of snow.

Yuri points out his window.

"the Syr Darya," he says. "only water we have around here." i c the slow, wide river flowing black as ink thru the flat Kazakh landscape. there are few trees: everything seems blasted, scoured—a desert in the true sense of the word. i notice an animal wandering along the course of the river, looking miserable. its own breath clouds above it. it's far away, i can't quite make it out.

"what's that?" i say.

"camel," says Yuri, when he sees what i'm pointing at.

"wow," i say. "i thought pretty much all the wild animals were extinct."

"not camels," says Yuri. "camels are too fucking stubborn to die. my granddad raised them & i always hated them. stupid *vorchuny*."

"*vorchuny?*" i say.

"like, grumpy people," says Grandpa.

"people?"

"well, camels in this case," says Grandpa.

i watch the river as we pass it. the glassy surface. "lots of water too," i say.

"yes but cold," says Yuri. "when people fall in, they die." he laughs. "sometimes other people jump in to help them. they die too. hypothermia."

cheerful, i think.

Grandpa leans over & whispers something to Yuri.

Yuri shuts up.

he told him about Orion, i think. & i feel oddly embarrassed, like my friend-brother-whatever's death is something to be ashamed of, & then i feel ashamed in turn of that burning sensation in my cheeks, & i lean against the window, feel the cold of it against my forehead, the smoothness of the glass.

the desert unfolds itself before us, a constant rolling carpet of thin scrubby grass & sand.

gradually, a city comes into view. first a sketch of shapes on the horizon—blocks, rectangles, towers—& then resolving into huge buildings, cranes, houses.

"Baikonur cosmodrome," says Yuri.

& i realize it's not a city; it's a rocket center. this whole town, growing as we approach it, is constructed around the old launch sites that used to be here. then the great space city is around us, warehouses & what look like apartment buildings flashing past on either side, & i wonder how many people must have lived here last century, when the space race was at its peak, & when the ISS was being built.

there are very few people here now tho: the odd rusting car, a man huddled in scarves limping along the road, packs of stray dogs roaming the streets, dust blowing in the wind. i breathe into my hands, to warm them.

we drive right thru. over to our left, i c a tall gantry-like structure that may once have been a T-shaped rig a rocket would be attached to before liftoff. there's a train station of some kind too, abandoned cargo containers on tracks, big flatbeds that would have taken equipment where it was needed. weeds grow between the railroad ties.

then the city is gone, & we're past it.

Yuri keeps going.

"we're not stopping?" says Grandpa.

"we're going somewhere else," says Yuri.

"where?"

"u'll c," says Yuri. "trust me."

23

indoor clouds

Yuri doesn't say anything more—just keeps his hands on the wheel. the road is long & flat & poorly maintained. the occasional shack flicks past the windows. everything seems forgotten, left behind, the whole road & outbuildings & poor run-down houses like toys discarded in a playroom no one has visited in years.

there's a forest, ahead. dark, thru the windshield. tall pine trees. they are the first really big trees i have seen, & we're basically in a desert, which makes me think they were planted for a reason. Yuri turns off the main road & onto a rougher 1, which curves toward the forest, & it fills the windshield & then we're in it, suddenly plunged into shadow & shade, the temperature in the car lowering another degree & i put my hands under my arms.

trees press in on either side.

Grandpa turns to me & shrugs. he doesn't know what's going on either.

ahead, the road, & the woods flanking it. a knife of light thru the forest.

then there's a sense of a clearing ahead, & tall concrete walls, & then Yuri pulls into a cracked parking lot & stops & i peer out of my window, then open the door & look out & catch my breath.

in front of us is the biggest structure i have ever seen. a hangar of some sort. it is a kind of monumental rectangle, gray, blocky. it dwarfs any of the buildings at the base in Nevada, makes Mountain Dome look like an architect's model. i have to get out of the car to c the top of it, high up in the sky, skyscraper high.

"300 ft.," says Yuri, coming to stand next to me, seeing me looking up. i am leaning on the car door, keeping most of my weight on my good foot. "& 500 ft. on side. it rains in there, sometimes."

"it *rains*? in a building?"

"yes. it's so big that it has its own weather systems. water turns to vapor, rises when the sun heats the lower sections of the metal walls. condenses in the cool above. it needs to be very large. in here is where we stored the things we didn't want the others to know about, during the space race."

Grandpa is staring up at it too. "it's massive. how could we not have known? this thing must be pretty visible to a spy plane."

"u knew, i think," says Yuri. "but u didn't care. u knew we would run out of money & then—kaput—no more space program."

"which is what happened," i say.

"yes. until glasnost & then the ISS anyway," says Yuri. "then we began to work together. but there are still . . . secrets in here."

i look at the enormous, mind-bendingly large building. i can imagine it.

"come on, then," says Yuri. "let's go in."

he walks toward the hangar, & Grandpa & i follow. it rears up like a cliff above us, as we near it. ahead of us there's a surprisingly small door, riveted metal, set into the long side of the rectangular shape, tho i notice that the entire end wall of the building is on some kind of huge wheel runners—so that it can slide open & let out whatever is inside.

Yuri goes to a new-looking keypad next to the door & taps in a code, then presses his thumb to a screen. there's a *chunk*, & then the door swings open. we go inside. we don't go right into the hangar tho. there's a steel wall in front of us; we're in a small stairwell, cobwebbed. Yuri hits a switch next to him & lights flicker on overhead, fluorescent tube lights. stairs lead up to the right, shiny silver metal, lozenged with raised shapes, for grip.

"up," says Yuri.

he leads the way. Grandpa takes my crutches under his arm & offers me his shoulder, to lean on.

we climb.

switch back.

climb some more.

my breath comes hard & labored, my heart thudding. sweating even harder now. i remember climbing the stairs with Soto, back in Nevada. it feels like a lifetime ago. i start shaking, like a shiver that doesn't stop. weird.

we come to another door, which seems like it must open into the hangar, but higher up. Yuri enters another code, his thumbprint again. the door *shushes* open & we step thru.

& my breath stalls again, in my throat.

we're on a kind of platform, steel mesh, so u can c thru tiny holes to the bare concrete floor 100 ft. below. my head spins dizzily. i look up: the gray steel roof still seems cloud-height above us. birds wheel, cawing, away from walkways & rigging, black swatches of silk in the wind, screeching, turning & flapping & then settling, on bars & steps farther away.

crisscrossing the space, extending from the platform we are standing on, halfway between the ground & the roof, are gangways, metal bridges spanning the void.

& suspended, propped up on great structures of tubes & cinder blocks, smeared with dust, the gangways surrounding them to give access to their doors & engines & panels, dripping crowshit & lit by sharp columns of light spearing down from plastic lights in the roof far, far above, are . . . shuttles.

space shuttles.

sleek, massive objects like airplanes, but bigger, & with rocket engines at their rears.

3 of them, laid out in a row.

i'm in a building big enough to have its own weather, & dust hangs in the light all around me, & there are 3 space shuttles the size of small apartment buildings in here, rust-stained & worn by age.

"Jesus," says Grandpa. "part of me didn't really believe it."

Yuri sweeps a hand, proprietorial. "the Burans," he says. "the name means snowstorm. developed at end of space race, as a competitor to ur shuttle. but shelved when democracy came."

Grandpa frowns at them. at least 1 of them is missing a wing. there are open panels with wires poking out. rust everywhere. an engine has fallen off 1 of them, & lies in a pile of broken scaffolding & dust on the ground.

"we're taking 1 of these?" he says.

Yuri laughs. "no," he says. he points to the far end of the building, to our right. "u are good with distances, Freeman," he says. "does that look like 600 ft. to u?"

Grandpa squints. we're looking along the wall of the building, to where it ends in a sheet of steel at the end. he whispers to himself, his finger moves, as he counts along the gangway that runs from where we stand all along the wall, ticking off the ft. under his breath.

"no," he says. "more like 400."

"correct," says Yuri. "follow."

he sets off down the gangway, & we follow. we walk for what seems like a long time, my leg aching, my lungs rasping, but i feel like i can't complain. we pass 1 of the Burans, its conical nose almost within touching distance at 1 point—we can c thru the big wraparound windshield, to the shadowed darkness inside, an impression of seats & instruments.

i trudge on, the pain in my leg bad now, gravity dragging at me, wanting to pull me thru the hard mesh rattling walkway to the ground below.

Grandpa turns, sees that i'm struggling, & falls back. "u ok?"

i suck in breath. nod. but my leg has turned to an iron rod, & i can't bend my knee.

"no," i say eventually. "too tired."

we're only halfway along the walkway. Yuri & Grandpa exchange a look, don't even talk to each other, employ some kind of astronaut ESP. then Grandpa says, "hold ur crutches."

i gather them into 1 hand, concentrate on not toppling over.

then Grandpa & Yuri get a hand under each of my arms, 1 of them on either side of me, & suddenly i'm in the air & they move forward, carrying me between them, so it's as if i'm floating along the gangway—if u green-screened them out i'd be levitating, moving smoothly thru the air. the noise of their feet on the floor dims out; it's like my ears are blocked, as if by pressure change. there's a distance in my vision too, like everything, the whole world, has taken a step back.

before long, we are past the other Burans & at the end of the hangar. in front of us is another door, another code panel beside it. Yuri taps it. thumbs it. it opens, & there is darkness beyond.

Yuri steps thru.

Grandpa & i follow. me on my crutches.

Yuri swings down a small lever on the wall.

& the floodlights come on.

"holy shit," says Grandpa.

24

Soyuz

it stands before us.

we're in a circular space, built within the walls of the rectangular hangar, i guess—a hidden compartment at the extremity of that vast building that is itself the size & height of a skyscraper laid on its side.

the walkway curves to the right & to the left, hugging, bracketing a cylinder of air that stretches dizzyingly from the ground to the roof, like:

()

& we are at the bottom end of the parentheses, looking into the column.

but it's not an empty column of air.

at various points, like the spokes of a wheel, the walkway forks inward, allowing access to the center of the vertical hall, where *it* stands, its tip almost touching the roof.

birds rustle, somewhere in the shadows, high above.

somewhere near the tip.

because it's a rocket. a Soyuz rocket—i recognize it immediately. toward the end of the ISS, after NASA scrapped the shuttle program & before the Company took over, it was the only way for astronauts to reach the space station.

i walk to the railing in front of us, & lean over, & look down.

80 ft. below, the tail fins fan out, the thrusters below them, unseen.

i look up.

the rocket tapers as it reaches up to the artificial metal sky.

i notice some things.

i notice it's clean. no bird crap. no streaks of rust.

i notice the walkways are gleaming.

i notice there are no missing panels, no wires protruding. it's sleek, & smooth, & complete.

"how many people are still working at the base?" says Grandpa.

"enough," says Yuri.

"& they'll help us?"

Yuri smiles. "they will be happy to."

Grandpa shakes his head in disbelief. "we're going to just help ourselves to a Soyuz & fly up to space?"

Yuri shrugs. "that's always been the plan, no?"

Grandpa shakes his head. "the plan was a Buran. a shuttle. take off like a plane, orbit a bit, dock. easy. a 2-man job."

"well . . . ," says Yuri, "i may have misled u slightly. telephones can always be monitored, yes? the Burans are fucked. more rust than metal. we cannot fly them."

"we can't fly a Soyuz either!" says Grandpa. "it's a goddamned rocket."

"we have done it before, have we not?"

"yes, but then we had NASA behind us. ur space agency. ground crews. governmental support."

Yuri taps his nose. "u are not the only ones who have problem with the Company," he says. "with the monopoly."

"so who's going to help us? & when do we go?" i say.

Yuri makes a teeter-totter gesture with his hands. "i am

working on it," he says. "making calls. but first we find beds. have food. sleep. then we do logistics."

Grandpa takes a step forward, grips the rail with his hands. he leans closer to the rocket, almost seems to breathe it in. he has a faraway look in his eye, his mouth has twitched up at the edges, at the corners.

"i thought they were all destroyed," he says softly.

Yuri smiles. "well," he says. "obviously not."

25
transition

i am in a daze.

my memory is like a time-lapse vid:

the hangar peels away, around us, we climb back into the car, & then the forest swallows us & spits us out & we dart across the desert, it rolls by monotonously, the car speeds along, & then buildings appear & streets & we are back in the cosmodrome.

Yuri turns left, then right, then drives some more.

i close my eyes for a moment & lose some time. 10 minutes? more? when i open my eyes, i know i slept for a while even tho i didn't dream, it was just blackness.

then Yuri slows, & stops.

it's the edge of town.

the driver's door opens, & Yuri gets out. he pops the back door, & i haul myself out & onto the sidewalk. Grandpa gets out from the passenger seat.

ahead is a drab building, maybe 5 stories, institutional, like a school or a local government office. a sign in old-fashioned letters, each letter 6 ft. tall, hangs above the door. 2 of the letters are missing.

COSM NAUT'S HOT L

it reads.

an old woman opens the door. she is wearing a black dress, a dirty apron over it. she is holding a bucket in 1 hand & a cloth in the other. she nods, as if our appearance confirms something she has long, & unhappily, suspected. she retreats, leaving the door open.

i stand there for a moment. to my right, far away at the end of the street, which seems to just stop at a certain point, give way to sand, i can c the desert. a complicated arrangement of structures towers above it. i recognize it as a launch facility.

"this is where the cosmonauts used to stay, before going up to the ISS," says Yuri. "we have stayed here before, u & i," he adds, looking at Grandpa.

"of course," says Grandpa. he is looking up at the building with a strange look in his eye. like seeing someone he once loved, but now has complicated feelings for. or an old family member who left, who walked out. i don't know. something like that. dirty white curtains hang in the windows.

Grandpa puts his hand out & takes mine. he frowns. lifts his other hand & touches my forehead.

"what?" i say.

"u're running a fever," he says.

the air is cold, & it smells of ozone & oil, of the airfields i have come to know, an industrial smell, with something else too. something wild. Snow, perhaps. or the long-distant breath of camels.

Yuri walks up to the door & indicates the opening with his hands. "come," he says. "we stay here briefly. until we take the Soyuz." he points to the sky. it is starting to darken, to purple, & thin, long wisps of cloud almost like enormous aircraft contrails are tinging to the colors of a bruise, as a pale crescent moon stands out sharp against the glossy metallic sheen of the sky, as if branded there. "& we go up there," he says.

interlude
a storm

i'm 6, i think. maybe 7.

i'm playing hide-&-go-seek with Libra & Orion. there are no adults around; they're probably on the bridge or in 1 of the modules, conducting an experiment of some kind. we have the run of the main cross of the space station, barreling around, so small that we can fly. we do fly—we power thru the modules like birds, swooping.

right now, Libra & Orion are hiding. they won't do it separately. they do everything together, even hiding, even seeking. they are a unit. their mother is not 1 of the adults who is here, on the station, at the moment, & when she is on earth they are even more 1 person.

i am looking for them. i torpedo past the hydroponics, past tiny lettuces & beans growing under bright light. no sign of Libra & Orion. i go thru our dorm module: we all sleep together, the 3 of us, in 3 little cots attached to the walls. i look under the cots. nothing.

the clock on the screen on the wall reads 10:21. i know how to read the time. i learned before i learned to talk, almost. Virginia taught us, with a watch she brought up to the station that had a blue hand for hours & a red 1 for minutes.

time is important: here, there is no night & day, or rather there is, on the earth below, but day & night succeed 1 another so fast, 14 times in 10 hours, that without a 24-hour clock u never know when it's time for playing, or napping, or sleeping.

now, it's time for playing.

i keep going. no Libra & Orion in the dark energy sensor room either. i pause in the cupola chamber, the inverse glass dome an eye & i am inside it, looking down thru it. we are over an ocean, & small islands dot the blue sea. a tiny fleck might be a cargo ship.

i hover there & watch the earth turning below me. i can hear no one & c no one. i am alone in the space station. i'm small, just a child, & for a moment i feel scared, i feel like maybe i really am all alone, floating up here forever with no one around me. it's a feeling i've had before, but never this strong.

the black depth of space frames the earth. the distant stars speckling the darkness, tho i don't know they're distant. at this age i think only that they are small things, dusting the universe that surrounds the place i live. they have always been there, since i can remember. the moon too.

my mother has not always been here. & when she is here, she is not like Libra & Orion's mother; she does not hold me, she does not whisper to me, she does not kiss me or ruffle my hair or tell me stories or any of the things their mother does. & i have no idea who my father is either; it's like i have no parents. it's like i belong to the stars.

so i watch them, the stars.

& i feel a strange sensation, just for an instant, like i'm older than i am, like i am seeing thru some secret door.

i am in the moment, but at the same time i am aware that i will remember this moment in the future; it pulses with significance, a beacon in the black sea of time.

like 1 day, i will be alone again, up here. like this is what is meant for me.

then i hear a noise, from somewhere down the x-axis of the

station, just faint, but audible. i plant my feet on the edge of the cupola & launch myself in the direction where the sound came from, arms stretched out in front of me; a diver.

i shoot thru a sleeping module & then i enter 1 of the spectrometer modules & i c that the door to a white cupboard built into the wall is ajar, & i open it & Libra & Orion tumble out, Libra somersaulting end over end, tucked into a ball, & Orion careers into me & we spin in the air, laughing.

"ur turn," he says.

"no," i say. at that precise moment i cannot bear the idea of being on my own. "let's do something else."

Libra is at the window. "look," she says. "a storm."

we look out. a chain of islands is below us, & approaching it, a dirty white flaring circle of clouds, spiking almost, feathering, from the force of the wind that is cycloning inside it.

right in the middle, there is a core of stillness, of blue sea, surrounded by whirling energy.

the storm is moving quickly, toward the islands, patches of green in the wide ocean, in the sunshine, suddenly seeming terribly vulnerable.

i shiver, imagining being on 1 of those islands, imagining being in a house by the beach, watching the storm approaching, feeling the breath of the wind, hearing the rattle of the shutters.

i'm up here, i remind myself. i touch the wall of the module.

i hold Libra's hand.

scoot closer to Orion.

i'm up here.

& i'm safe.

in-between 1

i open my eyes, & Grandpa is looking down at me.

"we've given u some acetaminophen," he says. "to bring down the temperature."

"i'm sick?" i say.

"yes."

i am dimly aware of my body shivering. i burrow down under the covers. there are brown-patterned walls. i think i'm in the hotel. wait. what hotel? an image floats in front of me: COSM NAUT'S HOT L. on the bedside table is a half-empty glass of water. half-full. half-empty. above is a flickering light, an old-school 1, incandescent bulb, with a tasseled shade.

"where's Yuri?" i say.

"meeting people," says Grandpa.

i try to sit, but fail. "this . . . is it the earth that's making me sick? is this it?"

"it?"

"am i . . ."

"dying?"

"yes."

he smiles. "no. i think this is just a virus. u didn't have much exposure to them up there. any exposure."

"i had a cold at the base," i say. "in Nevada. it didn't feel like this."

"did u have a fever?"

"i don't know."

"then u didn't have a fever," he smiles. "this time u did."

fever.

it makes sense. i think of the word *feverish*. the idea of a certain restlessness, a motion within that can't be stilled. i feel it, in my bones. deep inside. it rattles me, like the window of Yuri's old car rattles as it drives.

"are we still going?" i ask.

"yes," says Grandpa. "but only when u're better. can't risk taking a virus up there. it would circle around forever."

in-between 2

i wake up.
    it's dark.
    no one is here.
    i go back to sleep.

in-between 3

i am sitting up when Grandpa comes in. my body is still, my muscles no longer trying to shake off my skin, to slough it away.

i am sipping water from the glass. i feel hungry.

"i feel hungry," i say.

"good," says Grandpa. "Yuri will be pleased. he wants u to try some mutton dish the cook is making. it smells . . . interesting."

"oh great."

Grandpa winks. he sits down on the side of the bed. "here," he says. he passes me an unrolled screen.

i look at it.

there is a message there, in big type. i assume Grandpa zoomed it for me.

go, Leo.

fly.

fly, & don't look back.

it would be inaccurate to say that i am proud of u. u *are* my pride. u are the best of me, walking around the world. but the world isn't the place for u.

so fly.

love,

ur mother.

"u told her?"

"kind of had to," he says. "they are freaking out hard at Mountain Dome."

"it would have killed her to sign it 'Mom,' i suppose," i say.

Grandpa smiles. but i am smiling too.

26
launch, part 1

i don't know how many days we lost, but i'm better. not feverish anymore, anyway.

the Americans used to fly from here too, back when the United States & Russia were still collaborating on the international space station.

back then, the astronauts would have been quarantined for days before a launch, to make sure they didn't catch colds & things—a cold on a space station could be disastrous. no gravity to help clear the nostrils, which meant infections lasted a long time & a circulating air system constantly pumping germs back into the bodies of the other astronauts on board.

so it's a good thing i'm feeling better. we're just going to have to hope Grandpa & Yuri are ok too.

Grandpa & Yuri have spent the last 2 nights going over the flight rules for the Soyuz, refreshing their memories. i heard them murmuring when i briefly woke up, saw the glow from their lamp as they sat in the corner of the room checking rule after rule after rule. it reminds me of the death sims up on Moon 2, the endless meetings going over every detail of a mission.

"in the old days we would study this for at least a week," Grandpa said.

this time they will have less. we know we're on the clock: the

Company will have made calls already, will be speaking to the Kremlin, coming after us.

now, a Kazakh woman knocks on the door & enters with a cart. she says something in her own language, & Yuri translates. "breakfast," he says. "important we eat."

there is something called *tvorog* that Grandpa tells me is basically cottage cheese. also fruits, caviar, nuts, coffee, oatmeal.

Yuri goes over to the curtains & opens them. to my surprise i c the Soyuz rocket lying on a huge flatbed train near the launch pad that is maybe 500 ft. away. it wasn't there a couple of days ago. carts & cranes drive around it, people mill around.

Grandpa sees me looking. "that was quick," he says.

Yuri nods.

"a lot of people seem to be helping us," says Grandpa. he points to the breakfast cart. then back at the rocket. "the trains. hundreds of people. technicians."

Yuri nods again.

Grandpa looks worried. "they *know*? the government?"

"this is Russia," says Yuri. "maybe they don't exactly *not* know that we're doing this. maybe they don't exactly *not* want to take opportunity to piss off the Americans."

Grandpa sighs.

"u want to go to space or not?" says Yuri to me.

"yes," i say.

"ok. then we need the help," says Yuri. "come on. time for us to go. our government has eyes. but so does urs." he points up, to where satellites orbit the world above us.

"go?" i say.

"to space station," says Yuri.

"now?" i say.

"u want to wait for ur 18th birthday, have big party? no. we go now."

i look at Grandpa—he doesn't seem surprised. "u knew it was today?"

"when i saw the ship," he says. "the Russians believe it's bad luck to c ur rocket before the day of launch. like . . . the groom not seeing the wedding dress before a wedding."

"ah!" says Yuri. he seems to remember something, goes over to the cart. there's a silver bottle on it, like a thermos flask. he unscrews the cap & slings the water out of 3 glasses. then he pours something viscous from the thermos into them. into 2 of them he also pours something from a clear bottle.

he hands a glass to Grandpa, then to me.

"drink," he says.

i sniff mine. it smells like gasoline.

"come on," says Yuri. his expression conveys urgency.

i knock it back & gag. it tastes like gasoline too. i cough for a minute.

"what is that?" i say, seeing Grandpa grimly downing his.

"gasoline," says Yuri. "rocket fuel actually."

"it's for luck," says Grandpa, in a slightly strained voice.

"i don't feel very lucky," i say.

"ha," says Yuri, clapping me on the back. "i left the vodka out of urs."

we go downstairs & out into the clear air. the sky is Pacific atoll blue above us. it's so cold that almost immediately i feel my eyelashes freeze, feel them go hard & unwieldy. there's a bus waiting, a minibus, with its door open & exhaust & steam fuming into the air behind it.

we get on. Grandpa runs thru the launch scenario with me, prepping me on the stages. i am not really listening.

the bus drives us to a nondescript, flat concrete building, where we go inside & are met by stony-faced men in day-glo uniforms. there are pressurized space suits on a big rack behind them.

"*Sokhol,*" says Yuri. "suits for mission. it means falcon."

the men measure us with tapes, then pull out helmets & suits, & help us into them. quickly i am feeling hot, a stark contrast to the chill outside. sweat starts streaking my face.

we get back on the bus, Yuri & Grandpa supporting me, clumsy in our bulky suits, boiling up, holding our helmets in 1 hand. we drive an absurdly short distance, then get out again, on a flat piece of concrete, the launch pad ahead of us, the train tracks to our right.

then, in front of us, are 2 long, high pyramidal shapes formed from sand—meant to absorb shock waves if there's an explosion, i guess. they are arranged like brackets leading to the launch site itself, almost as if illustrating perspective as they narrow toward the pad where the Soyuz will blast off from.

if we blow up, those long pyramids will take some of the flame, some of the force, & stop it from reaching the city. they will soak in particles of us.

the rocket is strapped to the train, like a macro version of the 1 that Wile E. Coyote ties to his back in 1 of the cartoons.

that makes me think of Libra.

i wonder what she is doing right now. without me, without Orion. she will be with their mother, i think, & i am glad & sad at the same time.

what *i* am doing is watching as the train slowly starts to move, hauling the rocket toward the launch pad, belching black fumes from its heavy diesel engine. the rocket moves backward—the end of it is facing us, the tail fins facing the pad. it takes a long time. i am still sweating & i start to wish they had done this before getting us into our suits.

after an eternity, the train stops, just short of the pad. enormous robot arms turn & move to the end of the rocket. there are vast clamps at the ends & these descend, the pace still leisurely, & men & women in hard hats oversee as the clamps attach to the rocket & begin gradually, gradually, standing it up.

now i realize why it's facing backward: so they can lift it into place, stand it up from its position on the train onto the launch zone.

more time passes.

the robot arms whir away, move back on their slots. whirring. the train backs up.

now the rocket stands alone, next to a high scaffolded structure shaped as a tall *C*—the gantry—steps switchbacking up the lower part like a fire escape, the upper part sheathed in steel. i realize this is it. this moment. those are our steps. this is our rocket.

27
launch, part 2

"come," says Yuri.

we cover in ten minutes the distance it took the train to cross in maybe 1 hour, even with my bad leg. i lean on Grandpa as i walk—the exo-structure of the suit seems to help too. there's no ceremony, no one to wave us off. a technician of some sort comes forward from 1 of the robot arms & says something to Yuri.

Yuri nods.

then Yuri leads the way to the steps & we climb up them. this feels surreal. like i'm still in my bed in the hotel & Yuri & Grandpa are still poring over their rule books & i have imagined all of this, dreamed it.

the side of the rocket is right in front of me, stretching in a curve away on either side. the thin metal of the stairs is slippery & i concentrate on not falling. the rocket catches the light at odd angles, refracts it, & it dawns on me that it is covered in a coating of ice, inches thick.

"is that a problem?" i say.

"what?" says Yuri, ahead of me. stopping.

"the ice."

he shakes his head. keeps climbing.

when we reach the top of the stairs, another taciturn technician shows the way to a small elevator—it's hard for us all to fit in with our suits on but we manage it. the technician salutes, steps back. *"schastlivovo puti,"* he says.

"what does that mean?" i say.

"bon voyage," says Grandpa. it occurs to me that he is translating 1 language that is not our own into another, & i giggle, & reflect that i must be mildly delirious.

"thank u," i say to the technician.

he nods, & turns & leaves. we are alone in the elevator, the 3 of us.

there is a *clunk,* then a worryingly creaky sound as the elevator goes up. it jerks to a stop, & when the door slides across, there is a round hole in front of us. the door to the rocket.

it's small, so we have to crawl thru & into the module, being careful of the big pressure regulator valves on the front of our suits. it's the orbital module—i know that from what Grandpa & Yuri told me last night. most of the rocket is taken up with fuel & engines, parts that are jettisoned before reentry. the actual space for us is tiny—more like a car than what u would imagine in a rocket.

Yuri squeezes past me & shuts the door. flips a big lever, then turns a lock that is small & incongruous, silly-seeming in the scale of space flight.

i almost laugh. it's so ordinary.

shut the door behind u.

but this is a rocket.

it's a rocket that is going to blast off into space.

i keep saying it in my head, but there is still a part of me not believing it.

we make our way inside. everything is perpendicular to normal, of course. the seats have their backs facing the ground, we will be effectively lying down for takeoff. Yuri takes the leftmost of the front seats.

"i'll be pilot," he says to Grandpa. "u be copilot."

"of course," says Grandpa.

"what do i do?" i say.

"u sit & watch," says Yuri, but not unkindly.

"i lived almost my whole life in space," i say.

"yes," says Grandpa. "& we want to keep u living there." he pauses. "tell u what, if we black out, u take over on the radio, ok? do whatever mission control says."

"ok," i say.

i squeeze into 1 of the 2 seats behind them. it's weird being oriented like this. i fasten my belt.

"right," says Yuri. "fuel levels ... normal. expected thrust 220,000 lb/sq-in. let's calculate engine shut-down times."

they recite numbers to each other for a while, making notes on a piece of paper.

a voice crackles over the radio, & Yuri answers, then has a brief conversation in Russian with the person at the other end.

Grandpa flicks switches & writes things down & taps on screens.

launch protocol.

it takes forever.

it worries me how cramped it is in here. small. even worse than the module we came down in. i start to remember the spinning as we fell to earth, the way everything was up & everything was down, switching & switching, over & over, the speed & the chaos of it, & i start to breathe more rapidly. what if this thing explodes on takeoff?

"u all right, Leo?" Grandpa says.

"uh-huh," i say.

"don't worry," says Yuri. "beauty of the Soyuz is that we are flying in the landing module. if fuel explodes, this section detaches automatic. thrown clear. then parachute activates,

& we float down. very safe." pause. "oh. check parachute, please."

Grandpa looks at a screen. "check."

"has that happened?" i say. "the fuel exploding?"

"oh yes," says Yuri.

"but the module detached?"

"yes," says Yuri again. "both times."

"oh good," i say.

"the first time, the parachute did not deploy, admittedly," he adds. "shame. cosmonaut was Vladimir Komarov. a good man. friend of my grandfather's. killed instantly when the module hit ground."

Grandpa sighs.

i close my eyes & focus on the seat, the feeling of my body against it, the glow of the many lights against my eyelids. try to be purely in the moment.

"bigger problem is if the engines fail after maybe 2 minutes," says Yuri. "early catastrophe, u detach, u float down. once thru the atmosphere, u bounce along it on reentry, slows u totally. but in between? 2 minutes up? before atmosphere? u come down like rock. 24 g, 25 g. probably we all black out & die."

"Yuri!" says Grandpa.

"yes. sorry. but it is possible. if it happens i hit this switch here"—my eyes are open now of course & i c him show me a joystick on the panel in front of him. "take manual control of attitude boosters. try to roll ship to reduce g force. if i am conscious of course."

"u don't have to take him thru the whole boldface," says Grandpa.

"no," says Yuri. "but u & i need to go thru it all."

boldface is written in blood, i think.

i close my eyes again & block out the two old astronauts as they go thru every possible permutation of how we could be horribly killed.

time goes by.

then:

"helmets," says Yuri.

i take mine from next to me & put it on. *"dva zaschelka,"* says Yuri. "2 clicks. it is not secure till u hear 2 clicks."

i fasten the right lock.

click.

then the left.

click.

"connect oxygen," says Yuri, his voice now sounding as if it's coming thru a speaker on the space station, from another module, & for once there's a space life analogy that works better than any earth simile.

Grandpa turns & shows me where the tube comes down, how to click it into the port on my suit.

"now regulator," says Yuri. "test pressurization."

i press the button of the regulator on my chest & feel the suit inflate like a balloon—my ears pop almost immediately.

"wait 3 minutes," says Yuri.

we wait.

Yuri thumbs the radio. "ok?"

"ok," comes back the message from the ground.

"good. open helmets," he says.

i flip my visor. now we know the suits won't fail once we're outside earth's atmosphere. it will take us a day or 2 to orbit up to the space station, accelerating in order to rise, feeding fuel to the rockets.

"u have a toy?" says Yuri to Grandpa.

"no," says Grandpa. "u?"

Yuri shakes his head. "damnation," he says, an old-fashioned word i've only seen in books. "not good luck."

"what?" i say to Grandpa.

"we used to bring a little toy," says Grandpa. "like a Beanie Baby or a doll on a piece of string. u tie it to the instrument panel & when it floats up, u know u're in 0 g."

i touch my chest. thick space suit. i wish i hadn't just locked my helmet. i flip the visor & reach down inside & stretch my fingers as far as i can; they brush against thin smooth silver, cool & slick as water. something starts to pull in my arm, from the unnatural movement—i wince—but i push my hand farther & manage to snag the chain, pulling it up & out.

a bit of jiggling, & Libra's locket comes free. "here," i say, passing it forward.

"perfect," says Yuri. he loops the chain around a lever on the control panel & the silvery vial hangs down over him.

loud noises are coming from outside—clicks & bangs & scrapes. the gantry being dismantled & moved away from the rocket.

time passes.

the noises stop.

"ready?" says Yuri.

"ready," says Grandpa.

"then let's go." Yuri removes the clear plastic covering from a big red switch.

"what, that's it?" i say. "no countdown?"

"no countdown," says Yuri. "close visors."

we do.

he flicks the radio switch again, says something. the hissing voice speaks back in Russian.

"myagkoj posadki."

"myagkoj posadki," says Grandpa.

"myagkoj posadki," says Yuri.

"what does that mean?" i say.

"it means soft landings," says Grandpa. "they always say it. for—"

"luck," i finish.

"exactly," says Grandpa.

then Yuri flips the red switch.

28
launch, part 3

the rocket rumbles around us.

"outer engines firing good," says Yuri. "lighting main thrusters."

the vibration & the noise increase, & we start to smoothly move up into the sky—i can tell mostly from the sensation, because there's no visual frame of reference; our windows are just looking up at the sky, at the blue of it, the scattered clouds of it.

i was expecting more force, actually, more of a dramatic sense of—

& then it comes: suddenly we are thrown forward in our seats, as if stopping, & i am about to yell to Yuri to ask if there's a problem when he says, "first stage engines separated," & i realize that we have jettisoned our first set of boosters.

"second stage engines: ignition," says Yuri.

&—

with a roar—

my seat pushes up into me, slamming into me, my organs yank back down toward earth, my ears pop as we are propelled with colossal power up into the blue. the seat wants to push thru my body; wants to burst thru my chest.

the clouds race down & we race up—

we tear thru the clouds, enveloped in white—

then we're out, in darkening blue—

another lurch forward, the seat harness biting into my chest—

"second stage engines separated, firing third stage."

roar.

this time i am battered back into my seat; it feels elemental, total, like being hit by a mountain, as we accelerate at a rate that seems to want to pull my eyeballs thru my skull & out the back of my head.

& then, suddenly:

the blue outside the windows is gone & we're in the black, the speed of the rocket alchemizing light into dark.

"turning off stage 3 engines," says Yuri.

from the corner of my eye, i c Grandpa lean forward in his seat. "detaching Soyuz module," he says, & there's an oddly quiet thudding sound as the bulk of the rocket is ditched, leaving just our little reentry capsule.

"look," says Grandpa.

i look. the silver chain has gone slack, & Libra's locket, with the earth in it, has risen up as if come to life & is floating, bumping into the instrument panel. 0 g. i realize why this simple device is useful: we're strapped in. we can't feel it, the weightlessness. i think of Libra, & how precious this tiny canister of earth was to her. but now she has the whole earth, i suppose, or a small part of it. a garden.

i'm glad i have this piece of it tho.

of her.

i look out the window. i can just c the curvature of the earth, the blueness & greenness of it, surrounded by lacy white clouds. everything else is black, punctuated by stars & planets. the moon is behind the earth, only a sliver of it visible, so bright & gleaming as to seem like some kind of molten metal.

"check pressure," says Yuri.

"pressure a-ok," says Grandpa.

"ok, shut off oxygen."

"shutting off oxygen," says Grandpa.

a little time elapses, & then Yuri & Grandpa unlock their helmets & take them off, so i do the same. i c movement out of the corner of my eye & register confusing sensations from my body's balance system; i glance at the window: the earth appears . . . fills the view . . . & then is gone. deep space is in front of us. then the earth again. we are spinning around, rotating.

my heart jumps.

"what's happening?" i say.

Grandpa laughs. "we've switched to solar panels. the module turns to always get the maximum amount of sunlight."

"it's making me feel sick," i say.

"don't worry," says Yuri. "soon i do orbit adjust burn, & we can say *do svidaniya* to the solar panels."

he's right. i feel nauseous for maybe half an hour, & i try not to look at the window, but then he & Grandpa fire the smaller boosters in the landing module & we are catapulted into a higher orbit, moving up a little closer to the space station, the windows showing not a turning, tumbling world but the endless emptiness of space.

once u're in orbit, Grandpa explains, u don't go up by turning. u go up by accelerating. it's a whole different physics of movement.

i knew that, but i let him explain all the same. i like it.

Yuri & Grandpa get out their pads & their screens & maintain a constant background conversation, making calculations & inputting numbers to the systems, working out the amount of fuel & number of burns needed to get us to the station.

after a while, Yuri seems to notice that i'm just sitting there. "u can take off ur harness, u know," he says. "move around. have a proper look from window."

i unclick the fastenings & carefully maneuver myself out of my seat. the ceiling of the module is not high, but just high enough that i can float without too much impediment. there's a toilet, a small supply section with ready meals for us, a cargo hold that would normally be filled with equipment going up to the space station.

i close my eyes.

weightless.

weightless again.

i am home.

gravity is gone, but i feel another weight lift too: a rock that has been on my chest is suddenly removed, & i breathe in deep. i am free. i tuck up my legs & roll, in the air, then turn onto my back. it's like the hot tub at Mountain Dome but it's so much more: it's 360 degrees of freedom & every direction is open to me & there is no down & nothing pulling me into the ground. the single plane of existence has dropped away & once again i am in every dimension—i am a fish, thrown back into the sea.

i c drops floating in front of me, sparkling in the equipment light, & realize that i am crying, & that i should stop, because there is nothing to dry my tears, or make them fall away from me.

i push off from the seat back with my feet & glide over to the window. i look out. the stars are dense, a fine-spun web, covering the night sky, as if glittering with dew. i look closer. & with a lurch of recognition, of disorientation, i c that these aren't stars at all; it's some continent below us, lit by electric light, the threads & filaments of roads, the fireworks of cities, spreading their gleam out into the darkness.

i turn my head, & from the glow of the coming sun can make out the edge of the earth, the long bow of it, & then the more intense black of space, where the real stars burn, in their random patterns, in their chaotic brightness.

home.

"how long till we reach the station?" i say.

Grandpa turns. "a while. 2 nights. u may as well get some sleep."

as soon as he says it, i become aware that i am terribly, crushingly tired, that every part of me is aching for sleep. i drift back over to my seat & climb in & do up my harness.

i press myself into the seat. i have to, because gravity is not going to do it for me.

i close my eyes.

sleep is no longer below me, is no longer something to fall into, something whose direction is downward—it is everywhere, all around, & i have only to point myself at the stars, at the distant constellations, & launch myself out of my body & out, into everything & nothing.

dimly, i hear Yuri talking to Grandpa. "prepare for second orbit adjustment burn."

then i am gone, into the black.

29

click

i wake on the second morning to a bright star outside the window that grows until it's Moon 2, a shining cross in orbit.

the last day has passed slowly. looking out. floating. sitting. sleeping. Grandpa & Yuri constantly working, taking shifts to get some rest. i have tried to help as much as i can—i know some of the physics, the theory—but i don't know the flight manuals & i've never flown 1 of these things before.

"1,600 ft.," says Yuri. "1,300."

"activating automated docking aids," says Grandpa. "peripheral booster control . . . on."

Yuri peers at the screen that Grandpa turns to him. "anticipated docking in 2 minutes," he says. then he taps various numbers & scrawls something on a pad—the pencils are tied to the pads, for obvious reasons. "final orbital burn," he says. "13 seconds."

Grandpa hits a switch, & the module accelerates as we climb up a notch—we are a dog, leaping into the air to catch a Frisbee, crunching numbers in its brain, predicting & extrapolating curves.

"i wonder if they still use the same frequencies," says Yuri. he takes a radio mic from the board in front of him; it's attached by a coiling cord. he presses a button on its side. "Moon 2, this is Soyuz 23, approaching ur x-axis left port. do u copy?"

fizz.

"this is Moon 2. we copy loud & clear, but we don't understand. we have no rendezvous on the deck."

"u have 1 now," says Yuri.

"u can't—"

"just get ready to open the hatch," he says.

"u said *Soyuz*?" says the voice on the other end of the radio. faint Asian accent.

"i did."

"but that program was . . . that was shut down 20 years ago."

"well," says Yuri, "i guess no one told me."

he turns off the radio & laughs, & Grandpa & i laugh too—it defuses the tension a little. the craziness of what we're doing. burns off some of the rocket fuel in our veins. my heart is frantic in my chest.

"30 seconds to manual," says Yuri.

he watches the time tick down on a display above his head.

"manual control please, Flight Officer Freeman," he says.

"me?" says Grandpa.

"u were always the best," says Yuri.

"that's true—i was," says Grandpa.

he smiles again, & takes hold of a steering yoke in front of him, then inputs a complex series of keystrokes on a keyboard to his right.

"i have the module," he says.

"bring us home, then," says Yuri.

it's an expression, but it rings a pure, clean note in my head. home.

Grandpa is obviously steering, making minute adjustments, but it's not like u would notice. he constantly keeps an eye on a dozen different displays & readings, the angle of the earth relative to us, star charts, data pinging back from radio waves fired at the space station, laser attitude sensors. & he steers.

"strap in," says Yuri. "helmet."

i slide my harness fasteners shut. lock my helmet down. shut the visor.

"pressurize," says Yuri.

i hit my regulator. feel the thick fabric inflate. i am Wile E. Coyote, putting on an Acme space suit, but this time i am going to catch the Road Runner; this time i am not going to fall to earth.

gradually, the space station looms larger & larger. we are going so slowly, & yet i know this is a highly dangerous operation. i mean, i saw what happened to Brown. it suddenly strikes me that i haven't thought about him for a long time, about his body drifting alone thru space, forever. maybe i should have. but then again i didn't really know him. it seems cruel. to die up here, & not even be remembered.

& it still might happen to us.

Grandpa & Yuri go very silent as we cross the final few ft. the hatch is a round circle in front of us—thru the window & displayed on a screen on the instrument panel. hashmarked with hooks & latches, like the minute markers around a watchface. silver metal & white pipes. bright against blackness. then it swings away, as Grandpa turns the module sideways, reading out numbers all the time, Yuri whispering instructions.

then:

"15 ft.," says Yuri.

"13 ft."

"10 ft."

"6 ft."

"& . . ."

"docking."

there's a thud—surprisingly hard—& we come abruptly to a stop. i feel part of the seat harness bite into my hip, am thrown sideways. Grandpa breathes out, loud & slow. "check readouts," he says.

"all fine," says Yuri after a moment. "felicitations. u still have the touch."

"i don't know," says Grandpa. "that was a little heavy."

Yuri pats his stomach. "we have all grown a little heavier," he says. he leans over the panel of switches. "engaging assembly system."

click.

click.

click.

the hooks & latches close, a noise perhaps like very large insects shutting their mandibles.

click.

click.

"docking complete," says Grandpa. "now we'll c if they let us in. Leo, unlock our side, would u?"

"sure," i say. i grab the seat top & use it to propel myself toward the round door we entered the rocket thru. i flip up the heavy lever, then turn the lock to the ◀ OPEN position.

for a long time, nothing happens. then there is a *clank* from the other side, & the door swings open into the air lock of the space station. the others unfasten their harnesses & we swim thru, me first, then Grandpa, then Yuri.

on the other side of the air lock, beyond the glass, 2 astronauts stand, in casual gray sweatpants & white Company t-shirts. 1 of them is Asian & male, & the other is a woman in a headscarf. "identify urselves please," she says, thru the speakers mounted in the hull beside us.

"Commander Yuri Bogdanov," says Yuri.

"Flight Officer Freeman, retired," says Grandpa.

"& i'm Leo," i say. "i was born here."

the woman seems to shake her head.

there's a pause.

then she activates the switch to close the door behind us, & there's a hiss as air is forced into the chamber. i look up & c jets of it, of vapor, shooting from the walls.

we wait.

"pressure normalized," says the woman. "opening air lock."

she presses something else, & the hatch to the space station itself opens. we take off our helmets & torpedo thru. i notice that i am quicker here than Grandpa & Yuri, my movements more sure, & it's not just that my leg doesn't have to rest on the ground here; it's that i am more graceful too, more suited to my environment.

this is my home, i remind myself.

i am home.

30
trouble

i flip over in the air when i reach the 2 people, come to a stop next to them. thru a window in the curving wall of the space station's arm, i c the moon, bright as a white paper lamp, circling the earth, as it always does. below it, half-shadowed, is the dome of the earth, jewels of electric illumination sparkling on the dark side, the light side a wonder of green & blue, shaded with clouds.

"they warned us but i didn't believe . . . ," says the woman, but then she doesn't seem to know what to say next.

"u guys are in so much trouble," says the Asian man.

"really?" says Yuri. "what are they going to do about it?"

the man doesn't answer.

"i'm Sara," says the woman. "i attended 1 of ur lectures, Flight Officer Freeman. on laser guidance systems. u signed my book afterward."

"ah," says Grandpa. "i'm afraid my memory is not what it was."

she waves this away like it doesn't matter. "this is Ku," she says, indicating the man, who only scowls. "we'll take u to the bridge. Boutros wants to speak to u."

they lead the way, & we swim after them, thru several modules, before turning at the y-axis & going up toward the bridge. we pass the vegetable trays, the UV lamps over them glowing purple,

& i think of Libra, but all the time i'm thinking too i'm home i'm home i'm home.

when we reach the bridge, Sara goes over to a screen spread out on the magnetic table. i follow, Grandpa & Yuri behind me.

Boutros is on the screen.

or rather, his face is, blotchy above a green tie & a white shirt. sweat is springing from his pores.

"Leo," he says. "what the hell do u think u're doing?"

"coming home," i say.

"this is . . . this is . . ." a vein starts to pulse on his forehead. "Freeman, don't think i don't c u lurking in the background there. u'll be . . . u'll be . . . u'll be disciplined for this."

Grandpa barks a laugh. "u're going to dock my pay, is that it? make me sit down with HR? please."

"there's not enough room up there for all of u," says Boutros. "u're going to have to come down at some point."

"of course," says Grandpa. "Yuri & i will be returning in the landing module. u can wait for us & slap my wrists then if u like. i always like meeting with HR."

i look at Grandpa. he's leaving? well, of course he's leaving. why wouldn't he? it's logical. sadness flares in my stomach, & i force it down. come on, Leo. u can't have everything.

"u're leaving?" i say.

Grandpa turns his gentle eyes on me. "i have to," he says. "the cows. the calves. they need me. i need to make sure that fence is secure, c to the mothers that are calving . . ."

he tails off. he's speaking with his eyes. looking for forgiveness. which is not something he needs to ask for.

"of course," i say. "of course u have to."

he thanks me, still with his eyes.

& i take a breath.

425

i say to myself:

u're home.

u're home, Leo.

that's what counts.

Boutros turns back to me. "the Company has invested billions of dollars in u & ur upbringing. we can't just let u go. u need to come back."

"i'm nobody's property," i say.

"i didn't say u were, i said—"

"i'm not coming down," i say.

pause.

"we can force u to, u know," he says. his voice kind of cracks at the end. like he knows he shouldn't have said it, but it came out anyway. like the words crumbled in his mouth.

"i very much doubt that," i say.

silence.

"what are u going to do?" says Yuri. "train some marines to fly a shuttle? send a drone? this is a space station. it's not some *khalupa* in Mukhosransk."

Boutros sighs. he is pale. i almost feel sorry for him. "do u have any *idea* of the problems u have created? the president is on the screen to the Russian premier as we speak. they're talking about it on Moscow news like they righted a gross ethical violation. there is a major fucking international incident unfolding here. not to mention the media & the—"

"i'm sorry," i say. "i don't really care."

"u don't *care*?"

"the Company brought me here in the first place," i say. "u're responsible. u're just going to have to deal with it."

Boutros starts opening & closing his mouth. "this isn't over," he says eventually.

"of course not," i say. "i have my whole life ahead of me."

Boutros closes his eyes. it's like seeing the gradual collapse of his corporate shell, of the covering that sustains him. "this is insane," he says. "Leo, think about this. u're just going to orbit thru space till u die."

"yes," i say. i reach out my hand, ready to cut the vid connection. below me, the earth spins at 177,000 miles an hour.

i pause.

"but how is that any different to u?" i say.

& then i press OFF.

epilogue, part 1

"goodbye, Grandpa," i say.

he hugs me. already my body feels stronger, less fragile. on earth i was a baby bird u could crush in ur hand if u weren't careful; here i'm flying.

so why is it that i feel like i'm holding myself together? why is it that the word *goodbye,* when i say it, feels like the precise note an opera singer sings in 1 of Libra's old cartoons to make a vase shatter? only now the vase is me.

"goodbye, Leo," he says. "u know i would stay if i could."

"i know," i say.

"but the cows . . . the land . . . i have responsibilities, u know?"

"i know, Grandpa," i say. "really."

he smiles. it's ok. i don't need him to stay. he got me up here, & that's what counts. of course he has to go back to the farm. of course he has to make sure that Mother is looking after things ok.

"i'll vid u as soon as i get home," he says.

"u'd better. & say hello to Comet for me."

Yuri swims over & gives me a bear hug. "wave whenever u are over Russia, ok?" he says. "i will wave back."

i laugh. "bye, Yuri. & thanks for everything. i'm . . . i can't believe what u did for us."

he shrugs. "it was that or the repainting of my window frames. i should thank u. for bringing me here again."

"u're welcome anytime," i say.

"i don't think i will be leaving home again," says Yuri with a half smile. "the Americans have landed in Baikonur, i hear. no more hidden rockets."

i feel bad. that's my fault. but Yuri claps me on the back.

"u made Russia proud," he says. "plucky cosmonauts, helping child return home. the news vids from Moscow talk like u are national hero. don't worry."

a national hero.

what a strange idea.

Sara & Ku come along as Grandpa & Yuri head to the Soyuz landing module to begin their journey home. the Company will be waiting for them of course. Grandpa insists they won't be arrested or anything tho: too much media attention. still, i expect he will get a serious talking-to. i almost wish i could c it. i almost feel sorry for Boutros & the others who will have to do it.

my grandpa is not to be trifled with. the old-fashioned words make me smile.

Sara & Ku, i suspect, only want to make sure that Grandpa & Yuri really do leave. they wave, & Sara closes the hatch to the air lock. the 2 old men finish climbing into their suits, put on their helmets, & wait for the chamber to depressurize.

"good journey," says Sara thru the intercom.

they nod.

i drift to the intercom & ignore Sara's protests as i press the button myself. *"myagkoj posadki,"* i say.

Yuri beams & gives me a thumbs-up.

then the door to the module opens & they wave 1 last time, before floating headfirst thru it. i c them start to settle into their seats, as Sara closes the hatch.

Sara, Ku, & i return to the bridge—me in front, because i torpedo so much quicker than they do thru the turns & narrow apertures of the station, know all the handholds & the places i can use my feet to boost off, the points where angular momentum can be redirected, like a swimmer turning under water & kicking off the end wall of the pool.

on the bridge, i watch Grandpa & Yuri on 1 of the screens as they go thru their preflight protocol, checking the manuals & all the readings in the landing capsule. soon Sara is there & she starts calling out data to them, checking numbers; she's the astronaut. Ku, it turns out, is a meteorologist, here to set up some kind of net of minisatellites that will provide more accurate predictions, especially for places where global warming is driving extreme weather events.

Ku, therefore, just hangs back like me & watches.

minutes pass. finally, every safety check has been done, every relevant piece of data has been recorded.

"decoupling," says Grandpa. he hits a switch on the board in front of him & i wait for the module to detach, to float away from us for a while before it's at a safe distance to fire its thrusters.

but nothing happens.

1 second.

2.

3.

4.

5.

still nothing. it's like an inverse countdown with no outcome, no climax.

Sara scoots over to the mic. "Soyuz, what's the problem?" she says.

"we don't know," comes Yuri's voice. "we are attempting to unlock from peripheral assembly but it is not working."

Sara starts tapping keyboards, checking different screens.

"servos seem ok," she says. "power fine. have u tried pressing it again?"

"what do u think?" says Yuri.

"ok ok . . . ," says Sara. "hatch is still showing as locked. could be an electrical fault?"

"running diagnostics," says Grandpa.

i push off from the table & move toward her. i pull down a screen she's not using. "here," i say. "there's a camera on the y-axis truss. on the robot arm, for guiding it? if there's a problem with the latches on the hatch, it might show it."

Sara looks at me for a moment. "good idea," she says.

i bring up the camera menu & then camera 241, which i know is the 1 mounted for monitoring of the remote-controlled arm. i tap in the code to take control of it, then tilt & pan—but it's too close to the body of the space station; it doesn't give an elevated enough view to c what's going on with the docking port.

i indicate the screen on which Sara has been looking at the servo readouts. "u mind if i use that 1?" i say.

"go ahead," she says, with a faint, only slightly ironic smile.

i pull it over to me & launch the subsystem that gives me access to the arm. i put my fingers on the multi-touch sensors & ease up the slider that turns it to manual. they had an accident once when the end of the arm damaged a shuttle that was docked to the station because they hadn't thought to limit its range of motion. now it's got a defined window of rotation in each axis, but u still have to be careful with it.

gently, i lift the first joint of the arm up & away from the wall of the space station. the camera is on the next joint, so i turn that 1 next, up & sideways. at the same time i keep glancing over to the other screen & adjusting the camera angle.

1 more twist of the arm . . .

zoom & tilt on the camera . . .

. . . & there it is, the end of the station's crosspiece, the module attached to it by the standard androgynous assembly, the ring of hooks & latches.

i zoom.

"there," i say.

Sara comes & looks.

"c the problem?"

"yeah."

the latches have all popped up with the exception of 2, on the port side. they are still clinging to the Soyuz, preventing it from leaving.

Sara clicks the intercom. "we have a visual on the hatch exterior," she says. "the latches are not releasing properly."

"all of them?" says Yuri.

"no, just 2 that we can c. maybe try locking it again? & then unlocking?"

on 1 of the screens i c Grandpa hit a button. nothing happens.

"nothing," he confirms.

"dammit," says Sara. she turns & takes another mic, which is connected to Nevada. she presses CALL. "hey," she says. "give me engineering."

"this is Singh," says a familiar voice. "we're watching. u've got a problem with the latches?"

"yes," says Sara. "is there a flight rule on this situation?"

"we'll check the database," says Singh.

silence.

more silence.

outside, stars wheel past. the aurora flickers like fire on the earth.

"the latches can be manually opened," says Singh eventually.

"good, ok," says Sara. "where's the control?"

"u're not understanding me," says Singh. "*manually*. it requires an EVA."

Sara's mouth opens, & then shuts. "i can't do that on my own," she says.

"no & it would be against protocol anyway," says Singh. "maybe Freeman can leave the module & help u, then return to . . . ," he tails off. "no. as soon as the latches are opened, the module will detach."

"& Yuri will be on his own," i say.

"hmm," says Singh. "& it takes 2 pilots to fly that thing."

"what's happening?" says Grandpa over the intercom.

Sara grabs it. "somebody has to EVA. to unlock it. but if 1 of u does it, u'll end up stuck here while the other 1 leaves."

"we can't do that," says Grandpa. "neither of us can pilot this alone."

"we know," says Sara. "i'm sorry. it looks like u're stuck here."

she looks sorry too. maybe she'd rather Grandpa & Yuri weren't around: she's a very tidy person, very neat, & i can tell Yuri grates on her nerves.

i think of the look on Grandpa's face whenever he sees his ranch over vid call, the mountains, the fields. i think of Comet, down there with my mother, & how my mother's meant to be rotating up here soon with another astronaut—the Company is still going ahead with its new program, putting young people in space for 2 years, it seems like they never learn from their mistakes—& how then Comet will need someone else to be with him, to take him out running, to scratch behind his ears.

"no," says Singh.

"excuse me?" says Sara.

"no, they're not stuck there. the hatch is not locking again. it is between 2 states, in mechanical terms. it is not open & it is not closed."

"right . . . ," says Sara.

"which means that the inner hatch door will not open. it thinks it is in space. so it won't let them out."

"oh," says Sara.

"we didn't plan for this scenario," says Singh. "but unfortunately, unless those latches can be manually detached, the module is locked there & the 2 men are locked in it. the EVA is the only solution."

"i can do it," i say.

Sara turns to me. "do what?"

"the EVA. i can do it with u."

she frowns. "u're a kid."

"i've done it before," i say. "twice."

she keeps looking at me.

"ok, once really. but i'm good. don't worry. & i'll follow ur commands."

she sighs.

on the second intercom, Singh's voice comes thru. "sitrep please," he says.

"Leo is saying he'll do it with me," says Sara.

"i can't advise that u—"

but then another voice comes across the thousands of miles of air & blankness. it's Boutros. "in my experience," he says, "there's very little u can do to stop him, once he gets an idea in his head." his voice is weary, but is that a touch of humor too?

"we heard that," says Grandpa. pause. "listen, Leo, u really think u can do this?"

"yes," i say. because it's true.

"well, that's good enough for me," says Grandpa.

i love u, Grandpa, i love u.

i think it but i don't say it.

Sara looks at the ceiling, then down again. "u do everything i say," she says.

"of course, captain," i say.

she sighs.

"i must insist, however," says Singh, "on proper prep this time. 24 hours pure ox & 11 bars pressure. i know Leo decompressed last time & it was ok but we're not risking both or 1 of u getting the bends."

"i second that," says Boutros. "Yuri, Bob, u're going to have to sit tight for 24 hours."

"it's ok," says Yuri. "we have a deck of cards."

i don't know if he's joking or not.

epilogue, part 2

Sara & i leave the decompression chamber 24 hours later, & Ku is hovering outside, watching us anxiously.

i am feeling pumped, excited. i even managed to sleep a bit in there, mind spinning out into the star-filled sky, from all the oxygen filling my lungs. i don't think Sara slept. every time i turned to her little bunk, i saw her looking up at the ceiling, hands tapping on the military-grade canvas strap keeping her in the bed.

now she rubs her eyes & yanks in a deep breath while closing her eyes, like after a night in the chamber she's trying to bring some measure of normality into her body with the air.

of course, this air is artificial too. it's mixed with nitrogen & we shouldn't breathe it for long or it will undo our prep.

"come on," i say. "we need to hurry."

Sara nods.

"take the bridge," she says to Ku.

"um . . . ok," says Ku, coming over to the consoles. "what do i need to do?"

"nothing," says Sara. "just keep the radios on."

we torpedo to the x-axis exit hatch. we'll have to travel down the truss & then on to the other section of the cross—we can't exfil from the end where Grandpa & Yuri are, of course, because the landing module is in the way.

i'm quicker at getting into my suit than Sara is—i guess i have had more recent practice. i climb in & then shut the heavy back behind me, the pack with the oxygen tanks & water-cooling engine in it. then i put on the shirt of water pipes, before closing up the whole suit & lowering my helmet into place. i palm the button for the hatch door & float into the air lock, & Sara joins me maybe 3 minutes later.

she closes the door.

"visors," she says. her voice is short, clipped.

we lower our visors.

"oxygen."

i activate my supply.

"ox check," she says.

i look at my heads-up display, the LED readings floating in the air in front of me. "readings ok."

she hits depressurize.

hiss.

the air lock empties of air & we float over to the exit hatch. i turn to her. "it's going to be fine," i say, "it's easy. i promise."

she doesn't say anything. but i think i c her smile, behind her visor.

what i want to say, but it would sound too arrogant—she's an astronaut with decades of training—is that i will look after her. i mean, this is my home. we're safe here.

it's true tho. i will look after her. even if i don't say it.

"clip on."

i clip my cable to the rail running along the wall.

"opening exterior hatch," says Sara. it fish-eyes outward, a clear window now right onto an infinity of mostly nothing. we move toward the opening. Sara hesitates when we get there, holding back.

i don't. i unclip from the rail, hold on to the side of the hatch, & swing out, into space.

it hits me less hard this time but it's still monumental: floating out of a white-walled room & into a universe. my breath catches, & i focus on clipping myself quickly to the exterior truss, eyes on the small carabiner-style lock as it snaps onto the tubing of the armature.

i turn:

–earth below me, vast green-blue sea & small surf-ringed islands.

–moon beyond it, half-obscured, pale purple & huge.

–velvet black space all around, jeweled with stars.

–& just slowly coming out of the space station & clipping on next to me, Sara, her eyes wide inside her helmet.

"it's kind of overwhelming," i say.

"it's in-fricking-sane," she says.

i smile. she is a somewhat surprising person, Sara. she's in a band, she told me, when we were locked into the decompression chamber. a hardcore metal band. she does downhill mountain biking in her spare time.

it's just as well she's fun: i'm going to be up here with her for a while. she was due for a 4-month rotation, & she's only been here a month.

the quickest thing is to take the RCV, so we head a little down the y-axis section, sliding our clips along as we go. when we reach the small cart on wheels we hold on with 1 hand & transfer our cables to it with the other so that we're secured to the truss translation unit.

Ku could control the RCV from inside, but Ku isn't an astronaut, so instead i pull myself over to the other side of the flat vehicle & take the simple BACK ← → FORWARD lever that drives it. i crank off the hand brake & put a thumb up to Sara with my head cocked to 1 side.

ok?

her thumb goes up too.

ok.

i slowly engage the motor—the speed is limited anyway but i don't want Sara to freak out. even now she keeps turning, looking out at the incomprehensible depth of the galaxy, the sheer mind-spinning scale of it.

my breathing is loud inside my helmet. i keep an eye on the LED readouts: pressure, oxygen, temperature. at the same time i'm scanning the sky, for little meteoroids that could strike us as we work, or satellites, or anything—i have learned from an early age that everything outside this space ship wants to kill me, & that the outside of this space ship can very quickly become the inside, if the systems fail or are damaged, or the hull is compromised.

so i am watching for danger at all times.

we grind along the horizontal bars of the truss, the tiny clamped-on wheels of the RCV turning slowly.

the space station maintains its attitude.

the earth spins below.

the moon grows larger, rising up from the earth's curve & into space.

i am hot, sweating inside my space suit, but i am also free. my leg & my wrist are dragged by nothing here, subject to no authority of weight & direction.

when we reach the x-axis we have to unclip again in order to clip onto the next RCV—they only go up & down each crossing arm of the station, they are simple back-forward machines & can't handle the 90-degree turn.

just as we detach, there's a shudder from the station—atmosphere drag? i don't know & probably never will. some combination of boosters & gyros kicks in to kill the external torque, & the station twists—not dramatically but enough to make Sara let go.

she floats away, out into the blank blackness between the arms of the station.

that's not right. that's not meant to happen. she must not have fastened on properly, or she accidentally undid her clip.

"Leo!" she says over the radio. "Leo!"

her arms & legs flap, uselessly, against nothing. the gap widens.

widens some more.

the space station has imparted its momentum to her, its velocity, but now that she's not on it she's losing that speed quickly, is separating moment by moment from Moon 2.

"get this under control, Aziz," says Boutros's voice over the radio. "use ur training."

but Sara doesn't respond.

"activate ur booster," i say. there are small engines in the pack at the back of the suit—enough to power an astronaut back to the station. i hold up my left arm, where the little keypad is built into the suit. i wave it.

but Sara is still making uncoordinated movements, panicking. "oh my god," she says. "oh my god."

i think of Brown, his body preserved forever, orbiting the earth.

"i'm coming for u," i say. i undo my clip & take a deep breath. i look down at the earth, then at the moon. then i pat the sleek outside of the ship with my gloved hand. i take another breath, & kick off. immediately i am adrift, my anchor gone, nothing to propel me or hold me in place.

"Leo, what the hell are u doing?" says Boutros.

i, too, don't respond.

i flip open the cover on the keypad & press the red switch that fires the boosters, then use the directional buttons to steer. there are 2 boosters—1 at the top of the pack & 1 at the bottom, each with 90 degrees of vertical movement & nearly 180 degrees horizontal. depending on their orientation i can move up, down, & sideways.

i move up, toward Sara. i can hear her still in my helmet saying oh my god oh my god like all other words have been wiped from her mind. Boutros is also there, a disembodied voice, shouting things to me that i am ignoring.

i've never used the space suit's boosters before—but i know the theory.

the theory.

my fingers are clumsy in the enormous gloves & it's hard to properly feel the resistance of the buttons. i poke them too hard at first, find myself shooting upward, pointlessly, away from the earth & from Sara, who is close to the Soyuz now, threatening to crash into it, in fact.

i fire the opposite booster to slow my ascent, then some more, then adjust the steering as i finally get my vertical direction roughly right. it is, very literally, like being strapped to a small rocket. i feel the thrust thrumming thru my chest & back.

closer.

closer.

she is pinwheeling now, end over end—i can only assume she tried to fire something but has just sent herself into a flat spin. 20 ft. from the Soyuz. 15 ft.

i hammer down on the power, sliding both buttons so that the rockets are firing their soft sparks of fuel & exhaust directly behind me. the inside of my visor is steaming up with the panting of my breath. i make a final horizontal adjustment & then stretch out my hands—

&—

collide with Sara, wrapping my right arm around her neck, which is not very dignified, but allows me to reach the panel on my left wrist & turn us around before firing both boosters on full power behind us, dumping our speed so suddenly that our heads are thrown back.

i keep the boosters on, finessing the steering, so that as we keep slowing we angle toward the point where the Soyuz & the station meet. if nothing else, we've skipped the slow journey on the RCV, i think almost hysterically. then i grip Sara tight while turning us around again so that we're facing Moon 2. the station looms up, massive & heavy & very, very hard.

with the boosters behind me, there's no way to slow *forward* momentum. so i just have to hope i braked us enough before we turned around, or we're going to crash into the side of the station with an impact that could shatter us.

6 ft.

3 ft.

but as the body of the hull swings up, the Soyuz attached to the end, i realize it's ok: we've slowed sufficiently & i'm able to catch the rail with my left hand, turning as i do so that it's my back that takes most of the blow & the pack, Sara kind of rolling over the front of me & i say,

"grab hold!"

& she does, which is a relief because i don't think i could have held on to the station & to her. she pivots off me & seizes the rail with 2 hands & bumps to a stop.

i hang there, breathing hard, right at the extreme end of the x-axis. the RCV is back at the joint between the 2 arms, so we're going to have to hand-over-hand it all the way down the 3 modules to get back there, but that should be ok too. i look at my HUD. 20 minutes of oxygen left.

slowly, i get my bearings. i take my cable clip & attach it to the rail & motion to Sara to do the same.

"thanks," she says, a little shakily, as she clips on. "i kind of . . . lost it there."

i gesture at space. "it's scary," i say. "it happens."

"well, thank god u were there," she says.

i feel a glow spread thru me. i am useful for something. i have a purpose. i am not just imprisoned in a dome in the mountains. i drink in the endless vastness of space all around me.

of course, i remind myself, if i hadn't been here there would have been no need for the EVA in the first place. which kind of punctures my feeling of triumph.

"sitrep, please," says Boutros, very loudly, in my ears.

i turn from space & to the hatch, & can c the 2 latches that have not released properly. beyond, thru the window of the Soyuz, i c my grandpa & Yuri, both watching me intently, Grandpa with a slight smile on his face. he wipes his eyes, & i look away.

"we're both connected again," i say. "i can c the problem with the peripheral docking assembly."

"& Aziz?"

"i'm ok, sir," says Sara.

"hmm. right. get the job done," says Boutros gruffly.

we edge over to the hatch, & Sara takes a multi-tool from her belt, which she uses to lever 1 of the latches open—it's surprisingly easy; there's a screw bolt that must have been too tight & she just loosens it & then gets the tool under the latch & pries it till it pops up.

she hands me the tool, gets into position for the next latch.

thru the window of the landing module, Grandpa mouths something.

"Leo," says Ku. "i'm patching the Soyuz thru to u."

silence.

then Grandpa's voice comes over the little speakers inside my helmet. "u did good, son," he says.

my eyes well up, hotly. "thanks," i say.

"goodbye, Leo," says Grandpa.

"yes, goodbye, Soviet hero Leo Freeman," says Yuri. "we will toast u with rocket fuel & vodka when we reach home."

"we might leave out the rocket fuel," says Grandpa.

i laugh.

"goodbye, u 2," i say. "thank u for everything."

"no. thank u," says Grandpa.

he lifts a hand & gives a salute, a sharp snap off the forehead. Yuri echoes the gesture.

i turn to Sara.

"do it," i say. i hand her the tool.

she unscrews, levers, pries.

the latch clicks up.

the Soyuz remains there, for just an instant, as if frozen in time & space, & then begins to float slowly away from us.

Grandpa waves.

i wave back.

space enfolds me & embraces me; all around, the stars are everywhere. i watch Grandpa & Yuri shrink, the landing module too, falling away & then turning, & then trailing sparks & comets & meteors as they fire the boosters & sparkle-burn down toward the blue & the green.

i think of Orion, & Libra, & how Libra said we would be angels when we died, floating, looking down on the earth. i feel Orion by my side & i turn to him, inside my mind, & smile, & i picture Brown too as he circles the earth alone, & at the same time not alone. i'm the same. i'm alone but i will never be alone: my mother is coming soon, rotating in, & Grandpa & Comet & Libra too in her garden will always be there, thru the window of the screen,

which is a hole that leads right down to earth & that u can speak
thru instantly—a kind of miracle; a kind of prayer.

    signals.

    transmission.

    speed of light.

    i turn, & i begin to head back home.

interlude

it happens when i'm in the cupola. i'm reading the poetry book, the 1 i gave Orion, & that he gave back.

& i realize his words weren't in the wrong order. when he said "most this amazing day," he was quoting.

i read the poem.

> *i thank You God for most this amazing*
> *day: for the leaping greenly spirits of trees*
> *& a blue true dream of sky; & for everything*
> *which is natural which is infinite which is yes . . .*

i stop reading.

my eyes are open, but i can't c anymore.

i turn to where i know the foreverness is tho, the stars. how can i have known, when i looked at him, about the yes? how can the same word have been in my head?

i remember when Brown died, how i looked at space & thought it was endless & had no judgment in it but also no kindness, & yet now all i can c is a beautiful vastness full of love & music always & held together by it & full of all this all this all this yes.

all this yes.

"hello, Orion," i say.

epilogue, part 3

i go to the hatch. i wave at my mother, & she waves back.

a pause, & then she smiles. it is as if she is putting effort into it. as if she has thought about it, practiced in front of a mirror to get it right.

well.

that's better than not.

i smile back. i hit the button next to me & the air lock starts to pressurize. oxygen hisses thru pipes, misting slightly. my mother removes her helmet. the other astronaut with her does the same. they hinge their suits & step out, both in their underwear, because of the heat.

i press the button to open the hatch, & it irises open, expanding, until there is a clear space for them to float thru & into the station.

"welcome to Moon 2," i say.

not to my mother, of course. she has been here many times before. she was here for over a year, once.

not to my mother.

to the other astronaut.

Soto floats thru the hatch, with a marveling expression on his face.

"fancy seeing u here," he says, smiling so his eyes crinkle at the edges.

something flips in my stomach, like a fish.

outside the window, the stars wink at me, in the darkness.

i have always loved, like the moon loves
the earth

now i know how the earth loves the moon

/end transmission/

Acknowledgments

Circles feature prominently in this novel, so it seems appropriate that I circled back to an editor I had worked with before: the wonderful Melanie Nolan at Random House. Thanks to Melanie for agreeing to edit me again, and for improving the book with countless perceptive, wise, and clear suggestions. Emma Goldhawk, at Hodder in the UK, also improved the story in innumerable ways, seeing links I had missed myself. I am deeply grateful to both my brilliant editors.

Thanks to Ray Shappell and Jason Heatherly for the *beautiful* cover. And to all the people at Random House and Hodder who work incredibly hard to get books into the hands of teenagers.

As always, thanks also go to my agents, Caradoc King and Millie Hoskins, who made the story stretch further, before any editor even saw it, and to Jane Willis for convincing several foreign publishers to take it, even though it is written in mostly untranslatable poetic prose with silly orthography.

Finally, and firstly—we're back to circles again—my profound gratitude to Hannah, my wife and first reader, who doesn't just help to make the story better, but helps to make it a story.